JUSTICE IS FOR THE DESERVING

JUSTICE
IS FOR THE DESERVING

A Kristen Kerry Novel

STEVE CLARK

RORKE PUBLISHING

Also by Steve Clark

Justice Is for the Lonely

"Once more unto the breach, dear friends, once more . . ."

Henry V, act 3, scene 1
William Shakespeare

ACKNOWLEDGMENTS

I OWE MANY THANKS TO EDITORS, Kate Ankofski and Robert Schmidt, as well as agent, Scot Mortensen, for editing and helpful criticism, and of course Nyssa Vasquez, who handles the many little things in writing a novel. My wife, Jane, has seen me through many versions and ideas and will have my lifelong love.

Again, my apologies to my Texas colleagues. The books were plotted before the citizens of that state lost so much of their right to trial by jury.

CHAPTER 1

I'VE HEARD THAT some people who stop breathing or whose hearts conk out sense they're being pulled down a dark tunnel toward a beautiful light at the other end. They say it would have been easy to let go.

It's true. I saw it when I died.

Of course, some of those who live to describe their deaths report only darkness. Maybe that's hell. Skeptical neurologists say the light is simply the last neurons firing in the dying brain. Catholics, like me, hope the light is heaven or leads to a short stay in purgatory for a little sin scrubbing.

But you can enter another tunnel without dying. That path leads to utter, complete despair where every dream you had of love, friendship, children, and honor dies. It's like being plunked into the middle of an ocean without a life vest, knowing you can tread water only so long. You yell and pray, offer Jesus all sorts of promises and deals . . . to no avail. No one helps.

Not even God.

For years I'd regularly experienced a nightmare—drowning with dozens of people on the shore watching, who are reluctant to get wet. A version of that nightmare became real for me. Unlike death, which can be sudden and painless, despair is slow and agonizing.

∗ ∗ ∗

"Kristen Kerry?" Someone shouted like my father used to when he was drunk and pissed at me. Only the accent was Texas, not Philly.

"Yes."

"*Attorney* Kristen Kerry?" Another voice, female, yelled Texas style, stretching each syllable to the breaking point.

Why the yelling? My suite only had three rooms—cozy, feminine rugs on cherry-colored wood planks. Pretty Delacroix prints. You didn't have to shout to be heard. It was practically a whispering gallery like St Paul's in London.

Three sets of feet pounded toward my office.

I stood, knocked my cup off my desk, splashing hot coffee on my shoes—my only slightly worn Jimmy Choos.

I looked up from my wet heels. A burly guy, with moon-crater acne scars and wearing a tweed jacket, flashed a gold badge. The taller, thinner cop leveled his 9mm pistol right at me, like he meant to fire. Their gung-ho approach seemed quite unnecessary.

Holy Crap.

"You're under arrest on the charge of murder in the first degree."

I knew from experience the cop's pistol magazine could hold thirteen rounds. But the really scary thing was how his wrist shook with obvious excitement. A retired detective once told me that most policemen never fire a weapon outside the range in their whole career. This cop looked like he hoped this was his chance. Like he was praying for a chance.

I prayed his finger wasn't on the trigger.

A uniformed female cop, not much smaller than the men, parted the two goons and stepped toward me. She dangled handcuffs with relish. For a second, I thought I'd stumbled into a bondage porn movie.

"Turn around," she drawled with authority. But I found myself nailed to the floor in fear. There had to be something smart to do or say, but I couldn't think of what it could be. While my arrest was not unexpected, I pictured a more civilized event, not a film noir pinch. I would've RSVP'd had they simply invited me to the station.

She must've tired of my rumination. Grabbing my shoulders, she spun me around and jerked one wrist into a cuff. An instant later, the other was snuggled into a matching stainless steel bracelet.

She ratcheted me toward the desk and frisked me.

In the window I caught the reflection of the two guys smirking, watching her hands roam under my skirt and over my chest.

With a shove they hustled me out the door, to the elevator, not even letting me flip the lock. She jammed the button.

We stood waiting. What do you say to cops who have just arrested you?

How are ticket sales to the Policeman's Ball coming along this year?

Finally the elevator light went on. The four of us crowded in with two other women, who stared at me over lunches in Styrofoam boxes, likely wondering if I was the drug pusher at their kids' schools.

Really great for a lawyer's reputation. I'd fallen lower than a used car dealer. Lower than a politician. Lower than shark shit at the bottom of the ocean.

I kept my gaze on my wet shoes until the doors opened again. Once through the lobby to more stares, and then outside, they steered me toward an unmarked car parked at the curb. People slowed, taking in the show. Every eyeball fixed on me. I felt stark naked, like everyone's recurring dream of showing up to your second grade class in your underwear.

The female cop jerked the back door, planted her palm on my head, and lowered me into the car, then bounced her butt beside me. The guys sat in front, their broad shoulders almost meeting.

Terror generated the serious need to pee. Bad. But I doubted they'd accommodate me. I squeezed every Kegel God gave me, and prayed we went somewhere with a toilet. Soon. They could have taken me to the Gulag, and I wouldn't have cared as long as it had a john.

I'd been a complete fool to get myself in this position, but I wasn't dumb enough to start flapping my mouth, so we rode in silence the six blocks to the Dallas County jail. On the outside the place looks like something Hitler and Speer would've designed for the future Germania—steel and concrete. No hint of human warmth. And none expected.

The driver whipped the car into the garage and screeched to a stop, like he had Al Capone inside. He popped the locks.

I wondered if they'd put me on suicide watch, because hanging myself sounded like a great option. Unfortunately my pumps had no shoelaces.

My backseat buddy levered herself out and grabbed my arm. I bumped my head on the roof. She didn't apologize and hauled me into a kaleidoscope of flashbulbs and microphones. Shouted questions jumbled together. Somebody had leaked to the media that a lawyer, and a fairly notorious one, was going down. A perp walk is perfect for local TV news.

Hardened criminal arrested. Streets now safe. Details at six.

"Are you innocent, Ms. Kerry?"

"Can you explain why a gun—"

"No statement," I hollered.

Determined to stare straight ahead, I thought of Saint Beatrice heading for incineration in the Roman Coliseum. Not sure I wouldn't have traded places with her.

Inside, we turned a couple of corners until we reached a holding area. I got handed off to a jail deputy, who slammed the steel door shut. She gave me another pat-down, then unlocked the cuffs.

"Everything off."

The jailer's bark was hoarse, full of phlegm. Her breath ruffled my hair and told me she had had onions, corned beef, and deli mustard for lunch. Her dark hair had been chopped an inch long. Probably had it done cheap at a beauty college. A short-sleeved uniform shirt stretched across her flat chest and displayed a skull tattoo on her bicep. Her leer was as penetrating as any I'd experienced from a drunk in a bar.

"Can I use the toilet, please?"

"When we're done, sweetheart. They're gonna test your clothes for gunpowder residue. Even your undies. So peel off. And they're fixin' to search your darlin' little house too."

Crap. My sister and I had just cleaned the place. The cops would probably track in mud on the pretty new Berber carpet that my lover-on-probation, Michael Stern, had bought for me after I bled all over the old one last year.

You're worried about the rug, dummy? How about the rest of your life?

I returned my attention to my fingers, fumbling with the buttons on my blouse. I once visited a *pro bono* client in jail, a mother of four arrested for bogus checks, and remembered the fashionable orange jumpsuit and flip-flops. Maybe my charge was serious enough that I'd be kept alone. I doubted a roommate here would provide much stimulating conversation.

Another smirking female deputy strolled in to the room, redirecting my thoughts. Gangly like an awkward basketball center who'd grown too fast, she desperately needed a mustache wax and had neglected moisturizer on her face for the last thirty years or so. The way the slender woman tugged the latex gloves on without a hint of reluctance made me realize that, unfortunately, she enjoyed her work.

"Look close. Lawyers always hide somethin'," the big one said.

I hadn't killed the man whose murder they were charging me with. Absolutely not *that* guy. But suspicion lingered around me for the unsolved murder of a miserable shit who had implicated me in the murder of Stern's wife. So I guessed my new friends thought I deserved whatever treats they could dish out. I had to be guilty of *something*.

Security cameras stuck in the ceiling likely recorded the peep show, later to be replayed for the amusement of the male deputies. I'd probably be on YouTube the next day and would put to the test P. T. Barnum's adage that there's no such thing as bad publicity.

The bigger jailer finally let me piss. Thoroughly intimidated, I thanked her profusely and sounded ridiculous.

Thank you, sir, may I have another?

Their stares and the lack of a door in front of the toilet didn't deter me. I think Marie Antoinette had to go in front of her jailers, so I was in royal company.

Feeling a bit better, I got up from the filthy pisser and unhooked my bra with all the dexterity of a high school boy on his first hot date and tossed it into the wire basket the jailer had plopped on the floor as the repository for my clothes. An air conditioner vent in the ceiling blew cold air in my face. The painted concrete sent a chill from my bare feet up my body, as goosebumps erupted.

I'm pretty tough—played some college basketball, have an advanced black belt, and three times fought for my life—but the big girl, her shoulders pulling her uniform shirt tight across her chest, could probably mop the floor with me. Only my shaky pride kept me from bawling. That probably would've made their day.

The bigger one grabbed my neck and shook me like a bottle of Pepto-Bismol.

"Come on, sweetheart. We ain't got all day."

The mug shots would be next, on file permanently, a public record for anybody to obtain for laughs. Prints, a DNA sample, and my chance for a phone call. I just hoped my sister, or Michael, answered the phone. And would still talk to me.

A heroine splashed over every Dallas news outlet less than a year earlier for revealing a fraudulent defense in the biggest malpractice case ever in Dallas, admitting her own client had lied, rescuing fourteen-year-old Sarah Stern in the dead of night from a kidnapper, and later killing the psychopath, was going to hit absolute rock bottom—a body cavity search at the county jail.

In ancient Rome, a slave would stand beside a triumphant general who was driving his chariot through the forum to the cheers of the crowd and the waiting senators. The slave's job was to whisper continuously to the hero: *Sic transit gloria mundi.*

All glory is fleeting.

CHAPTER 2

THE DEBACLE BEGAN when I decided to start my own firm—if two desks, an empty file cabinet, three chairs, and no clients can be called a law firm. Had I followed orders to double-cross Michael Stern in the *Layne* trial I would have stayed in the fifty-lawyer sweatshop and kept grinding billable hours.

With my nose in a computer screen I'd be fishing through medical records on some poor sod who sued his doctor, looking for something I could embarrass the plaintiff with in his deposition. Something like herpes or a script for Viagra would do. And resisting the temptation to pad my time entries.

Michael helped me get a deal on some nice space in NationsBank Tower that I couldn't afford just by popping into a leasing agent's office. Having been one of the big players in the medical defense racket before he lost *Layne*, he made calls to hospital administrators and insurance companies, talking me up, trying to get me clients, working hard for a guy on sex-probation.

Although I hardly needed introductions after my front-page notoriety, I appreciated his help along with his smooches, his encouragement, and his beautiful hands on my cheeks. As a junior partner at McGee's ancient firm, I'd never hustled business, so I felt as nervous as a freshman at cheerleader tryouts.

So on a bright early spring day, budding with anticipation, I set out on my quest like Pip with great expectations. Naïve Kristen thought medical providers would be falling over themselves to hire a lawyer who'd famously walked Adventist Hospital out of the most dangerous malpractice case ever filed in Texas. I figured I'd have to go out and recruit a platoon of young lawyers to help with the overflow. High six figures here I came.

Slicked up—fresh haircut, new suit, polished shoes—I met Michael for breakfast that first morning in business. What a pep talk he gave me. He should've coached at Notre Dame. I left IHOP fired up, steady-eyed. No way I wouldn't come back loaded with files and retainers.

The first place I went was a non-profit hospital chain that had mysteriously managed to procure incredibly fancy furniture in the administrator's office at the top of a new gleaming glass tower. Guess that's where all those *non*-profits wind up.

As I waited for the Big Cheese, a dozen people had to pass through the waiting area and stare at the chick who'd won *Layne*, found a kidnapped teen, taken a bullet, and killed a murdering rapist. I tried to smile back at the stares and act normal, though I wasn't sure what was normal in those circumstances.

When I finally got inside, I saw that the administrator and risk manager had invited six other people, some of whom I suspected didn't have anything to do with hiring lawyers to defend malpractice claims. The freak show had traveled to town and everybody wanted a look.

I heard, *We admire your courage. . . . You showed great integrity on* Layne. *How is your leg doing? You were so brave to rescue that girl. . . .* The way they panted, I thought they were going to ask me to hike my skirt and flash the bullet hole.

My voice never wavering, I pitched my experience to the risk manager and yakked about how hard I was willing to work. Figured I didn't need to say anything about having balls. They were all very pleasant, ending with, "We'll call."

But after five of those meet-and-greets in two weeks, I wasn't getting any calls. Maybe none of them had drawn a claim lately, or maybe I just *thought* the look-overs had gone well. Like having a great first date and never hearing from the guy again.

My depression returned, despite years of therapy. After I graduated and could afford it, I spent many hours on a doc's couch, talking through the events which caused me to flee Philly—testifying against my drunk dad and the nice way my mother told me to get the fuck out of the house. After years of tapering to almost nothing—I went back on my meds.

I had one last appointment at prestigious Presbyterian Hospital, although by then I felt as defeated as an Italian army in the desert. I dressed-to-wound, if not kill, and showed up early, but found myself just going through the motions. Got more *atta-girls*, and no business. Not even a promise of business. Even the good-bye handshakes felt hurried. I wondered if somebody had warned them I had some Asian virus.

Shuffling to my car, my blouse sticky in the Gulf humidity, I noticed a guy sitting in an ancient, dented four-door Oldsmobile parked next to my BMW. I couldn't make out much through the tinted glass, but the window had been rolled down a couple inches and I saw his beady eyes fixed on me. I nearly choked on the gray exhaust belching from his idling engine.

Something about the dude halted my breath halfway out my lungs. Why waste gas and pollute the world when he could wait for someone inside a nice air-conditioned hospital? Why the fixed eyeball stare? Or was he waiting on *me?* Stalking? I couldn't recall whether he had been parked there when I arrived.

Something about the way he sucked on his cigar was a little suggestive and made my belly lurch. I jumped in the car. In my mirror I saw him follow me out the parking lot. Took me two miles at 80 mph on the Central to lose him. I needed a slug of scotch when I got home.

* * *

After a few days the stalker faded from my memory and I quit periscoping every stranger. Probably just a lonely, dirty old man, eyeing any woman he came across. One night, after another day of butt-numbing inactivity, I went with Michael to his daughter's softball game. The team was missing a coach that night, so he volunteered to help and left me on the bleachers.

As Sarah let fly her last warm-up pitch, Michael peeked around the edge of the dugout and beamed. Early in our fling his smiles melted me, sent a wave of desire through every nerve fiber, but after a crappy day like I'd had, that smile felt *gemutlich* as Germans would say—a word hard to translate but "homey" would be close.

Our affair began after my shocking, but undeserved, win in *Layne*. After the verdict my boss ordered me to get out of town and away from reporters and prosecutors. He even let me have the use of his spectacular place in the Rockies. My old firm didn't like the truth, about how poor Layne died, being spilled in open court. Rather than go alone I asked Michael Stern, my former opponent who'd thrown the case for me, to come with me to Vail.

Before that morning we'd not touched each other—hadn't even trusted each other. We returned home to find his estranged wife dead, his daughter kidnapped, and us under suspicion—suspicion that still lingered in some people's imaginations.

Three months later I called him a son-of-a-bitch and dumped him. When I agreed to see him again, after the months-long murder investigation finally shut down, I'd insisted on no sex. Before we could do that, I had to know Sarah could recover from her kidnapping and helping me kill the man who had taken her, though I wasn't sure she ever would. She needed a father more than I needed a lover. And I had to *know* I could trust Michael before I slept with him again.

Plus I needed reassurance he wasn't with me out of *gratitude* for saving Sarah's life. Trouble was, I was punishing myself as much as him. How I missed those hands, his strong arm resting on me as I slept. As far as I knew, he'd been fulfilling his penance—spending his nights being a dad and staying out of bars and away from other women. To say our sex had been the best I ever had would be like saying you don't eat the wrapping around a tamale. And my ol' ticking biological clock sounded like Big Ben.

Ninety minutes later, Sarah flung the last pitch, a high riser, and struck out the other team's cleanup hitter. Sarah leapt off the rubber, pumping her fist. The only time the kid wasn't melancholy was when she was playing sports, or playing matchmaker between her dad and me. Michael had her on this big-time softball team and squeezed in soccer, too. Every weeknight she had an activity, and her weekends were more booked than a Kardashian's.

Sarah ran into my arms for a hug. I get choked up whenever I hold this kid whose life I'd saved, who had helped cauterize old wounds left from my miserable childhood. She had helped me quit fantasizing about unique ways of committing suicide that might fool the coroner so my spacey siblings could collect the life insurance.

"Come with us for ice cream," Sarah insisted.

She was fourteen, tall, blue-eyed, and gorgeous. She smiled that Stern family smile that says *You know you can't resist*, then tugged my wrist.

Over her shoulder, I caught the late-forties version of the same grin from her father.

"Okay." Not like I could beg off with complaints of too much work.

Michael took my hand as we walked. I glanced around, trying to see if anyone stared at the suspected *criminals* and illicit lovers. Nobody did. Maybe gossip had dried out.

"How are the interviews goin'?"

"Lousy. Nobody wants a hero."

He grimaced. "You're radioactive."

"You mean everybody's afraid I care more about the truth than defending them?"

He shrugged. "Yep, something like that."

We reached his Benz. Sarah tossed her bat bag in the trunk, then said she wanted to ride with Shelly. Teenage girls run in packs like U-boats.

After we buckled up, Michael patted me on the leg. "I got an idea."

His touch sent pulses of electricity through me. I figured he was going to suggest we pack Sarah off to her aunt's for the weekend and fly somewhere. Maybe Cabo or Vail. Although determined to say *no*, I wanted him to ask. Really wanted.

Give me a fantasy to dwell on tonight.

Instead he leaned closer, his blue eyes sparkling. "You could do plaintiff's work."

"Give me a break. Be a turncoat? Contingency fees?"

"You think there's a hospital in town that would piss on their lawyers if they were on fire?"

"How could I get started? How would I eat till something settled? It could be years before I got paid fifty cents."

The idea sounded crazy. If the phone wasn't ringing now, would people call about something I'd never done? I might as well announce my new specialty in admiralty law. No experience—and not many ships in Dallas.

He looked me in the eye and squeezed my hand. "Marry me."

Not quite what I expected. I swallowed hard. "You're trying too hard to get laid. Probation runs until July."

"I'm serious. I love you."

I hadn't completely gotten over the hurt, learning he had purloined sealed transcripts containing my testimony in my dad's medical trial, when we were still opponents in *Layne*. I don't forgive easily. Supposedly he wanted to know whether I was ruthless enough to double-cross him. Maybe I was back then.

The Michael Stern I'd met a year earlier wouldn't have proposed to a woman he hadn't slept with in four months. Nor would that guy timidly accept his probation in exchange for the pleasure of my company. I'm not *that* interesting. When I set the ground rules for resuming a relationship, I suspected he would tire of abstinence and resume his skirt chasing. Then I could move on knowing I'd been wise to doubt him.

I tossed the idea around. Money wouldn't be a problem, unless we blew seventy million. He'd done well as a lawyer and even better by marriage. Diana, a great-granddaughter of one of the developers of the East Texas oilfields, hadn't gotten around to changing her will or filing the divorce petition before she was murdered, a detail that got the police jazzed-up about investigating him.

I could be a hobby lawyer or work for Catholic Action, and be a mom. I always wanted four kids, like in my family growing up. *Tick. Tick.* The biological clock sounded in my head. But what if I turned out to be a lousy stepmom to the most important female in his life? What if he got bored with me like he had Diana? And would I always feel like I'd failed at my profession?

He interrupted my thoughts. "Are you ever going to forgive me?"

"I have. But we agreed. Summer."

He slipped the tip of his tongue along his bottom lip. He knew I loved that little move. "Feels warm already."

I resisted a smile and steeled my voice. "Not yet, honey. Give me some more time. And Sarah."

Second dumbest thing I ever did.

Chapter 3

I DECIDED TO VENTURE FORTH more aggressively. Try, try again. There are no failures, only quitters. As Churchill said, "Never, never, never, never give up." Couldn't think of any other folderol to pump me up.

Michael got me an appointment with the general counsel of a big hospital holding company in Nashville. My younger sister, Tina, agreed to skip some college classes and sit in my office all day to answer the phone. Usually she was only available afternoons, but I didn't want to take a chance on "the big call" going to a machine, making me sound like one of the TV advertising lawyers willing to jump on a helicopter to see your shattered tailbone.

Tina's my best buddy, even when we fight about her getting a real job or a boyfriend who doesn't hit her. She's forgiven me for breaking up our family and I don't bring up her former lap-dancing career—or her abortion. She's making headway cleaning herself up, and also is the loudest advocate for marrying Michael and getting familiar with the Dallas Golf and Country Club, the center of old-money Dallas. The cash in Main Line Philadelphia is a century older, and downright sedate, compared to garish DGCC—known locally as "The Cage."

* * *

A passenger at Gate 28 in the A terminal of DFW stared at me as I looked for a place to sit. Fiftyish, he wore khaki slacks—too short to cover his green socks—and an unbuttoned pea-colored golf shirt sprouting a forest of chest hair from the neck. His face sported a three o'clock shadow and the beginnings of a double chin. Fatty eyelids hung low, giving him tiny, suspicious eyes.

I turned away, strolled to an empty seat, and snagged the *USA Today* from the next spot. When I peeked around the paper, he was still staring, but he turned away when his gaze met mine. He looked like a cheap private detective spying on a straying spouse.

The weirdo got on the plane after me and sat several rows back. After half an hour I swiveled around and glanced at him. He peered into oblivion, like he was gathering his nerve to storm the cockpit, or me. I could probably have taken him, but hoped to hell I wouldn't have to. I *am* paranoid, but even paranoids have enemies.

After landing in Nashville, I hurried off, stretched my long, track-trained stride, making sure I lost the guy, and grabbed a cab. Twenty minutes later the driver pulled up in front of a glass fortress surrounded by fountains creating little rainbows. I checked my lipstick and changed out of flip-flops into the heels I'd stashed in my briefcase.

The security station directed me to the claims department, appropriately located in the basement. The receptionist there pointed me to a seat where I squirmed, read old magazines, and rehearsed my spiel. Claims are the lowest rung in any hospital organization. They are money *out*, not money in, but I would have thought the general counsel would at least have a window.

I had googled the photo of the man I wanted to see, and was surprised by a different face finally emerging from the bowels. This functionary wore a short-sleeved shirt and a clip-on tie. I thought those went out with leisure suits. His hair was cut military-style with white sidewalls, and his gut battled his belt. Nobody in such attire makes a decision more important than when to send his secretary to lunch. Assuming he had one. This was going nowhere unless he was screening me, then taking me to his leader.

My pressed suit was a tad short and tight. Hopefully eye-catching, but not slutty. My legs are my best feature. I'm almost five-foot-ten and slim. Lots of men have complimented my full lips before trying to move in. But my nose was broken in basketball and is a little crooked, and my cheeks are sort of fat. Tammy, the claims chick who assigned me to *Layne*, had told me all I needed was a boob job to entice Michael Stern. As it turned out, he liked legs.

The lawyer gave my outfit a leer of approval. I tried, probably unsuccessfully, not to look disappointed as he related the intractable scheduling problems of his boss.

After a full minute of sad-eyed apologies he led me down a corridor lined with secretarial staff tapping keyboards. Apparently they didn't dare look up or they risked being on the street. In his cramped office we settled into a polite interview. It reminded me of a college coach's fake chitchat in the days when I was still hoping for a full-ride D-1 basketball scholarship after I'd torn my ACL during my senior year in high school. They weren't interested, but they didn't want word to get out that they were rude.

I made no effort to prolong the agony and declined the offer to stay overnight, get dinner, discuss my "famous exploits," and try to catch the bigwig the next day, though I couldn't be guaranteed the man would show.

While he asked me out, the asshole tried to keep his left hand in his lap. Give me a break—I'd spotted the wedding ring when I walked in and I'm allergic to dorks cheating on their wives. Had I known the woman's number, I would've called and tattled on him, just because he wasted my time and a plane ticket. By the way—Michael's wife, Diana, had already retained a divorce lawyer before I seduced him.

Plus, hanging around looking desperate was pointless. No way they'd hire a lawyer who didn't already look busy. That's like accepting a weekend date on Thursday. Late Thursday. A girl who does that gets no respect.

Thanking him for his time, I declined his offer of a ride to the airport and got a cab.

I was lucky to catch a flight back without having to wait all day. In the security strip-down, a guy dragging his family through behind me stared at my bare feet while we waited to go through the machine gun detector. Either he had a fetish or his wife had lousy feet. Either way this was a nice change after weeks of people scanning my face, trying to remember who I was—the price of one photo in the paper and one interview on the news after *Layne.*

The big excitement in Dallas the previous year must not have reached Nashville, and I do have good feet. High arches, straight toes, no bunions, and a recent pedicure. I've never had to put up with men staring at my chest. Unfortunately.

While I sipped a Starbucks and waited for my flight, the same greasy dude who'd been on the incoming plane wandered into the gate area, clutching a boarding pass, apparently on the same flight back to Texas.

You gotta be shittin' me.

He eyed me, like a dog who hadn't been fed that week.

I remembered the Olds next to my car. Could it be the same man? Was he a hit man hired by the brother of the parolee I'd shot? Or an assassin paid by the doctor who lost *Layne* and had to file for bankruptcy? Some relative of Michael's former partner, whom some people think I killed? A pervert who'd fallen in love with my picture? And why follow me to Tennessee when I'm easy to find in my office?

The spook sat on the other side of the check-in counter and said nothing. I stayed tense the entire flight, but he made no effort to approach me. After we arrived at DFW, I hurried, almost running, to my car. As far as I could tell, I'd lost him.

I had time to make Sarah's game, but was too depressed to be good company and opted instead for an Asian massage place off Northwest Highway a mile from my house. But as I lay on the table it occurred to me that if I was really being stalked the jerk might know where I lived, since he apparently knew my travel plans. So much for relaxation. Before going into the house I checked with Tina, who said everything was fine at home. I pulled into the garage and wasted no time getting inside.

Later that night I called Michael and gave him a report on my fruitless trip.

He probably tried his best to sound encouraging. Our goodnight lingered with lots of sweet nothings. But I couldn't tell him I loved him. Not yet. Nor could I accept his proposal without feeling like a failure.

As I turned off the light, the image of the oddball at the airport flickered in my head. I went down and checked the locks again. Even with an Ambien and my 9mm pistol nearby, it took me an hour to fall into restless sleep.

* * *

The next day I called friends and classmates, wandered to the courthouse to hang around and watch sad people, argued with the copier company about its bait and switch rates, and hoped the phone would ring or that I'd get an email from Nashville.

No luck.

Needing a pick-me-up, I left early for the gym, where I sweated for an hour but decided to pass on an invitation to sub in a men's basketball league. I'd played before and acquitted myself well for a girl, but didn't want to risk a black eye or fat lip if St. Paul's Hospital called wanting to meet and discuss my fee. After all, some guys get bitchy when a woman drains a three over them.

I caught the last inning of Sarah's game. She dashed home on a squeeze play to win. Pretty cool. Afterward, I got a serious hug from her. Those little moments made me feel like maybe there was a future. Maybe. Sarah's happiness with me as a stepmom would be the *precursor in fact* to any marriage—more important than my forgiveness of her father.

I loved him. No doubt about that, but a new *mom* might send poor Sarah back into the whirlpool of grief. Truth is, I love the kid as much as I love the dad. Nothing like staring death in the face together to create a lifetime bond. I could imagine Sarah helping me change diapers on a baby half-brother or -sister.

Tick. Tick.

Michael smiled, the smile that—last fall—would melt me.

"Let's go to the mountains. There's still some snow."

I shook my head. We'd begun our affair with a long Vail weekend, but I wasn't an infatuated twenty-year-old coed. We still had issues to resolve. I had seen a rotten image of marriage growing up in the Kerry family and hadn't entirely erased those pictures from my mind.

"July," I answered, buying myself three months.

He leaned closer. "Sarah's got a tournament in Austin next weekend. She can go with Shelly's folks." He held up his forefinger, knowing I was about to remind him of his admonition to be a perfect dad. "I haven't missed a game or a teacher conference this year. I've relearned algebra and am on the school auction committee."

Mother Mary, I wavered. Money, charm, and good looks—what more could a woman ask for? Sarah had her own trust fund from her mom, enough to live on comfortably her whole life. My sister thought I was crazy. I mean even crazier than both of us admit to being. Men who really love you, who'd massage your feet and draw a perfect bath for you after a rough day, don't come along very often, but more importantly Michael was my best friend, the best friend I'd ever had.

He made a sad face. "You still don't trust me?"

The memory of finding my dad's trial transcripts, including my own testimony, in Michael's library flared across my vision like it happened yesterday. The DA even found out about the whole sordid mess while he investigated Diana's murder. But after I shot Marrs and saved Sarah again he had begged. Incredible. The town stud had *begged* me to take him back.

The ballplayers jabbered while parents tried to shoo them into their cars on a school night. Nobody was watching. I shoved the rerun out of my brain and kissed him. Really kissed him for the first time since probation began. Planted a hand on his tight ass. Electricity reached my toenails.

"I want you so bad," I said. And I did.

He pulled me against his torso.

I sniffed. "But I've got to prove that I can make it on my own." I didn't add that I wanted to make sure he loved me for being me—not for being Wonder Woman, who saved his daughter.

He blew a breath of frustration, and said, "I think I understand."

* * *

The next morning, as I sat at my desk and worked the *New York Times* crossword —anything to keep my brain active—my suite door opened. I jumped out of my chair like a condemned prisoner getting a call from the governor. Could it be that extinct entity known as a client? Someone who could pay real Union greenbacks?

Shit. I wished it had been Tina's morning to sit up front and play receptionist while she did her homework.

I stepped into my pumps and strolled to the front, trying to look like my office help were all out on important missions to secure justice.

As I entered the reception area, I froze, shocked to see the guy from the Nashville plane, chomping on an unlit cigar. The same freak who'd stalked me at Presbyterian.

He advanced. My heart raced faster. I readied myself to put him down and prayed he didn't have a gun.

CHAPTER 4

I TOED THE HEEL of my left pump, levering off the shoe, and visualized my assault. First a knee, then his nose, and his nuts if necessary. His sternal notch also presented a good target. He was big, but if I could keep the struggle going for a minute, he'd probably have a coronary.

Before I could get the other shoe off, he held his palms up. "Relax, Kristen. Please. I'm Sam Larsen. You'll want to hear what I got to say."

From his tone I think I had scared *him*. Balancing on one foot for a second I eyed the slob. He still needed a shave and looked like a hobo who had cleaned up in a public fountain. His tie slung loose, his collar unbuttoned, the plume of chest hair still poked out. Too bad he couldn't transplant some to his head.

He was right out of an old black-and-white gangster movie, like a low-level mobster running a protection racket. Was I going to have to pay him something or watch my office burn?

He stuck out his chubby hand.

Warily, I stepped back into my pump, feeling a little silly when I had to hop for a second. I edged forward and shook his rough mitt. His grimy fingernails were longer than mine. Thick calluses decorated his knuckles. Nothing is more revolting than bad, really gnarly hands on a man.

He reeked of thousands of cheap cigars. An asthmatic nearby would need an emergency inhaler. If this was my first client, I decided I would go back to giving kids basketball lessons.

He must have realized I needed to hear further *bona fides* for me to consider him safe. "Joe Bragg and I go way back. Did investigations for him for twenty years. We never lost a case."

"Uh-huh." I ignored the hyperbole. Bragg had been the plaintiff's lawyer on *Layne*. Not a bad guy . . . for a blowhard.

He added, "Joe told me you're a good gal."

I'd gotten used to the Texas propensity for using first names two seconds after being introduced, but the "gal" clanked off my eardrums like a golf ball on the cart path.

"Okay. Let's talk." I pointed toward my office.

His loafers squeaked across the laminate floor. I closed the door as he plopped into a chair across from my desk.

The effort seemed to have cost him his breath. He puffed out, "I hear you're gittin' into plaintiff's work."

I nodded as I took my seat. "Word spreads fast."

"Gittin' on the Lord's side?" Getting his breath back he jammed the cigar back between his dingy teeth.

I was desperate enough to represent the Mob. But I decided to show him I wasn't a wimp. "Why did you follow me to Nashville? Were you at Presbyterian? Sitting in a car next to mine?"

He chomped on his cigar. "Sorry to be so obvious, but I had to know."

I waited, tenting my fingers, signaling the explanation was totally inadequate. "Know what?"

"I been looking into your, shall I say, ability, and have a job for you, but when I heard you were goin' to Nashville, I guessed who you was seein' and had to make sure you got turned down."

"I guess you noticed how fast they tossed me."

"Could tell by your hangdog posture when you left that you didn't git anywhere."

A private eye had admitted to stalking me. If I'd had any sense, I would've tossed *him*. "I don't understand what tailing me to Tennessee had to do with whatever you have in mind."

"If there was any chance you were going to git defense work, I couldn't offer ya my deal and I need to move quick before somebody else horns in."

Even his drawl was sloppy and annoying. He must have had a six pack for breakfast.

I grew more suspicious, not less. "And how'd you know I was going to Nashville?"

He shrugged. "I called here the afternoon before to set up a time to meet. Your receptionist told me you'd be in Nashville the next day at a hospital corporate headquarters. I checked flights and spotted you."

I couldn't blame Tina for trying to make me sound busy to anybody who called. "Okay." More cautiously, "What's all this about?"

"I have some friends, clients actually, who have been horribly wronged by a hospital. You know a lot about hospitals."

I decided to play along. Grabbing a yellow pad, I scooted forward. "What happened?"

He pulled the disgusting cigar out. "Death of a child. Nice family. A real tragedy. Clear negligence."

"Which hospital?"

"You're not representing *any*, are you? Haven't heard back from those bloodsuckers where ya done auditions. Right?"

I hesitated a second before confirming my strikeouts. He was checking for a conflict of interest—a reasonable thing to do, even if the manner was unreasonable. "Seems like you already know all about me."

He smirked, a lingering smirk like he knew the extent of my bikini wax.

"Too much is ridin' on what we *de*-cide today. This case'll generate a million-dollar fee. It'll set you up big-time instantly."

I tried to look only marginally interested. A girl should never look too eager. "Bullshit walks, but money talks." A Texas expression I'd learned practicing law at my nasty defense firm. In other words, *Get to the point.*

"There could be companion cases. Some lawyer's gonna get rich. Why not you?"

I let that hang in the air a minute. "Why not call your buddy, Bragg?"

He jammed his cigar between his teeth, chewed a minute. "He's busy."

True. Bragg was on an island sun-burning his belly and enjoying his *Layne* fee. We might never see ol' Joe in Dallas again.

The silence was pregnant with triplets. What did this guy want, dangling millions in front of me? I'm a practiced cynic, nurtured through childhood abuse and nearly seven years of snot-slinging malpractice lawyering. He didn't pick me for my smarts. Dallas is full of smart lawyers.

He read my mind again. "I'd want to be compensated for my time, so to speak."

Ah, the punch line.

I drew a breath. It's unethical to share fees with non-lawyers. Years ago some guys in Houston had to surrender their licenses for using "investigators" to hustle widows after a plane crash and then cutting their runners in on the fees. It was okay for profit-seeking insurance companies to contact grieving widows as part of their business, but not for hungry lawyers.

"How much is your time worth?" I asked.

He chewed on the cigar that was getting mushier by the minute. Soon it would be oatmeal. I couldn't stand to look at it, but instead of turning away I watched him, determined to get to the bottom of this conspiracy.

He stared back, smug, like a tomcat with a mouse in its paws.

"A fourth of your fee."

I swallowed hard.

"In cash."

Shit. He was a real scoundrel, not just an imitation. Lawyers hire investigators all the time to look under rocks or intimidate (interview) witnesses. But you can't share contingency fees with them and they can't legally run cases to lawyers. You are supposed to wait smugly in your office for the client to come to you or answer your bloviating ad. Although I could ethically pay Sam $500 an hour—I couldn't pay him a percentage of my fee, making him more-or-less an unlicensed attorney for the Dunns.

Not only would I get disbarred if caught—worse—I could be indicted for conspiring in tax fraud since it was not likely he would want me to 1099 him. And if I paid him I wouldn't want a paper trail proving my deal with him.

How hungry was I?

We sat like kids in a staring contest.

He broke first. "Don't make a hasty decision. Think about it and call me."

I told him I would, mainly to get rid of him. I'd already decided. No way was I going to risk my Bar card. I'd spent a year waiting tables after undergrad in Oklahoma to get Texas in-state tuition. Not counting a thousand basketball lessons while I was in law school. My "See ya" hopefully conveyed the fact I *wouldn't* see him again.

He left his card, imparted a wink, and waddled out, his ass cheeks keeping time with his plodding steps.

Grabbing the hand sanitizer, I sighed with relief. I didn't even want to touch his card. Probably had E. coli on it.

* * *

That night, in his library, Michael said, "Certainly you shouldn't. You could get disbarred. And you don't know this guy any better than you do Vladimir Putin. Would you do a deal with *him*?"

I'd related the creep's pitch to Michael over a glass of cabernet in the comfort of his sanctum. I'd asked for his advice as a buddy, as the old, wise one—a role he relished.

I shrugged. "Right." That was all it took. I was done with that slime bucket.

"What did you say his name is?" Michael asked.

"Sam Larsen."

Michael chuckled. "I remember him. Randolph and I deposed him about ten years ago. We thought he'd hidden a witness and some documents. The guy was working for Joe Bragg's partner. You've probably guessed everybody's nickname for him."

This could be good. Randolph was the only one at Jackson, Stern & Randolph who'd stayed loyal to Michael during the murder investigation and was a stand-up guy. "What?"

"Larseny."

I laughed. How appropriate. "Glad I ran him off."

In my mind, from that point forward, Sam Larsen would be "Larseny."

Michael smiled. His face, when he looked right at you with that crinkle-eyed grin, could launch a thousand ships.

"On the other hand . . .," Michael paused, held my gaze, making me suffer.

I thought the decision had been made. Nobody was worse than me at rehashing every option, often years after the event. I still rag myself for taking the three-point shot in the state finals with a minute left against Jersey Gold, instead of driving the paint. And that was sixteen years ago.

"He's going to find *some*body to take his deal. Right?"

I suspected where he was headed. "I guess."

He shrugged. "Might as well be you."

"Christ, Michael. Don't say that."

He rose from his chair in front of the empty library fireplace, walked over to the bar, and poured another glass of wine.

I shook my head at his offer of a refill.

"The world's a tough place, kiddo. Nasty deals get done all the time."

"They just don't get caught?"

He sipped, then sat again. His library always felt cozy and safe even in the spring. We'd worked on *Layne* together there and I'd met Sarah in the same room. And our bitter breakup happened here.

"'Fraid not. I always suspected several prominent lawyers were sharing fees with runners, paying kickbacks to ER nurses, cops, or EMTs."

"Of course, it's not unknown in the defense business either."

He faked a shocked expression. "Surely not! Pay adjusters for sending business?"

"What about new golf clubs? Trips to Vegas for claims supervisors?"

He cocked his head knowingly. "All in a day's work, my dear."

I got up, paced across his gorgeous Chinese rug, and decided I needed another drink. Pouring cab, I asked, "You think I *should*? Really, Michael? Put my career in jeopardy? Again?"

I realized how stupid and weak I appeared, but at that moment didn't care.

"There's another option."

I took a good slug, hoping for an alcohol calm. "What?"

"Marry me."

I threw my hands in the air. "Michael! I have to prove to all those assholes out there that *I am no fluke*. Everybody in town thinks I won *Layne* 'cause you threw it to get in my pants."

He grabbed my hand as I stalked by. "Baby, nobody thinks you're a fluke."

I jerked away, suspecting he agreed with me—that he had thrown it, but not to get me in the sack. Worse, I worried he did it because he felt sorry for me after reading the transcripts from my dad's trial. Hell, I practically had to beg him to go to Vail. He'd been ready to write me off as a basket case and almost turned me down.

After a minute of contemplation I said, "Then why won't any of these hospital bastards, who act so impressed that I walked Adventist on *Layne*, who smile at the big hero, hire me?" Strange how a walk in baseball means you never touched the ball, and a walk in legal jargon refers to getting a defense verdict. I guess in both cases the person gets to leave with impunity.

Michael said nothing for a while. "I honestly don't know, but it's always tough breaking in."

"Part of me wants to take this plaintiff's case and ram it up somebody's ass. Some shit-for-brains who wouldn't hire me. See how they like paying me two mil when they could've paid two hundred an hour."

"I understand, honey. You know where I came from."

Yeah. I knew. A refinery town on the wrong side of the tracks. He'd married the wrong woman—at least the wrong one for him—out of lust and to get a head start in our cutthroat business. The late Diana had old Dallas money and connections traceable to the bloody Alamo. The Anglo side of the battle.

I calmed down. I came up behind him, massaged his neck a minute, and thanked him for listening. I pulled my hands away before they started roaming down his shirt.

He turned and articulated the nasty fear that had lingered in the back of my brain through all those worthless interviews.

"I wonder if it's possible someone's blackballing you. Somebody with a lot of stroke in the racket."

I didn't say anything. The obvious culprit would be Pete McGee, my old boss at Wright McGee.

He read my mind. "Pete may be glad you won, but he wanted a piece of my hide as much as a victory."

"I didn't exactly follow instructions."

"Telling people you don't salute and follow orders would scare a lot of potential clients off. He sure couldn't run down your ability."

"The Bible teacher wouldn't have to soil himself with a lie. I *didn't* follow orders."

"Realistically," he paused, holding my attention, "it's not likely you'd get caught. Larseny sure ain't going to tell, and if the clients are happy in the end, who would blab?"

I pondered, taking a seat in one of the matching leather chairs facing the fireplace, in his beautiful Highland Park mini-palace. I wavered. Slipped off my flats, curled my toes on the soft rug, cursed my stupid ultimatum. Here was a gorgeous rich man in love with me, probably more in love than I was. I could have those hands roaming my flesh within the hour. The hair on my arms went *achtung*.

Before I could drop my admonition, as well as my shorts, Sarah strolled in from her science study group. I got a hug. Michael got a kiss. What a great kid. Though she had her own twenty million in a trust fund inherited from her murdered mother, she'd rather have the latest Easton bat than anything from Saks. She'd gotten her dad's blue eyes and strong nose, but Diana's beautiful hair that bleached blond in summer and show-stopping legs. Poor kid still saw a shrink and often turtled into a shell, but was finally off anti-depressants. I was gradually feeling less and less like I was walking on thin ice around her.

I stayed for enchiladas that Rita, their Mexican maid, had fixed. Michael asked Sarah about school and an upcoming dance, but she withdrew again, her personality disappearing into one-word responses. Of course I wondered if I should have gone home, wondered if maybe I should forget the whole deal, but finally I risked, "Is Annie going to play with you again this year?"

Annie was the best player on Sarah's softball team and a fairly close friend. The kid was a cinch for a scholarship and got frequent offers as a pickup player all over the metroplex. Sarah looked up from her rice and after a moment smiled.

"What do you think she should do?"

My heart rate sped up. Sarah had asked my opinion like it mattered to her. I caught Michael's expression of encouragement, but knew I had to sound relaxed and normal.

"That's tough. Some years I played with friends. Others I tried out and made the best club I could. Sometimes I tried to do both."

"Which did you like better?"

"Hard to say. As it turned out I blew out my knee and didn't get any serious offers. So it didn't matter."

"Do you think I'm good enough to get a scholarship?"

Her earnest expression amused me. She needed a full ride about like Donald Trump's granddaughter, but I admired her competitive spirit. "I'm no expert on softball, but, Sarah, you're capable of anything you set your mind to."

I wasn't kidding. This was a kid who'd helped me take down a killer. She loosed a sly smile, warming my heart. Michael nodded his approval at my effort. The mood lifted. Sarah chatted away about her teammates. Her melancholy seemed to have retreated. Feeling optimistic again I left, deciding once-and-for-all to reject Larsen's deal.

I wasn't as determined, though, to keep putting Michael off. He was a helluva dad. I already knew he was a helluva lover. He was right. I could work for Legal Aid and feel useful. My only tough decision would be whether to hyphenate my name.

CHAPTER 5

BACK IN MY TOWNHOUSE, I sat awake in bed until Tina wandered in at midnight. Although I've long ago given up mothering my little sister, I always sleep better once she makes it home.

Tina is tall, like me, with thick brown hair, third-generation Italian, but except for her teeth she's probably better-looking. Her cheeks are not as plump and her nose is straighter, but by the time she needed braces, our parents were spending their money on cocaine, then on lawyers to keep Dad's medical license.

She climbed the stairs and poked her head in. "Yo, Adrian."

"Yo, yourself."

Tina smelled of cigarettes. You can still smoke in some bars in Texas.

I felt the need for a second opinion, so I relayed the Larseny story to Tina.

"Go for it, sweet cakes."

Tina's response wasn't a surprise. Recklessness is a common symptom of Adult Children of Alcoholics—we have our own worldwide organization—like entering a dark house to save a kid from a murderer or grabbing a lying witness by the arm and threatening to break it.

Tina had, for years, displayed the effects of her relationship with our parents through sex, street drugs, dropping out of high school, and table dancing at eighteen. Never a dull moment. But she'd had the guts to go with me on the rescue mission to find Sarah, so despite all her faults I'd be eternally grateful.

I hugged myself against my long T-shirt and asked why.

"Somebody's going to do it. The people really deserve a good lawyer."

"Thanks."

I wasn't sure how valuable Tina's advice was. She'd never let rules stand in her way.

"And you should make some real money."

"And if I get caught?"

"You're still young enough to pole dance naked."

I rolled my eyes.

She rolled back. "The real answer is a no-brainer. Get married, silly. Be a rich Highland Park bitch. Take up golf and Junior League."

That scared the crap out of me. Tina had just described Michael's wife, now in her grave. What frightened me wasn't the thought of being stalked by a bloodthirsty pervert like Diana had been. I'd killed that bastard. Rather, what scared me was the painful knowledge that Michael had become bored with that very woman and had cheated like a gigolo on an Androgel and Viagra cocktail. I should know. I was the last young thing he'd hooked up with the very weekend his wife got carved up.

Point being, I had to make a go of it, not just for my self-respect but to keep Michael Stern interested in me. Diana had been beautiful and rich, with the social connections in Dallas that take one to the top. My best references were from basketball coaches and shrinks I'd seen through my twenties.

She has progressed well. She's not nearly as unstable as when I first treated her.

So I went to bed unsure. Got up six hours later and ran five miles in the gathering morning light. I showered and went to the office, praying that some hospital would dangle half a dozen case files. I would have settled for an old classmate asking about a divorce.

* * *

No such luck. Larseny rang at eleven, wanting to know my decision. Right then. He had to know. He sounded like he'd just run a set of suicides on the basketball court. Sprinting the lines for those who haven't played.

I stalled.

"These people can't wait much longer. I can't control them forever."

"Uh-huh."

"Great cases like these come along once a lifetime. If you're lucky."

I knew he might be shopping around. Also figured he wouldn't set up a meeting with the distraught family until I'd agreed to his bargain. They might decide they loved me. Hire me on the spot, and he'd have nothing to prove our shady deal.

"Rumor has it there could be as many as three more kids who died needlessly. Do the math."

I did. We say in this business that liability drives damages. The same injury or death can be worth double in damages if the screw-up is egregious. Triple or more if they tried to cover up the error, lied about it, or repeated the error on another patient. Ask Joe Bragg, wallowing on the beach with his *Layne* money.

"Well, Kristen, do I call somebody else?"

I told Larseny I had a client walk in, that I'd call him back after lunch. I doubt he believed that, but I didn't care. I just wanted off the phone. I'd bought a couple hours to stew some more, then decided to do some snooping.

My old buddy Jenny Norton, from Wright McGee, had been a

nurse at three different hospitals and knew most of the gossip in the medical-legal racket or could find out what she didn't know. But she was out when I called so I left a message. We had parted badly. Just like our boss, Pete, Jen didn't care about truth. Frankly, I wasn't sure she'd call back.

The receptionist had sounded shocked to hear my name. Probably worried that I was headed there with my Browning automatic pistol and a couple extra mags. Pete McGee certainly deserved a round in the head for sending me to defend Adventist Hospital on *Layne*, knowing the defense was a lie.

I stared out the window at a plane leaving Love Field, as if the answer lay in the clouds. Then I saw the old Texas School Book Depository. Infamous Dealey Plaza. I'd seen the History Channel reenactment and could picture Kennedy's open limo cruising down the street. Nobody had ever found the mystery second shooter. If there was one.

Perhaps it wasn't likely the Bar would catch me paying Larsen.

The phone rang.

Wright McGee on caller ID. I answered.

"Hey, superstar."

Her tone surprised me, she sounded like the last year had never happened.

We spent a minute catching up, then agreed to meet for a quick lunch.

* * *

After Tina and I had carried Sarah out of the dirtbag's house, I packed my office gear and kissed my former best buddy, Jenny Norton, good-bye on the cheek, and then kissed the heavyweight hospital defense firm, Wright McGee, good riddance. Senior partner Pete McGee had given me *Layne* because he thought I was a cute girl who'd buy into a phony defense to keep my partnership, follow orders to entice Stern into a joint defense agreement, and then double-cross him in trial. I didn't even get the chance to decline the assignment like Mr. Phelps, and the tape didn't self-destruct.

Pete McGee had told me about an hour into my career as a malpractice defense lawyer that if I wanted a friend, I should get a dog. I never got a dog. As hard as they worked me those first few years, it would have died of neglect. Despite his admonition, Jen and I became friends. Her office had been near mine. We had each other's back.

Sometimes I asked the former nurse for help on medicine. Although my dad is a vascular surgeon—or was—I majored in English literature and history. So I ran medical questions past her, and Jen ran legal problems by me. And I dodged most of her attempts to set me up with every single male lawyer or doctor in town. A wonderful friendship until I learned she'd been in on the decision to put little ol' me on *Layne*.

I arrived at The Palm in the West End and nabbed a table. Jen hurried in a couple minutes later. We hugged, but it wasn't a real hug—it was more rote than warm. But after a while our small talk gradually became less forced.

I was glad to hear she was up for partner. Jen deserved it. She's smart and tough. She didn't ask about Michael. I'm sure she was appalled that I was involved with him again. Or maybe she was jealous.

After a bite of salad, I reminded myself to be careful with what I divulged. You don't learn much while talking. "Rumor has it there's a nasty dead kid case floating around."

I know that sounds like I was being callous, but that's how lawyers describe cases—leg off, bad baby, dead kid, cashed geezer, smash-up, etc. Nasty shorthand.

"Haven't heard a thing."

But she gave it away. An eyebrow twitch. A bit of a head bob, stopping a nod halfway down. I ought to go to Vegas and enter a poker tournament. Something was afoot. No point trying to pump her. She wouldn't tell me if one of her hospital clients had Jack the Ripper on the surgical staff.

It's standard operating procedure in the event of a big screw-up for a hospital to call its lawyers before the body is zipped up or ink dry on the chart. And someone had called Jen or Pete. The culprit could be none other than one of my old clients.

Even if she didn't know I was considering doing a Benedict Arnold and switching to plaintiff's work, she'd see me as competition for the defense of whatever was brewing. Jen was a true believer in defending medical providers. In her mind, all the good they did outweighed any mistakes. No hospital or doc is in the business for filthy money. They're all Albert Schweitzers deserving a Nobel Prize.

Right.

We changed the subject and chatted about a guy she might go out with and my startup shop. Though she pried, I dodged specifics and didn't admit I had no clients. We parted, promising to get together again soon. I wouldn't hold my breath. But lunch had been useful. I'd be surprised if there wasn't something big out there. Likely the case Larsen was dangling.

CHAPTER 6

A FTER LUNCH WITH JEN, I hiked back to the office, breaking a sweat while fighting a warm wind in my face. No messages, of course. Not even a cold call from a stock broker or legal research publishing company. I never thought it would be so tough. I'd figured I'd get calls just because I was sort of famous. Didn't have enough ego to think clients would come in because I was good-looking, but my therapist would have reassured me that silence didn't mean I wasn't darling.

The phone rang. Made me jump. Caller ID said *Larsen*. Five rings to decide. On the second ring I decided *no way* was I going to risk the license I'd worked so hard for. In law school, I went out with boring guys just for the free meal. Until I got an internship, I could only afford vitamins and table scraps.

Two more rings.

Tina's voice echoed in my head. *"Go for it."*

I answered. After stammering like a dolt I agreed to meet Larseny in a bar on Commerce at five, like spies rendezvousing in a Vienna coffee house, a zither playing in the background, whispered conversations and cash slipped inside menus.

I felt like a high school girl wanting to believe her boyfriend's promise to pull out in time. I'd be totally dependent on the word of a man I had no reason to trust. Guess I was more scared of failing at the role of wife and stepmom than being surprised at that dive by the Bar Association investigator. Better the train wreck you see coming than the one you don't.

Three hours later I walked down Commerce, in the shadows of skyscrapers, breathing exhaust fumes. The breeze had died, leaving oppressive Gulf humidity gripping me, like a wet wool coat. Dark clouds loomed to the west, the direction tornadoes come from in Texas. You haven't seen a thunderstorm until you've been in one in Texas. Hail the size of baseballs and eighty-mile-an-hour winds, the kind that scare you in Philly, are considered mild storms in the Southwest.

As I tuned out the traffic, the debate continued in my mind. My pace slowed the closer I got to the dive Larsen had picked. Perhaps some bright idea to get me out of this would pop into my brain.

Maybe some gorgeous guy would walk up and proposition me to duck into the Fairmont. Even a by-the-hour hotel. The closer I got, the less good-looking he had to be. If I was going to whore myself to Larseny, why not some stranger?

Alas, it was not my day to be picked up. Every man who passed was in too big a hurry to notice me. Should've worn a leather miniskirt and high heels—felt like a hooker anyway, getting ready to prostitute my license and integrity.

The storm held off until I reached Ed's Bar and Grill. I blocked the entrance for a minute, trying to decide whether to do a one-eighty.

A giggling couple bumped into me, knocking my hesitant ass into the bar. Rather than look stupid, I strolled on in.

Once more into the breach.

A shaggy guy at the piano tapped out an unrecognizable snappy tune. The crowd, mostly male and almost filling the place, was a mix of yuppies in rolled-up sleeves and slung ties and hard hats with grime stuck to their cheeks. Everybody in the place turned toward me, as if they knew I was planning something seedy.

As the stares of dozens of eyes crawled over my flesh, I spotted Larseny, chomping on his cigar—maybe the same one—alone and sitting at a tiny booth in the corner. Several guys continued staring as I trudged across the bumpy linoleum, trying to ignore their booze-induced lust. I picked up my pace, wanting to appear capable of handling a million-dollar case. After all this gut churning, I sure didn't want him to decide to find another lawyer. Always better to be the dump*er* than the dump*ee*.

Larseny hoisted his belly a few inches as I reached his booth. His triumphal grin suggested the moment when a frat rat nails the little sorority pledge. We made forced talk until a waitress, too classy to be working there, took my order for a Coors Lite. When trying to impress other lawyers or be one of the *boys*, I drink single malt Scotch. No need to impress Larseny. He had been reeled in . . . or maybe I had. Low-calorie, low-alcohol, diluted beer was adequate for this adventure.

After our waitress darted to a table of rowdies demanding another round, Larsen leaned close enough to blow cigar-fowled beer breath on me. He had to speak up over the din. "I think there's two more deaths."

"You've got control of only one family, right?"

"That's the beautiful thing. The others don't know why their kid died. Got fed a line of shit about blood clots and heart irregularities."

"If there's no autopsy, sometimes you can't prove causation."

He gulped his beer, leaving a foam mustache behind. "The liability's so bad, they'll be beggin' to pay."

The harried waitress slid my beer toward me and hustled to the next table, giving me time to ponder how the hell a sweet, former practicing-Catholic girl like me got herself into a dive like this, drinking with a dude like Larseny.

Can I have a do-over?

"Hospital lawyers can get awfully creative," I said. "I'm an expert."

43

"That's why I picked you," he dropped his voice. "You're fearless."

He made it sound like I had more balls than he did. I sure didn't want to check. Shuddering, I took a slow slip of bland brew to cover my discomfort. I let the sales job continue while trying to still the nagging voices in my brain.

"Too many old plaintiff lawyers don't really understand how hospitals can cover up mistakes."

Buying a little more time I stuck my lips in the suds. The more he tried to sell me, the more suspicious I became.

"And too many of 'em would take the first offer and head for the beach."

I banged the glass down. Give me a break. There were plenty of tough bastards who'd try any case. My bullshit detector had blared. I decided to bail.

Larseny's spiel halted as he read my defiance.

I scooted an inch toward the edge of the booth bench.

"Some plaintiff lawyers are sweatin' for a fee just to pay their back taxes."

He yammered on, but I tuned him out.

Deliver us from evil.

Fear flashed on his face and I suddenly realized he *needed* me. Why me?

Why, if this was such a great opportunity? I downed the rest of my beer, steeling myself to bolt.

"You need to think this over carefully."

"I have. Thanks, Sam. I'm flattered you asked me, but I really can't." I hoped I sounded like I was turning a nice but unattractive guy down for a date. No point being a jerk—and I *was* flattered he'd chosen me.

Sorry, getting my nails done that night.

I got up and made my way through the crowd without looking back. I felt clean, as if I'd showered and exfoliated all over. A new woman.

I drove home and slept the sleep of the just. Got up early and lifted weights at Gold's. Since it was Tina's morning without a class, I let her beat me into the office while I lingered over the paper and breakfast, not giving Larseny another thought.

My cell rang as I neared downtown. Tina.

I clicked on.

"Krissy, you have clients here."

What clients? Had somebody sent me a drunk-driving case because they couldn't pay a real lawyer's retainer?

"Have 'em fill out an intake sheet," I told Tina.

"I did. They want to sue Adventist Hospital."

"Ten minutes."

Adventist. My client on *Layne*. My old firm Wright McGee's biggest money-maker. I figured it must be a bullshit case. An infection. An old lady fell out of bed. The nurse was rude. Everybody told me that in plaintiff's work, you have to run through dozens of intakes before finding a keeper.

But I sped up as I reached Central Expressway. Whoever had wandered in was my first client. Even if there was nothing to it, at least I felt like a real lawyer again.

* * *

"They killed our baby. My beautiful . . ."

Dabbing her face with a Kleenex the pretty mom choked up, unable to say more.

The husband held her hand and added, "Our son."

Lawyers deal in tragedy. If nothing bad ever happened, half the country's attorneys would go broke. This looked *real* tragic. I listened, taking a few notes, trying mostly to maintain eye contact. I was very conscious of how I sounded, how they appeared to respond to me, but things started well. Kind of like a job interview, which it was.

The father did most of the talking. He was a beanpole, taller than me, and well-spoken. Poor guy looked like he hadn't eaten in a week. His tie was a bright regimental red and yellow, his blue shirt starched stiff, but loose around his neck.

The mom's face contorted as she struggled for control. When she did add something to the story, I had to turn my good ear toward her to hear. Already a tear had plopped, darkening her pink blouse. In their late twenties, they both looked haggard from sitting in the hospital, attending a funeral, and enduring the miserable days afterward putting away clothes and toys.

He related how their sixteen-month-old baby boy—a sick, febrile little guy—had been diagnosed with bacterial meningitis and admitted to the PICU—pediatric intensive care—at Adventist. He was moved to a regular peds floor after he improved. No fever, eating well. They'd been assured he was coming home the next day. He'd responded to antibiotics. He was in the clear, hearing and faculties intact. Prayers answered.

And then he died.

They showed me pictures. He'd been a darling kid with his mother's skin and beautiful curls. Their first. The dad, Bob Dunn, was an accountant at Chase. The mother, Laura, taught sixth-grade Spanish and spoke with a slight accent, which went with her dark good looks.

"It took us four years to get pregnant. Laura had to have surgery to unblock her tubes. Then she had two miscarriages."

I nodded, ready to cry too.

"We weren't told much about what happened. But a woman called after the funeral. Said she was with Adventist. That there was a cover-up, a big mistake had been made."

Laura cried, bending at the waist, wailing at the floor.

This was bloody awful. Representing defendants hadn't prepped me for this. Insurance companies seldom cry. I told myself to hang together. I needed to be objective—and I wondered who the hell called them. "What else did she say?"

"That somebody'd messed with the records, but she couldn't say more. Told us to call Sam Larsen for the details. He's an investigator. He told us to see you."

Shit.

Larseny had sent them. He was dangling these people in front of me. Letting me know the case was legit and the clients were great folks, the kind juries and plaintiff's lawyers love—and that scare defense lawyers shitless.

I knew from the way Laura's tears trickled down her pretty face, her lovely accent, and the difficulty conceiving their son, that Larseny might be right. The case could bring millions, if we could figure out what happened. And if it really was the hospital's fault. I suspected their mystery source had a deal or some relationship with Larseny.

We talked for over an hour. I told them how the process worked. We'd have to hire experts to review the records. Some of their opinions would be speculation until we could file the case and take depositions of the nurses and doctors. There'd been no autopsy, which always makes a plaintiff's burden of proving that negligence actually caused the death tougher. They'd been too distraught to demand one and probably didn't want their beautiful son carved up, even if given the option.

I didn't try to hogtie them and it wouldn't have worked anyway. They weren't the kind to buy the first car they looked at, no matter how smooth the sales job.

Clever of Larseny to send the Dunns in to tempt me. He must have had complete control over them and wouldn't refer them to me without confidence in their loyalty to him, though I doubt Larseny had told them he was demanding a cut.

These parents could handle a few hundred bucks to an investigator and likely had paid Larseny enough to make it look legit. Had they signed a retainer with me that day, I'd have been under no obligation—

moral, immoral, or legal—to cut Sam in on the fee. I only had to fear a bullet in the back if I screwed Larseny out of his take.

A lot can go wrong in a malpractice case and I told them that, but the meeting went well. Though I felt we had bonded, I suspected they didn't want to hire me until they talked to Larseny again. They thought he was the key to finding some inside secret about their sweet boy.

We shook hands, hers and mine lingering as we both sniffed at the same instant, then smiled at our embarrassment. Her left hand clutched the silver cross hanging from her neck, as if in a silent prayer. He thanked me for my time. It had been a great first date.

If I took the case, even if I only got the records and later changed my mind, I was toast as a hospital lawyer. Adventist had been my best client at Wright McGee. In their eyes, I'd be Benedict Arnold, Quisling, and Tokyo Rose rolled into one scumbag. Not to mention what the Bar would do if I did a deal with Larseny and got caught.

But I knew I'd never forget Laura Dunn and wanted to do anything I could for her.

CHAPTER 7

IT TOOK LARSENY A WHOLE HOUR to pop in after the Dunns left. I had hoped he'd changed cigars since I last saw him, but this one was mangled, like it had been in a head-on collision on I-35.

He grinned, flashing teeth more yellow than last time, before he spoke. "Nice folks, huh?"

Appalled at myself for getting into this mess I nodded.

He eased into the seat nearest my desk, his smirk still showing greenish-brown teeth. "Let's do business."

I said nothing, feeling the dread that comes before diving off the cliff at Acapulco.

He popped open a cheap, scuffed attaché case and pulled out a single piece of paper. He tossed it at me with the confidence of a car dealer who knows he has an eighteen-year-old hooked on a used Mustang convertible with twin mufflers and a hundred thousand miles rolled back to forty.

I picked it up, read it, and muttered, "Fuck."

Very articulate. Took me six and a half years at Wright McGee to learn such an arcane legal term.

Larsen stared impassively.

He wanted the fee kickback in *writing*—evidence, if ever

discovered, that would get my license jerked faster than spaghetti goes through a fat guy with a bowel resection.

My gaping expression asked, *What the fuck?*

He answered, "We don't really know each other."

"Give me a break, Sam."

He chomped his cigar, pulled it out, and said, "They trust me. I can still run the case to a dozen other guys."

"You're asking me to sign something that would get me disbarred."

He shrugged. "I'd have no reason to get you disbarred. There's gonna be other deals, other cases."

I should have thrown it back at him, called the Dunns, and told them their helpful investigator was a crooked hustler. I could, ethically, since I now had a relationship, if not yet officially endorsed, with them. Later there would be many more *I should've*s.

But as I remembered Laura's tears, I told myself nobody could pull apart the records and find out what happened at that hospital better than me, especially if the hospital was hiding something. And to get the case, I had to sign the dirty document.

On the other hand, if there wasn't a valid case, if it was just a bad outcome, I'd wish the Dunns good luck, and nobody would have any reason to care about Larseny and me.

I'm the straightest person you'd ever know. Told the truth and got my dad's medical license revoked when I was a kid. Uncovered the scam in *Layne* and told the judge. Had slept with only as many men as I've got fingers. On one hand. Fingers, not the thumb. Went to Mass every week until I left home.

Deliver us from temptation.

I wondered what the odds were on getting caught. The Bar probably had plenty of lawyers they kept their sites trained on. My record was as clean as a scrub tech's new glove. Except for breaking and entering two houses to find Sarah Stern and illegally accessing hospital records to ID the kidnapper. On second thought, my record wasn't all *that* clean.

But I supposed Sam was right—nobody involved would have any incentive to turn me in. I guessed the odds at about the same as a half-court shot at the buzzer. Most miss. I had gambled when I freed Sarah, so I figured I was on a roll. This rationale from a woman who had never set foot in a casino.

Seeing in my mind the mom's tears, I picked up the contract and scrawled my John Hancock. Larseny scooped it up like a car salesman who had made his monthly quota.

After he left, my gut began churning.

Why did you do that? Are you a total moron?

I pulled my hair until it hurt. Paced the floor, cursing myself.

Embarrassed, I texted Michael that I wouldn't make the game that night with a lame excuse about an upset stomach. It was lame, but true enough. I hovered over the trash can, thinking I was going to hurl. Though I didn't, I felt like I had puked my integrity.

*　　*　*　*　*

The next morning, the Dunns returned. We rehashed everything. She was like the Ancient Mariner, telling her story again in the same detail, but I was ready to bawl even on the rerun. They signed my contingency retainer. I'd get forty percent if there was a recovery. I had enough in my 401(k) from Wright McGee to fund a case and pay office expenses for a year, maybe two. Long enough. Hopefully.

I took a medical authorization to Adventist that afternoon and went straight to Records. I knew enough not to naïvely mail it and pray they would send a complete chart without any monkey business. Call me a cynic. *Call me Ishmael.* Call me a crook.

I pored over the original records, looking for erasures, white-outs, late entries on the electronic portion, or anything that looked suspicious. Nothing did. After an hour, I counted the pages, asked for a copy, and told the records custodian I'd be happy to wait, so she wouldn't have to trouble herself mailing the chart. And nobody would have time to make changes.

Trevor Dunn had been admitted with a stiff neck, vomiting, and fever, and had been inconsolable. Classic symptoms of meningitis. ER had appropriately done a spinal tap that was positive for bacteria. The little guy was admitted to the kids' ICU and started on IV antibiotics. All well done. His white count on admit was twenty-four thousand, with lots of bands, immature white cells cranked out to fight an infection. A sick little cowboy.

But the parents had gotten him to the hospital in what would usually be plenty of time. Over the next two days he got better. His white cell count improved to nine thousand, his temp dropped to normal. When he ate oatmeal, they moved him to a regular pediatric floor and planned to send him home the next day. Instead, he crashed late that night.

The clerk gave me the same number of pages I'd counted. I paid and left. Back at the office, I graphed all the vitals by time and made a synopsis of every clinical finding. After three hours I knew the Dunn chart upside-down, backwards, and sideways.

Useful work gave me the confidence to face Michael, so I checked my iPhone for Sarah's ball schedule, zipped to the field, and caught her game. She didn't pitch, but had two clean singles, two stolen bases, and a slick backhand stab at short. So sweet of her to catch my eye and grin. Gave me some optimism.

Michael wasn't coaching that night and frequently found an excuse to slip an arm around me or squeeze my leg with excitement when Sarah threw a kid out at first. I might have surrendered another time, but tonight I was pretty much all business and wanted Michael's opinion on the Dunn kid's records. So I invited myself over after the game.

While Sarah showered upstairs, Michael sat behind his desk, his signal that he took this seriously, and read the chart, while I dug into housekeeper Rita's fabulous enchiladas. I swear the Lone Star beer at Michael's was always colder than anywhere else.

He didn't ask any questions about Larseny or unethical fee agreements. Maybe he didn't *want* to know. I watched him study the records. Whenever he slipped into pensive thought, his forehead wrinkled. For all his bluster, backslapping, and joking, he has a sharp mind capable of intense focus.

For twenty minutes, a wonderful sense of serenity enveloped me, like a comfy down coat in winter or an open fire on a Philly December night.

He put the chart down. "You know as well as I, a clean chart doesn't mean a thing. Too bad you don't have an autopsy. Pathologists are usually honest."

I floated my best conspiring theory. "Any chance the labs are fake?"

He shrugged. "Anything's possible."

He flipped to the lab sections and studied a minute. "There's got to be a computer trail. These blood draws get logged in and numbered. Somebody would have to screw with the system."

"And it happens."

"His platelets and white count were improving, returning to normal before he quit breathing. Creatinine was okay, so kidneys were working. Nobody mentions petechiae."

If that was true—and only a post-mortem would've confirmed that—it meant the tiny blood vessels in the eyeballs were intact. He hadn't choked on anything or had swelling in the airway. Nobody had held a pillow over the kid's face.

"I checked all the med dosages, looks like everything is within recommended limits," I said.

"The pharmacy department keeps separate records on what gets checked out and returned unused. You'll have to subpoena that separately." He smiled and added, "Of course, they may claim the records are deleted after a month."

An all-knowing look. Years ago he supposedly lost pathology slides and original charts, which suddenly reappeared in time to win a case. One of the many reasons I had not trusted him during the Layne trial. He'd always told me the stories were exaggerated. I was never sure of the truth.

That was part of the reason I didn't topple into bed the instant I felt the attraction. And I didn't feel the pull until I'd seen he had a conscience, despite his reputation.

He put the copies down on the leather inlay and leaned back. "He had DIC from sepsis. The labs they drew when he started crashing are consistent with that. But I wonder why all of a sudden everything went haywire. He responded to the antibiotics."

DIC is the collapse of platelets in a patient's blood, caused by infection, resulting in internal bleeding. Clots form in distant vessels, depriving major organs of blood and oxygen. It can act fast. Often it's fatal.

"That last lab report shows platelets were normal when they moved him to the regular floor. Blood sugar is fine."

Even glucose, just sugar really, can kill a baby. They were running it into the kid by IV in the PICU. I'd heard of glucose overdose, readings on CBC of five hundred or more. Somebody could've hung the wrong bag or run it too long into the child. Of course, hyperglycemia would be a red flag on the next routine bloodwork, and all sugars were 90 to 110.

A child suffering from disseminated intravascular coagulopathy, kidney failure, or sepsis would look bad. Real bad. And according to the nurses watching him, he looked fine that evening. One more night, and he would've been out of the hospital. The more I thought, the fewer answers came.

I could picture his mom making plans for a special meal when he got home. Instead, he went south after supper and died at two in the morning. Now, thanks to the government, most nurses' notes are template-generated. The default on most programs is "everything normal." Unless a nurse goes to the trouble of entering a different finding, all she has to do is hit *enter* and all systems are A-OK—at least that's how the chart looks.

I had seen and used these programs when I defended hospitals. If the button got hit, we always claimed everything must have been peachy and that our nurse had carefully gone over every system— bowel sounds, heart rate, blood pressure, skin color, respirations, etc. Maybe things weren't okay, but right now we couldn't say otherwise.

Michael seemed to read my mind. "This kid should've been autopsied."

"Family was too upset," I said.

"And let me guess . . . nobody offered." He checked the death certificate again. "Cause of death is arrhythmia leading to cardiac arrest, secondary to meningitis."

The catch-all defense of irregular heartbeat leading to no heartbeat. The same defense we tried to peddle in *Layne*. "Think it's a case?"

He thought a minute. I waited with anticipation.

"What's odd is the kid seemed to be improving. Got moved out of the PICU. Then this big collapse, and a code is called."

I nodded.

"Get a pediatric infectious disease specialist to look at it. Maybe they gave him the wrong drug."

I set my empty plate on the ottoman. "But it's not a multimillion-dollar case."

He shook his head. "Right now it's not any kind of case. Even if you get a theory and someone to testify to it, it's not that valuable without some stink. Something gross. Something to piss off a jury."

He knew what I was thinking. Larseny had oversold it to me and the Dunns. Or was there something I didn't know? Something we were missing?

As I pondered, Sarah walked into the library, dressed in a striped terrycloth robe, her long, blond hair still wet. I took it as a sign of real comfort with me that she could stroll in, wearing only a robe, sit, and tuck her bare feet under her thighs. When Michael took a phone call, we talked about school and boys. Fortunately the prevailing theme was still how silly they acted.

She excitedly told me her pal, Becca, was coming to spend the week with them. Becca's mother, a buyer for Neiman Marcus, would be in Paris. Becca's dad had gone bust in some over-leveraged oil deal and had disappeared. Becca played softball with Sarah. She wasn't near the athlete Sarah was, but seemed like a nice kid, unlikely to be sexting boys or getting Sarah into alcohol. After Diana's murder and the rescue, Becca had been a real friend to Sarah—not too many questions and lots of support.

I thought about how easy it would be to move in, but caught myself wondering if Sarah's mother had bought the darling robe for her, like she'd decorated Sarah's room. I couldn't replace Diana and had no business thinking I could.

Sure sorry your mom got sliced up while I took your dad for a sex-filled weekend. Mind if I move my stuff in?

I tried to hide my own blues and said I had to go. To my surprise, in my funk, they both looked disappointed, and asked me to stay longer.

I gave in. Sarah made brownies sprinkled with pecans. We slurped them gooey out of the pan with cold milk and laughed about a goofy boy who thought he was in love with Sarah. For the hundredth time I wondered if I was making a big mistake playing with Larseny.

* * *

The next morning I awoke to reality—the reverie of the last night had evaporated. Something told me the façade with Michael and Sarah would eventually collapse. Either that or my big case would go haywire. I took Wellbutrin without any immediate effect and drove to work, rationalizing that an antidepressant was better than drinking at nine in the morning like my parents used to do.

Part of me was sure that life would be simpler if I got a job with some dull state agency and met some desperate dork in a bar. I don't know what chemical reaction in my messed-up brain caused despondency that morning. You'd think I'd have been recovered from Jersey after sixteen years.

As I stared down at the traffic below my office, I remembered an infectious disease doc I'd met on a Wright McGee case who'd asked me out after the suit was settled. I hadn't gone. One of those moods again. Tina has always lived on the edge to escape her own memories of Philly and Trenton—pregnancy causing her to lose a basketball scholarship, abortion, nearly OD'ing a couple of times. I shouldn't be so hard on myself for occasional blues.

I called the guy, then waited ten minutes to get him on the line. He agreed to look at my case, though he made it clear he wouldn't testify against a local defendant. But the opportunity to accomplish something snapped me out of my melancholy.

I rolled into his office after hours, and was greeted warmly. My return smile was genuine. He was a great guy. Half of current med students may be women, but the board-certified department heads who'd been out of training twenty or more years—the best experts— were almost all men. Which was one of the advantages of being a female lawyer.

He studied the chart for half an hour. He said the same thing Michael said. It didn't make sense that the boy's platelets would collapse so quickly, if the observations of the day before were correct and this kid was headed home. But the final labs were consistent with DIC from sepsis caused by meningitis.

I asked if the antibiotics were appropriate.

He shrugged. "Absolutely. The kid was getting better."

"Dosages look okay?"

"Yes, assuming they were actually given."

He cocked an eyebrow. It would be impossible to prove a drug checked off on the medication sheet had or hadn't been administered.

He said he'd keep the chart and study it more carefully. I offered to pay him for his time. He waved that off, then asked if I had time to grab coffee from downstairs

He was decent looking, better than decent really, but not the six-three hunk Michael was. I told him I was seeing somebody, making sure I let him down easy.

*　　*　　*

That evening, I worked out, wolfed down a deli ham and cheese, and accepted an invitation to sub on a men's basketball team full of lawyers. Had a great time popping a couple of treys and trading jabs, both physical and verbal, with some of the guys I knew from other firms. Nobody complained about letting a girl play.

One, who was pretty cute, suggested a beer afterward. Though I declined, all the male attention certainly picked up my mood. Nothing like having a bird in hand to attract a flock. I admonished myself—no sleeping pills that night or meds the next day. As I headed home the memory of a shampoo Michael had given me last fall after a night playing ball popped into my brain and brought forth a smile I couldn't repress.

In all the euphoria, I had forgotten to check my cell. While I slowed for an accident on the Central, I grabbed it.

Three calls from Michael.

Odd. Wasn't like him to act desperate.

I rang back.

"Kristen! Where the hell have you been?"

Usually that question irritated me to no end. Something my mother used to ask if you were two minutes late from running dinner to Grandmother Spinello, like we were going to get in trouble *there*. But he sounded more panicked than angry.

"What's the matter?"

"Sarah and Becca." He choked, his response dying in his throat.

My heart leapt in my chest. Nasty adrenaline filled my mouth. The memory of the kidnapping, rescue, and shooting flashed Technicolor in my mind.

"They got hit by a car. Hit and run. Becca's in surgery. The surgeons are trying to save her leg."

I could barely breathe but managed to ask, "And Sarah?"

He paused, which only made me tenser. *"I think she's okay. Scrapes and a nasty cut on her chin and a knot on her head. They're taking her for a CT."*

"Where are you?"

"Presbyterian."

"I'm on my way."

CHAPTER 8

I WHIPPED OVER THREE LANES, exited on Lovers Lane, ignored drivers honking at me, and did a quick turnaround to head north. No freeway in the world will let you reverse course as fast as those in Texas.

At the hospital, I found Michael in the surgery waiting room. Sarah had been admitted downstairs in a med-surge observation room. Michael relayed that they'd gone with another friend, Shelly, to find live subjects for an eighth grade psychology experiment. I recalled Sarah telling me they were doing a science project on short-term memory and would be interviewing random people.

Michael related more of the little he knew. They had wound up at Northpark Shopping Center for more "experiments." When Shelly's mom arrived to pick them up, Sarah and Becca went around the car to get in. Becca, farthest from the open door, took the major blow. Sarah was half in and got knocked face-down onto the cement.

The other car's front fender crushed poor Becca's leg against the open door. The driver sped away. After the ambulance left with the two kids Shelly's mom took her hysterical daughter home.

"This happened in the parking lot?" I asked.

"I haven't been to the scene. I met the ambulance here."

My paranoia perked up like a stag hearing a rifle shot. This sounded like no accident.

Michael rubbed his eyes. "Becca has a shattered leg, torn ligaments in her knee, and lots of soft tissue damage. Sarah's CT was normal, but they're calling it a concussion. She got stitches on her chin. Wrist x-ray was negative. They want to watch her overnight. She's more upset over seeing Becca's blood splashed on the street than her own injury."

I offered to go down to the first floor and stay with Sarah, just as a young doc in scrubs came in.

"Who's the parent?"

Michael stepped closer and said he had notarized authority from Becca's mom. He pulled the form from his pocket.

The surgeon glanced at the paper, seeming to take Michael at his word, and introduced himself as the chief resident peds orthopedic surgeon, who had assisted in Becca's case.

Michael, obviously antsy, asked how the surgery went.

The surgeon grimaced.

I held my breath.

It seemed forever before he said, "The tibial plateau was badly comminuted. There's extensive soft tissue damage. We put the pieces back as best we could. Four screws and a plate. Dr. Felty did the soft tissue work. The girl will need another surgery to rebuild the tissue around the bone. Maybe two."

We both stood in silent shock. I'd seen the kid at Sarah's games. Becca often rode the pine, but always had a great attitude and cheered Sarah's hits. I could tell Michael felt horrible, being responsible while her mom was gone.

"The leg?" Michael asked. The question didn't need to be more specific.

"Fifty-fifty. Streets are very dirty, so we're not in the clear yet."

Becca's softball career was over. We thanked the doc. I remembered it was not yet dawn in France. That meant we'd be in charge, making any decisions, for several more hours, unless Becca had another relative in town. Fortunately, Becca's mom had given Michael a medical authorization before leaving, though I'm sure a sore throat was the worst she had in mind.

Michael decided he needed to stay on the surgery floor until Becca was moved to a room. So I took the elevator down to the MDU—Medical Decision Unit—next to the ER. I was directed to a room where I found Sarah in a hospital gown propped up on the bed watching TV.

She smiled, but I sensed the slightest disappointment I wasn't a parent. Maybe I was imagining it. Maybe she was still dazed. She had a bandage over her chin and a looming black eye. I related what had happened upstairs with her friend before asking about her.

I probably reported Becca's surgery too optimistically, but figured Sarah needed to feel upbeat. When I asked how she felt, she shrugged.

"Like I ate a bad-bounce grounder."

Maybe in some alternative universe that girl could be mine. I talked her into turning off the set and trying to sleep. I plopped into the chair next to the bed. Neither of us got much rest, since somebody came in every hour to see if Sarah remembered her name. They probably wouldn't have kept her had there been a parent at home to observe for head trauma, but Michael was *in loco parentis* for Becca and had to stay at the hospital while her mother gallivanted over Europe.

I knew Northpark. Neiman Marcus always told me what to look for next year at Dillard's. Traffic is heavy. You couldn't get going fast enough in the parking lot to nearly kill somebody unless you really wanted to.

At one-thirty in the morning Michael came in, reporting that Becca was morphined up and stable. Michael told Sarah she could not go up and see her buddy.

"Go back to sleep, sweetie." I risked adding, sounding like a rookie stepmom.

"But I'm not sleepy."

Michael gave his daughter a hard stare. Sarah closed her eyes. I knew she wouldn't pick a fight with her dad with me in the room. She wanted to appear angelic to me.

Michael turned to me. "Baby, everything's under control. Thanks for coming."

Sarah's eyes opened again. I felt brave enough to kiss her cheek before saying good-bye and didn't get any resistance. I'm young enough to remember not wanting my own mother to kiss me at that age, so that was nice.

* * *

Instead of home, I went to Northpark. In the early morning hours, there was no traffic and it didn't take long to find the accident site. Somebody had made a half-ass effort to sweep up the glass. A strip of bent aluminum had been kicked to the curb. Becca's blood was still splattered on the concrete.

Shelly's mom had pulled up in front of an Italian restaurant on the south end of the mall to pick up the girls. Anyone hitting the kids would have had to come around the southeast corner. You couldn't get up much speed, unless you gunned it hard and weren't slowed by traffic in front, which might be possible at close to nine at night.

I got back in my car and circled back to the east side, made a hard right, and floored my BMW to the point of impact. Reached thirty, but I was really trying and my 5 Series is fast. Only a drunk on meth could have hit them that hard accidentally.

My stomach felt queasy at the thought. Someone had tried to kill the girls.

I wanted to talk to the investigating officer. He'd surely glommed onto the possibility this was no accident, but I'm seldom shy about offering my opinion and planned to do so. Michael had made plenty of enemies lawyering nasty cases. What better way to hurt him than to take out his princess?

* * *

Tina must have known I needed sleep. I barely stirred when she closed the door downstairs, must have gone back to sleep, but the landline rang and woke me.

Saying a quick prayer, I picked up, expecting Michael to give me an update on the girls, but it was Tina.

She said that Larseny had called and wanted to see me ASAP.

Damn.

I cleaned up and drove to the office. In the elevator on the way up, Michael called and told me that an over-read on Sarah's head CT had shown a tiny hematoma. With her history of head injury and the surgery to drain a bleed the previous year, they wanted to keep her another night. Nobody gets better care than a malpractice lawyer's kid, especially one whose father has represented half the doctors in town.

He said he'd located Becca's mom. She'd been on an escapade in Provence when reached and had to take the train from Lyon back to Paris to fly home the next afternoon. Dirty mind that I have, I guessed she had met a smooth-talking French charmer.

I smiled at Michael's obvious concern for Becca. Only a guy trying hard to mend his reputation would take a daughter's friend for a week, then live at the hospital until her mom returned.

I told Michael I'd be there later and called Larseny.

He wasted no time on pleasantries. *"Got another dead kid."*

His tone was the same as if he'd said he had another hemorrhoid. I didn't know whether to be happy or sad.

"What happened?"

"Take a guess."

I wondered the worst. "Adventist? Same day?"

"Bingo."

Larseny said he needed time to round up the parents and grandparents. Apparently there was an argument within the extended family over what lawyer to hire and who was going to do the hiring. Sam assured me he'd get control of the various parts and get them in. Beyond worrying about shady deals—the only ones walking through my door—I agreed to see him.

In for a penny, in for a pound.

I knew the game was afoot, the chase was on, or whatever cliché worked best. Something was going on—and I knew a little about cover-ups. Maybe God, in His wisdom, had selected the right lawyer to help these people and get to the bottom of this, ethics be damned.

I spent the rest of the morning on the Internet and in medical books I'd "borrowed" from Wright McGee while boning up on pediatric hospital care. I paced, thought, and paced some more. Made some calls and left voicemails to docs I'd met when I was at Wright McGee, who didn't practice at Adventist. But by 4 p.m. nobody had returned my call.

I closed up early and headed for Presbyterian. In Becca's room, Michael was napping in the vinyl chair next to her bed, legs stretched out, spine unsupported, his head drooping awkwardly over the arm. He'd need a chiropractic adjustment soon.

Becca's leg was wrapped and elevated, bare toes pointing to the ceiling. Nails were painted gold—the team color. The IV line had been moved into the upper part of her hand.

Frankly the poor kid looked like hell, pale, her mouth open, drooling, likely bonked out from a morphine hit. I checked next door—Michael had pulled some strings and gotten the girls back-to-back.

Sarah had her iPod in her ears and a textbook in her lap, but had nodded off.

I went in and sat next to Sarah. I'd brought a P. D. James mystery and started reading about Inspector Dalgliesh solving a murder in the English countryside. Maybe it would inspire me.

As I got to chapter two, Michael shuffled into Sarah's room.

I rose and kissed him. He smelled like he'd slept in a hospital chair, but I didn't care. I tugged his arm and we stepped into the hall to talk.

Michael rubbed his bloodshot eyes. He looked so tired, and frankly a little old. There are fourteen years between us. Sometimes I wonder if that's too many.

"Christ, I thought she was through with hospitals until I get to be a granddad."

I pursed my lips, cast aside the *old* thought, and said something encouraging, but didn't share my theory about the "accident."

"Nothing new on Becca's leg. Drainage doesn't look bad. Thank God her mom is on her way. I can't believe an aunt in Baltimore is too goddamn busy to come."

I agreed, remembering the story of Becca's dysfunctional family. Absent dad, mom more interested in drinking and playing cougar. Sounded familiar.

I motioned toward his daughter's room and whispered, "Is there anything to this new CT read?"

"It's stable. Pretty much an excuse to keep her here until Becca's mother arrives and I can leave."

"Is her chin going to scar badly?" I felt stupid that I'd forgotten to ask yesterday in all the excitement.

"It was very dirty. That's part of the official reason they kept her. Hard to tell an insurance company she needs to stay to support her pal."

I smiled. Michael could sell sand in the desert.

"Of course I'll pay it myself if they crank about it."

And I knew he would. "Anything else new?"

"I called a plastic surgeon I know. He wants to do a revision in a month. Doesn't think it'll be all that noticeable."

"That's good." I hugged him, really tight. I appreciated how he made me feel useful, part of the team.

"You go home. Get some real rest. I'll stay tonight," I said.

He seemed to mull this a moment. Sarah was all he had. No law practice, thanks to the *Layne* mess. We both knew from our cases that hospitals are dangerous places. If a family member is not there to advocate for the patient, pain can go unaddressed, dressings unchanged—and worst of all, medication errors can occur. Sometimes patients get mixed up. I'd hate for somebody to give Sarah a barium swallow while we were gone.

Michael fought back a yawn.

I tapped his chest. "You had all the stress of the first night. That was the worst."

He wavered.

I wrapped my arms around his waist and squeezed. "I want to help, honey."

He finally gave me the night shift, but insisted I get something to eat and change into comfortable clothes first. Easily wrinkled linen slacks and a starched cotton blouse didn't look to him like sleepwear.

I went to the cafeteria and ate, then retrieved my workout bag from the car. When I returned, Sarah appeared perkier and seconded my motion to send Dad home.

"Feeling better?"

She held up her bandaged palm. "My hand hurts more than my chin. It got scraped."

Sarah was lucky she hadn't broken her wrist on the fall. That would have been a psychological disaster, since it would have meant no ball games. We played chess on her iPad. Michael had taught her well and I even lost the rematch.

Around eleven, a new nurse came in, checked vitals, and gave her an antibiotic and some Benadryl to help her sleep and to prevent itching under the dressing. She took Sarah's temp via her ear and told me it was normal. I asked when the dressings would get changed. I could tell by her mechanical motions that she didn't think Sarah should be in the hospital. And she was right.

She sighed, as if she regarded me as a nuisance. "Are you also here for the girl next door?"

"Yes."

"What exactly is your relationship with these patients?"

I stuttered, not sure what to say.

Obviously impatient, she interrupted. "Are you family?" Her tone suggested she was considering calling security.

I hesitated. Semi-girlfriend of the father until his probation ended sounded worse than stupid. Daring superhero of this patient? Crazy woman who can't decide?

Sarah flashed a look of anticipation and hope, like a little kid on Christmas Eve leaving cookies for Santa. I made a split-second not to disappoint her. She needed some good news. Assuming she wanted me for a stepmom.

"I'm going to be her stepmom soon," I said, nodding at Sarah.

Sarah thrust her fists and almost leapt from the bed.

The nurse's lips stretched into a thin smile as she left.

Sarah started asking a thousand questions.

"Where will you go on a honeymoon?"

"Where will we live?"

"Do you want children?"

"Could I be a bridesmaid?"

I only gave a clear answer on that last one.

"Of course," I said. "I can't wait to see you in a bright, overdone dress."

I shouldn't have said that. It was foolish. You never know when things can go south, and they usually do for me.

I had been overwhelmed by the moment, but part of me knew I would arrive at this decision eventually. I couldn't imagine living without Michael and Sarah. Certainly not living without his hands wandering over my body and his arm around me when I slept.

A few weeks later, when I ended up in jail, I realized living without them was not just a distinct, but a likely, possibility.

CHAPTER 9

IT TOOK HALF AN HOUR for Sarah to settle down and quit playing wedding planner, but she finally crashed. I got up, my spine stiff and aching from the uncomfortable chair, went next door, and thankfully found Becca asleep. I placed my hand on Becca's forehead. She didn't feel too hot. I touched her foot. Toes pink and warm, so circulation was okay.

The same nurse came in, this time not as hostile. I guess I qualified as family now. She did vitals, reported temp at 100.1, and checked the IV site for infiltration of drugs into the surrounding tissue. I knew nobody would worry much about fever unless she hit 100.5. They were running antibiotics in a hep lock, a more permanent IV site, since she wasn't going home anytime soon.

Car wrecks produce dirty injuries and they were watching for resistant staph that could result in amputation or even death. It happens every day in every hospital in the world. Antibiotics are losing the battle with what docs call MRSA—resistant staphylococcal bacteria. Staph is probably on your skin, maybe even in your nasal passages, so it's easy to get it into an open wound.

The nurse confirmed that everything looked good, for now, smiled reassurance very pleasantly, and left.

Looking at Becca, I wanted to cry, but forced myself to stare out the window, into the darkness pierced by parking lot lights. Even if Becca kept her leg, she'd have more surgery and months of therapy, all very painful. Had her luck been worse, Sarah might be in the same boat with her pal. What a disaster it would have been for Sarah to lose sports after losing her mother.

I promised myself I would find the son of a bitch. I'd trained in martial arts for years. A couple of good kicks, and whoever did this to the girls would be fighting to save *his* leg.

* * *

I must've slept. The aide bringing breakfast was the next thing I remember.

Becca, not a girl you'd call slender, perked up and wolfed down two strips of bacon and scooped up every bite of scrambled eggs. She probably thought I looked drained, because she split the toast with me. I'd learned in the year I'd known Sarah not to change my voice pattern when talking to kids like some adults do or comment on how much she ate. I assured her that her mom would be in that day. Even teenage girls sometimes need their mother.

I went next door. Sarah had inhaled her breakfast too. Made me wish I were their age, when I could eat anything and not feel guilty. Perky as she was, even Michael Stern's daughter would get the boot that morning.

We slipped around to Becca's room, watchful for any Nurse Ratched, and kept Becca entertained by reading all the text messages they'd received. Under the circumstances, the kid was doing pretty well.

But the stimulation of food soon wore off. I could tell Becca hurt, but I decided Sarah's yakking was better for the kid than lying there feeling dejected.

Drowsy, I started down the hall for more caffeine, just as a different nurse armed with more meds ducked into Becca's room. I turned and followed. She shooed Sarah out.

She looked to be in her late forties, so I figured she had experience. Very thin with auburn hair and freckles. She opened Becca's heplock. Though groggy, I tried to peek at what she was injecting into the catheter.

The woman sighed in late-shift annoyance. "Ancef and morphine. She gets two milligrams every six hours. Just like last time."

I smiled, really trying not to be annoying. She had something in the other hand. "What's in the other syringe?"

"Heparin to flush the heplock. It's highly diluted, of course."

I nodded. Heparin would prevent clots forming in the line where antibiotics were delivered intravenously. A clot there could travel up the bloodstream to the lungs. A pulmonary embolism can be fatal. But too much Heparin would cause bleeding, like what happened to poor Pain Layne, turning him into a vegetable. But when a line has to stay in for days, Heparin is better than saline to flush any clots.

"I checked the dosage twice." She said it like an irritated teenager who had already picked up her room and was still being hassled.

I tried to be friendly. "I know."

She swiped the medication with an electronic gadget at Becca's wristband, getting confirmation the stuff was for this patient. She ran the meds into the teenager.

The opiate did its job. Becca's breathing slowed, eyelids drooped, hands fell to the sides of her limp body. Sherlock Holmes and Freud knew a good thing. I thanked the nurse, trying hard not to sound like a lawyer. Undoubtedly word was out that the kids had attorney involvement, one who knew something about hospitals.

Though I was too tired to think further about Heparin, it would come back to me later.

With Becca asleep I got my coffee, found some crackers for

breakfast, and went back to Sarah's room. Michael strolled in an hour later, looking rested. Sarah hopped up to trade hugs with Dad.

"Have you guys set a date?" Sarah practically shouted.

Michael gaped, probably wondering what had happened in the night.

I spared him having to come up with a response that might be embarrassing. "First he has to convert so we can get married in my church. No race to the courthouse for me."

That wasn't just to stall. I'd thought about it—what girl doesn't—and decided that even without parents present, I wanted the real deal, Mass and all. A couple of close encounters with the Grim Reaper had regenerated the faith I knew as a kid.

Sarah applauded. "I will too. The Pope is pretty cool."

Michael's eyebrows remained crunched in obvious confusion. Usually the groom knows when the proposal is accepted.

I gave him the *Yes I meant it* nod.

Michael kissed me, his hands hot on my cheeks. I love the way he pulls away ever so slowly. His touch always makes me crave more.

With Sarah so happy, I couldn't back out now. Oh, well. There's a lot worse that can happen to a woman than marrying a handsome rich guy.

CHAPTER 10

FEELING A BIT GIDDY I headed home for a couple hours of real sleep. Before turning in I checked my phone and found a message from Larseny, wanting me to meet his latest finds—and likely my new clients.

By one, I was in the office—tanned, rested, and ready, as aspiring politicians claim. Had a message from the Dunns, asking if I knew anything. Called back and told them both how hard I was working. Didn't tell them I didn't know any more than the day they came in. I'd have to think of a new excuse next time.

Excuses—they teach that in law school, right after contracts.

I called Larseny back. The new family was ready to meet with me at four. After I hung up, I stared out my window, telling myself it was time to ask questions.

First: *Where the hell was Larsen getting these people?* Cases like these come rarely, not because mistakes don't happen, but because a lot of errors never come to light. Larseny had to have a mole in Adventist. And the mole surely knew more than he or she was telling Sam, since he wasn't a good enough liar to be hiding much from me.

The deaths were either incredibly coincidental or something was seriously wrong with the system. Even my old clients don't screw up that much. I remembered Harry Bosch's admonition: no coincidences. So what had happened?

The actual cause of the deaths was unclear. People die in hospitals every day. So why wasn't the mole spilling everything? If the spy wanted the cases filed and the bloody hospital sued, why not help the patients' lawyer? It was like leaving a treasure map showing the beach, the pond, every tree, but without marking the X.

Larseny had to know the mole, but had a strong incentive to keep me in the dark until every potential case had been rounded up. Otherwise I could deal with the mole directly and work around Larsen's crooked agreement. And enter a different crooked agreement.

My brain spun like Holden Caulfield's merry-go-round, sorting possibilities. A nurse who'd seen a screw up? A doc on the morbidity committee? Somebody in administration who had seen incident reports? Regardless of the identity of the spy, we still had to figure out why these kids died. A coincidence wasn't worth ice in Alaska.

Second question: *What was the mole getting out of this?* And third: *Was Larseny cutting the mole in on my kickback?* He had to be.

Fourth: *Why had Larseny been so insistent on* me *taking the cases?* He might have gotten a third of the fee from another dishonest lawyer. While I was temporarily famous, the *Layne* glow would eventually fade and there were plenty of lawyers more experienced than I was.

Sam had done everything but learn my shoe size before walking into my office.

More questions banged off the inside of my skull. Did the mole know me? Was it a friend or an enemy? Who wanted to see me rich? Nobody, as far as I knew. My ruminations were interrupted by the fax—the medical authorization for Alberto Rodriguez signed by his parents, Sam's latest find.

I dashed to Adventist, producing the medical authorization and my ID. By the time I got my copy of the chart, I needed to get back. I only had time to flip through and see that the boy had been three when he died after elective surgery for a club foot.

* * *

Promptly at four Larseny popped in, leading a host of people jamming the reception area—far more than could sit in my office.

Fortunately, I'd planned for such an emergency by getting friendly with the lawyers across the hall. I called and they offered an unused conference room. I promised them a pizza for lunch the next day and led the pack over.

The Rodriguez clan consisted of a twenty-four-year-old mother, a husband a little older, her mother, her grandmother, two aunts, an uncle, and a grandfather and aunt of the husband. Wasn't sure I had it all straight, but plowed ahead.

They related that the father's parents couldn't get off work but would want to know everything we discussed. The aunt spoke perfect English and related that little Alberto had been at Adventist for elective surgery on his club foot. He developed a postop fever. They decided to keep him another night for IV antibiotics. Late on the second day he got sicker.

He'd died on the third day.

The young parents were slender, well dressed. The father had donned a tie to meet the Anglo lawyer. His wife wore a loose sundress and sandals. Shapely ankles peeked out from under the hem. Those in the next generation were heavier, more formal, the women wearing heels, the men in nice slacks. No facial hair or tats. Good. All the women possessed fetching cinnamon-colored skin. Even better.

The initial interview went like shelling Texas pecans. Lots of repeating and translating. Larseny's Spanish was fair. Mine nonexistent. I wasted college language hours on German and a little French— neither of much use in Texas.

Soon it was clear that Sam had the family under control and they trusted him. They would've hired the sleaziest TV-advertising ambulance chaser if Larseny told them to.

About all I contributed was making sure they saw my cross of St. John pendant and a lot of sad expressions—not hard to do.

Two hours later, after Sam had puffed me up as a legal genius and future saint, they signed up. Of course I autographed Larseny's cut. Why not?

The Rodriguez family couldn't tell me much about the doctors' explanations of Alberto's death. They probably used medical jargon most people, regardless of native language, couldn't understand. Docs are good at leaving the family in a London fog. They had been given a death certificate listing cause of death as cardiac arrest.

Which was a crock. Everybody dies of cardiac arrest. A cessation of breathing usually works too. Question is: *why* did the heart stop? *Why* did they quit breathing? Whoever floated this nonsense must have thought these people were unimportant or lacked curiosity to investigate what had happened to their son.

The family had not requested an autopsy. And undoubtedly none was offered. Medical providers who have screwed up never want an autopsy. It's the plaintiff's burden to prove error caused a death, and without an autopsy it's often impossible.

With much reiteration and translation, I saw everyone out. They seemed to like me and I was eager to help them.

* * *

Next day I got the girls' accident report online. I saw that no skid marks had been measured—evidence of my intentional rundown theory. If you don't brake for kids or cats, you don't leave marks.

I left a message for the cop who had worked the girls' *accident*. It was still assigned to Traffic, not Homicide—a bad sign. They obviously didn't think like I do.

The officer called back and agreed to see me. Lawyers handling smash-up cases tip the investigative officer a couple hundred bucks for half an hour of his off-duty time. *Wish I could've billed at that rate when I did defense work.*

* * *

Late that afternoon the cop, young, good-looking, buff, and a couple inches under my height ambled in. His mustache was trimmed thin and admittedly sexy. My sister would have called him hot.

Assertively, he gripped my offered hand. "Officer Ross."

Something about short guys. Tall women either frighten them into stammering folly or rev them into the greasiest charm. This cop represented the latter. He grinned, leaned into my space. It's like short guys have to prove they, too, have a penis.

I pointed him to a chair, handed him his check.

Ross made a grand show of unzipping a leather briefcase, slick enough to be a lawyer's.

"Hit and run."

I somehow avoided rolling my eyes. Somehow.

"Haven't located the other driver."

"What are you doing to find him?" I asked.

"Sent the standard alert to all area body shops. We interviewed the witnesses."

"I bet everyone was too upset to give you much."

He nodded. "Blue. Maybe black, big car. No confirmation on make. Going fast."

"That's it?"

"A guy across the street, going toward the Central, thought maybe it was a black Mercedes or Lexus. Not sure. Nobody very close. It's fifty yards across that street."

I didn't want to put words in his mouth, so I asked, "What do you think happened?"

Ross shrugged. "It looks like an impaired driver. Maybe a guy on a cell. Or a drunk."

"No skids. Not much traffic at that time," I pointed out.

He nodded again.

"Could it be intentional?"

He snorted skepticism. "Somebody after those kids?"

"One of the dads is a bit notorious. He's made a lot of enemies."

"Yeah, I suspected he hired the murder of his wife."

Until then I didn't know shit could be stacked as tall as this guy. I barely repressed the urge to walk around the table and plant his teeth in his gullet, but took a deep breath instead and queried, "Somebody wanting to get even with him could've gone after the most important thing to him—his daughter."

Officer Ross scratched his short-cut temple. "Do you know how difficult it is to intentionally run over someone?"

I shook my head. "How hard could it be with a car and a gas pedal?"

He leaned over the desk. I could smell his aftershave. The musky-gym scent reminded me of my high school basketball coach, my first big crush.

"You've got to find 'em, follow 'em, and catch 'em on foot in the street. No traffic between you and the target. No witnesses. It'd be a miracle. After a month of trailing them and risking getting made?"

"Looked pretty easy to me when I drove out there."

Ross leaned across my desk. "Okay. Find me and hit me."

Although I was tempted to take him up on the offer, I argued, "But I don't know where you live."

"You know where I work. You could follow me out of here. But finding me walking across the street with a clean shot at running me down, nobody in your way, no witnesses would be almost impossible."

"Sarah could've been followed for weeks, until someone got a chance to run them over. Maybe that wasn't the original plan, but they saw a chance."

"And not be seen?"

"Kids don't pay attention. They're continually hooked onto some electronic gadget."

He shrugged. "That's how they get hit. Besides, how do you know they weren't intending to cream the other girl? The one with the busted leg."

He had a point, since Becca was the kid who could have died, and her missing dad owed a lot of money to a lot of people. I backed off, listened, and took notes on his measurements of where bodies and car parts landed. He let me photocopy his workup.

After I finished scanning the report, he asked if I'd like to shut down the office and get a drink. I told him I had more people coming in. He looked skeptical, but I didn't care. He should find a gymnast, not a basketball player.

In the fifteen minutes he'd been in my office, Ross hadn't asked about either Sarah or Becca, which irked me.

"They're going to live," I deadpanned, mimicking his indifference.

"Yeah. I heard. It means I keep the case."

With another *sorry-you-missed-out* smile, he slithered out.

* * *

Michael called to report Becca's mom had arrived and that he and Sarah were headed home. I told him that I wanted to stay late and do some research on foot surgery, but would drop by to check on Becca and see if I could stir up trouble.

He chuckled and told me he loved me.

I almost said the same, but the words died in my throat. After hanging up I tugged my hair and cursed my stupid neuroses. I told myself to remember my therapist's admonition: *NMNS. You're not the Virgin Mary, and just because you're not doesn't make you shit. Not Mary, not shit. NMNS!*

I chowed a protein bar and drove to Presbyterian. Becca's mother, Donna, acted grateful, downright pleasant. Becca was about the same, which was actually a good sign. I didn't stay long. Things were under control, no sign of infection. I told Becca "good luck" and she rewarded me with, "Thanks for being with me, Kristen." Sweet.

Embarrassed over my verbal fumble with Michael, I decided to go home to a bag of salad, glass of wine, and an Ambien. Maybe tomorrow I'd find the nerve to trust, to roll the dice, and risk my precious hard-won psyche.

* * *

Before I reached my townhome, my cell rang. I checked the ID—Larseny.

Now what? At night? The IRS on his tail? The cops?

He asked if he could meet me in my office in an hour. Urgent.

"No problem."

I sped to my office and had time to straighten my desk before Larseny waltzed in.

Behind him trailed a couple, in their twenties, dressed in jeans, her Levi's shredded, holes exposing both thighs. She wore a halter top around her thin torso, without a bra, her small nipples clearly visible. I thought the grunge look had gone out a decade earlier, but maybe I hadn't noticed its comeback. Her long hair hung lifeless, needing shampoo. But with a little work, she could be lovely. A belly button ring matched the one in her nose. I'm old-fashioned and thought she was a mess. But later I'd love that girl like a little sister.

The boyfriend's sleeveless tee sported the concert schedule of a band I'd never heard of. His biceps bulging, he looked fit, like he worked outdoors. He needed a shave and haircut. His mouth hung open like a fly trap. A stubby nose, long chin, and big eyes reminded me of our family Labrador. I couldn't help smelling the bath he hadn't taken.

All in all, they looked like abandoned children of groupies following the Grateful Dead.

Larsen introduced them as Troy and Dana Sayers. I asked for mundane details. Dana had gone to a vo-tech school to become certified as a scrub assistant, but admitted she was working in a club, since it paid better. I was afraid to ask what exactly she did in the club; probably the same career my sister had once undertaken—lap dancing. Troy pounded nails. I hoped he sobered up before going to work tomorrow or he'd lose a thumb.

After some questioning, I learned they weren't officially married. Dana had simply started using his name. Sort of a "common law" arrangement, they called it. She assured me they planned on a ceremony soon.

Their daughter, Sierra Sue Sayers, age six, had died at Adventist. I thought the alliteration a little silly, but as they talked I realized they grieved just as much as the other families, despite their hang-dog, spacey appearance. *Don't be judgmental, dumbass.* Maybe Highland Park had invaded my brain.

It only took me a minute to figure out why Larsen was so jacked up. Sierra Sayers had died on the day after my other clients lost their kids. In fact, practically the same day, since it happened just after midnight.

Dana managed to choke out, "She broke her arm in gymnastics. They took her to surgery. Put in a plate. Told us everything was fine. She'd go home the next day."

Troy said nothing. I couldn't tell if he was on something or numb with grief. He had a bad case of sniffles and a hundred-yard stare that contrasted with his fingers constantly tapping my desk. Could be argued either way.

I asked more questions, feeling like Dana and I clicked. They must've had some money since the girl had been working out in a nice private gym. Dana's tips, probably.

Larseny interrupted. "There's an autopsy pending."

"I insisted," Troy blurted out. "I seen on TV how they cover shit up. And they were fixin' to bullshit us."

Troy may have looked stoned, had bad teeth, used poor grammar, and worn dirty jeans, but he wasn't stupid. I wished the other families had been so suspicious. Unfortunately, I knew we couldn't expect a report for another month.

Under Larsen's steely gaze, I explained the process of investigating a case, getting records together, and hiring an expert for a review. I promised to get to the bottom of what happened.

They seemed to understand it would be a long slog. When Troy asked how much money they were going to get, I had to prevaricate and mumble "Difficult to tell at this stage" and other legal blather. Throwing a number at them would have been legal malpractice. Some lawyers toss out millions to snag a case, but regret it when they have to lower expectations back to earth.

Larsen nodded his approval when I handed them the medical authorizations and a retainer contract. He related my *Layne* exploits, puffing me up. He made it sound like I had brass balls, or at least brass tits.

Their glazed eyes pretended to read it and signed.

I wasn't sure Troy could actually read. He looked like he was scanning the *Athens News* upside down. But I told him he'd made a wise decision to insist on the post-mortem, and I meant it. The autopsy, when complete, would tell us a lot. I reassured them one more time how hard I would work and that they wouldn't owe me any money if we failed.

I shook hands with Troy and hugged Dana. The interview had actually gone well under the circumstances.

After they were gone, I scribbled my name on another of Larsen's crooked contracts. Once one becomes a whore, going down on the next mark is easy. At this rate, three files in a week, I'd have a full file cabinet and have to hire a paralegal.

***

I figured that as long as I was keeping Tina fed and safely housed, she ought to be useful, beyond answering the phone. I was showing her how to tab labs, radiology, and consults in a medical chart when we were interrupted by the office door chime. I wasn't expecting anyone, but we hopped up off the carpet—you get so much more done sitting on the floor and spreading stuff out.

I let Tina reach the reception area first. When I heard Jen's voice I went in, not waiting on formality.

This time the "Hey, girl" was more like our old days at Wright McGee, especially whenever she asked me to cover a docket for her.

"Wanted to see your digs," Jen said.

"Not much to see."

"Coffee?" Tina asked.

To my surprise Jen accepted. Tina fixed a fresh pot. The three of us ducked into my office. We chatted and gossiped. My former partner, Ron, was apparently having an affair with a woman at a firm opposite Wright McGee on a big case. Imagine the temerity of getting romantically involved with an opponent? Made me blush.

I wondered if Jen was snidely throwing aspersions over my affair with Michael. At least we didn't become the double-back monster until *Layne* was over.

It was a pleasant hour, stretching longer and better than I would have expected a few weeks earlier. Still, I didn't have the nerve to ask how her friend, Casey, was doing without a nursing license. Or either of the other nurses I got shit-canned.

Jen, the former RN, downed the last sip of her Jamaican java and said she had to get going. We parted with a hug.

As the door closed Tina said, "You know, she's gay. Or at least bi-."

"No way. She went on dates when I worked with her. We even doubled once."

"You were too busy watching the witness to see the tears rolling down Jen's face when you had her pal on the stand spewing out the truth about Layne's night in the hospital."

"Huh?" I couldn't recall any hint that Jen batted both ways.

"I'm usually right, aren't I?"

I couldn't argue. It was Tina who told me during the *Layne* trial that Michael *really* liked me. Turned out he liked me enough to throw the trial.

"Surely she's not interested in me."

Tina shrugged. "She knows you're not on that wavelength. But she gets a kick out of looking you over. She likes your butt and those toned arms."

I frowned, still not believing her. Jen and I had worked out together. Showered at the gym. I didn't recall any leering, but I can be naïve.

"Maybe it's you she thinks is cute."

Tina laughed. "Me? The girls I danced with in Philly gave me a nickname."

"What?"

"Anita Dickey."

I rolled my eyes.

In a flash Tina looked pensive. "Whatever happened to the tall, butchy nurse after you got her defrocked? The one Jen was bawling over. What's-her-name?"

"Casey?"

"Yeah. The one whose arm you nearly broke getting her to the courthouse."

"I haven't heard."

CHAPTER 11

I FLASHED MY BAR ID and plopped the medical authorization containing the patient's social and birth date in front of the Adventist records custodian. She examined it like it was contaminated, then stared at me like she'd seen my photo at the post office.

We were getting to be real friends.

She ducked out, into an unseen maze. Five minutes later she returned, toting a yellow folder. The records clerk opened the chart and spread it over her steel desk. She scrunched her eyes and peered through the bottom half of her bifocals, comparing the signature on my form with the admit handwriting by the parent.

Finally, she pushed the chart toward me, eyeing me suspiciously through the top of her specs.

I practiced my best approximation of a Junior Leaguer smile. "Thank you."

She stared at me while I started flipping pages as if she thought I was going to snag a few sheets when she wasn't looking.

Most of the file was computer-generated stuff. I wasn't likely to spot any problems. Each entry, supposedly, was logged in as last modified, preventing alterations. Based on my cursory exam, none seemed to have been changed once entered. All systems charted WN—supposedly "within normal limits." Cynic that I am, I suspected it stood for, "We Never Looked." I was primarily interested in the handwritten notes, sparse as they were.

But nothing looked fishy. Even the backsides of the hand-written pages were uniformly identical. Indentions in back had been a clue to the *Layne* plot.

I looked at the labs, those reports that Michael and I confirmed were all fine on the other cases until the crash. Lab values are the canary in the coal mine. White cells, platelets, and hemoglobin were all potential clues to what might be going on clinically before busy nurses noticed.

Great thing about lab summaries is you don't have to memorize a bunch of numbers. Lab computers flag abnormalities either "H" or "L," and give normal ranges. Everything was spot-on.

I was about to slam the jacket covers together on the chart and leave. The chance of another *Layne* cover-up was damn slim.

But something grabbed my attention.

My guardian angel must've directed my vision to Sierra's social security number in the upper corner of the lab report. For some reason, I took the time to compare it with the number on the admit sheet and jacket.

Oh my God.

My heart thundered against my chest wall. I could hardly contain my excitement.

Breathlessly I asked for copies, smiled, and said I'd be happy to wait.

She scowled. After a sigh as long as the last twenty seconds of an NBA game, she jerked herself up and snatched the chart, her fleshy arms jiggling. I couldn't imagine that she had caught the discrepancy, but her attitude doubled my suspicion—and my excitement.

* * *

That evening I practically flew through Michael's door before he got it open. I was so excited I forgot to collect my usual sweet kiss.

"I've found it! They switched the labs."

Michael smiled, playing the Old Wise One who'd been everywhere and seen everything. He led me into his study, offered me a Diet Dr Pepper, and sat in his big leather chair. I was annoyed that he seemed in little hurry to see my discovery.

I thrust the reports in his face.

He slowly spread the labs and copies of the jackets over his desk.

One of the few things he occasionally does that exasperates me is playing the role of sage. I wasn't in the mood for G. K. Chesterton. I was pumped and wanted some flattery about my brilliance.

I tapped my finger impatiently at the social security numbers. "See."

"Yes, I see."

"I've *got* 'em."

He blew a long breath of patience, like I'd seen him do with Sarah many times, especially when she wanted something he thought too extravagant.

"They've mixed up lab reports. No doubt about it. But—"

"But what?"

"The values are all normal."

My voice came out screechy as I came around the desk and pointed at the paper, "But they must have changed them up with some kid whose *weren't*. The missing labs probably show the kid whacked out."

He shrugged. "Maybe, but you need the abnormals to prove your case."

"I just proved the *normal* values are a lie."

He patted me on the rump. Ordinarily a butt tap would be nice. Not then. "It could be a simple filing error."

"Michael!"

"Kristen!" He pushed my copies back at me. "You still don't know what killed these kids. You don't have a theory of liability or an expert. The hospital will come up with perfect labs that match the social security numbers after you file the cases. They'll say it was an innocent mistake."

The air went out of my blimp fast. I landed hard and realized he was right. They could make up something and I would never know.

Dejected, I declined to stay for dinner, telling him to spend time with Sarah. Depression is best wallowed in alone.

* * *

I had to resort to a pill combo to get to sleep. So much for being off drugs.

My last waking thoughts questioned whether I was really up to this. Too many people depended on me.

I got up early, ran, and wandered into the office.

An hour later, Tina interrupted my study of the Rodriguez chart.

"Kristen."

Instead of just yelling, she used the intercom on the phone for the first time, like we were a real setup. Made me jump.

"You have visitors."

A client? Maybe a live one with a valid claim who didn't get referred by a conman. Perhaps they could even pay up front, help with cash flow.

I stepped into the extra heels I kept under my desk, applied lipstick, put on my gold stud earrings, redid my hair tie, and, ready to represent Bill Gates, sallied forth.

As soon as I opened the door, I smelled trouble. Two people: a solid, barrel-chested man, late thirties, coat and tie, crew cut, who looked like a drill sergeant, and a woman, maybe late forties, suited up like she'd just left an Episcopal church, perched across from Tina's desk. The blepharoplasty, which somebody had done to suck the fat out of her lids, had given her the biggest, brightest eyes outside *Cats*. I was surprised she could blink. Another magician had sculpted perky breasts, perhaps modeled after Lara Croft's.

They sure weren't potential plaintiffs looking for a lawyer. More like ethics investigators from the Bar Association. My heart gunned higher RPMs. Nothing to do but fake it, so I offered a hand.

"I'm Kristen Kerry."

The woman elbowed past the guy, stepped closer in her peep toe pumps, and shook my hand. "Cynthia Perdue. New CEO of Adventist South."

My nose was right. This stank like a water treatment plant in late July after a power failure. It took me a second to recover, a second she must have enjoyed, for she loosed a nasty, nose-curling sneer.

Before I could think of anything coherent to say, she jabbed a beautiful fingernail toward her companion. "This is Robert Colson, the new risk manager."

He held back, not bothering with pleasantries or a handshake. Based upon the look he gave me, I wouldn't have been surprised if he'd pulled a switchblade.

Of course they were new. All the gangsters who pirated *Layne* had been fired. The DA had insisted.

I steeled myself.

Do not be intimidated.

I invited them back to my office, like I already had another mob's protection.

The CEO eased into a chair, like Victoria assuming the throne, and slowly crossed her legs, her skirt rising to mid-thigh. Nice gams for a broad her age. Her sheer hose swooshed. Any male would have been quite aroused. She scanned the office, like a real estate appraiser unhappy to see such shabby property. Her vision returned to me, fixed and annoyed.

I was determined to win the stare-off.

She lost.

"We were quite surprised to get records requests from you."

I played dumb. "Was something wrong with the forms? Weren't the signatures correct?"

She scowled. It said, *We are not amused.* Victoria again.

"When did you start representing *claimants*?"

The bitch uttered "claimants" like she was referring to Nazi war criminals.

I deadpanned: "When people like you wouldn't hire me."

"Now you'll *never* get a hospital or doctor for a client."

I smiled, let it hold a moment, then asked, "Did you guys come here to settle my cases or hang me for treason?"

"Kristen." She drew a breath, seeming to will comity. "The entire Adventist community holds you in the highest regard for the work you did last year."

She meant the *Layne* disaster. Now I was in "high regard"? "Funny, nobody from the community ever thanked me. Not even the nurses I helped negotiate suspended sentences for on their perjury charges. They could have done a year in prison, but might even get their tickets back someday." I couldn't resist adding, "Assuming they tell the truth."

There was a pregnant pause. I mean eight months pregnant. I fired a stare at them. Their gazes slid down to inspect the carpet, like kids caught surfing porn.

After a second of throat-clearing, the guy leaned menacingly closer to me. Close enough for me to spot the lunch stain on his tie he likely tried to wipe off with a paper towel. "We're offering some friendly advice."

"Don't do it," the CEO pronounced.

A year ago I would've cringed, intimidated by the Gestapo routine. *Ve have vays of making you quit.*

I would have tried to defend myself, pointed out that I'd busted my buns to get hospital work, and felt guilty as hell for turning. But after fighting for my life and killing a man, I'd gained a bit more self-esteem. *NMNS* wasn't needed as often.

I sat silent, not hiding my disdain, and rudely examined my week-old manicure. Considered getting out the nail file.

"Your cases have no merit," she said.

"Purely a coincidence that three children died of mysterious complications the same day?"

"I'm afraid so."

A little rattle in her throat revealed she didn't believe it herself, making me more determined than ever to get after them. These goons were going to have to bring lots heavier guns to back me off.

The dude edged closer. "We make a point to never settle a case brought by a former defense lawyer."

I matched his posture. "Great. Another trial win will be good PR for me." I experienced the wonderful sin of pride. Michael couldn't have done better himself.

"How're you going to finance three major cases? You're looking at a couple hundred thousand dollars. We can put you in bankruptcy."

I started to tell him my boyfriend had more money than the hospital, but decided to leave Michael out of this. He might want to go back to work someday and probably didn't care to be associated with Larseny.

"Guess I'll have to learn to table dance. It's better than working for you people."

She popped up out of her chair in indignation. "We had hoped you would see reason."

The risk manager rose slower, pointing. "Don't say we didn't warn you."

I forced that sorority smile, at least what I thought was one. We jockettes rarely had anything to smile about, unless practice was called off early.

"Thanks so much for stopping by."

* * *

After they left, I rehashed the exchange. By the second replay I found myself grinning from cheek to chubby cheek. I didn't get anything done the rest of the day and decided I needed a drink and my man. I called him and learned they were on their way to the ball fields for the early game slot. Sarah had been cleared to play, which suggested just what a joke her admission to Presbyterian had been. I darted in and out of heavy I-30 traffic to get there on time.

The evening was lovely, barely any wind and almost summer-like. A kiss on arrival from Michael and a wave from Sarah in the dugout were as good as a single malt whisky. Another player's mom actually smiled at me. Maybe my rep was improving. In those seconds, I knew I'd made the right decision on marriage and needed to firm up the plan. In other words, ask *him*. Also about time to use the "L" word.

You can do it, girl.

Between innings, I related my afternoon to Michael. He chuckled, not offering to be my gallant knight and slay those infidels. I took it as a compliment, implying I'd done well.

His hand crept up past my knee. "And?" I couldn't resist asking.

"You just learned you've got three great cases."

"You're not just saying that?"

"Of course not, goose. If the cases sucked, they'd be more than happy to assign them to Pete himself and tell him to spare no expense to jam 'em up your ass."

Couldn't decide which felt better—his reassurance or the hand on my thigh.

Sarah played a second game as a pick-up on an "eighteens" team and acquitted herself well with the older girls. Sarah made a headfirst slide at third, then came in on a sac fly to win. I felt the same pride as if she had been my own daughter. Michael nixed ice cream cones, since it was after ten—and a school night.

As we walked to the car, I dabbed at the dirt caked on Sarah's sweaty face. She didn't seem to mind that bit of intimacy, which seemed natural, far more so than if my mom had done the same to me.

At Michael's I noticed Sarah expectantly scoping out her father and me, watching for signals. I took that as a positive, that she would be happy for me to join the family. Finally, at about ten thirty she went to bed.

I made hot nachos and took them outside while Michael brought beer. We sat under the magnificent magnolia in Michael's backyard. But, typically for Texas, the warm April day had morphed into a chilly night. After a minute I went back inside and found one of Sarah's sweatshirts on top of the washer in the utility room. Since I'd made the big decision, I decided to advance things along a bit. I peeled off my short-sleeve shirt and bra and pulled the sweatshirt over my bare torso.

Outside again the yard smelled of dogwood and azaleas. Moonlight glittered off the pool. A woman would be a complete idiot not to move into this edenic place. Like tonight. I could hardly control my anticipation of his touch.

Every hot cheesy nacho called for a long swig of cold beer and every ounce of beer fortified my nerve. I finally screwed my courage to the sticking place, as Shakespeare would say. Waited a little longer. Michael looked quizzical.

Come on! Now!

I cleared my throat about a hundred times and said a little prayer to my mother. Not the biological one.

"I meant what I said to Sarah in the hospital."

I paused, hoping he'd take the lead and the pressure off, but he didn't. He only smiled.

"If the offer's still open, I definitely want to."

He said nothing for a while.

Does he want me only for saving Sarah? Am I an obligation?

Then . . . "Offers not immediately accepted are deemed withdrawn.

Basic contract law."

I think my diaphragm froze as I blurted something unintelligible. Took me a second to realize his blank expression was in jest. For a split-second I wanted to smack him. But my annoyance faded and I hopped up from the lawn chair and bounded onto his lap. One of the many things I love about Michael is how his height and powerful frame make me feel petite, and protected. Few men ever had

His kiss began slowly, then pressed his lips hard against mine. My heart must've thought I was back to running the lines on the basketball court. I ground my groin into his thigh, a move worthy of the high school make-out champ. If I got any wetter I'd slide off him.

His hand edged up inside the sweatshirt. I thrilled at his quick draw of breath as he discovered my bare chest. Probation, fear, hesitation went into a death spiral. He circled my breasts, gently tugging my nipples, taking my breath to the next county. I moaned like a woman deprived for months—which I was. My hand jerked his belt loose, but before I could unzip him a light came on in the kitchen.

We froze.

I just had time to tug the sweatshirt down and ease back to my chair before Sarah opened the door.

"I had a nightmare," she said.

Michael displayed no irritation at the interruption of our bliss and invited her to sit. My heart finally slowing, I told her I'd been cold and bummed her shirt, praying she didn't walk back into the utility room and find my blouse and bra.

Sarah's eyes betrayed that she had been crying. She sat next to her father and told us about her dream—another version of a monster in a dark closet—one only too real that I have myself occasionally. I could tell this had been a bad one and she probably wanted to talk about her mother. After a few minutes helping with the reassurance I decided this was a "Daddy" moment, kissed them bye, and drove home.

Although frustrated, I realized that I had to be the luckiest *chica* in

Texas—engaged to a gorgeous, loving man, hired on three big cases, about to be a stepmom to a kid I adored, and my demons and paranoia conquered.

I was dying to get my hands on Michael again, but on second thought, I didn't want our re-consummation to be a nooner while Sarah was in school. I needed to bask in his warmth, not eye a clock—and totally absorb him. Maybe Michael could arrange for Sarah to spend a weekend with her cousins, Diana's sister's kids. That would be heaven on Earth.

CHAPTER 12

THE NEXT MORNING the phone interrupted my reverie before I finished my coffee. Caller ID showed a hospital in California. I picked up fast.

"Something went wrong."

It was the expert I'd sent the records to.

"I wish I could give you an answer, but either it's an incredible coincidence—and I mean miraculous—or they've covered up something."

For three grand, I'd hoped to get more than that. I wanted the definitive explanation.

I went over the switched labs again.

"That's a big problem for them, but it doesn't tell me what really happened."

I couldn't conceal my disappointment. "Yeah."

"I can give you a report that says there must be an error. Maybe some discovery will get to the bottom of this."

Sure, they'll tell ol' Kristen exactly what happened and write a six-million-dollar check.

I settled for, "Thanks for getting to this so fast. I'll ask for incident reports, whatever's not protected by peer review."

I hung up—not optimistic. Internal criticism can't be discovered. It's called "peer review" and shielded, supposedly so the hospital can improve morbidity and mortality rates. It's not kept confidential to prevent the hospital and doctors from being sued.

Absolutely not.

I hoped for some inspiration, but didn't get any. No other potential expert witness returned my calls. At six I headed to the YMCA for basketball. Sarah had her end-of-school open house. Although she asked me to come with them, I thought that should be a father-daughter night and didn't want to risk absorbing glares from other kids' mothers.

They had plenty of players and the game got rough, so I left basketball before I broke a tooth—or broke somebody else's—and decided to drive back to the office, even though it was after eight. I was ramped up and editing the three petitions I'd drafted would give me a semblance of doing something for my pitiful families.

I pulled into the underground garage in NationsBank. A few cars were still scattered around, but I didn't think anything of how empty it was. I'd often worked late down the street at Wright McGee and never considered it dangerous to go to my car no matter the time.

That's why I got out and strolled carelessly toward the elevator, my brain on the three kids and, alternately, on Michael's hands. As I pawed through my purse to find my security card, I sensed someone behind me—but before I could turn around, a hairy forearm was wrapped around my neck. Something pressed against the small of my back.

"Don't fuckin' move."

I'd trained for this scenario. I knew what to do. After leaving my abusive father, I had sworn that no man would hit me again.

Don't panic. Get ready.

But instead of springing into action, I lectured myself for being a mindless dumbass, oblivious to my surroundings, a victim waiting for a crime. That's how women get raped and murdered. Happens every day, but I thought never to me.

Finally I shook off the internal monologue and stomped on his foot.

He was smart not to use his hand on my neck, because I'd have broken a finger. Unfortunately he wore steel-toed boots and I had on basketball shoes. No damage inflicted.

I realized he was strong and likely experienced in grabbing women. That something pressed harder into my back.

My fright doubled. Foul adrenalin filled my mouth.

You have a black belt, dummy.

I turned, so I could toss him over my hip, but he rotated with me, tightened his grip, and used his bulk to lever me toward the floor.

I wasn't getting much air. Panic had closed off the air sacs in my lungs. The pressure on my throat prevented me from screaming.

I tried again to throw him over my hip, judo-style, as I went down, but he anticipated my move, sidestepped, and continued to pile-drive me to the pavement.

In a second he was grinding my nose into the concrete. I could smell and taste the oily grime imbedded in the cement.

I felt two sharp blows to my right kidney. He must have had a baton or club.

My heart pounded, echoing in my head.

Unless I came up with a plan, I was going to get raped and possibly get my throat slit.

I debated whether to quit resisting on the chance I was better off without making him angrier. The passive alternative won.

Hail Mary, full of grace. Pray for us sinners now and at the hour of our death.

Instead of jerking my shorts off, he smacked my sides three more times with his war club, sending my hips a couple inches into the air.

Shit fire, I ground my teeth against the pain.

Much more and I'd be peeing blood.

"Don't move or look up and you won't get hurt."

At that point, following orders was the wiser option, at least until I caught my breath. But foolishly, I tried to sneak a peripheral peek at my assailant.

He thumped me again right on the spine, even harder.

"I said don't fuckin' look!"

Yes, he had said that.

I glued my body to the floor, face down, and kissed the concrete.

"This is a friendly warning, counselor. Find somebody else to sue. Maybe start doing divorces."

He didn't want my body or apparently even my purse.

I managed to mumble, "That's what this is about?"

"You got it, baby. You got lucky tonight. My orders were to persuade you. *How* was up to me. I could've pulled those little britches down and fucked you in the ass, then gutted you like a fish. Right?"

I nodded. He sounded Hispanic. Maybe late twenties.

"Remember that. And if you look at me as I leave, I'll come back and make sure your memory is permanently impaired."

He grabbed a butt cheek with one hand, and squeezed it like a water balloon. The other hand smacked my tailbone so hard, I wasn't sure I'd ever walk again.

* * *

Relieved but still frightened, I waited a minute, hearing footsteps fade.

It took another minute to push myself to my unsteady feet. I picked up the security card I'd dropped, ran as fast as a cripple could to the elevator, and jammed the button, all before I started bawling.

In seconds, I was upstairs in my office calling Michael. Between breathless heaves, I told him what had happened. He said he was on his way.

I had some aspirin in my desk, which I wolfed down, laced with a swig of Glenfiddich I kept for emergencies.

By the time Michael arrived, I was through crying, had blown my nose, washed my face, and was royally pissed off. Whizzed at the slimeballs who had tried to intimidate me and even angrier at myself for letting the guy shove me around like a teenage girlie-girl. All those hours of training had been useless in my panic.

I'd given Michael a security pass when I first opened. Somebody responsible needed to be able to get into the place, if I got hit by a bus. Tina certainly didn't fill that bill.

He hugged me, let me suck in his warmth, and told me everything would be okay.

I didn't believe him, but it felt heavenly. For a few minutes he was not my lover, but the daddy I'd lost to booze and drugs.

"I was so scared." Another stream of salty tears ran down my cheeks. I'd forgotten mouthwash after licking cement. Hopefully the Scotch killed any germs.

He let go and looked me in the eyes. "*You?* Scared?"

I knew he was trying to buck me up, but my inadequacies made me mad. "Hell, yes. I nearly wet my pants." I pulled my T-shirt up showing him the welts.

He kissed my ribs on each side, just below my sports bra, smiled, his beautiful eyes crinkling, and let my emotions blow off.

After a minute he pulled me to his chest and stroked my scalp, smoothing my thick Italian hair. "It'll be all right. I promise."

He should have been a psychiatrist. "Maybe I ought to give the cases back to Larseny."

"Carry your pistol and shoot the bastard next time."

"I've shot all the people I ever want to shoot."

"I know." He stared into my eyes. "Believe me, if I thought they were really serious, I'd *make* you give the cases back. If something happened to you, I couldn't go on."

That tugged at my heart. I had to sniff like a horse with pneumonia. *He* couldn't go on without *me?* I might not last the week without him.

The previous night I was ready to cut short the probation, but tonight I didn't feel sexy. I just wanted to feel safe.

But Michael had to go back and get Sarah from the open house. I leaned into him again and let him hold me another minute. "I never knew they played so dirty."

Michael let me go, turned to the window, and stared out. It was a full minute before he spoke.

"It *is* over the top. I've heard of turning guys in to the IRS or the Bar, but never a mugging."

"Maybe they reserve special treatment for traitors like me."

"But hiring a thug to threaten rape?"

"Well, I don't want to have to look over my shoulder every hour of every day for the next two years."

He seemed lost in thought, then said, "You should get a conceal permit for your pistol. Nothing like a 9mm to discourage assholes."

Still a bit disoriented, I nodded.

"Better yet, get another pistol for your purse, or briefcase, a smaller one, a .32 or .25 you can stick in a pocket. Your 9mm is too big."

"Okay. I guess there's no point calling the cops."

He shook his head.

"You don't have a description. He didn't leave anything behind. They won't do squat."

I nodded. After the Marrs episode, I didn't have much more respect for the police than I did hospital administrators.

For half a minute, Michael stared into space, seeming to lose track of the conversation. "It doesn't add up. We're missing something."

Later I'd find out how right he was. We were missing a battleship in a bathtub.

"I'll walk you to your car," he said.

* * *

The next day, still too antsy to run even in my neighborhood, I hung around with an extra mug of coffee until nine when DFW Gun Range on Mockingbird opened. I drove there while constantly checking my mirror. Michael was right, my Browning 9mm wouldn't fit into a jacket pocket. I would need to get a concealed carry permit, but you have to sign up for classes. I planned to do just that, but I wanted something I could pack right away. Take my chances with the law. A common gamble for me.

My anxiety must have been evident. The salesman acted solicitous, like he feared I was being stalked. Keeping his tone soft he showed me a lot of different weapons.

"Can I try a couple?"

He bit his lip. "Sorry. Not on the new pieces. I do have some used consigned pistols you can fire. Save some money too."

I handled several. It came down to a .38 Detective Special—a little snub-nose revolver, easily fitting in a handbag —or a lovely .32 Beretta semi-auto. Both were small and light. The salesman handed me ear protection, then led me inside the firing range. The Italian piece ripped off a full mag without a hint of a jam.

Yes, *lovely* sounds weird when talking about a gun, but when you've fought for your life, a lightweight pistol burnished black is beautiful. Oil and steel smells better than any cologne. Even better after it's been fired. Don't believe me? Shoot a murdering rapist.

The Beretta was slightly larger than the revolver, but still smaller than my Browning. The revolver fired a bigger round and would handle hollow points better, but the Beretta's clip held eleven rounds. And it came with an extra mag.

Since a semi-automatic was technically legal as long as the magazine was out, and could be reloaded fast, I went with it.

The Federal ATF questionnaire asked if I was crazy. After some reflection, I marked the *No* box. The salesman used a computer website linked to the police to check my background.

While he waited for a response, a slender guy, my height, strolled up to the counter and began eyeing the merchandise. He had long blond hair and glasses a bit too large for his face. But his jaw line was sharp, attractive. He half-smiled at me and I returned it to be polite.

The salesman spoke to him, "I'll get someone to help you, sir."

"No rush. I want to see the consigned stuff first," he said.

The new customer turned away, concentrating on the array of weapons, enough to equip a battalion.

After hearing a *ding*, the salesman tapped the website off. I got an "approved." No warrants and no convictions. Thankfully the DA hadn't charged me last year for breaking into the murderer's house, nor had the Feds with privacy violations. Bad PR going after a hero.

My credit card cleared and I now had a small Beretta I could stow about anywhere. The purchase entitled me to half an hour of free range time, which I took immediately. I blasted away at pictures of hoodlums. It was cathartic, as I imagined the target was the asswipe who'd rubbed my face on the concrete. The pistol performed beautifully, cartridges flying out fast. I scored well from twenty yards.

I signed up for the class required to legally carry a concealed weapon, but they couldn't get me in for sixw weeks, until late June, a reflection on the state of public safety in Texas. Before I came to Dallas, gun control seemed logical to me. Now I tell every woman to get a heater. I'd be dead if I hadn't had one when Marrs got out of jail.

Feeling better, I slipped the new pistol into my purse and drove downtown. Must confess, I broke the law again—the magazine was snug inside, a bullet in the chamber. A real hardened criminal. Call me Bonnie. After I parked in the garage I looked around carefully, spotted no muggers, and headed upstairs.

Later, I would become less paranoid and leave the gun in my car, thinking I could retrieve it quickly, and surely I wouldn't need it in my office.

I took one more look at my petitions on all three cases. Pleadings are second-year law school stuff, no sweat to it. Everything looked fine—no misspelled words. I cut checks off my QuickBooks trust account to the court clerk for filing fees in each case. Document expenses carefully, the Bar says. No booze tabs tossed in. No detours to South Beach after an out-of-town deposition.

Several hundred cases a day are filed in Dallas County. Dog bites, fender-benders, whiplash, foreclosures, credit card default—all some form of human misfortune. Attorneys all over town humped their stuffed briefcases to the courthouse thinking of nothing special—another day another dollar. Every document a problem for some poor bastard and a fee for the lawyer. Others were returning, planning their evening—steak or frozen dinner, depending on whether they won or lost that day.

As I autographed the trust checks, an icy chill started in my brain, traveled south through my gut, and settled low, making me want to pee. Once the clerk took the petitions, I would cross the Rubicon. I would never represent another hospital or doctor again, and I might be risking my life.

Another reason for my panic was the knowledge that three families were counting on me. I couldn't bring their babies back, but I was expected to achieve some measure of justice. It was up to me to magically turn their pain into a check. And I had to do it under threat of getting my liver sliced.

I knew I could shoot eighty percent from the free throw line, whip most men . . . but could I win these cases?

I guessed I'd find out soon enough.

When I did defense work, I spoke the language and bought into the cynicism.

Does two million make you feel better than one? Does that relieve your pain?

The skeptics are right. Money wouldn't make my people happy, but I hoped it would let a sibling of the dead baby go to college, even become a doctor who really cared, or maybe a lawyer who followed the rules.

CHAPTER 13

SOMETIMES I WONDER if deep down we all still see ourselves as the little kid scared of wetting our pants because the store that mom is in won't let you use the employees' toilet. Like the student who walked into class and discovered the final was in five minutes, not next week, I felt inadequate, maybe not quite up to the challenge of the cases. I had no partners to ask for help—not even Pete McGee.

But I told myself that many lawyers I meet are barely competent. I'm pretty smart, finished in the top fourth of my law class at UT, a great school. I'd hidden at my cousin's house my senior year of high school, ridden a bus halfway across the country to a college where I knew nobody, made Phi Beta Kappa, and earned three athletic letters. I'd be damned if I'd ever let anybody call me a wimp after what I'd been through.

So don't call yourself one.

But success scared me almost as much as failure. What if I won? Risk my license by cutting Larseny in? John D. Rockefeller once said the most despicable man is the guy who, once bought, won't stay bought. After some thought, I decided that wouldn't be me. Once on my back, I'd stay a whore. If I got anything out of the cases, I'd pay Larseny and hope for the best.

I walked to the courthouse, the papers for the suits stuffed in the beautiful leather briefcase Michael bought me as a present for birthday thirty-two. People seemed to be taking a second glance. I'm not *that* good-looking. It was like they all knew something, making me feel like Peter Lorre strolling through Casablanca with the secret letters of transit.

While waiting for the light across the street from Old Red, the beautiful nineteenth-century Victorian-style former courthouse, a rough-looking, dark-skinned guy, needing to either shave or grow the beard out edged closer to me. Out of the corner of my eye, I saw him fixed on me. He kept on staring even when I turned toward him.

Give me a fucking break. Leer at somebody else.

I took a closer look. Was he the kind of dude who could slam women to the pavement in a dark parking garage?

His jacket was faded in the shoulders, from either sunlight or dandruff, and couldn't be buttoned around his thick torso. The loudest, widest tie I'd ever seen outside a gangster movie hung from his massive neck. For all I knew, he was a low-rung lawyer representing payday loan sharks. I looked away.

Sensing him edging closer, I braced myself for a shove into the heavy traffic.

I couldn't take my pistol into the courthouse so I had left it in the office.

"You got the time, lady?"

He sounded just like the guy in the parking garage, but his innocuous question disarmed me.

I checked my watch and blurted the approximate hour.

As soon as I did I realized I'd made a mistake.

"Got a big case today?"

Don't talk to him, stupid.

Then I spotted a bulge under his sport coat.

I'd worn slacks and flats, so I could run well, but couldn't outrun a bullet.

The light still said "DON'T WALK."

Was he going to plunge a stiletto into my ribs?

I sucked in a breath, maybe my last.

In a crowd like this, I'd be on the concrete bleeding, drawing everyone's attention, while he walked away unnoticed. Or maybe he was just hitting on me. I nodded, for want of anything better to do.

He grinned. "You got to be careful on big cases. Big cases are big risks."

The signal finally changed. I flew across the street like a baby lawyer late for her first hearing.

Glancing back, I saw that he didn't cross—only stood there smirking—satisfied he'd delivered his message. I detoured to the coffee shop in the courthouse before going up to the clerk's office, stalling and giving myself one more chance to change my mind. One more chance to call the families and tell them they needed somebody else.

One cup turned into two and a donut. A classmate came in and we chatted until she had to get back to work. Finally out of excuses I reminded myself *NMNS* and decided I couldn't live with myself if I bailed out. Picturing the distraught moms, I bounded upstairs with the petitions in my briefcase.

* * *

Over the next two weeks I put off sleeping with Michael or, more accurately, sex with Michael. Not that I didn't dream of it and make full use of the jets on my Jacuzzi, but a quickie didn't seem appropriate for the love of my life—love I knew I'd never duplicate. Every evening he was busy with something of Sarah's and that was how it should be; indeed it was how I had *insisted* it be. Thankfully Michael didn't fuss and let me set the pace.

Nobody threatened me or chatted me up on street corners during that time. Since the suits were filed, perhaps they had decided there was no point trying to run me off, at least for a while.

I went to Sarah's games, edited Tina's homework, and waited. Time dragged. Each day an interminable wait for the coming explosion. The stress built up like a six-foot line of dominoes.

Adventist had twenty days to file an answer, but more importantly, forty days to respond to my discovery requests. Answers in civil suits use legalese to say, in essence, "Piss off, we never heard of this patient." But . . . the well-drafted discovery request can be treasure, especially if a young defense lawyer assigned to the discovery responses makes a mistake and actually tells you something.

I'd drafted mine tight as panty hose two sizes too small. No way they could squirm out of telling me what happened, what investigation had been done, and who was responsible. Right. They'd confess as soon as the Catholics elect Jimmy Swaggart Pope.

Obfuscate, prevaricate, lots of "-ates" are what defense lawyers are hired to throw back to a plaintiff. I knew, because I'd been one. Mine would be the beginning of a paper war, not as bloody as the Crusades but probably as fruitless.

A couple weeks after the filings, I lowered the threat level a notch to yellow and quit checking under my car before starting it. I stopped driving in circles to shake any tail. I left the Beretta in the glove compartment in my car while keeping the Browning by my bed.

Time with Michael and Sarah felt like family.

Michael's volunteering with Legal Aid may have been a way to keep busy or might've been his atonement for past misdeeds. I'm sure many foreclosure lawyers and Judge Judys were stunned to see the Prince of Darkness in a three-thousand-dollar suit stroll into court, representing some impoverished soul. Like picking a bar fight, only to discover the guy you annoyed was a Navy SEAL. Made me respect Michael even more.

But things weren't always perfect. One evening Michael had to do night traffic court as part of his *pro bono* gig. I volunteered to handle

Sarah's game. On the way to the field I noticed Sarah tapping the armrest and risked a banal question, "Excited?"

She turned. "Were you nervous before a game?"

"Always."

"Did you worry about playing bad?"

I had to think for a second. "It depended on who we were playing. Maybe I worried more when the other team wasn't very good. That sounds silly, doesn't it?"

"Like if the pitcher is slow you think you should hit a homer every time. If you strike out you feel like a loser."

I chuckled. "Yes, I felt pressure to get a double-double. Especially if we were playing a team that liked to dribble the ball off their size-twelve feet."

Sarah laughed—a laugh that warmed my heart.

I added, "One trick for me was to think of something funny while warming up. Like my little sister smearing jelly all over her face or pouring bubble bath until it ran over the tub."

Sarah laughed. "I'd like a little sister."

She'd made my day. "Well, that might happen."

We traded knowing looks. The atmosphere felt relaxed and natural all the way to Mesquite. We talked about what kind of car she wanted when she turned sixteen and whether she should lifeguard that summer. I found myself totally relaxed, unworried about what to say.

She had two hits and turned an unassisted double play on a liner at her. I was proud of her effort, as if she were my own. Afterward, as she stowed her gear in the trunk, we both noticed a woman walking with one of the other team's girls. Around forty, bronze skin probably from watching ball games, good figure, her brown-blond hair was cut short, darling really, with a wisp of bangs at her forehead.

Sarah's hands froze over her bat bag. It took me a second to realize the woman looked a lot like Sarah's mother. I'd never met Diana, but Sarah kept her photos in her room. I couldn't think of anything appropriate to say. What *do* you say to a kid whose mother was murdered?

As the woman strolled to her car, Sarah's eyes filled with tears. I didn't know what to do.

Holy Mother, pray for this girl.

Palpable pain marked the ride home. Sarah wiped her nose occasionally on her shirttail while staring out the passenger window, not once turning my way. I could tell she was trying hard not to cry—or at least not to let me see her cry. I almost told her to let the tears roll. She sure didn't have to act tough for me.

I know something about childhood trauma and depression, and how words are seldom helpful, so I decided not to attempt conversation. Events like these stirred my doubts about the whole arrangement. I wondered if marriage would make things worse for Sarah. If and when I became an official stepmom, I'd have to help handle problems with the kid, instead of hoping they would go away.

Perhaps dealing with a teenage girl, whose mother had been murdered, was the real reason I put off sex with Michael. Or maybe Sarah was just my excuse and the issue was me. Once we did it, I'd be all in, as Texas Hold 'Em poker players say, my heart part of the pot. If something happened again to break us up, I'd *probably* survive, but how would Sarah respond to me appearing in her life, then disappearing again?

* * *

Sarah visited Becca every day. Her friend got around on crutches with a great attitude. Kids are resilient. I should know. But Becca obviously hadn't thought about the long rehab and the scars. No miniskirts—and stares at the pool.

I hadn't heard squat from the cops about the hit-and-run, but continued pestering, calling every other day. Sergeant Ross finally called back with, *"No reports of any unusual damage at any body shops. Nothing on the tip line."*

Sure. Like if I'm willing to run over a couple of kids, I would just roll into a repair shop and say, "Fix the dents and never mind the blood. I hit a stray dog."

Larseny constantly checked on his investment. I promised each time to let him know if anything happened. He was more antsy than the clients. I killed time pouring over the records, thinking, trying to find the smoking cannon with no luck.

Like most plaintiffs' lawyers, I already had the money spent. No ostentatious Ferrari for me; the Kerry Trust for Children of Alcoholic Parents just needed a board of directors and a check. I smiled at my joke. Lord knows there'd be no shortage of patients.

Then, four days before the answers were due, the secretary to the Adventist CEO called, requesting an urgent appointment. Though stunned, I pretended to scan my busy schedule before agreeing to meet the next afternoon with my adversaries.

I couldn't stop smirking the rest of the day. There could be only one reason for a visit, so Tina and I celebrated my moral victory that night with cold beer and hot Texas ribs. Cholesterol be damned.

* * *

The next day Ms. Never-Pay-A-Penny and Mr. Take-No-Prisoners strolled into my office. This time they were all smiles. No threats, no knives. No apology either for their boorish behavior, but I didn't expect one. His tie sported a new stain, probably ketchup dabbed with a wet napkin this time. No bulge in his jacket where a pistol might be hidden.

She wore a delightful turquoise linen suit and pink blouse, her eyes still big and beautiful. I hoped I'd look that good in fifteen years—preferably without having to pay a ton for surgery.

I showed them in, offering coffee, which to my shock they accepted.

It took a couple of minutes to get cups poured and everybody settled. During the entire time we were all as friendly as Rotarians at their monthly meeting.

Big Eyes started the festivities: "We appreciate that you didn't go to the media and sensationalize these tragedies."

I nodded. I'd thought of making a few calls, but had decided to wait until I really knew something more than the kids died the same day. Better to talk when I had something to say. I still had some contacts at the paper and TV stations, so that was in my back pocket.

A minute of silence. I was determined to let them spout first.

She started, then stopped. He drew a breath but came up short of words. I still didn't help them.

After another moment long enough to give Proust a good start, the risk manager flashed a slick smile worthy of any used Chevy salesman. "We believe the deaths were a horrible coincidence. But a coincidence nevertheless."

I wanted to say, *Of course they were. You could never acknowledge any error. We never did when I represented you.*

I settled for a leaden expression.

"But we do want to help the families." Cynthia Perfect Boobs said.

Another long wait. Monks vowing silence would have been more chatty.

I guessed she was going to offer lifetime membership for the families in their barebones HMO with unlimited yoga classes, but she surprised the shit out of me.

"We're prepared to pay a million dollars."

I nearly choked on my spit. I had expected some kind of offer, but something piddling to start negotiations.

Big Eyes cautioned me, "Not per case, but total for all three to avoid the bitterness of litigation."

The smarmy claims guy thrust his barrel chest forward and added, "It would be entirely your discretion how the money was divided."

He meant I could take as much fee as the Bar allowed—or I could get away with after so little work—and they wouldn't squawk.

I knew two things. First, they weren't paying for any reason other than because someone had screwed up. Perhaps an internal review had revealed the mixed-up labs on the Sayers girl, or somebody had blabbed and they weren't sure they could keep a lid on the story—one juicy and macabre enough for the media to play with. Local TV would run a long piece. They'd interview each family for the tears, and me for the details.

I nodded like I believed it. Second, I knew if their first offer was a million total, eventually they'd pay that much for each case. It didn't take long to calculate my fee, minus Larseny's cut, of course. Hell, if they thought I'd get to the bottom of the mess, they might pay a lot more. They wanted the story buried with the kids.

"We'll have to have a non-disclosure agreement," she added as if I was a clueless rookie.

"We can have the funds in ten days once the releases are signed," the man blurted out, like he thought my electricity was about to be cut off.

"That's our best offer." she insisted.

I knew that statement was for show. Joe Bragg, the Layne's lawyer, would have snarled back to them, "Make it ten million. And not a dime less."

Instead of Joe's approach, I calmly said, "I'll confer with my clients. I appreciate you coming in."

We made small talk about mutual acquaintances at Adventist, people I'd known while representing them, and finished our coffee. I showed them out with the grace of a southern belle.

Not thirty minutes after my charming guests left, Larseny popped in, his chest heaving with each inhale. I thought he might erupt like Vesuvius, only less gracefully.

"Anything new?"

I wanted to laugh. He was such a bad bullshitter. He'd probably been hiding around the corner from my suite.

Nah, Larseny, hospital reps walk in every day and offer me a million bucks. Sometimes twice a day.

I decided to play it straight. "You just missed the cabal."

"The what?"

"Adventist's CEO and risk manager."

"No shit?"

Sincerity is the hardest thing to fake and he failed miserably. If I ever get as lousy at acting as Larsen, I'll have to start teaching aerobics.

"They offered a million for all three cases."

"That's all?"

This guy was dumber than a rock.

"That's a helluva starting bid for dead children. I'm sure they'll pay at least double that," I said.

I could see the calculator whirling in his pea brain. A quarter of a mil had to be enough for him to pay off his house and the loan sharks. Too bad he couldn't buy a new Olds, since they quit making them.

"What're we gonna counter with?"

We? I wanted to ask: *When did you pass the Bar?*

I allowed myself a slight breath of annoyance. If I was going to have to pay this bastard, I ought to get a discount for putting up with him. Like the sign in a car repair garage: "$35 an hour. $50 if you watch. $75 if you help."

"I've got to talk to the clients first."

"They'll do whatever I say," Larseny insisted.

This time I rolled my eyes. I may be unethical but I won't be dishonest.

"Sam, I'm going to do this right. By the book. They're entitled to legal consultation on something as important as settling and it's *my* job to give it to them."

He reddened, looking sheepish. "Right."

I let him suffer a moment before I said, "I'll keep you posted." My tone said, *Bye-bye.*

He didn't take the hint.

I was sorely tempted to ask my new pal if he'd been staking out my office, but decided it was pointless since he had been and would lie about it. Maybe he'd be around the next time somebody tried to take me down. He could be useful in the thirty seconds before he had a heart attack.

Larseny promised lots more exciting cases after these. I nodded and bobbed fake enthusiasm. He finally ran out of bullshit and left. I hoped I would never run across him again after these Adventist kids were settled. Like bumping into a bad one-night stand a week later at the same bar.

CHAPTER 14

STEPPING INTO MY OFFICE, Roberto and Adriana Rodriguez greeted me deferentially, calling me, "Miss Kerry." They declined my offer of sodas.

I refilled my coffee, taking extra time to rehearse. This would not be easy, convincing them I knew what I was doing and could be trusted. It was only our second meeting. Settlements are easier to sell after two years of litigation, when people are exhausted by the process.

They stood by the chairs opposite my desk until I sat. Their faces bore pain mixed with a tinge of hope. She clasped her hands in her lap. He leaned forward expectantly.

I'd lost sleep the night before, worrying about how to handle my first big negotiation for real people, not a big "non-profit" institution. But I didn't have my hopes up. I learned a long time ago that most things don't work out like you want. After all, "Life is nothing but the slow extinguishment of your dreams." I don't know who originally said that. Maybe I did.

"Roberto, have you ever sold a car?"

This was as good a lead-in as I could think of. Weak, but I didn't want to ask Michael what I should say. Time to grow up.

"Yes," he answered cautiously.

"You didn't get the amount you were asking, did you?"

His brows furrowed. "No."

Adriana shifted in her chair, obviously wondering what I was getting at.

"The buyer bargained, right? And you bargained back."

"Sure."

"Well, that's what we do in these cases."

I went into a long exposition about how we weren't putting a value on their kid, but attempting to consider the risk of going to trial, an appeal, biased juries, outrageous case expense, and a lot of other legal mumbo-jumbo. My punch line was the fact that hospitals and doctors win over eighty percent of the cases tried in Dallas County.

I also told them that they shouldn't get discouraged by the opening offer, that often it was insulting. Just as they had scooted to the edge of their seats, I sprung the third of a million on them.

Roberto squinted in anger. Adriana oddly appeared relieved, looked ready to take anything to get it over with.

"That's all?" he asked.

"Okay," she said.

They glared at each other a moment, arms folded.

She spoke in Spanish. He fired back at her. She listened with teeth clenched. I couldn't follow the conversation, but was glad I wasn't going home with them.

I wondered why she was so eager. I'd told them that their lives would be opened up to about anything the defense lawyer thought to ask in depositions. Maybe she'd been married before and hadn't disclosed that detail to her second hubby, or perhaps she'd had a child and given it up for adoption long before meeting Roberto. An old criminal charge might surface. Plaintiffs keep no secrets.

I interrupted the finger pointing. "Guys . . ."

He slapped the desk. "For my son?"

"They will pay more," I spouted. "It's like buying a car. The hospital is negotiating."

"I thought we'd get three *million*. Not three hundred thousand. They're discriminating because we're Hispanic. I am a *citizen*."

Adriana shook her head and tapped his arm. "Roberto, listen to Miss Kerry."

I told them about the other cases and that the offer was the same for the Anglo kids. They were, as I expected, shocked that two other children had died the same day—I'd held off on that detail, because I didn't want any of them reading too much into the so-called coincidence, like there was a plot to kill children at Adventist. You rarely get a case settled by telling your client how great their claim is.

And each case would likely have to stand on its own if taken to trial. A judge would probably rule it was too prejudicial to talk about any other death in each trial. But I wanted to take the racial element out of the negotiation and that seemed to work for now.

He folded his arms. "Tell them we want five million. If that lady who spilled her coffee at McDonald's can get millions, we should too."

Ahh. The *cause célèbre* of tort reform, Stella and her outlandish verdict. The media never reported that the FDA had warned McDonald's that their coffee was too hot for human consumption. Spilling it on skin would cause third-degree burns in seconds. Hundreds had been scalded before Stella had multiple skin grafts on her crotch, costing a hundred grand to recover her vulva.

I told them how the far greater number of defense verdicts never get any publicity. Unlike Stella's case, they were "dog bites man" stories.

He didn't seem to get it, but she repeated: "Roberto, listen to Miss Kerry."

"No amount of money can bring your son back. Often it's emotionally healing to get a case like this behind you."

She bobbed her head while I prattled on. He scowled.

After listening a minute more to my gibberish, he interrupted, "I'll take four."

This wasn't going well. I didn't know of many verdicts in Dallas County offering more than a million for a deceased kid.

"We can start for whatever you want, but just like selling a car, you don't want to run the looker off with an unrealistic number. If I'm trying to sell my Ford, I don't start at fifty thousand."

Oops, that may have been a mistake. Their kid a Ford? Should I have called him a Bentley?

They conversed again in Spanish for a couple of minutes. I couldn't catch much, despite having lived in Texas for ten years. It was clear, though, that he was pissed and she was not backing down.

Roberto's moving company uniform had faded. Adriana had probably dressed up to come to the lawyer's office. Her dress sported pretty flowers and might have been hand sewn. They could use the money. I got the impression she was telling him they could try for another boy. Had the kid not been male, he might have been more reasonable.

I wondered if the hospital had thrown the early offer out to shake the clients' confidence in me. If so, their gambit might work.

After a while I broke in. "We don't have to decide anything today. Let's meet again tomorrow."

They agreed. We parted amiably. I think Adriana and I had connected, but a lot of effort remained in dealing with Roberto, whether the case settled now or went on for years. It wasn't that I was scared of litigating against the hospital. I just knew that the chance of finding out what really happened was slight. It had been my job to keep bad shit secret. And I had been pretty good at it.

*   *   *

The next day, I met with the other two families, both totally distraught. I hugged and consoled the moms. Like Señor Rodriguez, the dads were angry and wanted more. The moms just cried, so it wasn't just him.

Mr. Dunn said he wanted a full explanation and a public apology as much as money. Like that would ever happen. Maybe when hell had snowmen.

Dana Sayers wanted an assurance that no other kid would ever die like hers. From what I'd heard these were common reactions, and usually impossible to achieve. In the end it was all about money, and anybody who tells you "It's not about the money" is lying.

I'd resisted running my approach with the clients by Michael. Pride, the gravest of all sins, prevented me from consulting the ol' wise one.

After I'd met with all three, including the whole Rodriguez *familia* again, I didn't have the nerve to call CEO Big Eyes or Risk Management Nazi with a counter of fifteen million.

Maybe I needed to go back to therapy, the *NMNS* again. *Not Mary, not shit.* One good remedy when I become neurotic is talking to Tina. My sister's life, in all its chaos, makes my problems pale.

We enjoyed a quick dinner before she had to go back to a lab. After bouncing it all around, I concluded it wasn't fear but realism that made me hesitate. That made me feel better about myself. I hadn't just fallen off the turnip truck.

I'd seen enough courtroom drama to know a middling settlement was usually better than a great trial. Countering for too much would run Adventist off and there would be no further negotiations for two years.

Still, old-fashioned manners dictated that I call the hospital back.

I was leaning toward the honest approach. *It's too soon after the deaths for my people to talk to you in numbers you would be interested in hearing.* That way I kept my options open. And perhaps time would help heal my folks' wounds.

Michael and Sarah were leaving for a tournament out of town—a big one. They would play a gold team from Katy, a Houston suburb, where Olympian Cat Osterman played. I debated, paced around, then decided: *What are lovers for?*

I got there as they were packing.

After a bit of flirting, an update on the outlook for the big games, and asking about Becca, I gave Michael the two-minute version of my dilemma and my proposed non-action.

"I've had guys use that against me. It's not a bad tactic."

"Okay."

"It'll keep them receptive and a little off balance. Not sure what you're up to, especially if you keep pushing discovery."

I felt proud that I'd come up with the right solution. There's that pride thing again.

No sooner than my mind was made up, he came back with, "The trouble with that is you don't find out how bad they want this to go away."

Now I felt stupid.

"This is a potential public relations disaster for them if it comes out. Especially after *Layne.* How much do you suppose they spend on advertising?"

"Beats me. How much?"

"Millions. Many millions."

"So what do you suggest?"

"Tell 'em the only authority you have is twelve for all three."

"Christ, Michael, they'll think I'm nuts."

He chuckled. "They're used to dealing with loons."

"That would be far, far more than any case like this has ever settled for in Texas."

"When they snort, tell them you're from Jersey and know thumb breakers in the mob."

I crossed my arms, wishing I hadn't come, had gone with my gut. "Michael, I'm serious. What should I say?"

"The good thing about the soft approach is you imply that you're working to get the clients reasonable, but don't have realistic authority yet. You're the good guy—*I'm workin' with you.* But throwing out a huge number means that whatever it settles for, you'll know you didn't leave anything on the table. It's a Joe Bragg technique."

"I remember."

"Either approach is okay this early. It's your call."

My call. That made me feel a little more competent. We chatted another minute, me savoring his sexy voice and forgetting how I looked like a ninny who couldn't handle her cases.

As I was wavering in my decision not to go with them—I had decided sleeping with Michael with Sarah in the hotel wouldn't look good—when my phone beeped. Larseny. Splendid. More idiotic questions about money—the root of evil. I got off the phone with Sam after five minutes, assuring him all was under control, heading off a Saturday office meeting.

* * *

The weekend slowly simmered in uncertainty. I missed Michael and Sarah, although I practically got a play-by-play over the phone and talked to Sarah after each game. I got the impression she wished I had gone—nice. Saturday night Tina and I saw *Richard III* for a little culture. *Now is the winter of our discontent.*

On Sunday I ran a 15K and finished a minute off my college time. When I reported the result to Michael, he joked, "Maybe you're too young for me." Michael called late Sunday night to tell me they made it home. That felt like family.

Before I poured my coffee on Monday morning, the door opened.

In walked my old boss, Pete McGee of Wright McGee and *Layne* fame. When I signed on, he'd been the kind, all-knowing father I hadn't had growing up. Patient with my questions, initially solicitous, asking if I had adequate social time. It didn't last.

Years later, when *Layne* came along, I figured out ten seconds after he assigned the case to me that I got the job because it was unlikely

Michael Stern would find Pete attractive. Later I learned I was, in their words, "cute enough to entice Stern, rookie enough to follow orders and hose Stern."

I hadn't seen the weasel since I'd quit his highfalutin' firm and could've gone the rest of my life without his company. Such is the wrath of the woman scorned. Everything about him was phony as far as I was concerned, including the noon prayer meetings in his office and his status as former county Bar president.

He sported his usual three-piece suit, movie-style Roman haircut, silver cuff links, and blinding shoeshine. His mannerisms reeked of Texas aristocracy, like the guys on the old *Dallas* TV show.

"Kristen, may I have a couple of minutes?"

May I. if you didn't know the man, you'd think he was the perfect southern gentleman. His demeanor had been one of the things that sold me on working for him. But I knew him well now and was sorely tempted to toss him out of my reception area. He was shorter than me and out of shape, so it wouldn't have been hard.

Curiosity won.

I motioned him into my office without bothering with pleasantries.

He eased his stocky frame into a chair, showing perfect capped teeth. I noticed he'd had Botox or dermal filler since I had left. Cheeks and jowls nice and firm, he could pass for forty-five.

"Thanks for seeing me. I think it'll be worth your while."

"No problem." Hopefully I communicated he *was* a problem.

Slow on the uptake, it dawned on me that he didn't come with the long overdue apology for getting me into whatever level of hell Dante reserved for lawyers who put perjurers on the stand. He was here for Adventist, one of his best clients, to talk about the kids. No wonder Jen had been so coy, so damn friendly when she just happened to pop in. She'd reviewed the records long before I did, and likely caught the lab mix-up.

I decided to play unimpressed and uneager. I inquired first about several of my former partners, paralegals, and associates—even his family, which seemed to please him. He pointedly didn't ask about Michael, his arch enemy.

After I ran out of deflections, he got to the point.

"I was surprised to learn you were suing your own former client."

I stared at him like he was a ref who'd blown a charge call.

What game are you watching?

"Quite surprised," he added, as if I was hard of hearing.

I wanted to fucking scream. He could've given any number of hospitals a nod, getting me defense work, but he wouldn't want new competition, even from a pup like me.

He probably had torpedoed my chances, since he hated Michael and was pissed over the *Layne* outcome, even though I had won the trial for our client. A lot of faces turned pink when I spilled the beans. Several folks could've gone to jail for perjury, including Pete and Jen.

How I wanted to lay into him. . . . I let my venom go undisguised. "Beats small claims court."

He offered the slightest scowl. "Well . . . the Adventist people and its insurance company thought I might be of some assistance."

Despite his carefully manufactured upscale image, he pronounced "insurance" like a Texan—"*in*-surance." I tried not to look like a novice poker player holding a flush. "How?"

"Of course, if we're able to work out something it might cost me a very large fee. Maybe I shouldn't try very hard to talk you into anything."

I didn't match his gooey grin. I figured he'd be well paid if he kept this disaster out of the paper. I certainly had zero sympathy for his financial interest. Lord knew I'd made him plenty. Summarizing depositions on Christmas Eve. Outlining records till midnight. I'd flown to every city big enough to have a Wendy's while he sat at his desk playing Caesar.

After a moment of dead silence, I said: "What do you have in mind, Pete?"

"Kristen, I realize you're still angry. I told you back then how proud of you I was. Still am. I hope we can put those events past us."

What a load of crap. He reminded me of how Churchill described the Huns: "Either at your throat or at your knees."

I didn't give him the satisfaction of looking contrite about leaving his den of cutthroats. "How much do they want to pay?"

He wagged a finger like I was a naughty girl. "They gave you an offer. It's your obligation to make a reasonable counter. They showed exceptional good faith making the first move without even an initial demand. Without even an expert report."

If he thought I was going to agree, he was fucking goofy. This was crunch time. Did I have the balls, as a baby plaintiff's lawyer, to eyeball him and be totally unreasonable?

There are two ways to get respect in barroom brawls or lawsuits. Or the basketball court. Either be the biggest, meanest bastard in the room, or look crazy—crazy enough to do anything.

"They would have to get somewhere around ten to get all three done."

I did it! Holy Mary, it felt good. I looked crazy—completely insane. He couldn't hide his shock. His jaw flapped open.

Sweet little Kristen, who a year earlier could have been manipulated into defending any lie or taking any amount of shit from the miserable clients, who could be worked half to death, had gone whacko. I pictured him telling the troops back at the office about me. Everybody would gape with astonishment, like I'd gone to Vegas to take over for Siegfried.

"You know as well as I do, that's totally ridiculous."

"Like the *Layne* verdict." I smiled, enjoying watching him squirm.

Although Adventist hadn't gotten hit for the eighty million-dollar verdict, Bragg had appealed the jury-finding for the hospital. Adventist couldn't take further risk. So it had to kick in serious dough—along with the doc's policy and his vacation home—to get the case settled.

After a full minute he said, "I didn't expect you to become another Joe Bragg." He smiled and added, "You're far too pretty."

That joke landed like the *Hindenburg*. Third grade girls are *pretty*. I'm a lawyer who'd been in the shit storm of *Layne*. I'd been through hell as a kid. Nothing he threw at me could be worse.

"If they don't want to get serious," I said, sounding tough, "we might as well schedule depositions."

"You don't have any evidence of malpractice."

Then why are you here?

I settled for a sly smile.

"Kristen, if you countered, possibly in the area of three million or so, I think we could do business somewhere in between."

Damn. I'd made some pretty serious money in twenty minutes entertaining this over-dressed pirate. I decided I'd cut out early and swing by Northpark, treat myself to something snazzy. A girl can't have too many shoes.

"Pete, I really appreciate you coming. I'll visit with my clients again."

He stood, shook my hand, gripping it a little too tight, like a mob boss offering a deal I couldn't refuse. I detected a threat hidden behind a flash of capped teeth, but what could he do? Fire me? Blackball me from every hospital in Texas? He'd likely already done that. Keep me out of the country club? I don't play golf.

I used sterilizer on my hands after he left, wondering if Pete had hired the guy who threw me to the pavement. The timing worked— scare the crap out of her, then dangle a cheap settlement that she'll take to avoid getting cement overshoes.

After a minute I decided no way. He teaches Baptist Sunday school.

CHAPTER 15

WHILE I WAS ON A ROLL being a mean girl, I called Ross, the detective investigating Sarah's "accident." His voicemail clicked on, and I left a message.

To my amazement, he called back within a minute, but his tone spoke exactly what he thought I was—just one more annoying victim keeping him from doing his job.

"Not heard a thing from any body shops. No response to the reward money your boyfriend put up. The tip line was empty as of ten minutes ago," he said.

I tried, really tried, not to sound sarcastic. "Is that all you can do? Wait for the guy to get his car fixed?"

I was met by dead silence. Maybe I didn't try hard enough. I started again, but he interrupted. *"Counselor, unless a witness comes forward or the driver flaps his gums to somebody willing to call us, that's all we can do. The perp's probably smart enough to keep his car locked in his garage and ride DART."*

"I didn't mean to imply you weren't working the case. It seems to me though that if it was intentional, fixing it wouldn't be worth risking twenty years in prison."

I could almost hear his shrug of total disinterest.

"One out of a million wrecks happen on purpose."

I decided not to argue. Michael had left this up to me and I had accomplished a grand total of nothing.

"I understand." I hung up, wondering if there were a better solution than waiting for whoever it was to make another attempt.

* * *

I immediately relayed the "offer" from Pete to all three families and told each that I'd be happy to get together Saturday or Sunday so they wouldn't have to take off work again. Roberto said the extended family might need to meet with me. The others didn't—their positions were set in stone like Excalibur, and I was no King Arthur. Still, it felt good to deliver good news and let them know I was working. They sounded pleased.

Wednesday, I took the call from the expert in pediatric infectious disease and got the usual response.

"These kids shouldn't have died. If you can get more information, I might be able to help, but I don't see a blatant error."

Give me a break.

I took notes. She didn't have a better explanation for the lab discrepancies than I did. She was pleasant, sounded like she'd make a good witness. Her suggested deposition questions were helpful. I promised to get back in touch and asked her to send a bill. All I could do was keep plugging away.

* * *

I got into the office early Thursday. Spent the morning grinding out deposition questions for whoever had seen the dead kids. Ordinarily at a big firm this work would be put off for months, but I didn't have anything else to work on.

Later Michael and Tina walked in, laughing about something. I loved how they got on so well, not that I had much worry about Tina hitting it off with my handsome guy. She had made sure long ago that she got the credit for insisting I take Michael to Vail. Had it been up to me I would have wimped out and spent the rest of my life wondering "what if?"

Sarah had started calling my sister Aunt Tina. Cute. Although Tina is thirteen years older than Sarah, their maturity level is much closer. I'm sure Sarah saw Tina a bit like a big sister.

They poured themselves coffee, chatting away like best buds. It seemed Michael had helped Tina earlier that morning with her finance class paper. Tina's show-stopping gorgeous and four years younger than me, and had once pole-danced under the *nom de guerre* of Long Tall Tina.

As Michael strolled back to my office the phone rang. He joked that it was probably Pete apologizing and offering more money. Their animosity long pre-dated the *Layne* case. Pete's younger sister had been friends and sorority sisters with Diana and had urged her not to marry a truck driver's son. And Pete had helped Diana select divorce lawyers—the nastiest he could find. To put it bluntly, Michael was rich because the jerks didn't get a petition filed before Diana died.

Michael kissed me. I reached for his neck. His hand wandered down to my rump. We hadn't had any time alone for weeks and Tina wouldn't have cared what we did around the corner from her. I was sorely tempted.

I heard Tina pick up. "Kerry Law Office."

She buzzed me. "It's Sam."

I caught my breath, eased away, and picked up the receiver.

Larseny asked if I could swing by his office.

"When?"

"Now. Please."

I was nonplussed. He'd never been so polite. And I'd never been to his office. "What's up, Sam?"

"It's really important." He practically shouted.

"I've got a conference call with a nursing instructor."

"As soon as you can. Won't take a minute."

I sensed desperation. What was that about? "Can't you tell me over the phone?"

He hesitated, as if searching for words. Sounded short of breath.

"G-got a new case for you."

"Another kid?" Even as I asked, I hoped there wasn't. How much more tragedy could I deal with?

"Uh . . . yeah."

Odd. The bullshit had always come fast and furious. I promised I'd be there in an hour. He gasped, *"Thank you."*

Hanging up, I told Michael about my appointment and asked, "Want to come?"

"See that bandit? I'd rather be tarred and feathered."

So would I.

CHAPTER 16

A TEN-MINUTE WALK, into strong spring wind, brought me to the east edge of downtown, an area that fifty years ago sported stores and movie theaters. Lee Harvey Oswald ducked into one after shooting Kennedy and then the cop. But shoppers had headed north long ago and many of the retail places had been converted into inexpensive office space beyond the prestigious towers in the center of downtown. Storefronts had morphed into pawn shops, tattoo parlors, and cheap detectives.

How to describe Larseny's place? Rat hole? Pit? Close, but still too nice.

Inside the three-story faded brick building, the directory in crooked letters said Sam's place was on the second floor. The elevator looked like it had missed the last inspection, so I opted to hop up the stairs. The stairwell smelled like a wet collie. Worn edges on the steps invited a slip-and-fall case.

At the second floor landing, I turned the knob of the access door, only to find it locked. Sure looked like a fire code violation to me. Back down, I got on the elevator, pushed the button, and hoped I wouldn't spend a week in it dying of thirst.

It groaned, rising like a half-beaten boxer at the nine count, and lurched to a stop on two. I bounded off, guessed left, but had to turn back right when I hit a dead end. The linoleum on the floor bore a thousand scuff marks and likely dated to before the war. *Some* war anyway.

I noticed an odor. Had a toilet overflowed? It grew stronger as I neared his office. I thought maybe it was rat shit, which would be appropriate.

Larseny's old-fashioned half-opaque glass door had his name stenciled on it in black. Sam Spade would've been completely at home. The knob squeaked and sufficed for a doorbell.

I stepped inside. No receptionist and the furniture in the waiting area must have been repossessed since there was only one chair spilling its stuffing. I guessed Larseny ran most of his racket on the fly out of his car trunk.

I called out: "Sam?"

No response.

I wandered farther in. Speaking louder this time, I walked toward a closed door I assumed was his inner sanctum.

Was he was out chasing another ambulance? Unlikely, since he'd hung like a spider monkey in a tree on my offer to come immediately. So why wasn't he out here pumping my hand with his gnarly claw?

After hesitating a moment, I cracked the door and knew immediately somebody had died. Lunch erupted up my esophagus. It was only with effort I kept it from escaping.

I tiptoed over to the roll-top desk, as if I would disturb the dead. Larseny lay face-down, a purplish puddle surrounding his head. A clot congealed on his neck, where he'd been shot at the base of his skull, execution style.

You'd think I could remain calm. After all, I'd shot a guy myself and had searched another wasted body after a gunfight.

Nope. The room spun. I braced myself against the desk. I needed several deep breaths to regain my balance. I gagged again, turned away from the corpse, and leaned against the wall. After a minute, I regrouped enough composure to touch Sam's carotid—a pointless gesture.

Still warm. No pulse.

Now what?

I retreated a few steps, grabbed my cell, and called Michael. No answer.

I tried Legal Aid and left a message. *Please call immediately.*

In my panic I tried the house landline, Sarah's softball coach, Sarah's cell, the country club, and Michael's favorite downtown bar, where he often met old colleagues.

After ten minutes barely keeping my stomach under control, my phone rang. Michael.

"Larsen's dead!"

"What?"

"Somebody fucking shot him!"

Michael paused a second. I could almost see him thinking. Always calm whatever the disaster.

"Kristen, call the cops. Then get out of his office and somewhere public where you can be seen."

"Shouldn't I wait for the police?"

"I'm not telling you to leave the area. But get somewhere safe. Whoever killed him could be nearby."

I felt stupid. Why hadn't I realized I might be in danger? "Michael, come over here. Now."

"Sure, honey. Tell me where you are."

I sputtered the address to him, promised to be careful, and clicked off. He'd been on his way to the teaching gig he'd volunteered to do at SMU Law School, so it would be a while before the cavalry arrived.

I hurried out, calling 9-1-1 as I fled.

Fortunately the elevator still sat on the second floor and rattled all the way down.

To my utter relief, the doors groaned and opened.

I ran out onto the sidewalk and walked up and down the street in plain sight. When going south I leaned into wind that must've been thirty miles an hour as it whipped around the downtown towers. Unfortunately it wasn't strong enough to dry the cold dampness under my pits and across my face.

Larseny had been no friend, but he wasn't a guy who'd tried to rape me or the one who shot me last year. I felt horrible for him and whatever family he had. I could picture Sam's fear the moment before the murderer pulled the trigger. Been there. Had his executioner been holding a gun on Sam when he called me?

I saw the pulsing police lights half a mile away and felt a surge of relief. As the cruiser neared, I pulled myself together enough to call Tina and give her a quick briefing. I told her I didn't have any answers to her multitude of questions and asked her to keep things under control at the office. And to lock the door.

∗ ∗ ∗

I led the uniformed cops up to Larseny's office, my legs so wobbly they probably thought I was tipsy. Pistols drawn, they took a quick gander all around the floor, then went in and checked Sam. Satisfied he was dead they called for a murder scene team. Then they started in on me.

First they eyeballed my driver's license like a bartender scrutinizing a seventeen-year-old's. I pulled out my Bar Texas Association card, hoping that would back them off, but the other guy asked to snoop in my purse. I shrugged permission. Not finding a weapon, the cop eyed me up and down and must have decided a pat-down wasn't necessary. Thank you.

I gave them the one-minute version. They sat me in the chair in Sam's reception area and closed the door to his office. One stood guard over me like I might flee and the other went outside to meet the detectives. *Why do I always need to pee when under stress?*

In ten minutes, two plain-clothes guys in tweed sport coats showed up. They were right out of central casting, in their late thirties, and wore cynicism like sunscreen. One was tall, decent looking; the other sported heavy stubble, lousy posture, and drooping lips under a mustache, causing a permanent sneer. His chin was so square, he reminded me of a horse.

Mercifully they took me downstairs, out of the smell, to question me. The lobby was empty, so the interrogation started there.

I related what had happened, straight and to the point, leaving out only why I was there. Told them I didn't see or hear a soul and that I'd gotten a call from Larsen an hour earlier. Thankfully, I remembered not to call him "Larseny."

It took them two seconds to ask what I was doing in his office.

"He was working an investigation for me."

"What kind of investigation?" the six-footer asked.

Somewhere in the back of my rattled little brain, the idea of a privilege popped up.

"I can't say. Attorney-client privilege."

They looked at me like my third grade nun did when we got caught chewing gum.

They surrounded me, pressed me for more information, blew chili breath in my face. I folded my arms against my chest trying to look tough.

"I can't divulge client secrets."

Absorbing their incredulous stares, I retreated to a corner near the elevator, a wall to lean on if my legs got weaker.

The rougher guy piped up as he moved to my left, boxing me in. "We don't want to know any secrets, lady. We want to know why you were here."

"To talk about a case."

"What case?"

"I *said* I can't tell you."

They exchanged glances. "Let's go through what happened again."

The sneer grew sneerier.

The way they treated me, I might as well have said, *We were plotting to blow up Cowboys Stadium with Jerry Jones and eighty thousand people in it.*

I knew they were trying to grind me down, keep me talking. See if there was any variance in my story that they could seize upon.

When I finished they started in again.

I needed somebody to tell these guys to piss off.

Hurry up, Michael.

A female should be just as firm as a man. I've been in high-pressure situations many times and acquitted myself well. But nothing I did would impress these Columbo-wannabes like six-three, broad shoulders, and a power voice.

Slowly, I was glomming on to the idea they suspected *me*. How could they when I acted as if a screw bounced around my empty skull? I must've been throwing off really bad body language—probably because I felt guilty over ever messing with Larseny.

"Guys, he was investigating a serious death case on behalf of my client."

"This is a murder, not a civil case."

"The privilege applies even if it's a hundred-dollar small claims case." After I said that, I wasn't all that sure.

"We'll see what the DA says," the bad cop said.

The tall cop's smile was as phony as a Nigerian prince needing money. "We'll need a formal statement and I know enough law to know you can get a privilege waiver from your client. That is, if you really want to cooperate."

He had me. The attorney-client privilege protects the client, not the far-from-innocent lawyer.

He grinned, nodding at his partner, obviously spotting my discomfort and enjoying his brilliance.

My brain was on strike. *Keep yakking or shut up?*

While they stared me down, I saw Michael screech his Benz to a stop and jump out.

Hail Mary, full of grace.

Michael hustled into the entryway of Sam's building. He brushed his hand through his wind-tousled graying hair, smoothing the delightful little waves on the sides, and squared his broad shoulders. I took my first deep breath in an hour. My knight had arrived. I didn't mind him thinking me a wimp.

"Who're you?" the sneering cop demanded.

"Her lawyer," Michael barked right back.

The cops exchanged questioning looks, likely wondering how I could get representation so fast, and impressive representation at that.

Before they could decide how to handle Michael, he asked, "Anything else?"

The sharper of the two smiled. "Not now. How about you think it over tonight and drop by the station at noon tomorrow, counselor?"

"Then we're leaving," Michael said. He grabbed my elbow and hauled me out past the incoming crime scene people.

* * *

Two minutes later we were in the same dive where I had met Sam, dark and perfect for my mood. Dim lights cast a green tinge over the place, probably matching my complexion. Craving a drink, I collapsed into a booth while Michael bellied up to the bar.

He returned with two Scotch whiskies. My hand shook as I downed half of mine. It tasted like it had been aged in a chamber pot, burning all the way to my appendix. After a minute, a fiftyish woman with hunched shoulders brought us a bowl of chips and salsa. Guess it was too early for the cute waitress. I crammed a handful of chips into my mouth, not bothering to scoop salsa.

Every calorie in my bloodstream had been spent. I tossed the rest of my whisky back and waved my empty glass at the waitress.

"Slow down," Michael said.

My voice came out like I needed speech therapy after a stroke. "They treated me like a suspect."

"Of course. You were handy. If Mother Teresa found the stiff, she'd get grilled."

I mumbled agreement I didn't really believe.

He squeezed my hand. "We'll be okay, baby."

"Something tells me I'm in a world of shit."

"Don't worry. You've burned through enough bad luck for a lifetime."

Right. *Life's but a walking shadow . . .*

The nausea that had erupted when I'd first seen Sam's body now returned. Maybe the foul taste emanated from me and not the whisky.

The woman brought another round. What I really needed was a soft rug to collapse on.

Michael shrugged. "Larseny had a lot of enemies. Most of his clients were divorce lawyers who specialize in pissing people off. He'd probably caught a thousand husbands cheating. Even a few wives."

But I had a motive, too—the crooked contract I'd signed. I prayed Sam kept it at his house. Based on Pete's offer, I owed Sam a couple hundred thousand bucks that I couldn't legally pay. Larseny's death would save me a bundle and get me off the hook for a Bar investigation. A bead of icy sweat gathered on the nape of my neck.

"Will you come with me tomorrow?" I asked.

"Give me a break."

That made me smile. My own favorite phrase. "Should I tell them what he was doing, and, uh, what I was doing there?"

Michael sipped his drink, waiting before answering. "We need to think about this."

That response told me Michael knew I could be pinned with

a motive. But I didn't have anything to worry about. I hadn't shot anybody. The Texas legal system is fair.

Yep, shore 'nuff, pard'.

After letting me slobber a minute, Michael asked, "You didn't sign anything with Larseny, did you? About the fee split?"

"No."

I lied to Michael, my lover and best friend. Why? *Why?* Because I didn't want him to think me a fool. Hadn't I learned last time I dealt with police that one lie begets another? That a lie once uncovered makes you appear guilty, even if you're not. And you'd think with all the wedding talk I could trust him with my worst secret. You'd think I could walk into the bathroom and piss while he shaved. No, not there yet.

And I would have expected complete honesty from *him*. Liars tangle themselves in a web like trapped flies, but I felt so damn stupid—I gambled once more that I could get away with it.

Vegas probably listed the odds at six to one. Against.

* * *

I declined Michael's offer of a quiet evening at his house. Instead, he drove me home, since I was too blitzed to drive. All the conflict running in my mind made me lousy company. I wasn't mourning Larseny's death, and felt horribly guilty that I wasn't. At home I could get shit-faced without worrying about Sarah finding me passed out.

I stared at the walls, my brain firing starbursts. While I might be off the hook for my illegal bargain, Larseny could have a widow who might demand her money, or worse, expose the deal and give the cops a real, live suspect.

Later I made a pot of strong coffee and ate a bagel. After I felt a bit better, I checked in with Tina between her night classes. Nothing had happened at the office. None of the clients had called. Maybe the word wasn't out yet, pending notification of relatives.

I changed clothes, ran four miles, and sweated off the booze—and some of the worry. A hot shower felt wonderful. My car was still downtown. I could've called Michael, had him pick me up and take me to the garage, but decided to get it the next day. So embarrassed that I had lied to Michael I would have squirmed in his presence.

When Tina got home late, we fixed manicotti from our Italian grandmother's recipe. I was still as nervous as the shit sweeper in the tiger cage and confessed to Tina my fib to Michael. She assumed the role of big sister, telling me in no uncertain terms how I was headed for trouble again. I took my ass-chewing like a man, told her she was right, and promised to walk straight by telling the truth the first time—this time.

Even with an Ambien I slept little, and got up at a little before six. After a bite and a shower I popped into the guest room, poked Tina awake, and asked her, big sister style, to drive us to work. After a minute of cursing and a cup of coffee she complied. We were downtown before eight.

Tina pulled into the NationsBank garage. I directed her toward my BMW. Although at that hour there were spots closer to the elevator a terrible premonition had dominated my mind on the way downtown. I'd left the new Beretta in my car. I knew my big pistol was still at home—I'd seen it that very morning, but was my Beretta still in the car? Was it used to kill Larseny?

I leapt out, almost before Tina put it in park, and dashed toward my car. The glass appeared intact—a good omen.

In one swift motion I jerked the door open and flipped the glove compartment.

Thank the Blessed Mother.

My new small automatic pistol was still there. Unless somebody had a key to my car, shot Larseny, and put the gun back, I was in the clear. The interview would be a piece of cake. I only had to worry about an overzealous ADA turning me in to the Bar. Only.

CHAPTER 17

O N THE WAY to our appointment with the cops, I told Michael that both my guns were present and accounted for. He nodded but said nothing, seeming thoughtful, not as confident as I'd hoped.

Inside Dallas Police Headquarters, after identifying ourselves and escaping the metal detectors, Michael and I were led by a darling young female officer into an interview room. If she hadn't had on her pressed uniform, I would've expected to see her with a pierced nose and dragon tattoos, working at Abercrombie. She eyeballed Michael, then looked away, likely deciding he was too old to be interesting. Little did she know.

With the bored affect so typical of her generation, she opened the door to a small room and motioned us inside. The same two detectives, absent their tweed jackets, ties pulled loose, sat nearest us at a long steel table, waiting like hunters in a duck blind.

Perhaps too nervous to sit, a skinny guy, as tall as Michael, but forty pounds lighter, leaned one bony hip against the far end of the table. This had to be at least day four for his wrinkled dress shirt. An inch-wide tie was probably retro-cool. Rolled sleeves revealed forearms with less hair than mine. A mole decorated his smooth chin. Give him two A-cups and he could have been a Paris runway model.

He darted around and offered a hand to Michael, like he knew the secret lawyer handshake. His voice rattled with excitement, "Jack Orf, from the DA's office. I've heard a lot about you, Mr. Stern."

He didn't shake *my* hand and his lisp made me at first think he'd said, "Jack Off."

Neither cop bothered to rise.

Michael shrugged off the comment and plopped down with an "annoyed to be here" look, obviously playing the heavy. As I slid into a chair, the shorter and nastier of the two detectives switched on a video recorder.

ADA Jack Off beamed like a trainee broker we were asking to open an IRA. "We appreciate your cooperation, Mr. Stern. You too, Kristen."

I detected contempt in his voice, even if we also were now on a first-name basis. Michael's expression remained frozen in an Easter Island scowl, treating them like they'd filed a frivolous suit against his favorite doctor client.

The other detective stated into the record that I was not being detained and had come voluntarily. I knew that meant they didn't have to read my Miranda rights, but they could still use anything I blabbed against me.

Jack asked me to go over the story of finding Larsen again. I took my time, and thought I did it without any discrepancies.

After a few follow-ups from the cops, the ADA asked, "Would you please tell us about your relationship with Mr. Larsen?"

This was where Michael had told me not to volunteer, but even more forcefully warned me not to lie. As many folks were in prison for lying to cops as for what they actually did. Ask Martha Stewart.

Well-rehearsed, I spoke clearly and slowly, maintaining eye contact with the ADA. "I had retained him to investigate the deaths of three children at Adventist Hospital." My expression was fixed. I congratulated myself. Nicole Kidman couldn't have done better.

ADA Jack scribbled on his pad, looked up, and smacked his full, pretty lips. "Did Larsen bring you the cases?"

Michael and I had prepped this response too. "Mr. Larsen knew of the deaths before I did and told me about them."

"And ran the cases to you?"

Finally—the implied accusation that my relationship with Sam might be more than talking to witnesses. I wondered what they had on me. Michael tapped my arm, signaling me to keep my trap shut. I did.

His strong baritone voice dominated the room, "I want to know two things. Are you going to keep my client's answers confidential?"

Jack waved a hand. "I'm not interested in a Bar complaint."

"And second . . . do you consider my client a suspect?"

The underlying tension enveloped the room, like a cloud of World War I mustard gas.

I held my breath.

"Yes."

Jack had spoken in a trembling voice, like a teen gathering his nerve to tell Dad he'd wrecked the family car. *Holy crap.* I should have known the second he declined a chance to report me to the Bar that he had bigger ambition. My last experience with the law told me that once they trained their sights on you, they cared only for the conviction and their scorecard, not justice.

Michael hopped up. "Then we're out of here."

"But, Michael, I just need to ask a few more questions," Jack Off pleaded.

In the second it took me to stand, the crooked-lip detective blurted, "Ma'am, do you own a .38 Detective Special?"

"No, absolutely not."

Michael grabbed my arm and pulled me to the door. The other detective, the better-looking one, snickered like he knew something we didn't.

"Had you agreed to pay Mr. Larsen some of your fee?" the ADA called after us.

Michael tossed me out of the interview room and slammed the door behind him.

I was smart enough not to say a word until we'd weaved our way out of the police station. Clearing the doors without getting stopped brought a wave of relief. When we got in Michael's big Mercedes, I started blabbering how I could have convinced the ADA and the cops how utterly innocent and what a wonderful, caring human being I was. If only he'd let me talk.

"Shut up," he barked.

That's just how he said it, hurting my little feelers—I sound more like a Texan everyday.

Since I knew I was in deep shit, I didn't say, "Don't speak to me that way." Or maybe, "Fuck you." Thought about it, though.

Michael whipped the steering wheel hard out of the garage near the station, almost hitting a panhandler dressed nice enough to find a job.

"Are you mad at me?" My question had come out wimpy like a kid asking her father if she was going to be grounded.

He sighed heavily out of obvious exasperation, but didn't answer.

I knew I was in trouble with *Dad*. Maybe Sarah could give me pointers.

"If we explained—"

"Kristen, you know how cops work. They settle on a suspect they *know* did it, and then look for evidence to support a conviction. Nothing you could say would help."

"They can't believe I killed Larsen."

"You're a perfect fit. You had motive and opportunity. He died right after you got a big offer on *his* cases. His death saves you hundreds of thousands and the risk you could lose your license by paying him. People have been murdered for far less."

"This is such *bullshit*," I shouted.

When Michael didn't respond, only staring at the street, looking pensive, I began beating my fists on the dash. He ignored my tantrum.

"Something ties you to the murder weapon they must have found near Larsen's office. Undoubtedly a .38 revolver. Not so far that they wouldn't look, but close enough they'd stumble over it."

I mumbled into my palms. "I don't have a .38."

"Well, they must have something we haven't thought of."

"You don't think I did it, do you?"

He rolled his eyes. "Of course not, baby."

"Thank you." I said it with plenty of sarcasm while I crossed my arms like a spoiled brat. Much more and I'd look like Sarah's *little* sister.

He ignored my shitty attitude, like he'd probably done with a thousand clients. If another fit would have gotten a response, I'd have kicked the floorboard.

"I've never even touched a . . ."

Holy Crap.

A chill, menacing and visceral, gripped my whole body. My airway constricted. I thought I might pass out. The revolver I tried out when I bought the .380 semi-automatic. The man standing at the counter watching me buy the Beretta—I recalled how patient he had been, waiting for me to finish the paperwork. And how his glasses seemed too big for his face.

I dropped my head between my knees, gagging on gastric juice, trying to keep from vomiting.

"What is it, honey?" Michael asked.

I realized they had a great case. My prints on the murder weapon, my signature on the crooked deal with Larseny, my appearance at the scene, Pete's settlement offer. It all fit for them. Add the lingering suspicion surrounding Tony Caswell's death and even Jack Off could get me indicted. Somebody had set me up—and done a hell of a job.

Monday afternoon the police came to my office.

CHAPTER 18

ONE ADVANTAGE to being charged with a capital crime is you get your own cell. I must've been on suicide watch. No blanket. Heavy paper sheets that would likely tear if I tried to hang myself with them. Yeah, it crossed my mind.

The cell sported few amenities. Water dribbled out of a rusty sink, like Chinese water torture, even with the faucet fully turned off. A matching metal toilet didn't have a seat and was little more than a hole to pee in. Although it flushed, the smell of urine still permeated everything. They honored me with a short stack of thin toilet paper.

I paced for what seemed like all night. Maybe I did. Time had no meaning. I'd never felt such despair, even when I fled my home at sixteen. Even on the lonely bus ride from Philly to Oklahoma. Even when testifying against my drunk dad.

Finally, I plopped down, exhausted. I lay sleepless and sweating on the wafer-thin mattress. The racket was unending—prisoners hollering and guards stomping down the hall. I was afraid to close my eyes. Until you've been in jail, you never appreciate the wonderful ability to simply walk into another room, or mosey outside and breathe fresh air.

I must have finally drifted off, because breakfast caught me by surprise. A gal in the same delightful jumpsuit as I wore, who must've been a trustee, shoved a plastic tray through the slot in the door. No smile. No "Enjoy." Tips must be lousy. Still, I'd trade jobs with her. At least she got to roam around.

The toast was so cold, they must have imported it from Minnesota. The eggs ran like they were trying to escape. The butter looked more like pure lard. Coffee, lukewarm. I didn't feel like eating, but remembered a Jack Reacher maxim: "Eat when you can." I choked down the grub. I might need some energy later.

I quaffed the last of the coffee, nearly gagging on the floating grounds. After a couple hours, the nasty female jailer and a uniformed male deputy appeared at the door and barked at me to move. They cuffed my wrists and ankles and motioned me to follow.

"Got a visitor, sweet pea," the jailer said as I struggled down a long, sterile white corridor. The bright lights burned my sleepless eyes, but as we progressed the foul smell waned and I prayed my Hail Marys that they were taking me to see Michael.

But, it occurred to me, this was his chance to dump me like a six-ton load of gravel. A gorgeous, rich, single guy would do fine without a nutcase chick charged with murder. I wouldn't have blamed him a bit if he had only sent me a note. Hated him the rest of my life, but not blamed him.

Another metal door swung open at the touch of a keypad by the deputy. My hope and simultaneous foreboding ratcheted up.

She shoved me inside and snarled, "Ten minutes." Then added, "No touching. I'll be watching." She slammed the door shut.

My eyes instantly watered at the sight of Michael, tall and beautiful, standing next to the bolted-down interview room table. I wanted to fall into his embrace, impaired as I was by the shackles, but remembered the jailer's admonition.

"Are you okay, baby?"

"Yes. I'm fine." I sure as hell wasn't *fine*, but thought I carried it off fairly well.

I was determined not to bawl. Nobody likes a crybaby and I needed Michael to like me, to love me, as at no time before. I had to be the brassy law bitch Michael had been mystified by, not a simpering weenie.

I sat. *So far, so good.*

He whispered, "I'll get you out of here this afternoon. Whatever it takes."

That did it. I lost it. So much for the tough girl who'd shot murderers, fought hoods, and played basketball with men. A tennis ball rose in my throat.

"Go ahead and cry, honey."

It was all the invitation I needed. The long night had unnerved me. Though I felt like a pussy, I saw how people broke and confessed to anything, even shit they didn't do. Isolation is more effective torture than the rack.

Half our time was wasted by my bawling, and I mean three-year-old falling-off-the-swing crying. When I finally calmed down, Michael told me I'd be arraigned at one.

"Can you really get me out?"

Michael hesitated a moment, a moment that made me quake. Did I want to hear the answer?

"The DA's being a jerk. They're asking for no bail. They'll claim this is potentially a capital case."

"Like execution? For something I didn't do?" I must have stumbled into an old Western movie. The sheriff yells to the mob outside the jail, "We can't hang her yet! She's gotta have a fair trial first. *Then* we'll hang her."

He waited a while before saying anything. It was a long while and I knew more bad news was coming. I sniffed and braced myself.

"This is serious, honey. Deadly serious. They have a lot of incentive to go after you. They think you murdered before."

"Caswell." Tony Caswell was Michael's former partner who helped the cops dream up a murder-for-hire plot to implicate Michael and me for Diana's death. As if Michael would arrange for Sarah's mother to be sliced to death. Tony had been shot supposedly by a tall woman, and nobody had ever been arrested.

"Yep."

Unable to look at him, I plopped my forehead down on the table.

Never had I felt so low. I berated myself over my stupidity. If I'd had a whip I would have given self-flagellation a go. Why had I ever had a thing to do with a snake like Larseny? Why hadn't I married Michael, worn him out with Vatican Roulette sex, had a Catholic-load of babies, and spent leisure hours doing *pro bono* for poor folks? Why? Why?

Hand me a cyanide pill. I'll swallow before the jailer can get in.

Michael let me hold a pity party for a minute before he told me to pull it together.

I more or less did. "What have they got on me?"

"They found a revolver with your prints. Ballistics show it's the gun that killed Larseny."

The Bar requires fingerprints before giving you a license, so that had been easy for the cops to find. "Someone is framing me. Some guy bought the .38 right after I fired it."

His expression hardened, his lips tightened as he muttered, "And they have the agreement you signed with Larseny."

He was kind enough not to remind me that he'd told me not to put anything in writing, but I could tell he was livid. Probably more angry that I had lied to him. His strong jaw hardened. He didn't blink for a long time.

I bucked up for the worst, determined not to cry again. The big dump had to be coming. Surely not as lame as, *We need to see other people. Date around before we get too serious.* Of course, those lines beat *Sorry, I don't date musicians, women with six kids, or convicts. It's not you. It's me.* No typical lines came—not yet anyway. Give it a couple days. And I wouldn't blame him.

But he wasn't half as angry at me as I was. Maybe I deserved maximum security for the rest of my life for the crime of being an idiot.

* * *

That afternoon the same nice lady who'd herded me back to my cell came and shackled me again. I tried to cooperate, stood at attention, like one of the guards at Buckingham Palace.

But still she barked, "Feet closer!"

My guts rebelled against the gnarly damp sandwich I'd gnawed at for lunch, but this was crunch time. I had to get out of there so that I could try to prove my innocence, or else I would sit in jail and rot for months awaiting trial. By the fall docket, I'd be trying to eat the bars.

I shuffled along behind the jailer, eight-inch steps at a time, steel chaffing my ankles. After a long hundred yards and an elevator ride, I was ushered into a sterile room half the size of a basketball court lined with bolted-down benches packed with inmates bound like me. All looked wrung out and scared. The guys needed shaves, the women a shower. The place reeked like the boys' gym after a full day of PE.

A big-screen TV decorated one bare white wall. On it, the camera was directed at an empty judge's bench. I realized this was how they did arraignments in these days of tight security and assembly-line justice. I had no chance to stand innocent before the judge or even look pitiful, which would have required no acting. All the prisoners stared at the screen, like we were expecting a smash Hollywood production to begin, starring us, a cast of dozens.

A judge entered the picture to the "All rise" and mounted the bench. She sported wild, permed red hair, which made her look angry, and lines etched on the alabaster skin under her eyes. I guessed her to be around forty. You don't get elected judge in Texas without promising to lock 'em up. I had zero experience at criminal work, so I'd never seen her before. Doing arraignments would put her low on the judicial pecking order.

A clerk called the first name. The deputies pulled a scraggly black girl toward a camera mounted in our romper room. She stood slumped, defeated, crushed by the weight of the system.

The judge read the charge. A young runt lawyer with a gallon of goo in his hair moved into the picture. The sleeves of his jacket were too long, making it look like he'd borrowed his dad's suit. Obviously a public defender, he put up little fuss to the ADA's demand of a hundred- grand bond on the drug charge. The judge happily went along; the girl buckled further and was led out. She wasn't going anywhere but back to her cell.

The litany of woe continued. One snazzy-dressed defense lawyer appeared to be a committed idealist, got red in the face with his argument, but still lost. The holding room emptied. Few in the parade would likely be bailed out. A bond runs ten percent of the bail. Five or ten grand to most of these people was a fortune. I realized I was being saved for last.

Alone, except for the deputies. So alone.

I heard rumbling in the courtroom. The judge hopped up, left my view, but didn't dismiss court. A guy strung a cord across the screen. I heard jabbering about lighting and testing.

Shit fire. They were going to put Michael on TV tonight. Also I realized they could splice tape of me watching the proceedings and put my sorry face and limp hair in the picture.

Christ, Mary, and Joseph.

My name was called. I leapt up, determined not to look beaten and probably not succeeding.

The judge reentered the picture and sat. A different ADA, and not Jack Off, appeared. This one was older, more cocksure. They'd obviously kicked me up the ladder. I'd get the real- deal DA if I went to trial.

Judge Redhead glanced at a file, then spoke forcefully, "Kristen Kerry, you are charged with first-degree murder. How do you plead?"

I think every woman views her man differently at different times— friend, lover, companion, or frustrating, narrow-minded male who doesn't unload the dishwasher, but that day Michael was my knight errant. He towered over the ADA. Michael's silver-tinged hair was razored straight in back. Strong nose and jaw aimed straight at the prosecutor, as if challenging the guy to a duel. After a second, Michael turned back to the judge.

"Not guilty, your honor." Michael's deep voice filled the room.

"We request the court deny bail," the ADA bloviated like a carny barker. *Step right up, folks, and see the world's most dangerous woman. Only a dollar!*

The judge's eyebrows floated up, in apparent surprise. She looked down quizzically at Michael.

Michael drew a breath. I'd seen him argue a point many times, always pausing to ensure he had everyone's attention while carefully choosing his words.

He spoke slowly: "Your honor, the purpose of bail is to guarantee the defendant's appearance, not to punish before a conviction." He sped his pace, "I will personally promise she will be in court for any trial, any time."

The ADA scoffed. "The law does not allow attorneys special privileges."

The judge tugged her chin. "This court remembers Ms. Kerry's exploits on the *Layne* case, and her subsequent heroism."

Junior prosecutor's voice rose. "Your honor, there is evidence of premeditation for the worst motives. Money and the potential loss of Ms. Kerry's Bar card. We will seek the death penalty."

I squeezed my Kegels to keep from wetting myself. They really do execute people in Texas. About forty a year. One or two might have been innocent. Cameron Willingham, the guy who supposedly burned his kids probably was.

An image of all I would lose flashed through my mind—Michael, children, marriage, my siblings. Standing became a struggle. I fought to breathe. My diaphragm felt paralyzed.

Michael allowed a stare of derision to settle over his face. I'd seen him toss it at opponents with weak arguments. Only I wasn't confident their case was all that thin.

"Y'all can file whatever charges you think you can prove. My client can surrender her passport. But there is no reason to keep her stewing for months at the state's whim, when everyone knows she will be back for a trial anytime, anywhere."

The judge studied my file. I could tell my chances were a coin flip. Michael must have sensed her indecision and jumped in again, dominating the scene. "How 'bout five million dollars?"

The judge rocked back in surprise. I may have just set a record. There may have been higher bails set, but not likely any that size had been met.

A low murmur rose from the gallery. It sounded like dozens of people whispering, *Can you fucking believe that?*

The ADA curled his nose but said nothing. What could he say? *Make it six and we got a deal?*

"I'll personally deposit a cashier's check within the hour."

Michael had tossed out a number so stunningly large, so casually, and offered cash, he could hardly be denied. Brilliant. Absolutely brilliant. One of the reasons I love him so much.

The judge smiled. "Very well, Mr. Stern, so ruled."

A wave of gratitude and relief crested over me.

Hail Mary, full of grace.

Although the tears rolled down my grubby cheeks, I felt the tiniest glimmer of hope, like I was clinging to a life raft on a dark ocean and had seen a cigarette lit miles away.

CHAPTER 19

I SIGNED FOR MY CLOTHES and changed. The deputy glared and said, "Thanks for staying with us."

Unable to think of a snappy comeback I simply shrugged and stepped into the warm Texas sunlight. My eyes involuntarily closed. When I opened them again, there was Michael waiting next to his car.

I held it together, looking straight ahead, marching like a marine, ignoring the shouted questions and the mini-cams thrust into my face.

"Why was your pistol found near the body?"

"Did you kill your own private eye?"

Michael had parked close, in Judge Crawley's place. They played golf together and had been at UT at the same time. Crawley had probably loaned him the spot to shorten my reverse perp walk. I ducked in without a word to the stalwarts of the First Amendment.

The instant Michael started his silver Mercedes and put it in reverse, and I knew we were really leaving, I started shaking. A seven on the Richter. I hugged myself, squeezing into a ball, like if I just got small enough, the evil world couldn't spot me.

Tears welled and then rolled down my cheeks. Before my face looked like Niagara Falls, Michael put the car back into park, scooted closer, and dabbed my cheeks with his red silk pocket square, his big right arm around my slumping shoulders.

"It's okay, baby. It's okay."

I couldn't talk, just kept fighting tears.

I'm not a crybaby. Never cried through two serious basketball injuries and several hard blows in martial arts. Didn't bawl when I got shot or during the fat hand-rape in Marr's closet. But I'd never felt so helpless.

He squeezed me harder, quieting my soul. His embrace drew some of the sting away. After a minute or two, maybe ten for all I remember, he drove off, keeping a hand on mine.

I couldn't imagine why he loved me so much. Wouldn't have blamed him if he dumped me the instant I got home. Ninety-nine percent of men would have. I worried my deposit of good will and love for saving Sarah was rapidly running out and the account would soon be empty.

I pictured myself falling to my knees, hanging onto his slacks, begging him to take me back. Believe me, at that point it would not have been beneath my dignity. Because I had none.

* * *

We arrived in Highland Park. He steered me inside to one of the big leather armchairs in his library and covered me with a soft quilt. Though the afternoon was warm, I shivered.

He walked over to his bar and held up a bottle of red wine and a decanter of Glenfiddich. I pointed at the Scotch.

Michael poured half a glass, maybe remembering how I'd impressed him by ordering whisky the first time we'd had a drink at the Fairmont more than a year earlier.

I tossed down the booze in about four gulps. I could've been an alcoholic like my father, given a few wrong turns here and there. Being hungry and exhausted, I felt the room spin. My memory of the last couple days dulled, but physically I felt worse.

"Thank you. Thank you," I whispered. I told myself not to say anything gooey, not use the "L" word. After all, I was far from being in the clear . . . and who'd love a jailbird?

"The frame must be tied to the wrongful death cases," I said after a long while.

"Of course. Larseny couldn't find his ass with both hands, but he had contacts."

"Somebody fed him the cases knowing I'd buy into his deal?" I asked.

He poured me another drink.

"No, that would be taking a chance on where he'd take them. My guess is whoever learned of the deaths dangled them in front of Larseny on the *condition* that he take them to you."

I took another big slug of Scotch. "Who wants me done in that bad?"

"I don't know, but if we unravel the cases, use discovery to find out what really happened to the children, that answer might lead us to who wants you to spend the rest of your life in prison."

"Maybe." I wasn't sure the earth was still round.

My eyes felt heavy and I realized that I was drifting out of our conversation. Michael pulled me to my feet. Before I could topple he swept me up into his arms and carried me upstairs. I'm *not* small, five-ten, pushing one-forty, more on Mondays. I mumbled a warning about his back, but up the fabulous staircase I went, like Scarlett O'Hara.

He eased me onto the edge of his Jacuzzi, levered my shoes off, and began massaging my scalp while he filled the tub with bath beads and steaming water. I slipped into Neverland in minutes. He undressed me and got no resistance from *moi*. For the first time in months he saw me naked, but I wasn't embarrassed. Or excited.

I luxuriated in the warmth and amaretto scent. The jets pounded my neck and soles of my feet. After half an hour, he helped me out and dried me off. I never knew rich people had such soft, hot towels.

Michael wrapped me in a thick terrycloth robe that hung on the door. It had probably been Diana's, but I didn't care. I was just able to walk to the big canopy bed, with Michael's assistance.

Afternoon faded to night, then morning.

I woke to a house that was incredibly quiet. No neighbors' car alarms going off. No dogs barking. No kids outside throwing rocks at each other. *Paradiso*, as Dante would say.

My bare body lay wrapped in Egyptian cotton sheets. I realized that only an idiot would have hesitated one second to move in here. And I certainly qualified.

Tina had brought some clothes and necessities. As I dressed, I dilly-dallied, not sure how to act as a bailed-out, accused murderer. Would everybody leer at me? Snicker behind my back? Spit in my face?

Michael drove us to the gun store where I had bought the .380 Beretta and fired the revolver that must have been used to shoot Larseny. We parked near the massive awning over the white edifice. Guns are big business in Texas.

It took twenty minutes to track down the salesman who had sold me my pistol and let me fire the revolver. The man beside me had likely not bothered to shoot it. "Just go ahead and wrap it up," he had probably said.

The salesman cocked his head in semi-recognition of me. But as I feared he had no memory of the man after me. I have long legs, thick hair, olive skin, and either chubby cheeks or prominent bones, however you want to call it. So I get noticed and sometimes remembered.

Truth was I couldn't describe the man myself. I'd been mugged the night before, wanted a weapon and didn't want a man. Already had one. So why remember the dude? He wasn't fat. He wasn't thin. Not short. Not tall. Vaguely I recalled he didn't look bad, wore big glasses, and needed a haircut.

"We know the date and approximate time it was purchased. Can you search your records?" Michael asked.

He shook his head. "Sorry, sir. Purchases are confidential by law. And there's no registry law in Texas."

"Don't you have video surveillance?"

"Yes, but those discs are kept by the security company."

"But you could ask for them?"

"No, sir. They are only for law enforcement. We do all we can to protect the privacy of our customers."

Michael seemed to repress a sigh of frustration, then peeled off four Ben Franklins and gave the guy his card. "Thanks for your time. If you think of something."

He snatched the cash. "I'll see what I can do."

Discouraged, we left, hoping the salesman might decide there were more where those bills came from and get creative.

"Can you tell the DA the gun came from here?"

"Sure, but it'll have more impact if we can wrap it up and hand them a better defendant."

I knew he was right. Prowling through gun purchases in Texas would be politically sensitive. And DAs face the voters, including lots of NRA members.

"Maybe your gun dealer pal might do some research himself and call us for some more cash."

"Yeah. Maybe."

As Michael drove me into downtown, I didn't realize things could get worse.

* * *

It was after eleven when Michael dropped me off at my building. I looked around before getting out, like I was making sure I wasn't going to get mugged. But it wasn't thugs I feared; it was folks who watch the news.

Heart thumping, I entered the elevator. Halfway up, four people I didn't know got on. One did a double-take, then cocked his eyes toward the woman next to him.

She sneered, as if to say, "Yes I see her."

I popped into the office and immediately caught the frightened wide-eyed expression on Tina's face.

What the hell now? They couldn't put me back in jail this fast.

It took a second to comprehend that the Rodriguez *familia* filled the reception area. Roberto, Adriana, an aunt, both grandmothers, and an uncle.

"They'd like to visit," Tina said in a tone suggesting she knew the bad news that was about to smack my kisser.

I smiled, shook everyone's hands, and ushered them across the hall to my neighbor's conference room. As I closed the door, before I even sat, Roberto blurted out:

"We've decided to get another lawyer."

I tried to keep the panic off my face and out of my voice, probably without success.

"We're making headway. I'm sure they'll pay more."

They only scowled, even the grandmothers—frozen like they had undergone Soviet-style torture before the show trial. They all acted like they'd seen me kill Larseny and hide the gun.

Who could blame them? Had I been in their position, I'd have done the same thing. Why use a lawyer whose energy will be consumed the next few months trying to avoid death row for killing the PI who had discovered the case?

I sputtered out a piss-poor sales job, emphasizing the new offer from Pete . . . but my heart wasn't in it. Call it Catholic guilt.

I summoned my old therapy—*NMNS. Not Mary, not shit.* But it didn't help.

After five minutes of stammering and getting little response, I told Tina to put their file together and make copies. They were kind as we parted, wishing me luck, making sad smiles. One of the grandmothers kissed my cheek. I wanted to cry, but I had no tears left.

* * *

I stared at the walls, deflated as a bald tire with two nails. I fielded a few calls from sympathetic friends, an old teammate in college, and Ron from Wright McGee. Their reassurance that all would be well helped some.

Should I call the Dunns? Would I look desperate? Would they listen to anything I could say?

I decided to do that the next day when I felt better.

Tina left for class at two. I hung around another hour, then zombie-walked to my car. I drove to Prather Park, where I'd given Michael a second chance back in February.

I felt tugged to the darling pixie statues, so delightfully innocent. Staring at those steel kids that day and looking back into Michael's stunning blue eyes, I had wilted. His probation had begun before we left the park.

What I wouldn't give to be ten again, before my father started boozing and snorting. We still lived in Philly. My brother, Brandon (second in birth order) and I actually got along, and we adored the little girls, Tina and Beth. Dad, Brandon, and I shot baskets almost every summer evening, when he could let residents run the hospital. Relocating to Trenton and opening a private practice would make us rich. Money had been Dad's downfall—and it looked like it would be mine.

I found a quiet, shady spot and prayed the Rosary. Realizing I could soon be without the sun for the rest of my days, I slipped off my shoes, rolled my slacks to my knees, and moved to a bench in the sun. Had it been legal, I would've taken off my shirt and bra. Then I chuckled. What more could they do besides charge me with murder one? I settled for tugging my blouse up to sun my belly.

The breeze over the sweat on my face cooled me. I guess Wolfe was right. *You Can't Go Home Again.* After an hour I decided I didn't need a sunburn and headed home.

I was too humiliated to call Michael, but when I pulled up, there he was at my front door.

"Yo," I said, avoiding his gaze.

"Yo, yourself."

My voice trailed off as I looked at the pavement and said, "Got fired by Rodriguez today."

"Yeah, Tina told me."

He drew his lips in, like he was saying *Ouch*, feeling my pain.

"I'm sorry, but the world didn't end. We've still got an avenue to get to the bottom of this."

I started to tell him an asteroid was only a thousand miles away and getting closer by the minute. And Bruce Willis wasn't around to save the world.

He came over and hugged me. I didn't hug back. I felt undeserving of his love.

Michael placed his palms on my ears and tilted my head, forcing me to look him in the eye. "Quit feeling sorry for yourself."

I blinked.

"We're going to get proactive. We're going to get the other clients in and head off problems. We'll use discovery against the hospital to find out who the culprit is. Who learned about the kids and followed you to the gun range."

I didn't believe him. I knew I'd lose the other cases and that I was fucked. I let my self-pity show. My lips drawn in tight, my chin dropped to my sternum.

"Let's get a really cold beer and something spicy to eat."

"I need some time alone, honey," I said, pushing away my only protector, as if I had a surplus of allies.

Michael stalled a minute, made a forlorn face, nodded, then slipped away.

After he left, it occurred to me I might never see him again, that I'd run him off.

You're a genius, Kristen.

CHAPTER 20

ICOULDN'T CONCENTRATE on the Cara Black Parisian mystery, which I'd started on a better evening. Though hungry, I didn't deserve to eat. No dog to kick or cuddle with, so at about eight, I decided to drive to Michael's. Maybe I could score a neck rub. Maybe Sarah and I could play an Xbox game and take my mind off my troubles.

Highland Park is only ten minutes away in late-evening traffic. As I turned onto Cornell, my guts nearly turned to water. Michael's house sat third from the corner, giving me a few seconds to drink in the scene. In the front yard Shelly—a kid on Sarah's team, the third girl in the car "accident"—and Sarah were tossing a ball. Becca, still on crutches, laughed at something with them.

But what chilled my heart and seared my skin was the sight of Becca's mom and my man leaning against her car, not a foot between them. Their smiles matched, like high school kids who'd been going steady for weeks.

Undoubtedly she had brought the kids home from practice, because Becca had wanted to see her teammates.

I spotted a bounce while she chuckled and realized she didn't have on a fucking bra. Erect nips pointed against a thin cotton shirt. The guy who'd done Donna's boobs had not gone berserk like so many surgeons. Likely fifteen years older than me, she probably colored her hair, but had done a good job. The short cut was cute. Capris shaped her legs nicely.

I slowed the car. She kept tapping his arm and leaning into his space. Her almost-bare tits rubbed against his side. Michael laughed at something she'd said. So involved were they in their flirting, they didn't noticed me.

I wanted to stop and gouge her eyes out. The divorced, randy slut probably hoped he was on the market again, since the nutcase was headed for jail.

If I'd had *any* self-esteem that night, I would've parked, walked up the driveway without a care, and given the whore the stare-down. Right before planting one on Michael's lips. A big sloppy one so she could stew in envy.

But I couldn't. Just couldn't.

Becca was Sarah's best friend. Who would make a better new stepmom than Becca's mother? Sarah would tell her dad, "Please, marry Donna. We'll have lots of fun."

And I'd be alone on death row eating horsemeat boiled in axle grease for the rest of my miserable life. Wouldn't even have a cellmate for intellectual stimulation.

Ducking, I sped away, praying that they wouldn't notice me on the other side of the wide Highland Park street. Maybe I could evaporate. Or drive off the nearest cliff. Maybe I could arrange a head-on with a semi. Leave a mushy body for Michael to identify, one he'd see in his mind every time he mounted Donna.

I drove aimlessly. Lost track of time. It was a miracle I didn't hit anybody, since my eyes blurred with tears. Back when I was in therapy, I often told my doc that the idea of suicide *had* occurred to me. They always ask you that as part of a depression test. But being Catholic I believed in hell and feared I might go there if I offed myself. On that drive, though, it sounded like a reasonable option, a chance worth taking. Hell might even be better than a Texas prison.

The radio was on a '70s station Michael had gotten me hooked on, although I hadn't paid any attention to it until I heard Kenny Loggins singing about time to stand up and fight. This *was* it. My back was definitely against the corner.

I brushed my eyes with my sleeve and told myself it wasn't over. All I had to offer was blood and sweat, tears, and toil, as Winston said, but I'd go down fighting. Fighting for my man and fighting the criminal justice system. They might haul my carcass away, but there'd be bloodstains on it and on whoever fought me.

Whipping the car back to the south, I drove fast for Mockingbird. My tires squealed my arrival at Michael's.

Becca's mother still hustled, like a mare in heat, but looked up and eased a couple inches away from Michael as I got out of the car. I played college basketball against women over six feet tall and outweighing me by fifty pounds. I know how to say, *That elbow in the mouth didn't hurt, bitch—but don't try it again* with just my expression.

And I did. Walked up the drive, head high, jaw clenched.

Donna probably thought I was as insane as Lizzie Borden. I detected a slight cringe of fear. No, I take it back, nothing slight about it. After all, I had four inches on her and fifteen pounds of well-honed muscle. And a black belt. And she knew it. And she probably thought I was crazy.

Nevertheless, her "Hi" sounded like she had addressed the cleaning lady.

"Got any more buying trips planned?" I asked with a smile.

My question reminded her that I was the one who'd spent a night in the hospital with her daughter, while she moseyed back from France, likely leaving a trail of satisfied French gigolos.

She glared right back with her big brown eyes, sighed, and said, "We've got to get home. Too much homework." She threw in a nervous giggle and one more gooey grin at Michael, before adding, "Come on, girls."

It took a minute for her to round up the kids, getting the usual "Not yet. Please. A little longer."

Finally Becca hobbled to her mom's car. Shelly followed, exchanging another round of teenage conversation with Sarah.

Donna's C-cups wobbled as she waved at Michael. I promised myself if I ever saw her around Michael without a bra again, I'd rip her shirt off.

He said, "Bye-bye."

I ignored her as she did me.

I didn't look at Michael until they were gone. Steam erupted from my ears. My face had likely turned as red as a drunk Irishman's—like my dad's.

Michael told Sarah to get started on her finals homework.

I held my fire until she was in the house.

"You like that slut?"

"Huh?"

"Don't 'huh?' me! She was coming on to you like a whore on Hollywood Boulevard. And you were fucking enjoying it."

"Kristen, don't. We've got a lot more to worry about than her."

My hands shook. I was even more pissed about his know-nothing innocent look.

"If you want her, go ahead. She's ripe for the picking. You'd get blown before the dessert arrived."

I paused, gauging his reaction. The lack of anything further incensed me.

"Just don't plan on seeing me again!"

He grabbed the finger I'd been wagging in his face. "Would you calm down?"

His voice came out smooth, effortless. Why the hell wasn't he upset? I had done my best to be the bitch from the wrong side of town, demanding more child support. I jerked my finger loose and shoved him. Hard. Right there on the curved walkway, in front of the whole world—or at least the rich snots of Highland Park.

He grabbed my shoulders, but I executed the perfect spin move—the precursor in my training before hammering a guy's throat. Thank God I didn't.

"Kristen, get in the house."

I turned my back, heading for the car, like a brat denied ice cream on her Cheerios. Again he tried to grab me, this time around the waist.

He gripped my belt and jerked me toward the door.

Though I struggled with all my worth, soon he had me half-inside, holding me with one hand, opening the door with the other.

I lost it, took a swing at him. Went for his jaw with a closed fist. Fortunately I couldn't get much force, swinging with my back half-turned. I missed or he ducked, but an instant later a sound from the house froze us both.

With a scream, Sarah flew through the half-open door.

In that instant I assumed she was going to let me have it, but good, for trying to slug her dad. Lord knows I deserved it. I guessed my relationship with them was over.

Finis.

I braced myself, trying to summon a defense she might accept, other than insane jealousy.

Instead, to my utter shock, she jumped on her father.

"You leave her alone!"

Sarah's small fists pounded on Michael's chest.

"Sarah, it's okay," I said.

I tried to pull her off Michael, but she was a demon. Her fists and feet flailed in all directions.

Another lame attempt: "It's a misunderstanding."

You could have heard Sarah downtown. Downtown Fort Worth.

"You're not going to treat her like you did my mom!"

Michael looked as shocked as if Sarah had suddenly become possessed by a demon.

Holy crap.

I didn't have a clue what to do. The time bomb from her mother's death had gone off.

Michael's face paled. It took him a full minute to get a good grip on the kid and haul her inside. I stood there utterly useless.

Finally I followed, guessing half the block had seen the tussle at the Stern house. And the other half heard it. So much for the paradise of new love.

By the time I closed the door, Sarah was wailing incoherently about her mother, accusing Michael of killing her. Tears streamed down both their cheeks. A scene from the infernal regions and it was at least partly my fault.

While trying to calm Sarah and reason with her, Michael's breathing raced, his face flushed. I feared Michael was going to have the big one. His blood pressure must've been pushing two hundred. And why wouldn't it? The two most important females in his life had dumped all over him.

I got a grip on Sarah's wrists and she quit trying to KO her dad, but in between gasping sobs she repeated over and over: "You killed her."

Michael tried to pull her to his chest, but she jerked back.

This can't be happening. Please, Lord. Please.

"Honey, you know that's not true," Michael begged.

"But kids at school said so."

"Does that make it true? Some mean girls were trying to hurt your feelings. I loved your mother."

Sarah paused, hopefully considering the possibility some girl was being horribly nasty.

"No, you didn't. I saw you guys fighting all the time."

Michael let go of her arms. He ran his fingers through his hair, obviously at a complete loss how to deal with this. Unfortunately what Sarah said carried a ring of truth.

"Now you're hurting Kristen," she stammered.

"No, he's not, Sarah." I sounded pathetic, but let go of her wrists. She let me take her hand on the third try.

I blamed myself for this mess, but looking back, Michael wasn't completely innocent. Still, I'd rather go back to jail than hurt Sarah—the girl who'd saved my miserable life.

Instead of confronting Michael calmly, like an adult, I had replicated a scene from my childhood—parents abusing each other and the kids at the same time in front of the whole world. I was heading for crazy and getting there fast.

"Sarah, it's my fault, not your dad's."

She glared at me in disbelief, but the crying slowed.

Michael told her adults do stupid stuff too.

I assured her over and over that my silly temper went nutso. I finally got a shaky nod from her.

I knew she didn't believe Michael had killed her mother. But it was a heck of a way to get attention to her long-simmering pain—and her own guilt. She and Diana had tangled many times in the year before Diana's death. Call it hormones.

Sarah had been so strong, so tough after all she'd been through, a collapse shouldn't have been a surprise. We should have been better prepared. Once we had the kid upstairs in her room, the storm receded. She finally quit sobbing and halfheartedly started on some computer game.

Kids are resilient. I should know.

Sarah's cell rang. She composed herself and answered. The chat seemed harmless, so Michael and I went downstairs and settled in the kitchen.

"Are you interested in Donna? Or anyone else?" I tried to sound detached, like I was taking a deposition of a medical records custodian.

He tilted his head like I'd asked if he liked warm beer. "Of course not."

I read his denial as legit. His eyes held steady on me, but I decided to prolong the discussion. "Because if you are, I want out now. I'm sure I can get another lawyer. Someone good will want the publicity."

"Kristen, I'm sorry."

He'd said the words slowly, his eyes locked on mine. He seemed sincere. I wanted to believe, but trust is hard for me. When your boozing dad knocks the crap out of you, it sort of gives you an unhealthy picture of people who supposedly love you. And Michael had come with his own baggage—town stud.

He drew a long breath. "Donna has had problems. Her husband lost a lot of other people's money. I realized too late she was flirting. I didn't want to be rude and shove her away, especially in front of Becca."

"You don't have to *shove* to let a chick know you're not available."

"She kept moving in like a lonely spaniel. Suggested we take the girls to some dumb movie. I said I couldn't. Twice."

I sucked my lips, drawing in my anger. "For this to work, you'll have to get in the habit of pushing women away."

He spoke with the solemnity of the Gettysburg Address. "I know. And I will."

I thanked my guardian angel I hadn't slept with him since announcing the probation. With all the pressure I was under, I couldn't risk a broken heart.

"I want every woman in town, young or old, divorcee, or hot young thing, to know you are *mine*."

"Yes. I am."

"Go check on Sarah."

* * *

I didn't sleep well, even with a pill. I dreamt Sarah and I were in an airplane plummeting down, because the pilot had bailed out. Obvious symbolism in that.

In the morning, too tired to run, I drove downtown, knowing I had to do something, anything, to keep from being fired on the two other cases.

I thought that if I could get an expert witness to commit, I would have positive news to deliver and have a reason to call my clients with something other than "Please don't fire my ass."

Before I could get to my desk I saw a fax sticking out of the machine. I fixed coffee first. Even a rookie like me gets junk faxes.

After sipping some Colombian, I detoured to the machine before calling my expert witnesses. I picked up the single piece of paper, noticing it was on plain paper, not someone's stationery.

You are discharged as our attorney.

The Dunns were only a day behind the Rodriguez family.

I sat at my desk and stared out the office tower window, too jaded and beaten down to cry. Unfortunately, the damn thing wouldn't open. Didn't want to throw a chair through before I leapt out. Chairs are worth something. And I didn't want to land on some poor innocent on the sidewalk.

CHAPTER 21

AFTER A LONG HOUR OF DESPAIR, I called Michael. I had become a real Cassandra of bad news.

He picked up, sounding so fucking cheerful I was damn irritated.

I stammered, "The Dunns fired me." I sniffled and asked, "Want another crack at Becca's mom? *She's* not going to prison."

He ignored my sarcasm and said he'd be right down. Told me to gather the remaining file and meet him in the lobby.

He picked me up downstairs, acting like this was a small problem easily handled, a scheduling conference on a dime-sized case. His annoying confidence interfered with the mood I wallowed in.

We drove toward Garland where Dana Sayers supposedly lived.

I didn't have much hope. My blank stare made for lousy company, but Michael kept up the charming chatter anyway.

Forty minutes later, Michael pulled up to their house, his S-Class starkly out of place in the early '50s neighborhood filled with beat-up pickups and sedans as old as me. The two-bedroom brick affairs sported one-car garages, where the garage hadn't been converted to another room. Peeling asphalt shingles mostly covered the roofs. Despite the age of the neighborhood, few trees had ever been planted, as if nobody planned on staying long. Six-inch-high purple spring weeds and dandelions overran the yards.

Michael marched up to the porch and rang the bell. I trudged behind him, dragging my imaginary ball and chain. I thought the music roaring from inside was old acid rock. Maybe someone had been to one too many concerts and lost their hearing. Troy? I readied myself for a blank stare.

Nobody answered. Michael banged on the screen door louder, shaking it. After a minute, an elderly woman cracked open the door. The lines in her face reminded me of a windshield after a wreck. Liver spots probably caused by cheap booze decorated her hands.

He asked for Dana. When the elderly woman spoke in a voice that sounded like a jackhammer on concrete, I realized she wasn't that old, just the victim of thousands of cigarettes, which permeated her and her clothes, and lots of sun without any screen. She probably was only a little older than my man.

"She ain't here."

I overcame my inertia, stepped forward, and explained who we were and that it was important.

"You'd think her ma would know where that li'l tramp went, but she lit out of here without a word."

"And Troy?"

Her lips parted with a sneer, showing crooked yellow teeth. "That's why she split. Gittin' away from that little shit. I s'pose she told you they're *married*?"

I wasn't sure whether to defend Troy or not. He was my client after all. "Yes."

"Bullshit! That guy's trouble. Can't hold a job. Can't stop hittin' her. Probably fixin' to go to jail."

"Do you have any idea where she is? It's about her case against the hospital where her daughter died."

She leaned toward me, peering closer. "She gittin' money?"

Her greed was as palpable as the spit flying out of her mouth.

Michael had backed away a step. Did the woman offend him, or did he think this was a job for me?

I carried on. "There's a serious settlement offer from the hospital."

Her eyes brightened like I had morphed into Ed McMahon. "How much?"

"I can't give you details."

She folded her arms against a dingy white T-shirt, loose over her droopy chest. "She owes me a ton. I supported them whenever that bastard got fired. I paid for her to have that baby. I ought to git half."

No concern for her dead granddaughter. A real piece of work. I gave her my card with careful instructions to call me when she heard from Dana.

As we walked to Michael's car, he said, "The good news is, if she doesn't know where Dana is, neither does whoever's behind this."

I sucked a breath. "You think the guy who framed me got the clients to fire me?"

Michael rolled his eyes, a gesture that always irked me. Wisely I resisted a smart-ass comment and let him answer.

"Well someone probably edged them into the decision. We've got to find Dana first. If we don't have a client . . ."

* * *

No answer on Dana's phone, but the intake form in the file showed Dana worked at a club called The Green Door. Call me innocent and you'd be right. It wasn't until we pulled up and I spotted the massive bouncer and the line of horny desperados waiting to get in that I realized it was a strip joint. I swore under my breath. Hopefully Adventist wouldn't find out where my client worked, assuming I kept her as a client.

Michael was less judgmental. "Don't scoff. She probably makes more than a schoolteacher. And some lawyers."

Michael approached the door and got out his wallet, but the bouncer grinned at me and waved us through without having to pay. Maybe it was amateur night and he hoped I'd mount a table.

A bunch of sad-looking drunks nursed beers and stared at the stage. A woman wearing too much makeup and nothing else spun herself around a pole. Hopefully she was older than she looked.

Michael ordered us two Coronas from the bar, then asked if Dana was working. The bartender shrugged, said he didn't know where she was. When Michael waved off the change for his fifty, the guy volunteered that she hadn't been in for a week, then pointed to a girl bussing tables. Said Felicity was her best friend.

We perched at an empty table in the back. I felt the eyes of every loser in the place. After a while, they lost interest in me, figuring I wasn't the gyrating type, and redirected their attention to the stage. Knowing that Tina had once made ends meet working in a dump like this made it even creepier.

Michael threw back his beer fast, then banged his bottle on the table. Felicity wandered over.

She beamed at my good-looking man. "Howdy, y'all. 'Nother?"

He pulled a fifty out and pushed it over. His sleeve rose exposing his Presidential gold Rolex.

"I don't dance." She scowled, the accent suddenly gone.

Michael smiled. "That's okay. I just want to find Dana."

Her hand stopped short of the U. S. Grant. "I don't know."

"We're her lawyers on the case against the hospital. You know, for her daughter." Michael used his smooth-as-motor-oil voice, "We've got to find her fast, Felicity."

I doubt that was her real name, but Michael's charm won out again.

She slipped into the chair next to Michael, leaned close, and spoke over the clanging music. "She's running from Troy. I told her to get out of town, but she probably won't."

I decided to pipe in, reminding her I was present so she wouldn't climb onto Michael's lap. Shooing off women was looking like it would become a full-time job. "Any idea where? We've checked with her mom and she didn't know."

"Dana doesn't trust her mom not to tell Troy where she is. She's had a rough time, losing her girl. Troy got pissy when she wasn't bringing home much money as a scrub tech, so she started back dancin'—but her heart wasn't in it and it showed. You gotta pretend you're gettin' turned on to get the big tips."

Michael nodded. "I understand. Any other suggestions?"

Felicity seemed to ponder a moment. "Knowing Dana she'll be at another club before long. She likes to drive a nice car and Troy will hit her up for the money he owes everybody."

We thanked her, left the fifty and my card, and fled. A dead end.

* * *

Over the next four days, Dana didn't answer her phone, so Tina and I dropped into bars and strip joints all over northeast Dallas. I had no idea there were so many dives. Everywhere, we struck out. At least we never had to pay a cover. Always wanted to exfoliate as soon as I got home, though.

Most places, the girls used fake names and worked for cash, so we were wasting time, but I had to be doing something.

Luckily for me some guy killed his girlfriend and her three kids, kicking me off even the metro page. Hopefully, people had forgotten me.

Michael checked with Dana's mom again. No joy.

For a break, I went to Sarah's game. As I reached the ballpark, my cell buzzed. I didn't recognize the number, but punched on.

"Kristen, I need help."

I couldn't place the voice and asked, "Who's this?"

"Dana. Troy's after me. Says he's gonna kill me. Can you hide me out a few days?"

"Where are you?"

She told me she was working at a "gentleman's club" in Richardson. I got directions, and headed north, not calling Michael. I wanted to prove I could do something right without him.

I arrived half an hour later. The lot was paved with real concrete. The building had been built of handsome stacked stone with no aluminum siding, an improvement from her last gig. I ducked in, getting a freebie and a leer again. The place was almost empty, too early for the regular crowd.

Without asking permission, I slipped through a door behind the stage and trailed my way down a hall lined with closet-sized dressing rooms.

As I reached the end, Dana, in bikini panties and a tank top, flew out the last door toward me. How nice, I thought. She was glad to see me.

"He's gonna kill me!"

She darted past me, grabbed my waistband, and ducked.

It took me a second to realize I was being used for cover. What insanity had I stumbled into?

A second later Troy ran out of the dressing room, carrying a small revolver. His face aflame, he shouted, "Get out of the way! She's dead meat."

My heart thundered. It looked like he meant it. It was her or me. Or probably both of us. The hammer was cocked and Troy looked half-cocked.

I attempted to sound calm, "Troy, settle down. Put the gun away. We need to talk."

He tried to angle himself around me to get to her.

Dana circled to my side, using me as a tree.

The gun was maybe a foot from my head.

He squeezed the grip so hard, the muscles in his forearm quivered.

I kept trying the cool approach, an acting role worthy of Grace Kelly, because I was damn scared.

Troy, getting impatient with the game, grabbed my arm and tried to jerk me out of the way. I ripped my arm back and kept Dana behind me.

In my Krav Maga training years ago, I learned how to take a gun away, but they warned me it was a lot riskier than grabbing a knife. One tenth of a second of error and you get a hole the size of a quarter in your heart. A mistake with a knife might only get you a dozen stitches.

"Get out of my way. She's dead! No bitch cheats on me!"

I slapped my palms on his chest, locked my fingers on his shirt, and if not edging him back, at least kept him from getting to Dana. "Troy, there's been a settlement offer. A big offer from the hospital. We need to talk."

He ignored me. "You're dead, cunt!"

I had to shout over Dana's constant wailing. "Troy, there's a lot of money at stake."

I hoped the mention of money would throw water on the fire, but no luck.

When he stuck the gun over my shoulder and fired, the ante went up. Way up.

Dana screamed.

I leapt a foot.

Fortunately, he'd fired near my bad ear, on the side of my head Dad had slugged after I wrecked his car while driving his drunk butt home when I was all of fourteen. But the hot flash singed my neck.

Most gun owners have never fired a handgun in an enclosed space without ear protection. Takes them a second to realize the thing didn't explode. And I got that second.

I grabbed his wrist. The instant of reckoning—I could lose either a hand or my frontal lobe.

Keeping his wrist firm, like a fulcrum, I pushed the hot barrel up with my left hand, praying he wouldn't pull the trigger again. The wrist is a weak joint that can be overcome with leverage and in a half second, I had the gun. I threw it down the hall and sidestepped Troy.

Eyes wide, he stood mute, stunned that a lawyer, and a female at that, had disarmed him.

Who's the cunt now? I wanted to yell.

While he hesitated, I whipped my leg around his and rocketed my hand into his throat, slamming him to the floor on his back.

The gunfire finally brought the burly bouncer trotting toward us. I suspected he didn't stir from around the corner until he knew I'd gotten the pistol. Now he flew like Batman, pinned Troy to the carpet, and started slapping his face with what looked like a police baton.

"Call the cops!" Dana hollered at me over and over.

I hesitated, unsure what to do and wondering if I had the strength to pull the bouncer off Troy and save his worthless life. And did I really care if Troy got his head beaten in?

Every time Troy tried to wiggle free, he got hit even harder. The bouncer had to outweigh him by a hundred pounds or more.

The bouncer snarled, "No cops!"

I decided not to argue. They didn't like me anyway.

The pounding continued. Blood splattered the floor as Troy squirmed and hollered. I watched, thoroughly appalled.

"That's enough!" I finally snapped.

He eased up on poor Troy, moving from a head-bashing to a tongue-lashing.

"We don't fuck with the police, but you *ever* show up here again, you're history. I look after my girls."

By now Troy had a swollen eye, bloody lip, two broken front teeth, and a nose pointing to the side. The truncheon was stained maroon.

I couldn't decide where my duty lay. They were both my clients and I needed them a lot worse than they needed me. Even Dana seemed to feel sorry for Troy. I stepped closer and told the goon I'd take Troy home. The bouncer shrugged and got off.

Retrieving the pistol, he said, "He's all yours, doll-face."

Suddenly concerned for her "husband," Dana grabbed a towel. We helped Troy out the back door. In the parking lot, Dana cleaned him up a little and stuck him in the backseat of my car. He blubbered incoherently, barely able to sit up and hold the towel against his face.

Dana asked for the night off and piled in the back with Troy, keeping him upright. We drove to Parkland Hospital. The poor bastard needed his nose set and a head CT at a minimum.

Fortunately I knew the ER doc from a case when I was with Wright McGee. We hopped to the head of the line. The fact that I whipped out a credit card to pay the bill probably helped. They get a lot of deadbeats. An orderly wheeled Troy to radiology. Half an hour later I got the report on the CT—negative. At least his brain wasn't bleeding.

They set his nose and recommended he see a dentist. Until then Troy would eat soup. Four hours after we arrived, Troy shuffled out. While Dana no longer seemed scared of the guy, she didn't want him to know where she was staying. And I didn't blame her.

So, I drove Troy to a flophouse south of downtown where he'd gotten a room after they split. Somebody should have checked on him every hour, but truth was, I didn't give a shit about the bastard. The fact that he was alive when we dropped him off more than satisfied my conscience.

Dana asked me take her to a friend's apartment where she crashed occasionally. On the way I told her things were going great on her case. Had I been Pinocchio my nose would have grown a foot. Though I'm not sure she understood anything anyway. She seemed spacey, maybe on something. Troy had gotten a dose of narcotics in the ER and they both acted about the same.

I walked Dana up to a dreary second-story apartment and declined her offer of a drink. Despite my hand gripping the doorknob, Dana gave me a full rundown on their troubles. It seemed Troy was jealous, didn't like her working in clubs, but didn't mind the money she brought in. After a few minutes of self-justification, she admitted that humming a customer had something to do with Troy's attitude and the end of nirvana.

I must have looked aghast, so Dana assured me she had not swallowed. In her mind, this mitigated the offense.

Too much information.

I was too wiped out to hear any more and told her we needed to talk tomorrow.

She thanked me, actually sounding grateful for saving her life.

I still had a client, a case, and a chance to prove I didn't kill Larsen.

* * *

I slept poorly, dreaming of guns. In my visions, Troy still had the pistol and I cowered in the corner, helpless.

After breakfast I called Michael. Gave him a slightly watered-down version of the night before, but under interrogation, remembering my honesty vow, I admitted to grabbing a pistol from Troy. Michael said nothing for a long minute. I assured him I was fine.

He agreed to meet at my office right away. I dabbed on concealer and wore a hunter-green polo shirt that went well with my eyes. Maybe Michael wouldn't notice I looked like hell.

He sat across from my desk, proofreading my discovery requests to the hospital in the Sayers case. I was proud of the legal work I'd done and, like a rookie, hoped for a compliment.

"They're good, but knowing Pete McGee, all we're going to get is obfuscation, prevarication, and then plain ol' lies."

I knew Pete well and realized Michael was correct. I was on my third cup of coffee, trying to perk up. "Pete may lie, but when we depose the nurses and staff, we'll learn more. Folks sometimes get nervous about perjury." I said this hopefully, not completely believing it.

"Some . . . times," Michael stretched the word emphasizing his doubt.

I feared even Michael was worried. Would he tell me if he was? Lawyers withhold bad news all the time.

The reception door opened. Since Tina was in school, I stepped out of my office. To my surprise, the bruised and blue Troy stood at the front desk. He didn't look much better than he had the night before, except for sporting a slightly cleaner shirt. His bruises were a darker shade of purple.

I expected a word of thanks for getting the bouncer off him, keeping him out of jail, and paying his ER tab. Silly me.

He wiggled his index finger at me. "You stay out of shit 'tween me and Dana."

I started to count to ten, made it to three. "Troy, you could get twenty years for attempted murder. Even if Dana doesn't press charges, I could for aggravated assault. Your bullet missed my head by an inch."

He combined a leer with a shrug. "We could keep in touch through the fence."

"What?"

"How can you be our lawyer when you're fixin' to go to prison?"

Shit. I'd screwed up by not telling them. But when could I in all the excitement? I stammered about my innocence, and my wonderful qualities.

He interrupted my spiel, "I want our file back. I wanna new lawyer."

I stood mute, feeling my world going down the shitter.

"Listen, dumbass!"

Michael moved across the office toward Troy like Wyatt Earp striding down the middle of OK Corral.

"That's some thanks for keeping your sorry ass out of jail. Kristen's wrong. You could get life. Attempted murder, plus aggravated assault. Thirty years minimum. More if you already got a record, which I suspect you do."

Troy's mouth hung open, speechless.

Michael kept coming. "I got a buddy in the DA's office. All I got to do is call him and you'll be locked up in twenty minutes. I doubt you can make bail."

Troy backed up a step, surprise plastered on his stubbled face.

Michael towered a good six inches over Troy. "And now you want to fuck up your case? We've already got big bucks on the table, more than you'll ever see again in your whole miserable life. You want to see the offer withdrawn, start all over, and fight this case for the next three years?"

Troy kept retreating, stammering.

"The same assholes who killed your baby are trying to frame Kristen for murder."

"Well, I don't know—"

"Who told you about the charge against Kristen?"

Troy hum-hawed.

Michael was now a foot from him as Troy hit the wall and could retreat no further. Troy was strong, like a bricklayer, but Michael had the momentum.

"I asked *who*, jerkweed."

Troy looked like he feared Michael was going to slug him. I wasn't sure myself. I'd never

have the nerve to talk to a client I desperately needed like Michael addressed Troy.

"Got a call this morning. They didn't say who it was."

"Who's *they*?"

"Don't know."

Michael paused long enough for me to reenter the conversation.

"Male or female?"

"A chick."

Michael pulled on Troy's tee and then shoved him against the wall. "She leave a name?"

"Uh, no . . . sir."

"Can you get the number off your phone?"

"No. She called me where I was workin.'"

I made sure my tone was reassuring.

Be the good cop.

"If you'll stay with us, we'll get you everything you deserve for such a terrible loss." I wondered what Troy really deserved. Sierra's death had saved Troy twelve years of child support and maybe a contempt charge when he got behind.

Troy looked up at Michael, then back at me, seemingly for comfort. "Okay."

"Tell me everything this woman said to you," Michael demanded.

Troy shrugged. She went and asked, "You want a killer for a lawyer? How can she represent you from jail?"

Michael demanded to know if that was everything.

Troy, suddenly coherent, said it was.

My darling man jabbed a manicured finger at Troy. "Stay out of trouble. We'll keep you up to date on the case. But I don't want to hear a peep out of you."

Troy seemed unsure what to do. He looked at me.

I nodded, faking sincerity. "I'll be in touch."

Michael pointed to the door. "Pard', get out and don't come back, unless we call you."

Troy shot a forlorn glance at me, then hustled out the door probably one second before Michael threw him out.

Once Troy disappeared I thanked my lover, then blew a long breath of relief. Unfortunately, I had named Troy as a plaintiff along with Dana. I didn't know how much influence Troy still had over Dana after last night. Maybe none. If I had Dana I still had a case, but I worried that if she'd stayed with Troy for years under threat of abuse, she might go along with firing me.

But despite my worry and desperation I appreciated my dauntless man even more.

CHAPTER 22

WE WAITED IMPATIENTLY for the hospital's discovery responses. I treated Dana like the Queen of Sheba, dropping in several times, answering all questions legal or otherwise, and encouraging her to find better-dressed employment. She shrugged off my rendition of my troubles. Nothing like facing a gun together for bonding.

I even provided free marital counseling: *Get rid of the guy.* I wanted to ask if Troy really was the father, but decided I didn't want to know.

Michael met with the DA, suggesting, then pleading that they subpoena gun purchase records for the day I bought mine. He got smarmy shrugs in response. They had their woman.

As I suspected, we didn't hear a peep from the gun dealer.

The hospital's answers finally arrived. Breathlessly, I opened the thick manila envelope from Wright McGee. I gathered my strength before reading, telling myself I'd likely be disappointed. *C'est la vie.*

Was I ever. Michael had been prescient. Objections to everything I asked, except the address of the hospital. Awful even by Wright McGee standards. Pete had signed the responses himself—his way of saying *Up yours.*

I could take their non-answers to the judge, where they would be embarrassed. But the rules require a conference before filing a Motion to Compel.

I called Pete and had to leave a message with his paralegal. I stressed the importance of my call.

She sounded annoyed. Actually worse than that, like she hoped I would die soon of bubonic plague.

No response all day. Big shock.

That night Michael lit a fire under my ass to just show up. He didn't need to. I'd already decided to pop in to Wright McGee and wait him out, even if cobwebs grew around my face.

I arrived at 8 a.m. Pete made me stew for an hour. I knew he was always there early to study his Bible before starting the day. Hopefully he was on the commandment about bearing false witness. I suspect that one day lightning will strike him while he reads.

Cindy, who had been the receptionist when I worked there, was sweet and told me he *was* in, knowing Pete was playing a power game. She fixed me a perfect java and we chatted about her baby.

After far more than long enough to piss me off, his snooty paralegal came for me, snarling my name, treating me worse than when I was a new lawyer. Many paralegals resent baby lawyers. They know more practical stuff than the pups toting their shiny plaques. And she had been the worst.

She led me down the hall like I was the janitor and she was Queen Liz II.

Pete, without bare civility, stood from behind his desk and directed me to the small conference area at the other end of his digs. How many times had I been there, hoping he'd tell me I'd done well? How things change.

Before I sat, I said, "I want everything I'm entitled to."

He smirked. "That wouldn't be much."

I glared, wanting to tell him what a sorry, slimy scum-sucker he was. But I resisted. Somehow.

With no pleasantries or mention of old days, we spent half an hour haggling over his pathetic discovery responses. I wanted policies on lab reports, incident reports, sentinel event notices given to the Joint Commission on Hospitals, and the personnel file of everyone involved in her care.

He had to pony up all of it. He knew it and finally caved, insisting on a protective order requiring me not to disclose anything I learned— particularly to any lawyer representing the Dunns or *la familia* Rodriguez. They could get no help from me.

When we finished, he patted my hand, ever the sweet old dad I never had.

"I'm so sorry to hear about your troubles, Kristen."

I didn't believe him for a second. Indirectly, he had started the ball speeding downhill a year earlier. As I pulled my hand away, I wondered if the Bible-toting prig could be behind the whole plot to put me away.

* * *

Three days later, McGee's runner dutifully delivered the agreed-upon documents. The speedy response told me they had already put it all together before I met with Pete. That morning's fuss had all been for show.

Assholes.

On Friday evening, I picked up Sarah's favorite pizza and hauled the paper dump to Michael's house. Becca was there for her first sleepover since leaving the hospital. Unfortunately, I missed Donna when she brought Becca. Sure wanted to say "hi."

We spread the documents on the floor in Michael's library, looking for anything suspicious. Sarah and Becca participated, asking distracting questions, but it was heartwarming how much they wanted to keep me out of prison.

At ten, Michael sent the girls upstairs to get ready for bed. I got up and grabbed us beers. Employee files are uniformly tedious. My eyes already glazed over.

The teens ambled back down the stairs in pajamas, came back in, and looked over our shoulders. But, after a while, their interest waned. They went to the TV room and put a DVD in while Michael and I kept looking for needles in the haystack. After an hour or so the girls came back and offered us popcorn.

As I snatched a handful, Becca asked, "When will this place where they gave me the IV smooth out?"

Michael waved her closer and looked at the back of her hand. "Could be a little infiltration under the skin. It's nothing serious."

"Okay." Becca didn't seem entirely convinced and hobbled over to show me. I affirmed the prognosis.

And so the seed was planted.

* * *

I put my shoes back on an hour later and somehow levered myself to a standing position. We were tired and had kicked around every conceivable theory about what happened to the children to the point of talking in circles. I reminded him I'd promised to check on Dana when she got off work.

Michael's blue eyes stared at me a moment before he kissed me good-bye. Those little crinkles around the edges drive me nuts. His hand roamed my back, then wandered down to my rump.

Very nice.

I thought my nether regions might explode. No two people needed a weekend away more. A weekend without cases, crimes, or dead kids.

* * *

At the So Fine club at about one in the morning, I sent Dana a text to the phone that was now working, telling her I had arrived. I parked near her Corvette. The last time I went in, the manager tried to talk me into dancing. I told him I didn't think I was qualified, trying to be funny. He'd scoped out my chest, shrugged, and said I had nice legs.

So I stayed in the lot. Saw no evidence of Troy.

I slumped against the headrest, my lids growing heavy. I'd been on Ambien at night and Wellbutrin during the day since my return from jail—leaving me groggy in the afternoon and a zombie at night, until I went to bed, when I suddenly felt wired enough to power a small generator.

I must've dozed off to the music coming from inside—"Stairway to Heaven." When I came to, blinking myself awake, the jukebox blared some sad-sounding country song. This meant a different dancer was prancing around the pole and Dana only had one more routine. I must have slept fifteen minutes.

But I didn't feel better. Now my neck ached from its awkward position, my mouth felt like sandpaper, and I was still tired. The music went rock again as I checked the dash clock. The order of songs never changed and Fleetwood Mac was Dana's last number. Stragglers staggering out and piling into their cars confirmed it was closing time.

A pickup pulled up and stopped near my passenger door. I heard Stevie Nicks give it up for the night. The pickup had parked at an odd angle, so that its headlights' reflected off the inside of my windshield. The motor was still running, like someone else was picking up a dancer. I didn't pay any further attention until the glass in my back passenger door exploded.

I knew immediately I'd been fired at and threw myself low across the center console. I heard a pumping sound, then the pickup eased closer, before the deafening second blast flew through. Shards of glass sprinkled over me. Whoever it was had a pump-action shotgun. Another explosion. My car windows were gone. I didn't dare reach for the Beretta in the glove box, fearing I might lose a hand.

The truck peeled out.

I realized I was still alive, but waited a full minute before peeking. Wasn't sure they weren't coming back to finish the job.

Warm fluid trickled down my face.

My driver's door opened and the car's dome light came on. I tried to shake off the shock. Dana stared at me, her mouth hanging open. The bouncer peered over her shoulder.

"Jeez, are you okay, Kristen? Look at me."

I pushed myself up and shifted around. Got a once-over from Dana.

The former scrub tech propped open my lids and stared into my eyes, then rotated my head.

"Talk to me," she said.

"I'm okay."

"Shit, darlin'?"

"Huh?"

"Glass clipped your ear and cut your scalp. There's a lot of blood."

At that point, I was just glad to be breathing and told her to call the cops and Michael.

"Don't you want to go to the hospital?"

My heart slowed. Breath came regularly. "No, I'll be okay." Wasn't completely sure I'd told the truth, but needed to buck myself up.

Dana eased me out of the car and she and the bouncer helped me inside the club into her

dressing cubicle. I looked into the mirror. She was right. My right ear had been nicked, an eyebrow bled, and some place in my scalp had been cut. Specks of blood decorated my hair and right cheek. Quite a sight.

I stuck my head in the tiny sink. The cold water stung and washed away the adrenaline. My hands shook and my ear hurt, like a welder had torched it.

Dana gave me a palm full of aspirin, which I gulped down.

I sat in a little wicker chair in front of the full-length mirror and leaned against the glass. My wet hair lay plastered to my head. Hands shaking, I struggled to steady my breath.

More warm blood trickled across my face. I went back to the sink and worshipped the porcelain a minute before I barfed. After rinsing my mouth, I felt a tad better.

Half an hour later two uniformed cops shuffled in. Their droopy eyes told me their shift had almost been over when the annoying call came in. Had it not been for me, they'd be on their way home or to a poker game.

Although I suspected I'd just been warned off the kids' cases again, I didn't share that theory with the cops. I had no description of the shooter and was vague on the truck. So the investigation was going nowhere.

They weren't exactly sympathetic and quickly grew suspicious, as if I must've done something I wasn't telling them. They asked questions about who I was seeing, where I worked, how long I had known Dana. Did I work with her? A compliment for a woman my age.

One of them speculated that whoever did it only wanted to scare me, since they only found bird shot pellets, not the bigger buckshot.

"I could've taken the full load in the face and been blinded."

"Then you got lucky," the lead cop blurted.

I didn't argue further. What good would it have done?

It took a minute to figure it out—they knew I was the bonded-out murderer with a rich, important lawyer boyfriend. Not exactly the most sympathetic of victims in their view.

I signed a single-page statement and they split. A few minutes later Michael hurried in. Finally, I got some TLC. He wanted to take me to the ER, but I didn't see any point. I'd had all the vaccinations last time I got shot. Nothing looked so deep it couldn't be treated with butterfly strips. I asked him to take me to his house and let me sleep in the guest bedroom.

Too frightened to go home, I wanted to curl into a fetal position somewhere safe.

CHAPTER 23

IT TOOK ME FOREVER to fall asleep. I was damn tempted to get up and sneak into Michael's bed. But that wouldn't be fair, since I didn't want sex, just snug safety. At around three I got up and took another pill from my emergency stash.

Daylight found me completely disoriented. I wandered into the kitchen, heard nothing, and realized the big house was empty and kind of spooky. The clock over the stove read eleven. Good thing I didn't have a court hearing today. Hopefully Tina was minding the shop.

I made a pot of coffee and found a pack of frozen waffles. After I ate, I showered and managed to look presentable except for the Band-Aids.

The front door opened. Michael walked in.

He asked if I felt better, but didn't smile. I could tell something was amiss.

"What?"

"Went to see the DA again," he said.

I wasn't sure I wanted to hear more. "And?"

"I thought the shooting at the strip club would convince them someone was framing you."

"And?"

He motioned me into his library and asked me to sit. I knew bad news was coming.

Michael leaned against the mantel. "They're spinning the shooting as something we concocted to make you look persecuted."

I covered my eyes, hoping this nightmare would end soon, that I would wake up, be in Venice on the Grand Canal in a gondola. The way my week was going, I'd have settled for Lake Texoma in a bass boat.

"No witnesses, no description, no motive. They think it's phony."

"Like I had somebody take a few shots for grins?"

"The hotshot ADA asked me how they could've missed if they really wanted to kill you."

"I don't know. Tell the DA to find them and ask."

He sucked in his lips a moment. I braced for more tales of woe.

"It gets worse. A gal who worked in the collection agency next to Larseny's office says she heard an argument. She says a woman was yelling at Larseny and she remembers the word *fees*. Also said the woman sounded young, thirtyish."

I leapt up. "How long before she heard the shot?"

"She didn't. Says she left right after that to get a late lunch. When she got back, there were already cops, so she got scared and left without going back upstairs."

"Jesus, how long was she gone? How long was it between the argument and when I got there?"

"Baby, if they have to, to make the time line fit, they'll claim you returned to look for the agreement you signed to split the fee. Then you called the cops when you couldn't find it."

"I guess they've got it."

"Yep. It was in Sam's safe under the rug."

"Forgot to look there."

He stared at me for the longest time, as if I was a worm he'd found in his candy bar. He was probably figuring out how to keep me from hanging on his leg like a toddler after he dumped me.

"I couldn't talk them into getting the gun records. Maybe ATF will help."

I sighed. "Maybe." Why would anyone help me?

"The DA wants to go to trial in September."

"Three months. That doesn't give us much time to find my enemy."

I knew Pete would stall and try to postpone every depo and hearing on Dana's wrongful death case. He'd do that on any case, just to bill the hours, but I'd get special treatment. Payback for being a traitor.

"If you want to waive your right to a speedy trial, I can get a delay till after New Year's."

The thought of this mess going into another year made my teeth hurt. "Let's go."

Michael nodded. "We won't waste a day."

* * *

I put on the previous night's clothes and asked Michael to run me to my place. Instead, he gave me the keys to his Benz SL550.

"I had your car towed to the body shop. Your gun's in the console."

"Thanks." He took better care of me than I did myself.

I got in the two-seater and zipped away. At the first light, I flipped the console lid and found my small Beretta.

Enjoying my upgraded wheels, I sped to the office. I'd already mapped out the names of the most important players in the Sayers baby's chart. Notices for their depositions went out that day, Tina hand-delivering them to Wright McGee. You have to give five days' notice, and I did, but I wasn't surprised by the call that came an hour after Tina returned. It was my old pal Jen.

"Kristen, there's no way Pete or I can do these depos next week. We're up to our asses in alligators." She added, as if I suspected them of intentionally stalling, "I'm not bullshitting you. We can't do these depos this month, let alone next week."

Despite the lunch and the drop-in a few weeks earlier, we'd not fully recovered our friendship. But I figured she still owed me for the *Layne* mess.

I cast a line. "Jen, can you get a drink after work?"

* * *

About six, Jen bounced into the dive where I'd met Sam, which was now my favorite bar. I stood and hugged her, towering over the five-two former nurse. Her freckles made her look younger than she was.

"Congratulations on your partnership," I said as we sat.

"I'm not sure whether it's a promotion or a sentence. It might mean I have to give up the night I spend each month nursing at Methodist to keep my skills up."

"That's the night I know patients get really good care."

I meant it. She was a great nurse.

After a quiet moment, Jen blushed. "Sorry about everything."

I waved her apology off. Tried to look totally unconcerned. *Tried.*

We chatted through the first round. She told me about the case they were working on that kept them from doing anything on mine. It was going well, almost like the good ol' days when I was two years ahead of her in legal experience, but she'd nursed for ten years before going to law school.

Two sips into the second glass, I went for it, maybe the best hope I had.

"I didn't kill anybody."

She stared a second like I'd told her I wasn't from Mars.

She took my hands. "Jesus, sweetcakes, next you're going to tell me you didn't kill Kennedy."

I had to gather myself, look humble, but not pitiful. "I can use any help you can give me."

She said nothing.

I waited a moment for a response, then felt the need to keep flapping, while she stared like I was a talking seal begging for a fish. SeaWorld might hire me—if I stayed out of jail.

I ended my plaintive pitch with: "Somebody's framing me. We think the answer lies somewhere in these kids' deaths."

She looked skeptical, but asked, "What can I do?"

"You can move the Sayers case to the front burner. I've got to get this to a head before the DA puts me on trial."

"Pete ordered me to give you as much shit as possible. Stall and fuss."

"His revenge for my departure."

"You got it."

This wasn't going well. Feeling sorry for myself, I added, "I win *Layne*, get everybody a suspended sentence on their perjury charges, and this is the thanks I get."

Jen frowned for half a second. I suddenly figured out she wasn't all that grateful. Brilliant, Kristen. How many months did that take? No good deed goes unpunished.

Her former supervisor and head of nursing at Adventist, Casey Denman, was one of the guilty, maybe the guiltiest.

I wondered if Jen realized I could've gotten *her* charged along with the nurses. Some gratitude.

Blessed is he who expects nothing, for he shall not be disappointed.

We finished our wine mostly in silence, punctuated by vignettes about some of my old colleagues. It was all forced, making me feel like our friendship was slipping from its high-wire act.

Jen polished off her last drop, set a twenty on the table, and slid out of the booth. "Got a lot to read for a motion tomorrow."

I added another twenty and slowly rose, not disguising my disappointment that I didn't get a commitment from her to cooperate. Even after their alligators got skinned.

As we stood facing each other, Jen said, "I can't buck Pete."

I mumbled that I understood. I knew that new partners weren't much higher on the rung than associates. But so much for getting a little help from my friend. I should correct that: ex-friend.

CHAPTER 24

A S I EXPECTED, the next morning I got an emailed Motion to Quash my deposition notices from Wright McGee, signed by Pete himself. In other words, consider my notices and subpoenas invalid. The accompanying brief said that *Rogers v Adventist* was going to trial in four weeks, depositions were scheduled every day until then, and the case would take two weeks to try. I wanted to cry. The motion was rock solid. No point even contesting it. My trial was little more than three months away and we'd just lost half that time.

I called Michael and gave him the details.

He listened, asked a couple questions, but didn't seem nearly as upset as I was, which irked the hell out of me. Of course he wasn't the one going to prison.

So, I begged off on Sarah's game or going over for dinner, telling him I wouldn't be good company. The honesty in the relationship thing. I fiddle-farted around the rest of the day, feeling like the sword of Damocles hung inches over my head. A few calls came in. Nothing like notoriety, but none of the dangled cases amounted to anything. Only flakes call a lawyer facing a murder conviction.

At about 4:30 Tina buzzed me, telling me Jen was on the phone. I hesitated to take the call. She was undoubtedly wanting me to confess the Motion to Quash and save her a trip to the courthouse. I thought about blowing her off, making her walk over, but finally picked up.

"*Guess what?*" she asked.

I was in no mood for banter and thought her enthusiastic tone sadistic. "What?"

"*Want to do depos next week?*"

"What?"

She chuckled at my confusion. "*Funniest thing. The plaintiff's lawyer on Rogers called. Wants a continuance.*"

"Huh?" Articulate, I know.

It dawned on me after a second. Something good might be happening for a change.

"*Since now we can't tell the court we're booked, I talked Pete into honoring your notices. We'll start lining up folks Wednesday morning.*"

I blubbered, "Thanks."

In a minute, I had Michael on the phone, telling him the news.

"*Yeah, ol' Kenny Webber is never ready.*"

Then it dawned on me. Michael had called in a favor, contacting the *Rogers* attorneys, getting them to ask for a delay, so I could go forward. Michael had probably settled something with Webber years ago and called in a chit, or maybe he offered them some helpful insider info. He might've even paid their case expenses. Nothing stopped the unstoppable Michael Stern.

I managed to choke out: "Thanks, Michael."

"*Perk up, Sunshine. We'll get 'em.*"

* * *

We had a wonderful weekend, almost letting me forget all the trouble. Sarah had a doubleheader Friday night. Her team won both games and went for pizza. The parents eyed me suspiciously, but nobody said anything nasty, at least not that I heard. I felt really honored to go with Michael and Sarah, like I belonged.

Life got even better Saturday. Sarah's team won the evening game, which put them in the championship bracket and gave them Sunday morning off. Sarah asked to go with a teammate and spend the night, reflecting progress in her slow recovery. Michael winked at me as he told her, "Sure."

Michael sensed my need, but let me do the asking. I gathered my nerve. "Could *we* do a sleepover?"

Michael chortled, his eyes crinkling.

His victory smile amused, rather than irritated, me. Made me think he really wanted me—mess and all. He had certainly waited a long time. He drove us to the house. Had I been at the wheel we would have gone a lot faster.

I hurried to the front door, exasperated over how slowly he moved. Inside we headed to the stairway. I wanted to run, but he took each step methodically, building my anticipation. At the top landing I tugged him into his own bedroom, pushed him onto his own bed. I threw off my shirt and bra and dropped my shorts. That got his pupils expanding. I thrilled at his eyes feasting on me.

In seconds I had his pants off and his shirt ripped open. He fondled my breasts as I leaned over him; absorbing the wonderful tingling sensation of his hands circling my erect nipples. How much I had missed those hands on me. I tried to savor the moment, but couldn't hold myself back and slid onto him.

I used his body to feel in control, to banish my fear for a while, reaching a quick, almost agonizing climax, then rocking forward and luxuriating in another long, slow orgasm. He held back his own, letting me have my way. After my third I rolled off and let him pound away, enjoying submitting. Everything was messy and loud. Wonderful— literally full of wonder.

We took a break for pizza and beer and resumed in the library. At about one in the morning he asked, "Can we *please* go to sleep now?"

I bit his earlobe, getting a yelp out of him.

"Okay, big guy. But this cowgirl's getting back on in the morning."

He kissed me, telling me he loved me.

I hesitated. What if I went to prison? I wouldn't hold him to any promise or vow. But every minute of life, minute of freedom, had to be cherished, so I went for it.

"I love you too."

"I know."

I had to wipe my eyes—after years of therapy, Atlas had shrugged. Love's weight was off my shoulders.

Michael didn't seem surprised that I finally spit it out. To his credit, he understood my longstanding problems and had never pressed for the appropriate words. Of course, how he learned of those problems was still a sore spot we had never discussed since the day I probated him.

We spooned, and I closed my eyes, but I knew nightmares would come. Not my old ones of monsters chasing me, but new ones. Claustrophobic. Sitting in an even smaller cell, the walls closing in, crushing me.

At about three I woke up, sweating and hollering. Michael wrapped an arm around me, cuddled closer, and whispered that everything would be okay. I wanted to believe him.

* * *

The depositions of Sierra Sayers' nurses and aides began at nine on Wednesday. By then I had every line of the chart memorized. Michael said he didn't need more than an hour to get ready. How typical of him.

I started the first examination with Michael next to me. So ready, I was over-prepared. Everything I wanted to ask jumbled in my mind and I struggled to ask coherent questions. Pete glaring at me, making ticky-tacky objections, didn't help. Michael slid a note to me. *Calm down.*

The first pediatric nurse gave me the same horseshit I would've delivered had I been representing the hospital. The story was so pat, it could've been scripted.

"I don't remember anything other than what I wrote. . . . If this child had a serious condition, I would've charted it. . . . I have no idea why she died. . . . What an awful tragedy."

By the lunch break I felt defeated and turned the questioning over to Michael. At least there would be fireworks between him and Pete. Maybe I could glean something through the smoke. Michael took the RN on duty when Sierra coded. Same story.

"Everything was completely normal up to the code. . . . I would've charted any abnormalities."

We'd decided to save the contradictory lab slips for later. But I could see Michael getting frustrated, not just with the witness's evasiveness, but with Pete's smug expression. An hour into the depo, to my surprise, Michael reached around me and grabbed my briefcase. He rifled through it and pulled out the lab report with the wrong social number.

"When you tell me everything was fine, do you base that on the real numbers or these concocted lies?"

My mouth dropped open. *Now?*

Michael had used the indignant snarl he was so well known for. He shoved the lab slips at the nurse.

Pete grabbed the documents before she could pick them up. "You haven't disclosed these!"

"Pard', give them to the witness. I've got a question on the record and I want an answer."

Pete's square face reddened, his stocky frame leaned forward. His voice didn't waver. "This is the kind of stunt you are notorious for and I'm not going to put up with it from a newly minted ambulance chaser."

Michael glared back. "I said I want an answer."

"We *are* going to adjourn this deposition so we have time to analyze this." Pete signaled his nurse to step out.

I realized I may have been wrong. Maybe they didn't know about the switch.

"You mean until you've had time to think of a good story?"

"Stern—"

Michael pounded the table, interrupting. "You'll be violating my notice. I *will* seek sanctions."

Pete snickered. "An ethics complaint from you would really be rich. Any judge would laugh you out of the courtroom."

Michael, his teeth locked together, face flushed, hands clenched into fists, shoved his chair back and headed around the table for Pete.

Pete paled. Michael undoubtedly learned to fight on the wrong side of a refinery town. Probably the only thing Pete knew about brawling was fussing over a golf scorecard.

McGee backed away. "Hit me and I'll get your license."

Michael strode closer. "Think I give a shit? I got eighty mil."

The court reporter and the witness hopped up and darted out of the line of fire.

Pete continued to retreat, but was feisty enough to spout, "All from your dead wife. Everybody knows you—"

Before Pete could spit out *had murdered*, I yelled, "Stop!" More at Michael than Pete. I didn't care if the self-righteous prig got the crap beaten out of him, but I needed my lawyer—with a license.

My shout slowed Michael enough for me to catch him by the shoulders and steer him from Pete. Pete wisely fled the room while I had a hold of Michael. But the depos were over. It would take time to file a motion—more precious time lost. While I understood how Michael could get so angry, he wasn't the one going to jail and I felt so fucking frustrated.

* * *

That night I tried to put the day aside while the three of us ate Rita's deliciously spicy enchiladas. She had worked for Diana and the family for five years before Diana's death. Rita always referred to her as the *Great Senora.*Looking back on all the horror, we wouldn't have gotten through it without Rita. It wasn't the cooking and cleaning, though that was nice, but her faith, her love of Sarah, and the moral support she offered all of us. Rita was partly responsible for me going back to Mass.

Michael had a rule that the TV had to be off while we had our family dinner, but after we cleaned up, Sarah flipped on the Disney Channel.

"Haven't you seen enough TV today?"

"This is one of my favorite movies."

"That you've seen a hundred times," Michael added.

I craned to see what Oscar winner they were arguing about and recognized Lindsay Lohan fussing with her father, played by Dennis Quaid. *Parent Trap.* The remake. I'm not old enough to remember the first one, though Michael says it was a lot better.

"One more time . . . ," Sarah semi-whined.

Michael rolled his eyes.

Maybe Sarah loved the movie because one of the twins had no mother. Becca essentially had no father, so it was a double hit. Sarah sent a text to Becca, who called as the movie started.

After they talked, I asked how Becca was doing. Sarah related that Becca's leg was awfully bad and her hand still hurt where they put the needle in.

Michael said, "Tell her the line could've been washed out better, but it'll go away."

I stared at the screen a minute. My brain scanned for the answer buried in my memory bank.

Think, Kristen. Think.
I blurted, "Oh, my God!"
I knew what killed the kids.

CHAPTER 25

DYING TO SHARE MY INSIGHT I paced over Michael's thick Chinese rug until he came back downstairs after telling Sarah good night. Ordinarily, my bare feet luxuriated in the sensation, but not then. I had tried to talk myself out of it, like a good lawyer examining the other side's argument, but the more I thought the more sure I became.

He must have spotted the wheels in my brain whirling. "Okay. What?"

I gave him a short version of my theory and how I got there. Tried to keep my pride at finding the Maltese Falcon from showing.

He expressed skepticism, but didn't say I was wrong.

After a brief discussion about my theory, Michael invited me to sleep in the big guest bedroom upstairs, Diana's old room after they began sleeping separately two years before she died. I was still too scared to go home, and we weren't going to bounce the mattress with Sarah in the house. Feeling guilty about interfering with daddy time, I took the small bedroom downstairs, so Sarah wouldn't know I'd stayed. Anyway, I was anxious to get to the office in the morning and look over the records again.

* * *

I woke before they got up, left a love note near the coffee tin, and sped downtown in Michael's slick roadster. Not hearing from Tina since I'd told her to stay away from the condo, I tried her phone again and got her recorded response. Tina had said she'd hole up with a guy she'd been seeing. I hadn't met him and only remembered his first name—Dave.

I figured Dave was unemployed, decent looking, and some kind of artist who hadn't sold anything yet. That, or he played in a band needing more gigs. I started to worry, realizing I should've asked more questions, but by the time I pulled into the downtown garage, Tina had slipped out of my mind. I slid the new pistol into my purse, and after looking around carefully got on the elevator.

In the office, I pulled all three charts. Keeping a copy of the records on the cases I got canned on had been one of the few bright things I'd done lately. I wasn't supposed to have them, but what could they do? Charge me with murder?

I went over every detail, slowly, like Holmes with his magnifying glass.

And then I saw it.

Somebody noted bruising to the buttocks of the Rodriguez boy and charted them as pressure marks. Odd for such a short stay in the hospital. Very odd. But I had to credit the nurse for her diligence looking and charting.

On the Dunns' child, one bruise was attributed to diapers and another discoloration under the arm was called a birthmark. I'd gotten the delivery records on the baby from the year before. Every newborn gets a thorough going over, with a check on everything from genitals to the number of digits on each limb.

The delivery exam didn't note any birthmarks. Not likely one would be missed. Had to be a bruise. And recent.

The switched labs could have shown elevated creatinine consistent with kidney damage or platelets whacking out, since Heparin causes bleeding. If full chemistry had been ordered, calcium and sodium would be off too. Then the kidneys would start to shut down. Distant vessels would occlude as the body fought to save the brain and heart, resulting in DIC—disseminated intravascular coagulation. The kids would die if nobody reversed the effect.

Michael didn't think it likely Heparin had been used to flush the kids' IVs. But he conceded the Dunn kid, who had been in the hospital the longest, was the most likely to get a hep flush. The longer an IV stayed in, the more it needed flushing. And their baby had been the first to die. Was his death the first mistake, repeated twice?

Although many hospitals had switched to plain saline, Heparin was more effective if the line was left in for more than a few days. Unfortunately, too much of it causes lower platelets, bleeding, and possible DIC.

Years ago, Dennis Quaid's twin babies got an adult dose and died. That's why the movie jarred my brain into a possible solution. The disaster generated publicity, resulting in new protocols at many hospitals. I could imagine the pharmacy making a mistake. Errors happen. Hospitals are dangerous places. Medical screw-ups kill a hundred thousand people a year. More than car wrecks.

I'd convinced myself that somebody had switched the labs to make the chart look clean. But why blab it to a fool like Larseny? Why then run the cases to me? Why? Why? An enigma wrapped in a riddle.

My cell phone rang, interrupting my thoughts.

It was a neighbor from my condo complex telling me she'd heard hollering coming from my place when she went out this morning to get the paper. She'd called the house and gotten no answer, but the noise continued. She had no idea what it might be.

Our townhouses are well built, not the new junk thrown up this century. She was pretty sure it wasn't a puppy or another animal. We didn't have a pet.

I dashed out.

At a red light, I called Michael and begged him to meet me there. Bless him, he didn't need to be begged. Darting through traffic on the North Tollway, I was able to hit eighty and was lucky enough not to get stopped.

Michael, holding a pistol at his side, was already at my house when I arrived. I grabbed my gun from the console.

"I heard something through the window, but didn't want to break it if you were nearby," Michael said.

I inserted my key. As I opened the front door, Michael pushed ahead of me.

The sound of a wounded animal echoed down the staircase. No words were discernible, more a groaning for help.

Michael took the steps two at a time, his weapon raised to shoulder level.

My heartbeat echoed in my brain, my pistol grip damp with sweat. "Shit!"

Even before I heard Michael's exclamation, I knew it was Tina and that it wasn't good. Rounding the corner into her bedroom, I saw her on the floor, tied and with a gag held in place with duct tape. Her shirt had been ripped.

I hoped having her shorts on meant she hadn't been raped. She had apparently bitten her way through the rag and become audible. The smell of piss told me she'd been trussed up for hours.

While Michael kept his gun trained on the doorway, I put my weapon down, knelt beside her, and began ripping off tape.

Tina sported welts on her arms, legs, and neck. One eye was purple, but I didn't see any active bleeding.

Michael jerked a blanket off the bed and wrapped Tina in it while she sobbed against my shoulder. She shook so hard my body synchronized with hers.

"It's all right, baby. You're safe now."

As I held my little sister, Michael called 9-1-1, then said he wanted to search the rest of the townhouse.

He came back in a minute. "Looks like somebody came in through the back. Busted the back door from the garage. But the place is clear."

After another couple minutes, Tina began to talk in choppy sentences. I couldn't interpret much as she groaned and strained to stretch her limbs.

While I tried to calm her, Michael brought her some water. Tina chugged, like she had been in the Mojave for a week.

After she finished the glass, we learned she'd been tied up since the previous afternoon, when I was having dinner at Michael's house in Highland Park.

Guilt rolled over me. Why hadn't I checked with the new boyfriend when I couldn't find her the previous night? I knew why. Tina going AWOL had been typical of her for years, though she had straightened up some since she came to Dallas.

Coherent now, Tina arched her back while she talked. "There were two, but I only saw the one in front. He had a ski mask. They must have been standing behind the door when I walked in."

I tried every comforting word I could think of for my goofy baby sister. I'd changed her diapers and spooned her applesauce. Every muscle fiber in my heart ached for her.

Through staccato breaths, she said, "They hit me hard."

"Baby, did they rape you?" I dreaded her answer.

"Just kicked my crotch."

"What did they say?" I asked her.

"Only one thing."

"What?"

She hesitated. I knew bad news approached fast.

"Tell your sister to get off the case."

My greed, my ego, had gotten my sister beaten up. She could've died—all because I hadn't been ready to join Junior League.

I asked her to repeat it, hoping I'd heard wrong.
I hadn't.

* * *

Cops arrived twenty minutes after we called. They looked the place and Tina over, then called in detectives. Frankly I didn't think they were all that interested, like they thought the culprit might have been a pissed-off boyfriend. From what I knew of Tina's history, that could've been true, but boyfriends don't say, "Tell your sister to get off the case."

One of the detectives was female, blond, rather attractive—except for a nose that hooked down with too much cartilage on the end—and obviously bright. She listened when Tina told her story, but didn't seem excited. Nothing real juicy here. She took a couple of cell phone pics of Tina, scribbled a few notes in a little spiral book.

They called a crime scene unit. Those guys took prints off knobs and switch plates, combed the carpet in Tina's room, and messed around like they were working by the hour. The detectives sat Tina at the kitchen table and took a formal statement. Tina declined an ambulance ride.

The female cop told Tina that she really should go to the hospital for an exam. If she had reported a rape, they'd have insisted she go.

Typical for my sister, she shrugged it off. "It wasn't that much."

By the time all the excitement ended, I'd called a repair service and gotten the door fixed, not that we were going to stay in my place that night. Michael had left to pick up Sarah. He'd invited both of us to his house for the night, but I wondered how safe that was. If they knew where I lived, they could find Michael's.

* * *

"Are you sure you don't want to go to the ER?"

"I've been beaten up before. They shoot an X-ray of your head and tell you there's nothing in it."

What a tough cookie—she'd been a better basketball player than I was, before she got into so much trouble. She seemed able to move all her joints and converse normally, so I gave up and phoned Michael.

He was waiting in the car line to get Sarah from summer school and head for practice.

"I think we should all go to a hotel tonight," I said.

"Nobody's running me out of my home."

"Michael, I'm scared they'll find your house—and us in it."

His voice hardened. "If they do, they'll meet my friends, Smith and Wesson."

I paused, not wanting to deliver my bombshell, but I had to.

"I've decided to get out of the case."

"What?"

"Tina might've died. It's not worth it."

Like a brat who deserved the paddle, I clicked off before Michael could argue. Tina and I packed overnight bags and left.

CHAPTER 26

I DROVE IN CIRCLES to lose any tail, ran a light while watching my mirror. When I was sure we weren't being followed, I headed for the Galleria. We checked into the Westin, not where we'd stay indefinitely, but nice for a while. When the world knew I was off my last Adventist kid case, we could slither home.

We ate spicy Mexican at Cocina's and quaffed cold drafts. *Several* cold drafts. We only talked about the fun times growing up and laughed at shared memories of our neurotic mother and doddering Italian grandmother. Well lubricated, we walked across the street back to the hotel. I constantly checked our backs. No threat detected.

Strolling into the hotel lobby, I nearly lost my breath. Standing near the elevators was Michael. He didn't look happy.

Unsure whether I was angry or embarrassed, I demanded, "How did you find us?"

"GPS. I told Mercedes I thought my daughter had taken the car. They tracked you."

Deciding I was pissed, I tried to elbow past him. "I don't want to talk now."

"We can talk here or up in your room."

"You're not changing my mind."

"You want to spend your life in prison?"

I glared, trying to think of a clever response. No witticism came. Maybe it was the beer.

We were so loud people traversing the lobby stared, but I was damned if he was coming up to put the charm offensive on me. I shoved Tina into an open elevator and stood my ground.

I waited for her protest to die as the car left. "They can't convict me. With all these assaults, the DA will realize there's somebody after me."

He shook his head, like I was an annoying kid. "You think anybody cares about the truth? They want a conviction. You're the Great White Defendant. Some DA puke will see you as his ticket to Congress. His campaign ad will say, "I'm the one who finally got her."

"I can't risk Tina's life—or yours." I paused, and then delivered a roundhouse. "And especially Sarah's."

He didn't flinch at the mention of his kid and stepped into my space, forcing me against the wall next to some kind of indoor tree. "I fell in love with you because you had more balls than any ten men. I knew you'd have my back and you know I have yours. For the rest of our lives."

I slammed my palm into his chest, backing him off. "It's my problem. I screwed up. I'll work through it. By myself."

"Don't pull that martyr shit on me. What happened to all the shrink crap? Not having to be the Virgin Mary? Where are those Hail Marys and prayers to saints when you need them? Where's the faith you want me to convert to?"

People eyed me suspiciously. So much for my secrets.

My cheeks flamed. I had no idea he could dish it out like that. It was our second fight and the first time he fought back. And he could fight. I wondered if this was a replay of his marriage.

"Don't bring my therapy, my past, or my religion into this."

He finally retreated a step, but snarled, "Coward. Candy ass."

I absorbed the worst he'd ever said to me for a full minute, staring stone-faced at my lover. I told myself that I was a rock. I had no need of love. I'd gone years without a man or a lover and could go the rest of my life without one.

I turned away and pushed the elevator button. "You're right, that's me."

He grabbed my shoulder before saying something even more hurtful.

"Glad I found out now, before I did something stupid and married you."

His sarcasm and livid expression hurt like a flare gun had been shot through my throat and burned me from the inside. I'd taken my armor off the last few weeks and now regretted it.

When will you ever learn, Kristen?

I was too far into this crash to pull out now. "Lucky you," I said.

Where was the goddamn elevator to take me out of this awful scene?

Before it arrived, Michael nailed me good with: "You think Sarah will get over seeing you go to prison? After losing her mom? You're the second most important person in her life. You're her idol."

I pushed the elevator button harder, as if that would hurry the damn thing. Was there a fucking convention in the hotel? After what seemed an hour of agony, trying to hold it together, the car finally opened.

As the doors closed, the last thing I heard was, "Guess it was all phony after all. A big waste of time. Wonder what I'll tell Sarah?"

On the ride up I couldn't stem my anger. Shaking so hard, I had to lean against the side to stay upright. The question was: Was I infuriated at Michael or myself?

CHAPTER 27

I MADE IT TO THE ROOM and took a moment to breathe before entering—part of me feeling better, knowing I'd lowered the threat risk to the important people in my life. But another part felt like I was on the *Titanic*, down below in the hold with the Irish Catholics and no chance at a lifeboat, while the rich WASPs got off.

I'd probably made the second biggest mistake of my life, but had the satisfaction of proving how stubborn I could be. Didn't make all-conference in basketball, but was a lock for All-American first-class moron. I heard Tina running a bath and made myself a cup of coffee—sure didn't need any more alcohol.

After sipping half a cup I peeked into the bathroom where Tina was soaking her bruises in the tub. Foam rose to her nose and wafted toward me with each breath.

"Are you sure you're okay?"

"After three beers and fajitas? Of course. Those guys weren't all that tough."

"Tina, you don't have to be a hero."

She shrugged her bare shoulders. "I had worse from Will."

I shook my head, amazed. Maybe she was right. Will, her Santa

Fe boyfriend, had been vicious, though not as tough as me, as I proved with a fast thrashing.

She blew bubbles away from her mouth. "Bigger question is, are you?"

"Sure."

"Don't lose Michael, Krissy. No man will ever love you as much as he does. He'll be a great father for all the kids you want to have."

I sputtered something about not needing anyone. I'd always been alone. Never trust anybody. The same shit I'd told myself for fifteen years. But it all rang hollow.

She interrupted my self-justifications and sat up exposing a bruised breast. "I joke about sex, but I've had enough guys to spot love when I see it. Told you that during that crazy *Layne* trial when he couldn't take his eyes off of you. And that was *before* you found Sarah. His feeling for you will be there thirty years from now. He'll endure your hot flashes and you'll pick out his cane."

How could she not be doubled over in pain?

Maybe I'm not the tough sister. I had absorbed more of Dad's abuse, but Tina had probably fought her way through as much as I could handle.

"Tina, I can't let anything happen to you."

"And I won't let you throw your life away. You've already done plenty for me. I'd be dancing next to your client if it weren't for you. If I hadn't OD'd on something or been beaten to death by a crazy customer."

I folded my arms, my usual gesture with my three siblings to signal I was the oldest and the argument was over. "I've made up my mind."

Tina matched my gesture over her wet, slick chest. "They didn't really hurt me."

"That's what I'm worried about. What they could do next time. It's not me I worry about. I can take care of myself."

"But—"

"The way to hurt me is to injure someone I love."

I closed the bathroom door on the enveloping steam, ending the argument, grabbed my cell, and found Dana's number. Time to fly my Kamikaze into the nearest ship.

I left her a message. If she was working, I'd have to catch her tomorrow to give her the news that she needed a new lawyer.

Michael had given me some Xanax he had left over from when Diana died. Fortunately they were in my purse for emergencies. I gave one to Tina, then found Scotch in the mini-bar and washed my pill down. Even so, the nightmares came around two and Tina had to get out of her bed to shake me into coherence. I couldn't go back to sleep.

* * *

The next morning I cleaned up and sobered up with black coffee, then drove Tina to the glass shop to retrieve my car. I gave her Michael's SL and handed her the new pistol to go to class.

She made a pretense of arguing about the gun, telling me I needed it more. I reminded her I had my old Browning. She finally took the Beretta and I headed in to work. Tina notably didn't argue about the car. With a smile and an engine roar, she'd probably have a new boyfriend in thirty minutes.

In the office I drafted one more Motion to Withdraw. This was now a quite familiar document. I tried Dana again. No answer. Without any cases, there wasn't a thing to do but sit and feel sorry for myself.

I plugged my ears with my iPod and played some of my favorite sad songs over and over. "Alas, my love, you do me wrong, to cast me off discourteously. For I have loved you well and long."

I wondered how hard it would be to sublet my space. Could I get anything for the furniture? Could I go back to basketball lessons for eating money? Certainly no law firm would hire me.

Early that afternoon, Tina popped in to play receptionist at my disappearing firm. My scowl warned her not to restart our debate. I closed my door. A minute later Tina buzzed me that Dana was here. With trepidation, I told Tina to send her in.

I rose and gestured Dana toward a chair. She sat.

I spoke first. "Dana, I've made a decision."

"So have I," she blurted before I could spill my guts. "I want to settle. Get me the most you can, but I want it done."

Wonderful news. I could get paid. A lot. With the fee on Pete's last offer I could hire the best criminal lawyer in town. "I'll call today."

"I can't go on fighting Troy and dancing. I want a new start in a new town. I can go for a nursing degree."

I nodded. "Very well. I'll call Pete McGee and get it done. There may be some counter back and forth, but I'll get you everything I can."

"If I clear anywhere near a quarter million to my part, I'm out of here."

I did the arithmetic. Since she had to split the settlement with Troy I probably couldn't get Pete that high, but the word, "near" made it doable.

Dana left a few minutes later. Things were looking up. I didn't need a man or a case. I just needed to beat the rap and get the hell out of Dodge. Philly and baby Beth, my youngest sister, were calling me home. Tina would certainly follow.

I could taste a real Philly cheese steak. Genuine Tuscan pizza. Hills you could actually sled down in winter. Snow. Rivers, not glorified ditches. I'd never have to drive on the constantly-under-construction LBJ freeway again.

* * *

Pete wasn't in, so I asked for Jen.

She picked up her line, asking me how I was holding up, but I got straight to the point. I'd decided not to dicker. Pete had said he could pay something between two and three when I had all the cases. Working the math I assumed the offer was $600K. Maybe even $650K. Rather than haggle higher, I could cut the fee some and Dana would net as much as if I had bargained for a month.

Once I had the case settled I could probably negotiate a bigger share for her than Troy, in view of his criminal record and her greater efforts at parenting. Her net after fees and expense would be all she cared about and I thought I could get what she wanted quickly.

"We accept Adventist's offer on the Sayers case. The last one Pete mentioned. Six hundred."

I held my breath, hoping for a quick, "Okay, I'll draft the releases"— standard response in these matters.

A minute of tortured silence. Something horribly wrong. A foreboding chill gripped me.

Jen said, *"The hospital wants all three cases to . . . go away. I haven't heard anything from the new lawyers."*

"Jesus, Mary, and Joseph, Jen, I'm taking the deal on the table. He said something around two million for all of them. I divided—"

"Krissy, I'm sorry, but Pete made the offer when you had all three. Adventist's motive is to get all this shit shut down and out of the limelight. These other guys might grab all sorts of headlines if you settle."

I mumbled that I understood, trying not to sound like my dog had died.

Jen didn't help me save some pride, just offered utter silence.

I hung up.

So I was no better off than when I walked in that morning. I couldn't get Dana fifty fucking cents and had to quit because I was a worthless cream puff.

I called Dana and lied—told her negotiations would take a while. Hanging up, I felt even worse. I'd lied because I didn't have the guts to tell her the truth.

* * *

At about four, Tina told me she had a late lab assignment and was leaving, adding that she'd meet me later at Michael's and drop his car off. Having been through all my melancholy songs six times, I peered out the window, lacking the ambition even to get up and leave.

I had a case once, a *pro bono* for a young woman who refused to go to an in-patient psych facility. She liked to cut herself. Razor blades, knives—anything would do. She had horrible rope-like scars on her thighs and arms. I'd helped her family get the court to order her into a hospital. After she got out I kept up with her for a couple years until she slid back and went into another facility. I now understood what motivated her.

I clawed through my desk for scissors, not sure I really would have cut myself, but wanted them handy. But before I found them, the main door chimed, interrupting my search.

A soft knock sounded on my door. I pushed myself off my butt and opened it.

Sarah stood there, in her softball gear. Her expression was so serious, so *Stern*-like, I couldn't decide whether to laugh or cringe. I assumed Michael had dropped her off to act as mediator.

"Hi, Sarah. Did your dad send you here?"

"No," she said emphatically, then added, "I asked Shelley's mom to take me downtown."

She crunched her jaw and waited.

What was this about?

Before I could think of anything bright to say, she locked her hands on her slim hips and spouted, "I wanted to come here and tell you to your face how much I *hate you*."

No one anywhere in the entire world could've said anything worse to me at that moment. I had to retreat to one of the reception area chairs and sit, before I collapsed to the floor.

I told myself teenage girls could be monsters, but this knocked my skirt off. I could think of no response, but suspected worse was coming. And I was right.

Sarah stepped closer and pointed. "Some kids told me you got my mom murdered. That you and my dad were having sex before she died. She wouldn't have died if you hadn't been with him. The bad guy knew my dad was gone. Found out you had taken him to Vail."

This was the hydrogen bomb. I had hoped this conversation would never happen. But, "alas, my love."

I sat quietly for a moment, praying for patience, wisdom, and compassion. This was not really about me, but undoubtedly grief bubbling to the surface and I made a great target.

She demanded, "Did you?"

Her eyes glistened. I realized she wanted a denial but also a thorough explanation. She deserved one, especially if I fled town, or worse, went to prison.

I spoke as calmly as I could, "Sarah, we were not involved until after your mom decided to file for a divorce." I paused and looked her straight in her blue eyes as I continued my confession. "I've still got receipts for the plane tickets I bought. Your dad can show you your mom's calendar with her visits to lawyers noted. She hadn't decided which one was the, uh, most aggressive."

Sarah met me eyeball to eyeball for a minute before blinking.

I clasped my hands, prayer-like. "Of course that doesn't make it right. We shouldn't have and I've always felt guilty taking your dad to Vail the weekend she died. Maybe it wouldn't have happened if your dad hadn't been gone."

She edged closer—a good sign.

"Maybe they would've gotten a reasonably civil divorce."

She stared. I wasn't sure I had convinced her.

"So yes, they were still married when we slept together. He got the call from the police while we were in Colorado. But they were definitely going to get a divorce. I think you know that."

She wiped an eye. I had to do the same.

I bucked myself up as best I could. "Sarah, regardless of where we go from here . . . I'll always love you. I'll always be there for you—whenever or wherever you need me."

A long silence. She dabbed her eye again and walked over to the other chair, sat, and folded her arms against her flat chest. Her stare physically hurt.

I added, "That's the truth. The unvarnished, no-BS truth."

"And you're breaking up with my dad?" She was fighting tears, her face reddening.

I sighed. "Maybe. I guess that hasn't been decided."

She looked at me for a long, painful moment, then started choking, and sobbing, bent over, her head between her knees, rocking helplessly.

I had no idea what to do. Did she not believe me? Had she bought the kids' gossip? Should I call Michael? Hug her? I couldn't decide and found myself watching helplessly. I felt as useless as a one-armed juggler.

After a minute Sarah sniffed, regained some control.

"I . . . I remember everything now—rolled up in a carpet in a closet."

She drew a halting breath.

"Then hearing a bad guy slapping a girl. Me trying to keep quiet in that rug. And the shooting. Then another fight. Lots of screaming. A girl fighting a man."

I had to sniff. "Yes. I remember too."

"The woman who fought those killers wouldn't quit."

I kept quiet, wondering if Michael had put her up to this. Even if he had, it hit me in the gut anyway.

She sniffed. "I wouldn't be alive if it weren't for you."

That got to me. In the last battle with Leonard Marrs, I wouldn't have survived without Sarah's help. I had to look away to avoid a complete meltdown.

Amazing how teenagers are so like Mount Aetna—volatile when you least expect it.

She stood and pointed. Her voice rose in anger. "You think my dad will ever get over you?"

"Sarah, your dad will have women beating on his door the instant I'm gone. He'll need a traffic signal in the street and an appointment secretary."

"You think I want some dumb, greedy slut for a stepmom?"

"Your dad has good taste."

She glared. "You're the *only* one I'll let him marry."

She said it like she believed she had veto rights. Maybe she did.

I was speechless.

"I don't want some money-grubbing, divorced babe, with two kids, moving in with us and playing happy family. She'd probably bring dirty boys who'd mess up the bathrooms, or a girl with an eating disorder, throwing up every night and borrowing my clothes."

Another long pause.

"I want you. You're my," she gathered her breath, "buddy."

She was crying again and my resolve collapsed.

In the eyes of a fourteen-year-old, I wasn't a half-witted gold digger with a host of problem kids. What a compliment.

I walked over to her.

She sniffed, wiped her nose with her hand. "I want a scholarship, a championship ring, and a black belt. And to go to law school. Like you."

I wrapped my arms around her and hugged for all I was worth, drawing strength from her warm body. She let every muscle collapse into my embrace.

* * *

Sarah finished the Pepsi I'd gotten her. "Haven't you been thinking?"

For a second I didn't realize Sarah had changed the subject. "What?"

"Whoever is behind all this, like, framing you and everything could be part of the other deal. My mom and all that mess after."

Out of the mouths of babes.

I hadn't thought of any relationship between Larseny's death, the frame, and *Layne* or Caswell's unsolved murder.

Marrs, the parolee I'd shot, had a half-brother, but I doubted he claimed many friends. Betty Layne had to see me with mixed emotions. I'd uncovered the truth behind her husband's medical disaster, but she hadn't gotten much money out of my client, Adventist. Some nurses lost their tickets, including Jen's big buddy. Michael's client, Galway, surrendered his practice and went to some Indian reservation to do charity work. Pete McGee was still pissed.

A lot of people had reasons to hate me. We had an entire cast to consider.

After pondering all this, I made a decision. There were risks, and all I could do to protect Tina and Sarah would be done, but the way forward was obvious.

I asked, "Will your dad take me back?"

She grabbed a clean tissue from my desk. "As far as we're concerned, you never left."

We. A response worthy of Michael. Maybe he'd coached it, but it was good enough to carry the day. I smiled. "Okay, sister."

I called Michael and told him Sarah was in my office. He acted surprised and denied sending his kid to assault my conscience. I wasn't entirely sure I believed him, but plowed ahead.

I said we needed a face-off at a neutral site and insisted on nothing romantic. We agreed on dinner at an Italian place in Highland Village. I offered to take Sarah to practice and said I'd meet him there.

Sarah seemed happy—yakking all the way, but I worried I might be in the eye of the hurricane with more storm to follow.

As she popped the door, I called out, "Be careful."

Even though I dropped Sarah off, I still beat Michael to the trattoria. He didn't arrive for twenty minutes, saying he'd swung by the fields to double up the warning and advise the coaches of our concern. He told me that he got a "teen-girl eye roll" in response.

I held my fire until he'd ordered wine, then blasted away.

"You hurt me."

"Somebody needed to. That was the worst display of narcissistic martyrdom I've ever seen. Like you *want* to be convicted to prove you can suffer? I thought Joan of Arc died five hundred years ago."

"Closer to six."

"Whatever."

I leaned over the table and hissed: "You owe me an apology."

"I'm sorry I insulted the Pope."

I ground my teeth and strangled my glass stem. "That's not funny. Don't ever bring up my therapy again."

I realized I'd just conceded a point. There would be an *again*. Oh well, I had known walking in we'd patch it up, but hadn't planned on surrendering so fast.

"Kristen." His voice deepened to its unctuous, sexy mode. "I love you and I'm not going to let you go to prison. *We* are not giving up."

I felt the flutter in my belly he so often gave me, but still resisted. "I don't want anybody else hurt."

"The worst thing for any of us—me, Sarah, or your siblings—would be to lose you."

That tugged me into heartache. He said it like he meant it.

"What would your little sister do without you? And I don't mean Tina."

He had a point about Beth—still trapped in Philadelphia living with an aunt, but under the influence of our loony mother. After our trip to the Caribbean last winter, after the Marrs shooting, I'd promised to come get her for good once she finished school.

I switched the subject, telling him about Sarah's theory.

He shook his head. "Whoever set all this up had access to those kids. And some way to kill them. I can't think of any of the *Layne* players who could've pulled it off. My old client is at an Indian reservation in Arizona. The nurses all lost their licenses. Tammy, the former adjuster, couldn't get near a hospital if she had a flat-line EKG."

I let my disappointment show. I wanted a solution.

"But whoever did it probably won't hesitate to kill again," he said.

"You think somebody murdered the babies just to send me to prison?"

"Or they were on the inside and knew of an incredible fuck-up and ran the cases to Larseny on condition he nab you. Then once Sam hooked you, he became expendable."

"But why are they trying to scare me off the cases if they want me on them? Why the drama?"

"I don't know, but the more I think about it, the more I think the deaths are intentional, not a medical error."

"Then we're dealing with a serial murderer. A person who'd kill totally innocent kids to get to me." I verbalized what had been troubling me so much. It seemed impossible. "Who could hate me that much? Who could be that insane?"

He shrugged. "Got me, but we need to finish the depos."

He leaned closer. I could count his eyelashes.

"Together. Because I love you."

I absorbed what he'd said—heavenly.

"If I owe you an apology, consider yourself apologized to," he added without sarcasm.

My heart went pitter-patter. The waiter brought our dinner, letting me stall for a minute, as he fussed over water refills and sprinkling cheese over sauces. I took the plunge, like a paratrooper jumping out of a plane.

For the second time since our affair began, I said it:

"Michael, I love you too."

It had taken all the guts I could muster. Silly, I know. I felt the relief of seeing your parachute open after jumping out of an airplane.

He squeezed my hand. "Do you believe me now? That there will never be anyone but you?"

I forced all the neuroses out of my psyche and told myself to never doubt again, that I was all in. "Yes."

We ate, the mood lightening a bit. During the sharing of chocolate mousse for dessert, Michael dug into the outside pocket of his sport coat and produced a gift-wrapped box.

A really small gift-wrapped box.

Of course I knew what was in it. I'm not a nitwit. But how could he want a commitment before we knew I wasn't headed for the gallows?

My heart rate belied my caution. At my age, it was time.

He casually placed it in front of me. I scrutinized his expression. He looked determined, expectant, a little like when he watched Sarah bat against a good pitcher.

I toyed with the ribbon for a moment. My neurons fired randomly, like a computer infected with a Chinese virus. I had to ask, "Don't you want to see what happens to me?"

"Nope."

"I want to get married at Saint Thomas Aquinas. A full Mass. You'll have to convert and do RCIA."

He nodded. "Fine."

I stalled, knowing that once I opened it, I'd be Pandora.

I wondered if it would be garish, something a newly rich truck driver's son would pick out. Taking a deep breath, I grabbed it and pried the top up.

Stunning, absolutely stunning. Not too big, gorgeous settings, the diamond refracted the light a dozen directions. Fit for a princess. I suspected he'd blown thousands, many, many thousands, and they probably wouldn't let me take it to prison.

I choked up for the third time that day, but fought back the emotion and tried a lame joke. "You'll visit me in jail."

"Only on conjugal days."

"Then I'll be waiting by the gate naked with a mattress tied to my back."

Despite our repartee, I was scared—scared of the commitment to both of them, scared of murderers, and scared of prison.

I must confess that after I slipped it on, finding it a perfect fit, the tears rolled like Niagara Falls.

He smiled and told me he had borrowed my Big 12 championship ring to size it.

The people at the next table noticed. One of them started clapping, followed by everyone in the place. Michael beamed. I felt a blush and basked in the sweetness of the moment.

CHAPTER 28

THE NEXT DAY I took Tina to a gun range. I wanted to make sure she knew how to use a pistol and wouldn't blow her foot off. After a quick safety lesson, she shot three magazines at the bad-guy target. She gained confidence, learned to load, and agreed to take my small Beretta with her. I didn't tell her Michael's theory that our tormentors were capable of killing babies.

Tina had a standing invitation to bunk at her new dude's place. She jumped to take him up on it. Big shock. I demanded to meet the guy, but she replied snippily that I was still trying to boss her around like I had for twenty-eight years. I finally backed off, trusting that her taste in men had improved since the late Will Fett, who had died in the confrontation with the parolee.

At Michael's I insisted I'd sleep in the downstairs guest room. Sarah seemed happy with me hanging around and probably laughed at our hypocrisy. Kids these days know everything.

But I wasn't sure we'd driven a stake through the idea that I broke up her parents' marriage. That tale could come back to life with another round of gossip from another mean girl jealous of Sarah. I prayed for patience and wisdom in my new role.

The weekend was delightful. Michael didn't want Sarah leaving the house except for her games on Saturday. I didn't go, deciding to stay and guard the place, keeping my 9mm Browning in reach the entire time they were gone.

A huge thunderstorm rolled in that night, canceling the rest of her tournament. The rain began as a downpour and then got heavier, pounding hail the size of golf balls on the slate roof and shaking the windows. I scanned the horizon for Noah and the Ark. Texas thunderstorms still amaze me.

Unable to sleep with the racket, we watched movies well into the morning and wolfed popcorn, thankful we had a home.

Sunday Sarah and Michael accompanied me to Mass for the first time. They followed directions and got blessings during the Eucharist. I felt proud to have them with me. All very family-like.

Michael took us to brunch at The Cage. Pancakes for Sarah. Omelets and champagne for the adults. I'd never been in Dallas Golf and Country before, but I must say I could get used to the place. If anyone stared at the home-wrecking criminal, I didn't notice.

That afternoon we played Monopoly and baked brownies. I probably gained four pounds. Sarah won. Four railroads will send you to bankruptcy every time. She's going to be a natural hustler like her dad.

Every peaceful moment was heavenly. All the drama temporarily evaporated, like the puddles the storm left. *Temporarily.*

* * *

On Monday morning I called Jen and insisted we restart the depositions. I reminded her that nobody needed a sanctions squabble. Not good for either Michael's or Pete's reputation. Not that either had much reputation to lose.

"I'll check Pete's schedule."

"Jen, Pete is still under my notice."

She hesitated, probably realizing that Pete had technically broken off the last round—a no-no if you're under a valid notice without a protective order from the court. Although the beat-the-shit-out-of-you exception probably applied. I'm sure there's a Texas Supreme Court case on that.

"I'll suggest a deal to Pete. We'll resume Thursday, on the understanding you ask the questions and your boyfriend shuts up."

"He's also representing them."

"Take it or leave it."

"Okay, but I want all the pharmacy people on duty the day the Sayers kid died."

"Pharmacy?"

"Yes. Everybody."

"That's half a dozen people. Why pharmacy? Nobody in there ever saw your kid."

"I also want the pharmacy log for the entire stay for Sierra Sayers." The list of drugs released for a patient would not be in the official chart unless they were actually given. Meds could have left the pharmacy and been given by someone who didn't enter it in the record.

A long hesitation. "But there's no evidence of a medication problem."

I chuckled, trying to get her to lower her guard. The last thing I wanted was to disclose my theory to Jen. "Just fishing around, wasting time. Letting you get your hours billed."

"Right."

She didn't buy it. I pictured Jen finding Pete within two seconds and telling him what I wanted. That meant I wasn't likely to get it. At least not without a fight.

* * *

The next three days I stayed at Michael's. Tina at Dave's. I checked in with her often, urging her to be vigilant, probably annoying the hell out of her—but that's what big sisters are for. My engagement diamond constantly pulled my gaze. Pride I guess—and excitement.

Getting ready for the depositions was as much a matter of getting psyched up as poring over documents. I knew Sierra's chart and all the hospital regulations from dozens of other cases as their lawyer. I even knew about the secret privileged shit we never disclosed in litigation. Pete had to be worried about me.

* * *

On Thursday morning we dropped Sarah off at summer school. Michael wasn't on great terms with Diana's sister, but thankfully she agreed to pick up Sarah after school, which was okay with Sarah, who wanted to see her cousins.

That would give us the whole day and then some. We marched into Wright McGee, like Crusaders storming Jerusalem. I was more jazzed than the night my AAU team played at the Spectrum in Philly.

As we were spreading out in the main conference room, Jen waltzed in, sporting a smug expression. I immediately knew something was up. I wasn't wrong.

She handed me a pleading. Before I could even glance at it, Jen said, "Sorry, Krissy. Pete's orders."

I could've shit a concrete block. It was a motion to bar me from handling the case because of my prior representation of Adventist. I deflated like a hot air balloon doused with an extinguisher. I should have seen this coming. I guess I assumed they would be nicer to me than the average asshole plaintiff's lawyer.

Silly me.

I'd gotten so wrapped up in my indictment, conspiracy theories, engagement, looming danger to all concerned, that this possibility never occurred to me.

My gallant knight let her have it. "Counselor, is Pete afraid Kristen will get to the truth again?"

The reference to *Layne*, the power of Michael's voice, and perhaps her discomfort backed Jen against the wall. "I'm sure we can get an expedited hearing next week," she said.

"Why bother? I'll take over the case. Would Pete rather deal with me?" Michael asked.

Jen was ready for that. "You two are personally involved. The motion asks to remove both of you." She pointed to my rock. "Especially now."

"Well, let's get the depos going and sort this out later."

Reddening, Jen spoke to the floor. "Pete already sent the witnesses home."

I thought Michael might throw tiny Jen through the fortieth story window to go splat on the sidewalk. I hurried to repack my file, grabbed Michael's arm, and pulled him out. There was no choice—we could hardly depose Jen, though I'd have loved to know what she knew.

* * *

Michael regained his cool by the time we were in the elevator. I hadn't, but he's the wise one. I'm the spaz.

"Which judge did you draw?"

"West."

Michael thought for a moment, then said, "He's good pals with your buddy, Proctor."

That cheered me a bit. Judge Proctor presided over *Layne* and had called me "a credit to the Bar" after I spilled the beans.

"Also, I've seen him playing golf at The Cage. Probably a guest of somebody. I'll look into that."

249

Not likely a judge could afford a hundred-grand membership. Michael put an arm around me. His embrace bucked me up.

"What now?" I asked. "Until we get a hearing?"

"Let's go over those personnel files again," he said.

"I've combed through everything. I'm half blind."

"I want to match them up with the state licensing board files."

"Again?" My brain hurt at the thought of going back through that stuff, like rereading *Moby Dick*.

"Yep."

I didn't know what he had in mind, but I had plenty of time on my hands. No. I take that back. I had a few weeks, then I might have the rest of my life on my hands.

When we got back to my office, we nestled ourselves over the hundreds of pages of paper I'd been reluctantly given by McGee. There was actually more than I expected. Sometimes defendants throw in more documents than they are required to try to camouflage what's important. I'd prowled through everything so many times, I saw the files in my sleep.

I felt a wonderful enveloping sensation while Michael studied each sliver of paper carefully. I rested my back against the wall and enjoyed the serenity of watching the best trial lawyer in town work for me. I wasn't being lazy, just enjoying a few minutes of security I might never have again.

Around noon Tina waltzed in from class. She eyed my bare feet and dreamy stare. "Letting him do all the work?"

"That's why I hired him."

"Want me to get you guys some lunch?"

Michael barely looked up, then pulled a fifty out of his wallet. "Thanks. Get something for all of us."

I ordered turkey on rye. Michael, the Texan, wanted beef. Tina strolled out.

I decided I'd better look useful and started back on the files behind

Michael. I didn't know what he was looking for and didn't want to disturb his concentration.

Tina returned with a sack of sandwiches and chips.

She grabbed sodas for us and plopped down to join the club. I caught Michael's glance at Tina's legs as her skirt rose up. For an instant I felt a pang of suspicion, but told myself to loosen up. Tina has the world's best legs next to Gisele Bundchen and no man who still had a pair could be expected to resist a peek.

"Seen any murderers yet?" Tina asked.

Michael ignored her. I grunted, "No."

Between bites Tina said, "Funny thing. When I was in the snack bar downstairs, they had the radio on."

I swallowed. "And?"

"They said some woman was stabbed last night in the parking garage at Adventist."

That got our attention. We asked in unison, "Who?"

Tina shrugged. "Didn't give a name. Next of kin had to be notified." Tina snatched a chip, and added, "Said she was a hospital pharmacist."

* * *

Willing to chase any thread, no matter how slender, Michael and I hurried over to Adventist. In the main garage, the seventh floor was taped off as a crime scene. Two uniforms were keeping an eye on the area. That meant the scene people had come and gone along with the body and detectives. These guys had to be as bored as I had been summarizing depositions for Pete in the old days when I knew he already had sufficient authority to settle the case.

Michael strolled up to one of the cops with complete self-assurance. "Howdy, men."

The cops nodded back.

"Who's the assigned detective?"

The nearest policeman said, "Shooter. Shooter Sampson"

I was surprised that the cop, fortyish and burned-out looking, even answered, but Michael always knew how to talk the talk.

"He any good?" Michael asked conspiratorially.

The other cop grunted contempt.

I knew Michael caught it too.

"An ass kisser?"

"Yep."

The other policeman chimed in. "Nose is permanently brown."

To hear him when he went into this mode, you'd have thought he grew up next to a refinery, worked at a country club cleaning golf clubs, and had once toted an M-16 army rifle. All of which he had.

Turned out the cop had been a tank commander in Iraq. In a minute they were swapping stories about goof-up superiors. The policeman had also served in Germany, giving them more in common. He'd apparently been denied promotion over an evidentiary screw-up. Michael sympathized with him like he was his brother. After a lot of laughter Michael asked who died.

The cop stiffened. "Can't divulge that information."

"Yeah, I know. Y'all got rules."

Both cops nodded in agreement.

"We used to be the hospital's lawyers. Got to know a lot of the people doing the real work. We were concerned."

Michael went on about the unappreciated. He even mentioned that he'd worked his way through college fetching golf bags for rich duffers at the country club. But information really got greased when Michael handed the cops two crisp Franklins. Each.

"Paula Colson," the officer whispered, even though there wasn't anybody except his partner within fifty yards.

"Thanks. I can't remember. Young gal? Mid-thirties?"

The cop smiled, now eager to be knowledgeable. "Thirty-one.

Throat was slashed. They think it could've been a scalpel. Her scrubs were torn open, but she wasn't raped."

"Geez. Any suspects?"

"Don't know. No witnesses. Happened around five this morning. Another employee spotted her slumped in her car. They're grilling the security guards."

"Attempted rape? Robbery?"

He shrugged. "If so, he didn't get very far. Pants were still on. Purse still in the car."

Michael thanked him.

The ever-helpful policeman added on our way out: "They're checking the CCTV."

"Thanks again," I said.

We sped back to my office.

We found the victim's personnel file in my office. She'd been on duty in the pharmacy the shift before Sierra died. Her record indicated she'd been at Adventist two years. After graduating from pharmacy school, she'd worked at St. Paul's and was more than halfway through her master's, which would let her apply for a supervisor's role.

I checked the medicine log. Paula had discharged the kid's meds from the pharmacy before going off duty, two hours before Sierra coded.

"She's either the villain or another vic," Michael said.

I was absorbed in the file. "What?"

"Either Paula accidentally dispensed adult-strength Heparin— or some other drug that killed three kids—or she was murdered by someone who did to cover up their crime." After a pause, he added, "And that someone had to have done it intentionally. An accident wouldn't be worth slitting a throat."

"How do we know she wasn't attacked by a mugger or rapist?"

"Security in that garage is pretty tight. A rapist would more likely try his luck at a mall."

"Or come through a maze of halls in the hospital and go in directly," I added.

"Okay, true. But the woman couldn't have had much cash and the credit cards were still there. A thief would've at least tried to use them for a tank of gas before they got canceled. Even a half-wit thug probably would have waited for a doctor to come along."

I wasn't sure it was so simple, thinking the killer might not know how to tell pharmacists from docs, but we finally had a lead. If Michael was correct, poor Paula may have known too much.

CHAPTER 29

I F WE NARROWED OUR FOCUS to the pharmacy, we were left with nine people covering all shifts for all three kids. Hospitals dispense a lot of drugs. The stuff gets checked and rechecked. These days it's done electronically. No more errors, ever.

Right.

We did computer searches of all governmental records on line. Michael was pretty good at it for a guy his age. Of course I knew he'd done lots of snooping, since his spying almost ended *us*.

We found real estate information, taxes, and divorces. At eight, Michael had to pick up Sarah, leaving me alone in the office. He gallantly got my car out of the garage and parked it on the street in front of the building, legal at that time of evening. I kept my pistol close and the door locked.

By ten I was famished, my eyes and brain giving out. Fortunately, I'd saved half my sandwich from lunch. I knew all there was to legally know on every one of the pharmacy employees. But no smoking gun emerged. Just a few unpaid tickets, a bankruptcy, and two uncontested divorces.

My attention perked up as I left. Through the ground floor window I didn't see anybody around my car, but I asked the night security guy to watch me get in. I made it to Highland Park without incident. As my trial date approached I found myself taking inordinate pleasure in little things like a cold brew and reheated enchiladas. Not likely they served those in prison.

Michael came into the kitchen. "Got an idea. If our culprit hatched a plot to ruin your life, if it's someone really that nefarious, he or she may have taken a job at Adventist just to set this in motion. So we focus on new hires."

I was still trying to get my mind around the idea that I could be so hated. "If someone wants to do me in—why not just shoot me in the street?"

"Because they want you to suffer."

I slugged back the rest of my Corona. I needed a couple more. "It won't work. None of the pharmacy people or nurses, except for a baby tech, were hired in the last year. At least from the files we were given."

"Then we need to keep looking."

* * *

Not much got accomplished the rest of the week. Michael offered to hire a host of private eyes to do surveillance of hospital employees. But I'd had enough of those sleaze buckets and didn't think spying would help.

So we pondered, pored over records, and often experienced frayed nerves. Anxiety grew with each day.

Monday neared, bringing with it the big hearing on Pete's motion to kick us off the case and leave me in limbo awaiting justice—Texas style. I tried to savor every second and notice the little events that make up life. A new crimson lip gloss matched the manicure I sprang for. I sunned myself sans top in the privacy of Michael's backyard. Warmth on my skin felt delightful.

Saturday went smoothly. Sarah had a softball tournament in ninety-plus heat that kept us in McKinney all day. By the last game I looked like I had been tossed into a swimming pool with my clothes on and felt like a wrung-out dishrag.

Sarah's team was playing up in an eighteen-and-under gold bracket and got hammered by the older girls, but it was still fun. Her face was delightfully streaked with infield dirt, her jersey drenched with sweat. She'd gone 4-for-14 against stellar pitching. Not bad. Not bad at all.

Sarah got an invitation to spend the night with a teammate, and to my joy she accepted. Michael escorted her all the way to the other kid's car and left instructions with the parents not to let them roam. Without a long explanation they seemed to understand.

It was dark when we arrived at Michael's. He pulled into the backyard and parked next to the pool. Michael switched off the back security lights and, without bothering to go inside, we stripped down and dove into the warm water. I'd been so sticky all day I might have done the same even without the eight-foot fence surrounding the backyard.

He leaned against the side tile and watched me swim. I loved how he drank in my body, making all the gym time worth it. After a while we wrapped ourselves in towels and he began a heavenly back rub as I lay on a pool lounger.

Just as things were getting really interesting, my cell rang. I peeked at the number. Tina. I would've ignored a call from the President, but I still worried about her. I tapped on.

"Yes, baby."

"Krissy, there's some asshole following me."

"What happened to Dave?"

"He's worthless. I dumped him."

"Christ, Tina. Get somewhere public, call me, and I'll come get you."

Michael swore his frustration, which was certainly no greater than mine.

Pulling sweaty clothes back on I told him I'd go by myself.

"Like hell. I'm not letting you go out alone."

"What if somebody gets into the house when we're both gone?"

"I'll set the alarm, call the police, and have them do a drive-by."

"And the Highland Park cops want to do you any favors?" An HP detective had tried to pin Diana's murder on Michael. Some of them probably still thought he was guilty.

"I can't let you out of my sight."

I shrugged. "This sounds more like another Tina Kerry man problem. How would my enemy know Tina's boyfriend?"

He eventually surrendered. I promised to check in every ten minutes. I felt like a sixteen-year-old out with the family car.

Before I could get to the door, my cell rang. Tina told me she was at a Chili's only a couple miles away near University Park.

I told Michael, "I won't be long—and I'll have my pistol."

He kissed me and escorted me out.

Fifteen minutes later, I found Tina wolfing down Tex Mex and beer and chatting with two guys at the next table. She looked like her only concern was keeping the drafts coming.

Majorly annoyed at my pleasure being interrupted I let my irritation show, just as I had many times for the past twenty-eight years. I sat across from her and swiped a nacho.

"What is it? You sounded scared shitless." I wanted to add, "You interrupted my massage with a happy ending." But I didn't.

She shrugged. "I was, but when I got here I got a better look. The Porsche did a quick U-turn when I whipped in here."

"And?"

Tina slugged back more of her Corona. I waited impatiently.

"It was a girl. Or woman. Couldn't tell how old, but it had to be this babe Dave was seeing on the side."

"What?"

"I spotted an overnight bag in his spare closet with tampons and makeup in it. I threw it at him and drove off."

Although that was a typical Tina scenario, something seemed odd. "Did she follow you from Dave's?"

Tina shrugged. "I don't know. I drove toward the townhouse to leave my stuff. Halfway there I noticed this car tailing me, turned, and went the other way, but it hung with me. So I called you."

"Damn it, Tina, I told you not to go back home without me."

She swigged and banged the glass down. "Where the hell else am I supposed to go? Besides, it wasn't a chick who beat the shit out of me."

"What I don't get is why would some woman Dave is bonking on the side follow you?"

"Maybe she was trying to scare me off."

"Maybe." The wheels spun. "What's Dave's last name?"

"Rouse. Now I'll call him Rouse the Louse."

"Where's he work?"

Tina hesitated a moment, then said, "Funny, once he told me he owned a computer business. But another time he said he had some gig in a hospital while he went to PA school. I saw a pair of dirty scrubs in the bathroom. Almost forgot about that."

"Scrubs?"

"Yes."

"How'd you meet him?"

"What is this? You playing Mom?"

I thought for a minute, letting Tina order another beer. None of the nurses assigned to the Sayers baby were male. I'd been through the chart enough to have the thing memorized. So maybe it was just a coincidence that Tina had stumbled onto another two-timing liar.

But I persisted, "Tell me. I may need to know how to meet men someday."

Tina rolled her eyes. "I saw him in Starbucks reading the *New York Times*. Figured he must be smart and returned his smile."

"And?"

"That's the key, Kristen. You have to look available. Most men are too intimidated to approach a woman, except for the creeps. I can pull a man toward me with just a grin."

I thought for a second or two. This didn't smell right—even for Tina. "You go there often?"

"Every day after chem. My brain hurts too much to play receptionist without a cappuccino."

"Did you leave anything at Dave's in your hurry to escape?"

Tina waved me off. "Nothing much."

"Let's go retrieve it tomorrow."

Tina looked startled. "You're not going to pick a fight? It's not that important."

I smiled. "I just want to meet him."

Tina rolled her eyes again. "Kristen, it's over and done with. I didn't get hurt."

"But you could have."

She smiled. "Actually a *little* pain in the right places is not bad."

Somehow I broke off the argument without throttling her.

* * *

I insisted Tina come to Michael's for the night. She bunked in the downstairs guest room. Michael and I took up where we left off in his. I didn't share the theory I was working, deciding it could wait.

Tina fixed waffles the next morning—Mom's old recipe with cinnamon—making it seem as if we were in a country inn. Of course the Stern house had real maple syrup, not the fake stuff. I told Michael that Tina and I were going to Mass. He bought it, aware that Catholics wear jeans and what-not to church, and go at odd hours, unlike the Presbyterian he'd become when he married.

Tina gave me directions to Dave's house, twelve miles north of Highland Park. I was surprised by the neighborhood—much nicer than I would've expected for a part-time student, computer geek, or whatever the hell the guy really was. His place sat on a cul-de-sac in a brand new addition.

Some of the houses around his weren't finished. Most were for sale, part of the fading housing boom. It had to be four thousand square feet and worth over $800,000. No wonder Tina didn't argue about holing up there.

"Did he say he owned this place?" I asked as we pulled into the drive.

Tina seemed to ponder my question. "Don't remember."

I guessed she had been jerking the guy's pants down her first time there and hadn't paid any attention to details. But she'd been staying in the place for a week. Surely the topic came up. Had it been me, I would've known a little about the guy before I slipped between his sheets, but Tina would say his résumé didn't matter. Just the rise in his Levi's.

"He did mention something about getting a bargain from the builder," Tina said.

My suspicion went up another notch. We strolled up the walkway and rang the bell. Nobody answered.

"Hey!" Tina fished into her bag. "I've got a key."

She slipped the key in the deadbolt and tried to turn. Nothing happened.

"The bastard must've changed the lock."

"You're sure we got the right house?"

"Think I'm a stoned nitwit?"

Not wanting to comment, I walked two places down to a house that looked occupied. Cul-de-sac neighbors must know each other. A second after I rang, a middle-aged man opened his storm door.

I pointed to Dave's. "We're looking for Dave Rouse. Do you know where he works?"

Lines gathered in the guy's forehead. "Who?"

I repeated the name.

"The fellow said his name was Wells or Welch or something like that. Never talked to him much. I saw a U-Haul there last night."

"Did it look like he was moving?"

"Yeah. Funny, he wasn't here very long."

I thanked him, returned to where Tina waited, and looked through the front window. Dave's place sat empty. Not a stick of furniture. I smelled a rat.

CHAPTER 30

I HAD TO PUT THE DAVE PUZZLE ASIDE on Monday morning as Michael and I trooped into Judge West's courtroom. Pete and Jen were already perched there. Pete looked primly indignant at us. Jen seemed a bit sheepish, but had the grace to speak to me. Michael didn't honor either with a greeting.

Dallas County courtrooms are uglier than a fat guy on a beach in a Speedo. Photos of old judges loom over everyone. Many look like they'd been on the *other* side of the law. The linoleum floor must've been cheap when it was laid thirty years ago and is now worn slick, literally. The low ceiling adds to the sense of oppression.

Just as we settled in at the plaintiff's table the bailiff poked her head through the chamber door and asked us to come back. Unlike most bored civil court bailiffs, she seemed jazzed, like fireworks awaited.

Michael darted up. I followed him, toting my briefcase. I'd worn my law-tigress navy blue suit, but added a white blouse with a cute ruffled collar to feminize it a bit and short heels so I wouldn't be taller than the judge. Same outfit I'd worn the day of the *Layne* verdict.

Pete and Jen trailed us.

Judge West was standing behind his desk shaking Michael's hand as they got there. Michael was obviously schmoozing before Pete could strike a blow.

By the time Pete sat down, Michael and the judge had traded golf stories.

After acknowledging the defense lawyers, Judge West said, "What's this motion to disqualify about? Seems to me a party has a constitutional right to hire the counsel they want."

Michael, bless his heart, had indeed woodshedded the judge, probably through the guy's golf partner. More or less legal? Yes. Ethical? Doubtful.

Pete spoke up. "Your honor, this young lawyer," he jabbed his thumb toward me, "used to represent Adventist. She is undoubtedly aware of privileged information prejudicial to the hospital."

Judge West leaned forward and asked, "What information?"

Pete flapped for five minutes about peer review matters, adjusting claims, personnel issues, and risk management. He made a good pitch and I started to worry again. Pete was no slouch.

Michael appeared relaxed, his wrists draped on the chair's armrests, his long fingers hanging limp.

The judge stroked his short, gray beard. "Michael, what do you say?"

Michael had still not even looked at Pete. He waited for what seemed an eternity, adjusting his maroon pocket square, before answering. I wanted to defend myself, but Michael had instructed me to say nothing. More like demanded I say nothing.

"Judge, we've heard them pitchin' a fit, but they've not shown Kristen knows any dark secret privilege on *this* case."

Michael paused.

I knew the hammer was coming.

"Second, you remember the scandal surrounding the *Layne* trial last year?" Michael got a knowing nod from the judge.

Michael continued, thumbing toward Pete, "This law firm sent Ms.

Kerry to *this* very courthouse to defend a lie, a lie which I will always suspect Mr. McGee was fully aware of. Long before it was uncovered by Kristen." Michael now turned and glared at my former boss like he had caught Pete dealing off the bottom of the deck.

Pete's face reddened. His response faltered after a couple of syllables in protest.

I covered my mouth to conceal a smile.

Michael ignored the interruption. "The outcome of that case cost me my defense practice, not to mention time and expense to the county for a pointless trial. If anybody should be disqualified it should be them." Michael hooked a thumb at Pete and Jen.

The accusation hung in the air like a sewer backup. While Pete sputtered again, Michael continued. "But I'm willing to let the past stay in the past." He looked again at Pete, who glared as defiantly as Napoleon on Elba. "If the hospital wants Mr. McGee representing them, fine. That's *real* fine, but they should be embarrassed to want Ms. Kerry tossed when she was the attorney who showed incredible courage, bucking her own client and firm to bring the truth to this courthouse."

"Your honor! He has no proof I knew anything about *misstatements.*"

I thought that was rich.

Judge West signaled for quiet and stared at Pete a moment before saying, "I want to talk to Judge Proctor about all this. I only know what I read in the papers. I'll issue a ruling tomorrow." He stood. "Thank you."

I figured we had a shot. Proctor had been the *Layne* judge who'd said wonderful things about me—on the record. Most of it had even been true.

On the way out, I set a pick worthy of the NBA between Michael and Pete, keeping them apart and making sure my lawyer didn't slug the little shit. If anybody got to do that, it would be me.

* * *

Tina's story about Dave nagged at me like a commercial jingle you can't get out of your head. I spent the afternoon trying to find out who Dave was. I started by pulling up the county assessor's records.

The house had been foreclosed on. Odd—although in Texas, values depend on the price of oil more than interest rates. The previous owner was named Wilson Steiner. Wells Fargo now owned the property.

Checking the foreclosure case in the court clerk's file, I saw that the sheriff's sale was scheduled for the following month. I searched the county assessor's records for Steiner, and learned he had owned, or did own, at least a dozen properties nearby that he had paid taxes on. Probably a real estate speculator.

Google did not turn up a photo. Zilch on Facebook. I did find an office address in Farmer's Branch, a northern suburb. I grabbed Tina, locked the office, took the elevator to the garage, and drove north.

The place was a small storefront in a strip mall. "Steiner Properties and Sales" read a decal on the glass. The door was locked, nobody in sight. We got cones at a yogurt shop a door down and sat where we could watch Steiner's office through the window. By the time we were crunching the waffles, a guy pulled up in front in a racing-green Jag coupe and got out.

He looked like he was coming back from fraternity rush, wearing gray slacks and a snappy blue blazer, despite the heat. His preppy eyeglasses rested on a slender nose. Thick hair brushed back swirled in back at his collar. He was taller than me and flat-bellied. If he was Dave, Tina had chosen well.

"That's not Dave," Tina said, reading my thoughts.

I didn't think it would be that easy and was prepared. I hurried out and hollered before he could go in. "Mr. Steiner?"

He stopped and looked me up and down, grinning. "Yes?"

I must have passed inspection. "I'm interested in a house you used to own."

His smile faded. "I used to own lots of houses."

I stepped closer and gave him Dave's address.

He shrugged. "I mailed the keys to the mortgage company. Every house on the block. Got in over my head. Everybody's building stuff as fast as they can find the lumber. I decided to bail while prices are holding."

"Do you know who's been living there?"

"I have no idea, cutie. Bank must've stuffed somebody in there."

"Thanks." I turned away as Tina strolled out, looking the guy up and down like he was a glass of ice water in the desert.

He called out, "Got a phone number? I lost mine."

I held my left hand up, showing my ring.

He asked, "How about your darling sidekick?"

I tugged Tina toward the car before she could rape him.

* * *

You don't just walk into a place in foreclosure and set up house. Dave had to have a contact with the mortgage company, the lawyers, or the security people. Maybe the real estate agents—somebody.

Back in the office, I checked the court file again. The foreclosure attorney for the lender was identified on the clerk's documents. I called his number and, of course, couldn't get him on the phone. I left a message, stressing that I was a lawyer. Usually that expedites a return call.

Next I tried the lending company, pretending to be a neighbor complaining about intruders in "Dave's" house. After getting routed through four people, nobody could or would say much, but someone told me the mortgage company contracted for security at their foreclosures with another outfit and gave me the number. I phoned them and had to leave another message.

The more I thought about Dave, the more certain I became that he was a phony designed to get to my sister, then to me. Maybe he had been one of the guys who had beaten up Tina. Her discovery of tampons and a quick exit might have derailed their plans. If the guy was cute, Tina would have been as easy to pick up as litter with a sharp stick.

I drove back to the mystery house after Tina went to class. I rang every bell in the cul-de-sac and got one stay-at-home mom. She told me the house had been empty since it was finished last year, with a For Sale sign, until a guy matching Dave's description, driving a Lexus, moved in recently. She volunteered that he didn't seem to come around much, but had serial girlfriends. One had looked a lot like me. I thanked her and left.

I insisted Tina spend the night at Michael's again. We didn't need to waste energy worrying about her. Tina about matched Sarah's maturity level, outside of her vast hooking-up experience, and they had a great time playing some dumb card game with Becca that called for slapping cards and lots of hollering.

After the game, Tina strolled into the library, found the bar, grabbed a Corona and

settled into one of the oxblood chairs while I reported our activity to Michael.

Michael said, "The guy was a squatter. Somehow he got a key and set himself up."

"Why?" Tina asked.

"He didn't want to be tracked later," I said.

Pouting, Tina folded her arms across her chest. "The bastard wasn't interested in me at all? I'd like to cut his balls off."

I wanted to tell my beautiful sister that she could've exercised a bit more discretion, but had said that many times before without much effect. I think that deep down Tina doesn't think she deserves much.

Thanks, Dad.

* * *

I got up early Tuesday and bounced into the security company office. Nobody could tell me anything. Next I tried the mortgage people. Again, zilch. Of course the lawyer hadn't called me back. Since I didn't sound like a fee, I would be far down his priority list. So I headed to my office.

Toting my loaded pistol in my purse, I beat Tina into the office. As I strolled to the coffeepot, I saw the copier, which held a single piece of paper. I tiptoed closer, as if the machine might bite, and retrieved the document. It took a while to summon the courage to read it.

Minute Order. Defendant's Motion to Disqualify Ms. Kerry is DENIED.

My heart nearly flew out of my mouth. Before I called Michael, I scrounged in my desk for my Rosary, knelt, and prayed.

When I got him on the phone, Michael didn't act surprised. I wondered if he'd had the deal wired all along. He told me to light Pete up about finishing the depos. I called, got neither Jen nor Pete, but left seriously demanding messages with both to get rolling again.

While I plotted our strategy, my cell rang. The caller identified himself as Richard Mize, attorney for Wells Fargo.

I had my pitch ready. After I gave him the case number and address of the house, I said: "Your client might want to know somebody's been living there. My sister got involved with a guy who claimed it was his. She went back to the place to reclaim her clothes and it was empty, her things gone." I realized a third of the way through that the story sounded incredibly lame and he had no incentive to help look for Tina's stuff.

To my surprise he asked, *"Weren't you the lawyer on that football player case?"*

Nothing like notoriety. "Yes."

"That was really something."

"Yes." I hoped he had missed my perp walk on TV.

"I'm not supposed to share this, but"—a long, frustrating pause—*"Fargo had a claims manager who got caught running a rental business on the side. She was letting people live in houses pending sales. She claimed it prevented deterioration. Unfortunately she was keeping the money herself. Several thousand bucks a month."*

"What's her name?"

Another delay, then he answered, *"Nicolette Carlton."*

This was turning into a smashing day.

"Do you know how I can find her?"

"We've already tried. She owes the company thousands. Some developers are looking for her too. She was also renting houses awaiting sale."

Another long moment, then: *"This isn't about some gear of your sister's, is it?"*

From the tone I knew he also knew my latest career change—jailbird. "No."

"If I get a lead on her, I'll call you."

I thanked him and hung up. My pondering was interrupted by another fax. I darted over and nabbed it.

Supplemental Order. Defendants are directed to resume discovery. FORTHWITH.

I mumbled the word to myself. "Forthwith." How lovely. Bless his heart. Michael could probably fix a Cowboys game.

I had to lean against the wall a minute, catching my breath.

One more chance.

* * *

On Monday morning we were back in the main Wright McGee conference room. The first nurse was another Rip Van Winkle who'd slept through the week my kids were there and was a waste of time.

According to her nothing unusual happened. All she remembered was in the record. She sounded like one of my old witnesses. Try as I might I couldn't pick up any vibe that the automaton knew more.

We were trying not to tip Pete off to my theory. I casually asked the second nurse all the tiniest details of what she'd done on her shift for Sierra Sayers. Buried in the minutiae was whether she had flushed the IV. She couldn't remember whether she used saline or Heparin. Of course, if she used Heparin, she'd made sure it was a child's dosage. *Of course.*

We did an aide next, then a respiratory therapist who helped with the code when it was called. All pretty worthless. By the end of the day, everyone exhausted, I was beginning to think this was a dead end like the murdered pharmacist and "Dave." It looked like prison would give me a chance to restart *Anna Karenina*.

Pete rose and began packing his briefcase. "I guess we're finished," he said with a smarmy expression.

I caught a look from Jen, a look that told me something wasn't kosher. My exhausted brain went into overdrive, like the last half mile of a marathon. Then I recalled there had been a float nurse on the peds floor. Although she wasn't assigned to any of the kids, she was on duty when both the Dunns' baby died and the Rodriguez kid, as well as early the next morning when Sierra died.

"You haven't presented E. Peyton, whoever that is. She's listed as backup for the floor." Nurses typically sign with a first initial and last name. I recalled we had not been given a personnel file on her in the initial discovery response, since Adventist claimed she was an agency temp and not a formal employee.

"She worked for an agency we use for subs. She was on the floor, but wasn't specifically assigned to your client."

Michael leaned across the table. "Don't give me that crap. The court ordered you to bring everybody who ever saw Sierra Sayers."

I tossed in my two cents. "That's right, Pete."

I could tell from the way Jen turned away that she had talked to the woman and the woman knew something.

Michael, his jaw locked, pointed at Pete. "Get her here at nine tomorrow."

Michael may have missed Jen's tell, as poker players call them, but clearly enjoyed giving Pete orders. He'd kept quiet all day until then, letting me do the fruitless questioning.

"Or do we need to see the judge *again*?" Michael asked.

"Don't you dare raise your voice to me."

Michael walked toward Pete, as if resolved to pound him into a pulp.

I caught Jen rolling her eyes over the useless excess testosterone on display, a sentiment we had often shared when we worked together. Under different circumstances I would have returned her gesture with a knowing smile.

Before the fight could get going, Jen and I both stepped between them.

She spoke first, "Hold it! I'll call the agency. They can get her here, but it may have to be tomorrow afternoon, if she worked a night shift."

Michael backed off and we consented to do the last depo at one the next day and left. I didn't share my reading of Jen with Michael. It could've been entirely innocent or they could know something they sure as hell didn't want us to know.

* * *

The next morning we agreed to divide our efforts. Now that the DA had shared at least some of the investigation, Michael wanted to find the witness who had supposedly heard "my" argument with Larseny and see if he could shake her story. After he saw her, he then planned to go to the police station and try to get more on the pharmacist's murder. He promised to make another effort at the gun range to bribe the salesman.

While he was doing that, I had the task of finding our mystery real estate magnate, Nicolette.

I popped into the bank lawyer's office, looking the part of seductress with my engagement ring stowed away. The receptionist told me he was in a meeting. I volunteered to wait. She directed me to a coffee station, which I jumped on, since sleep was still tough to come by. I plopped onto a ritzy leather chair which threatened to swallow me, under a real oil painting of some Italian hillside.

After I'd downed two cups, Mize finally came out. He was how I imagined a foreclosure lawyer—skinny, with rimless glasses Ben Franklin might have worn, and pasty skin. He walked with his head thrust forward on his giraffe neck, like he spent too much time staring at a computer.

I don't know why it took me thirty-two years to figure men out. One plus one does equal two. So, I'd worn the gold stud earrings I'd bought with my first partner paycheck and my matching gold cross pendant. They're dynamite with a white blouse against my Dago skin. Two undone top buttons and a push-up bra made all things look possible.

As I uncrossed my legs and stood, he beamed at my knee-length skirt with the six-inch slit. He was all mine.

"Any new information on Nicolette?"

His hands quivered, his breath came in stutters. "Not a thing." I thought he might faint.

I lowered my voice into conspiracy mode. "I was wondering. . . . Her employment file might help us locate her."

He shook his head like I'd asked for the nuclear war codes. "Wells Fargo has a very strict privacy policy."

"I know. But if they made you a copy . . ."

He twisted slightly to get another look at the slit and nodded. "Well . . ."

I inched closer. "I think criminal activity waives any privilege."

He peered down my shirt.

CHAPTER 31

A S I LEFT THE BANK'S LAW FIRM I told Mize I'd look forward to a lunch. Hoped I gave him some confidence he could use in the future with a woman who might really be interested. I slid my ring back on once I reached the elevator.

I drove to Nicolette's last listed address in the employee file. Her place sat inside a gated neighborhood. Not mini-mansions—more like patio homes, I think they call them. Nevertheless, it was more than she could be expected to afford. I checked with a security type who probably also mowed the grass and unclogged toilets. He didn't know her.

Time to go back downtown for the last deposition.

I met Michael at my office. Before we could leave, the phone rang. The ID said "Unavailable." I picked up and listened to silence for a few seconds.

Finally a muffled voice came through, sounding like someone speaking through a sweater.

"If you don't get off the Sayers case, I'm going to carve up your little sister and mail her tits to you."

Without thinking of anything more clever, I shouted, "Fuck you, asshole!"

I slammed the receiver down. After a second, clearing my head, I told Michael what the guy said.

"That-a-girl."

Rage made my spine shiver. What was the goddamn point? Was it just to wind me up tight before taking the last deposition? I texted Tina and she replied that she was in class, and would drive straight back to Michael's when she got out.

As we marched to Pete's office, Michael gave me an update. The witness to the loud argument involving Larseny was in her fifties, overweight, and pissed at the world for making her unattractive. Michael guessed she'd been fond of Larseny and was going out of her way to help nail the woman who killed him. I figured if she was Sam's type, she wasn't Michael's and that he wouldn't get anywhere questioning her.

"Also . . . I waived a prelim or grand jury," he said.

"Why, for Christ's sake?"

"They can indict a ham sandwich and I think you've had your name in the paper enough," he deadpanned.

＊ ＊ ＊

Soon we were in Satan's lair watching the court reporter set up. I feared this was a big waste of time; that I should instead be out tracking down the leads I had on the mystery house guests. But we had planned to see all the depositions through and the Dave and Nicky chase could also lead nowhere.

Jen strolled into the conference room. The witness, the float RN who worked for an agency, trailed three steps behind.

Unlike the others we had deposed this young woman looked ready to jet to the Riviera. She wore black leather pumps, maybe Pradas. Her worsted wool slacks were creased like a knife; a silk tee, showed off yoga-toned arms. The gold Bulgari watch, worth several grand, caught my eye with every move of her wrist. She was maybe five-five, about a hundred and ten pounds. Sandy-colored hair was layer-cut shoulder length. Her skin shone golden as if she'd just come back from Canyon Ranch. A cute up-turned nose completed the *Shape* cover look.

I introduced myself.

She shook my hand. "Emma Peyton."

The voice betrayed no intimidation at the process. I could detect no accent, no Texas drawl, no dropped consonants, like she'd had elocution lessons at a fancy private school as a child. I glanced at Michael. His quizzical expression told me he also detected something odd beyond the designer look.

She was sworn in and I started in with the usual background. She'd graduated from Baylor only four years earlier. She was single and preferred working for an agency for the flexibility.

"Flexible to do what else?" I asked.

She shrugged. "Whatever I want to do."

Obviously not hurting for money. Under the rules, I couldn't ask if she had a rich boyfriend who was keeping her. I could ask if she lived by herself.

She knew what I was up to and leaned over the table with an emphatic, "Yes."

I guessed family money. Poor girls don't go to Baylor for a nursing degree, unless they can play basketball. You can get the full BA degree lots of places, instead of spending two hundred grand on private school tuition. But Baylor meant a good time. Contrary to the Baptist affiliation.

Emma had made only one entry in the Sayers chart and didn't remember anything about my clients. I recalled she had also worked the code on the Rodriguez kid, but when I tried to get into it, Jen shut me down.

"The witness is only here to testify about Sayers."

She was technically correct on the rule, so I retreated.

We shadow-boxed the entire examination. The nurse seemed to know something I didn't, but I couldn't drag it out of her. I think she sensed my frustration and grew cocky, giving me snippy answers and smart-ass looks. Also unlike most of the others, she didn't seem fazed by the three deaths. Not a whiff of emotion. Just another day at the hospital. Live bodies in—dead bodies out.

I asked Jen for a break, which she agreed to.

Michael and I slipped into the stairwell for privacy. "Something's amiss," I said.

Michael nodded. "I've seen this girl somewhere before."

* * *

We ended the session more perplexed than enlightened. The woman testified that she didn't know diddly. She couldn't recall any trips to the pharmacy or anything about her patients, and had no inkling why Dana's daughter died. No surprise there, but her cold demeanor made me wonder if she didn't like children. Unfortunately, neither of us could marry any details to our vague suspicions.

The next day we split up once again. Michael had to get Sarah to practice after summer school. He had a hearing on an eviction case in the morning. Some slumlord would be shocked to see Michael Stern, the Prince of Darkness, in court. I ventured forth on my own to tilt at windmills. Wasn't Don Quixote a crazy Catholic? Gives us a lot in common.

I kept thinking about the mystery nurse, picturing Emma Peyton's face and trying to place it. I nearly ran a stop sign on my way to find the first of Nicolette's references, and realized that if I quit thinking about Emma, the answer might suddenly come. The crossword is always easier the next day. I'd be more likely to reach my destination alive too.

It was probably useless, but I tried Nicolette's patio home complex again. The security station was now manned by an older guy who looked like he'd gone back to work after his 401(k) had dried up. I parked in front of the gate. He shuffled out, the flabby skin on his neck flapping back and forth. He didn't need to stoop to look into my car, so bent was his spine.

A coy smile. "I'm looking for Nicolette Carlton."

He looked me over. I wasn't sure whether he was leering down my shirt or had macular degeneration.

"Haven't seen her in at least a week. Been pickin' up her papers and mail."

"I've got a birthday present for her. Mind if I go in and leave it at her door?"

With effort, he stiffened his degenerating vertebrae. "Regulations say leave it with me."

I was ready for that. "It's heavy and I don't mind taking it in."

"Sorry."

I could take the guy down in half a second, but my conscience would have screamed at me the rest of my life. I doubt even the Pope would hear that confession. And what would I learn standing outside her door? I couldn't break in in daylight. I thanked him and left the wrapped box with him. He'd never know it held a brick inside.

My next stops were the references she gave. People might give me more in person, so I drove east. The minister at Free Will Baptist Church was doing the hospital visits when I arrived. I asked the pleasant, young, and pregnant woman at the church office if she knew Nicolette. Her perplexed expression told me all I needed to know.

A pastor reference would look good, though I suspected my real estate tycoon knew many references never get checked. The secretary called the reverend on his cell and asked him. He hadn't heard of her either.

Her second reference was a dean at North Texas. From my experience the dean at a good-sized university doesn't know any of the students, except football players and the Panhellenic chair, especially if she's luscious. So that was likely bogus. Probably the bank had tried the dean once and the call hadn't been returned. I didn't bother to drive to Denton.

Last was John Morton, identified as the manager of a Merrill Lynch branch office where Nicolette had once worked. It was to the west, toward Arlington. Traffic was heavy, and I probably couldn't get there by four-thirty, when stockbrokers go home, so I called him. When the receptionist gave me the third degree about why I wanted him, I told her I was concerned about a friend of his.

That got me through. To my surprise he was willing to talk and said he'd stay late.

Traffic on I-30 moved like a three-legged tarantula. If properly shod and dressed, I could have run to Arlington faster. I crept forward a few yards and stopped. On and on. I might not even make "late" at the broker's office.

Just as I saw a possible gap, I checked my rearview mirror to make sure I had room to squeeze in and noticed the Hispanic driver of a slick Camaro behind me. He sneered, his mustache curling in a nastier look than warranted by the frustrating traffic. For an instant I wondered if he was my friend warning me to "be careful." Had I been followed? I had to admit I'd been too absorbed in the Nicky quest to notice.

Despite angry horn-honking I whipped across the white line and slipped into a lane that was actually moving and hoped I had lost the guy.

I put my conjecturing aside as I reached the broker's office. The staff was locking the doors and putting away the derivatives and inside information.

Morton came to the front and showed me back to his office. He stood six feet tall, a little gray on the sides, a bit of a paunch in the middle, not bad looking. His smile showed off perfect bleached teeth, against a face developing folds around his mouth. I guessed mid-forties, and my dirty mind wondered if Nicolette had been involved with him.

I told him again we'd been pals. Took care not to lay it on too thick.

My suspicion was confirmed when he said: "I've been worried about her. Some heavies from a security outfit have been by, but you're the first friend looking for her. We had a misunderstanding a couple years ago, and she left, but I've tried to keep in touch."

Spotting his wedding ring, I guessed the little misunderstanding had to be that he wouldn't dump his wife. Not that *I'd* get involved with a married man.

I spread concern on my face and leaned closer. "She's not been home for over a week and left her job under bad circumstances."

I didn't know enough about the woman to fake my way through this, but the way the lothario drooled, he wasn't about to run me off.

His voice deepened, "I thought so. She was always living close to the edge."

Like getting mixed up with married assholes?

I pushed my concern to the next level. "To be perfectly honest, I'd like to find her before the police do."

His eyes gaped. "Cops?"

"Afraid so."

He peered closer, questioning.

I continued, "I'm an attorney. We were at North Texas together. I might be able to talk sense into her."

"I hope so."

His concern was as worthless as an Italian lira. He asked for my card. I smiled and got one out, very slowly, flipped my hair with the other hand, and passed it to him, making sure our fingertips met. I learned that trick from my little sister.

Practically slobbering, he took the bait. "Maybe we could get a drink. Someone as obviously successful as you probably needs to talk investments."

I tried hard to look disappointed. "Can't tonight."

"Maybe another time?"

This guy didn't give up easy.

"Sure. Any clue where Nicky might be?"

My guess of "Nicky" reeled him in tighter. "She had been seeing a guy in the computer business."

I had *Ex-Boyfriends for a Hundred* and took it. "Dave?"

"That's him. Lives in a high-rise by The Mansion on Turtle Creek. His shop's an old converted gas station on Maple. Writes billing programs for lawyers and CPAs. Did you know him?"

Bingo. I would've made a pretty good Philip Marlowe.

"Not really, but from what I saw, I didn't think much of him."

"Me neither."

Dodging any questions about either Nicky or mutual funds, I chatted a while longer. Then I excused myself for keeping him late. He held my hand a bit long in parting. We agreed to do lunch sometime.

His card landed in the trash bin in the lobby.

I had only a little trouble finding the former station once I was back in uptown Dallas. It was decorated all cutesy, painted in garish purple and yellow. Planters had replaced the pumps. Some kind of evergreens sprouted out of the potting soil. The front glass said "David Wells Computer Services."

My, my. How we go around in circles and come back to the beginning. This had to be the "Dave" Tina had been banging. He'd gotten the house through his other girlfriend, Nicky, who was renting property she didn't own. Had to be Nicky's twat-plugs Tina had spotted. And he thought nobody could ever trace him. He hadn't reckoned with me.

I retrieved my small pistol and strolled to the front door, finding it locked. A heap of mail inside the glass had obviously been shoved through the slot. The front room looked empty. I checked the side window. Nothing. Dave had split.

I walked around back, out of sight of the traffic on Maple. Behind the building, Johnson grass was ankle high in an alley just wide enough to back a truck into. Looked like it hadn't been mowed in a couple weeks, probably about the amount of time the catalogs had piled up.

The bottom windows had iron security bars, but a small window, maybe eight feet off the ground, wasn't barred. I didn't see any alarm sensors on it, unlike the lower ones. It must've led into some kind of loft in the filling station days.

How bad did I want in?

A steel trash dumpster sat five feet or so from the back of the building. Its odor should've been banned by the Geneva Convention. Ignoring the putrid crap inside for the time being, I guessed I could stand on the bin and jump. A ledge jutted out a brick length from the wall under the window. If I could grab it, I might be able to hold on and open the window at the same time. And I might fall and break an ankle.

Go to Michael's and get a ladder? Just bust in? Or forget it? What was I likely to find? Probably nothing for my trouble.

As I pondered, the odor from the garbage either grew stronger or I began to pay more attention to it. It really reeked, far more than ordinary rubbish. I'd smelled dead before. And this smelled worse than Larseny.

My hand against my nose, I stepped toward it.

A thousand flies buzzed. No doubt something had died, and probably not a squirrel. My fingers shook as I opened the side door. The squeak of metal nearly sent me fleeing. A wave of stench made me gag. It took a minute to summon the nerve to look.

Holding my breath, I stuck my head inside. Broken-down cartons and black lawn bags reached the height of the door. The thing hadn't been emptied in a while. Maybe Dave hadn't paid the bill or the trash collector had forgotten the place.

I poked at the pile, shuffling the box remnants around, stirring up annoyed flies, and, propelled by fatalism, I pushed more trash aside into the corner.

I hit something. A piece of cloth. Denim. Blue jeans. A tug revealed a slender leg in them. The body had been stuffed at an angle, head toward the bottom. I shoved aside a trash sack, revealing a ballet flat with a foot in it—the kind Tina wore around short guys—most guys in fact.

Blessed Mother, please not Tina.

I stopped clawing for a moment, telling myself it couldn't be Tina. Couldn't be. Nobody could deserve that much pain. And if it were Tina I couldn't live the rest of my life with the vision of finding her body. How I wanted to flee.

You have to look. You have to.

Drawing a deep lungful for courage I settled on a half measure. I pried the flat off. Red nail polish on scraggly toes and a painful-looking bunion. And only a size eight. Not a Kerry foot.

I breathed again. But I was beyond the grossness of the situation. I had to see who the woman had been. Swatting flies and swearing like a sorority rushee denied a bid from the Theta house, I kept digging.

CHAPTER 32

HALF IN THE DUMPSTER, I no longer worried about getting dirty. I tugged hard, flipped the body over, then slapped the remaining refuse off. A flying insect just missed my mouth. Another landed in my hair. The ghastly gray face looked like plastic boiled in olive oil. Gross. So gross.

The woman's hair had been dyed fire engine red. Bugs crawled in and out of her mouth and nose. Thank God it wasn't Tina. I crossed myself in thanksgiving, then again for the dead woman.

I bailed out, swallowing my lunch for the second time. A minute of spasms got my upper GI back under control. Foul-tasting adrenaline filled my mouth, sweat exuded from pores I didn't know I had.

I hurried back to my car in front of the shop, jerked open the door, and grabbed Nicolette's file. In the photocopied picture she sported a smile, not the flaccid, expressionless face of a corpse. But the nose was the same—wide for her face. A mole decorated her chin in the photo, just like the woman I'd found.

Well, at least one "mission accomplished"—I'd found Nicky.

Mice seemed to be scurrying around my brain and they couldn't find any cheese. I'm surprised the autonomic system worked and my heart continued to beat.

Hardly making a conscious decision, I hurried into my car and sped away, like Nicky could be a flesh-eating zombie. I lost track of how far I drove, but eventually spotted a convenience store and pulled in.

After trying Michael on my cell and only getting a recording, I got out, walked into the 7-Eleven, and bought a six pack of beer. While I waited for Michael to call back, I tossed down a cold Coors. You'd think by now I could handle problems on my own.

Into my second can, but not feeling much calmer, my cell rang. Michael.

I didn't give him a chance to say hello. "Somebody fucking killed Nicolette!"

"What?"

"I saw her. She's in a Dempsey Dumpster behind Wells's shop."

"Who's Wells?"

I had to will the patience to take a deep breath and recount my detective activities.

Michael interrupted a couple times for details, then said, *"Kristen, get the hell back there and call the cops."*

"I'm scared they'll think I had something to do with it."

"Don't think she won't be found! Whoever picks up the trash will smell her. By tomorrow, somebody driving down the street will."

"You already can."

"Jesus, honey. You've got a duty to report this."

"Come down here and go with me. Please."

"Okay. Let me get Sarah from Shelly's house and I'll meet you there. Give me the address, but get over there. Now."

I told him where the place was and agreed to go back, like a kid sent to the principal's office.

I tossed down the last of the second beer, reversed out, and drove toward Dave's, but hit a red light and had to wait the full cycle. After another half mile I had to stop again at another signal. Somehow I didn't recall having gone so far. Just as it lit green, red lights reflected off my rearview mirror.

A police cruiser, overhead lights flashing, whipped left of center and passed me. I eased forward, drove two more blocks, and nearly shit my pants. The blue and white unit had stopped at Wells's place. Two cops were already out of their car.

I kept driving to the next side street and found a curb to park against, slinking down in the seat and turning the mirror where I could watch the cops in the rearview. Sure enough they loped right to the dumpster. One jerked the side door open using his flashlight. It dawned on me that my prints were on the crime scene.

I called Michael.

"*Fuck,*" Michael responded to my latest woe. Not exactly a speech by Patrick Henry.

From the mirror I saw one of the cops poke his head into the dumpster. The other hurried back to the patrol car.

"What now?"

"*Somebody must've followed you and called in an anonymous tip. Dead bodies always get the cops' attention. Get somewhere safe.*"

"This spot is going to be swarming with police in another minute. What could be safer?"

He didn't respond right away. I assumed he was mulling whether I was too stupid to be seen with ever again.

"*I guess you touched every goddamn thing in sight.*"

"Don't use that tone with me."

"*Kristen, you've got to start thinking.*"

"How the hell was I supposed to know there was a stiff inside?" I hollered into my phone.

A long pause. Maybe he didn't want to go ten rounds, although I was pissed off enough to take on Ronda Rousey. The worst part of the nasty conversation was—I knew he was right. It had been the fear of seeing Tina and then the surge of relief that had caused me to be so stupid.

"Drive to the house. Don't hurry or do anything to get stopped."

"But what about—"

"I'll think of something."

I pounded my palms against the steering wheel, yelling at the world. Two more police cars screeched up, one an unmarked. I cranked my rant up higher. What the hell did I do to deserve this? Was the circus in town? Maybe I could run away and join it. They could surely use another clown.

* * *

By the time I got to Michael's, I felt dumber than the Three Stooges, even the fat one. Somebody had tracked me and I'd been pulled right along, like a heifer with a nose ring. Whoever my enemy was must have been right behind me every step. Even Tina had been sharp enough to notice she was being followed.

I used the key Michael had given me, trudged inside, and headed straight for the shower in the downstairs bedroom. Hot pounding water rinsed some of the stress away—some.

I found cleaner clothes than what I had been wearing and changed, then walked barefoot into the library and flopped on one of the leather chairs facing the fireplace.. The Trafalgar print drew my attention. I wished I could time travel and fight next to Horatio Nelson. At least I'd know who to shoot at.

After I stewed for five useless minutes, Michael came in. He poured whiskies—much better than Coors. I snatched mine up and downed a third of it before taking a breath. His loud sigh told me he was perturbed either at my folly or my drinking. I had heard Diana had won beer-chugging contests in college and had boozed all through their marriage. Did he wonder if I was becoming her?

He set his drink down on the desk, came around, and massaged my neck. Some of my fear settled into his hands. He plowed his finger through my hair, taking me to a better world far away. I felt even better when he worked my feet and almost forgot all my problems.

He sat in the other lounger and said, "We can't waste time feeling sorry for ourselves."

"Ourselves" sounded nice.

"I guess they'll find my prints on the dumpster."

"Yeah, you're at the top of their data bank."

I slugged down the rest of the Scotch. Had to cough and catch my breath.

"Slow down, Kristen."

Alcohol sped to my brain, numbing me. "They can't think I had any motive to kill some woman I didn't know. I'd never even seen her alive."

He hesitated and I knew bad news was coming.

"That's not the immediate problem. They'll revoke your bail."

I sprang up. "How the hell can they do that?" Even as I asked, I knew the answer.

"Sweet Pea, you left a crime scene. A rather serious crime scene. That's a felony you committed while on bail. I can't get you out again."

The room, the world, went blank. I saw nothing. My attempt to prove my innocence—an effort I thought was making headway on—was going to send me back to jail. Had I time-warped into a Kafka novel?

An image of jail filled my vision. Claustrophobia closing in, the bars threatening to squash me. I could taste mushy toast and hear the commotion of long sleepless nights. I would rather go to a Bangladesh sweatshop and make sneakers the rest of my life. I stifled tears and somehow even held back the scream that begged to be let loose. Nobody likes a crybaby.

He knelt, holding me tight. I regained enough control to ask Saint Teresa of Avila to pray for me. I tried to remember martyrs who'd suffered far more than spending their lives in a modern air-conditioned prison with a weight room and cable TV.

Despite my best efforts, I didn't feel any presence of Christ or saints. The cell tower connection to heaven must have been down. Through blurred vision, I saw Sarah hesitate at the door. I forced an embarrassed smile as she joined the scrum. She slipped her arms around me too. After a minute I managed to spit out, "How much time do we have?"

"Not much. Maybe only a day."

I wondered if after this latest screw up he really wanted to stay with me.

You've got his ring. Snap out of the self-pity shit. He loves you. Sarah's crazy about you. Don't puss out and let them down.

Michael leapt to the computer. I stepped over and saw he'd pulled up the County Assessor's website. Fortunately he was capable of productive activity while I slobbered on myself.

"What's the address again where you were?"

It took him five minutes to track down the property owner—Patterson Properties, Inc. Pat Patterson was the service agent. Other than the not-very-creative nickname, we had no other information, since the page only gave a post office box.

Michael searched for other properties, found several, then checked the court clerk. "The guy sues a lot of people for back rent."

Michael kept tapping keys. "There's a lawyer I know down the street who's at the firm Patterson uses."

He pulled up a number, then called from his landline in the library.

He identified himself and asked whoever answered if he knew Patterson.

Michael listened a minute and then put the phone down and tapped another number. Getting no answer he tried another.

After the fifth call, Michael thanked somebody, hung up, and said, "The guy owns and rents out a bar not far from the gas station. Stops in occasionally to ogle the girls. Let's go."

I made a cup of coffee, then we took two cars, in case we needed later to split up or get Sarah out of potential danger. Neither of us thought it wise to leave her. Michael and Sarah followed me. She wanted to ride in my car, but Michael insisted she go with him. I agreed. Someone was more likely to take a shot at me. Anxiety helped me sober up.

The place lay between us and downtown in an area where lots of houses dating to the '20s had been converted to offices for law firms and small businesses. We circled the block twice, didn't see anyone tailing us. I parked in a lot crowded with the remnants of happy hour. Michael found a spot near me and pulled in.

We debated who was more likely to get information. I won. I entered Tipsters. The joint was crowded and the clientele better dressed than I expected. I squeezed my way to the bar and ordered a draft. Left a ten for a four-dollar pour and waved off the change, then asked the bartender where Patterson could be found.

The good-looking bartender's nice tan might one day cause melanoma. A sharp goatee matched short, dark hair. He introduced himself as Brady and said, "He's never in this time of month. Probably out beating rent out of deadbeats on his properties around here."

I kept eye contact. "Did you hear about that body the cops found?"

He grabbed a half-lit guy's empty glass and refilled it from a tap before answering. "Yeah. The old gas station."

"The girl was a friend of mine. I'd like to know who was renting it."

He thought for a minute, then said, "A dude used to come in here, handing out cards saying he was in the computer business. I think that was his office."

I nodded encouragement. An old Stevie Nicks tune started blaring, making it harder to hear over her raspy voice. He had to fill another drink, but turned back in a minute. "I'm trying to think. He quit coming in a few weeks ago. Somebody said they tried to get hold of him to fix a program he installed and couldn't find him."

"Was his name *Wells*?"

Our conversation was jarred by two guys at the bar arguing about the Rangers' pitching and banging mugs, trying for the bartender's attention. He detoured from me and refilled the loudmouths' glasses.

Coming back, Brady pondered a second, grabbed an empty off the bar, then shouted over the racket, "Don't think so. That's close, but not quite right."

Damn. Should've known it couldn't be that easy.

The bartender continued, "He's about your height. Maybe thirty. Real slick type. Funny accent, English maybe. Always leaving with a girl."

"That's him," I said.

"Give me your card. If I think of his name or if I see him, I'll call you."

I retrieved a card from my wallet. Hopefully he didn't watch the local news.

"You might catch Patterson at The Elms apartments on Lamar. He likes to collect himself and get cash. Know what I mean?"

Ah—a tax cheat. I thanked Brady and left.

* * *

We found The Elms—brick apartments off the street, easy to miss if you're in a hurry. The grounds opened up into a tree-lined square on the inside. The place must've been trendy four decades ago, but had been eclipsed by newer buildings fronting them. There were maybe sixty units stacked two high. It was the kind of dive you flee to in a hurry when your spouse kicks you out, but don't sign a lease, hoping you can get back in the house once the angry fire fizzles out.

We wandered around, the three of us, seeing people come and go, nobody answering to "Patterson." Agreeing to give it an hour or so, we relaxed on a bench in the courtyard. I grew impatient, went off on my own, and headed toward the back row that bordered an empty grocery store, probably a casualty of Walmart.

A man around sixty, with bifocals and slumped shoulders came out of an apartment upstairs. He looked like he'd had a rough life and too many cigarettes. In another place, I would have guessed he was a retired teacher plagued by nightmares of juvenile delinquents. He toted a zipper bag you might take to the night deposit at the bank.

"Mr. Patterson?"

He nodded suspiciously, reaching behind his waist. I guessed he carried a gun along with the rent.

I spoke fast, trying to get my pitch out before I got shot. "A friend of mine, named Nicky, was found behind the old gas station you own on Maple."

He scowled, said nothing.

"Do you mind telling me who you were renting it to?"

He scrunched his face with annoyance. "I already told the police he said his name was Wells. Always paid in cash. Don't know where he is."

He hustled off. I matched his fleeing pace.

"But you don't think that was his real name, do you?"

"How should I know? He paid on time until last month."

"What happened?"

Patterson shrugged. "Started moving his stuff out. Last I checked it was near empty."

I figured this guy didn't ask for references. Cash spoke louder than a credit rating. "What's he look like?"

"Nice-lookin' feller. Seemed on the up and up."

I put my hand even with the top of my head. "About my height?"

"Yeah."

I thanked him for his trouble.

We were at a dead end for the night. My cell rang. I pulled it from my back pocket and answered.

"It's nine o'clock. Do you know where your sister is?"

Stunned, I couldn't form a reply before they hung up.

I looked at the caller ID screen. "Unknown."

I tried Tina's phone. No answer. No recent text either. I pictured the worst, ran to the bench where the three of us were to rendezvous, found Michael, and told him about Tina. Of course he urged calm, ever the wise one.

I knew it was possible the goofy girl was hustling some guy and her phone was off—contrary to orders.

Michael said the threat could be simply an attempt to pull my chain. Problem was my chain was already stretched taut.

Sarah listened to our stilted discussion. I saw in her wide-eyed stare that all sorts of evil images were flickering through her mind. Lord knows the kid had seen enough horror to write a Freddy Krueger script.

"She's got a pistol and a fast car," Michael said.

His tone didn't help. I had a bad feeling. "But I'm not sure she could really use it."

"Daddy, we have to find Tina!"

That shook Michael. Sarah only used "Daddy" under duress or when she wanted something she knew she couldn't have.

"We will, sugar."

"Take Sarah home. We don't want her in the middle of whatever is going on." I insisted.

"Let me stop at your place on the way."

My townhouse wasn't *on the way*. About three miles the wrong direction. "I've already tried the landline," I said.

"But . . ."

He was alluding to Tina's assault. If she was there and taking a beating, not likely she could answer the phone.

"Sarah?"

"She'll stay in the car," he said to Sarah, as much as to me. Sarah folded her arms. "I'm not a baby. I want to help."

I thought a second and came up with a strategy. Not likely the bad guys would come back to the townhouse. Too much chance they'd get spotted, after the neighbors had seen the commotion last time.

"Okay. You take my house. I'll try to retrace her route from school."

Driving around, even on the known roads she took, would probably be fruitless, but I had to try something. The phone call both frightened me and pissed me off. Odds were good this was just more immature irresponsibility, but I couldn't risk it.

However, I promised myself that if anything happened to Tina I would spend whatever time I had left as a free woman to find the culprit. And there wouldn't be any namby-pamby call-the-cops crap. Whoever hurt her would die.

CHAPTER 33

FIDGETING, TAPPING THE WHEEL, I drove to UT Dallas, about ten miles. As always the LBJ was under construction or destruction, making the trip take twice as long as it should. Halfway there Michael called and gave me the *all clear* at my house.

He rang again when they got home. No Tina there either.

I checked the campus Starbucks she liked, finding only bleary-eyed caffeine addicts cramming for exams. The school library. No Tina. I detoured to Dave's old house, or Dave's new house, whatever it was. Ringing several doors in the cul-de-sac turned up zilch. Nothing to do but move on. No idea where. After I buckled up, my cell buzzed. Michael.

"Tina thinks a woman is following her."

"Why the fuck didn't she call sooner?"

"Her phone went dead and she didn't have a charge cord in my car. I should have put one in it before I gave it to you."

"Shit!"

"I told her to go to the police station on Northwest Highway."

"I'm closer. I'll head over there. You and Sarah stay put."

I struggled to make any sense out of this. Emma? Why would whoever was torturing us let a space cadet like Tina spot her? Tina seldom paid attention to stop signs, let alone a car behind her. Yet Tina had made somebody. Twice. Maybe the whole tailing business was just to jerk us around?

I hurried out to the cop shop and found Tina sitting in the SL in the civilian parking lot. I couldn't decide whether I was pissed or overjoyed to see her.

I decided on pissed. "What the hell is going on?"

"Good evening to you too."

I rolled my eyes. "Are you sure you were being followed? Why didn't you call?"

"Yes. The woman behind me U-turned in the middle of the street when she saw I was pulling in here."

I swore that if I ever got out of this mess I'd quit drinking, learn to putt, and get pregnant. Not necessarily in that order.

"Sorry I let my phone die. My charger—"

I cursed again, interrupting her, and signaled her to get in my car. We sped to Highland Park. Mario Andretti couldn't have done better.

Michael hugged both of us. Me a little longer. *Thank you very much.* I'm glad he liked Tina, but then again, Michael hadn't grown up with her.

Sarah joined in the celebration of the safe return of the prodigal daughter. She and Tina began boiling pasta for dinner, carrying on, laughing about something some boy had said to Sarah. I enjoyed the distraction.

After dinner I made a *big* decision.

I strolled to the downstairs guest bedroom. Rummaging in my purse, I found my birth control pills. Without hesitation I flushed them down the toilet. Then I remembered reading about how they contaminate the water supply.

Damn, another crime.

I assumed the state would let me out of prison long enough to deliver a baby. They'd probably take me to the charity hospital once

I was dilated to a nine and not bother with an epidural. I knew it usually took a full cycle or two to get a bun in the oven, but miracles do happen and even if I never saw the baby again after I spit it out, I might give Michael the son he so badly wanted—or Sarah a little sister. If they wanted another ball player my genes would certainly top Donna's.

I walked into the library, sat, poured Glenfiddich, and contemplated my decision. I knew we'd have sex that night, even with Sarah home, since it could be the last time. Maybe the last time in my life. I tried to recall which positions were most likely to produce conception. Not a bad image to ponder.

After supper, Michael's landline rang.

I glanced at my watch. Nearly ten. A little late for calls.

ID said it was Becca's mom, Donna. The fucking whore couldn't wait until I got locked up? She probably had her vibrator charged and her finger on the start button ready for the sound of my man's voice.

I answered, as annoyed as the receptionist at the department of motor vehicles.

"*Who's this?*" Donna asked.

"Who's *this?*"

After a second she said, "*It's Donna. May I please speak to Michael?*" She hadn't even acknowledged my identity.

Slut.

Instead of driving to her place and breaking her nose I said, "I'm sorry, he's in the shower."

Another hesitation. "*Well, would you tell him Donna called and that I'd like to get the girls together for—*"

"Sorry, I don't have time to take a long message. I'm getting in the shower with him."

I slammed the phone down loud enough for Beethoven to hear. The only part of my day I'd enjoyed. I'd eventually get around to telling Michael about Donna's call—maybe at the girls' high school graduation.

Around eleven, Michael suggested we quit thinking about everything. The solution might suddenly pop into someone's head in the morning.

Tina took Diana's old room upstairs. With Sarah in the house I retired downstairs and waited until I thought Sarah was asleep. After peeking in her room and seeing no movement, I tiptoed into Michael's. We quietly made love. Wonderful. I could have lingered until morning with our bodies separated only by the perspiration we had generated.

But I crept back to my assigned spot downstairs. Sleepless in Dallas, I tried to organize what we knew. Assuming my theory was correct about the dead kids, someone had run adult-strength Heparin into their IV lines and intentionally killed them. If Michael was right, they'd done it solely to generate three big cases to send my way through Larsen. And I had taken the bait, agreeing to share the fees with him.

Then this psycho serial killer murdered three more people—the pharmacist, who perhaps knew about the adult-strength blood thinner; Larseny; and Nicolette, the shady real estate entrepreneur. She likely knew too much from staying with Dave.

But Dave didn't work at Adventist, so where did he fit? Was there another girlfriend? The one who left her overnight bag for Tina to find?

In the meantime, someone had mugged me and my sister, gently urging me to get off the very case that was the source of my woes. Everything kept spinning in my mind as I tossed and turned on the wonderfully clean and ironed sheets Rita had put on the bed. A glass or three of Rhone Valley sounded like the ticket to dreamland, although I knew I was drinking too much. Like father like daughter.

Michael came in without knocking in the morning. I glanced at the clock. Tina must've already left for school.

My mouth tasted like moldy grapes. I pushed the covers back and sat up. I saw genuine fear on Michael's face, an expression I'd never seen on Mr. Unflappable. "What?"

"The DA's office called. Your prints were all over the place."

Even though I knew they were there, sour adrenaline filled my mouth.

He folded his arms, clearly put out with me. "They've filed an emergency bond revocation motion. Maybe as soon as tonight you go back to jail."

I slapped my hands over my eyes, trying to make the world go away.

Please, God, give me a do-over.

"Might look better to surrender voluntarily," Michael said.

"They don't have any evidence to prove *when* I was there. Or that I found that woman."

"Except that the video camera in the squad car caught your car, plate and all, sitting down the street while they started their work-up."

I curled up in a tiny ball under the covers, hiding like I did as a kid afraid of the boogeyman.

What are the chances of getting across the border without a passport?

CHAPTER 34

I LINGERED IN BED, savoring security for another minute, then forced myself to shower and dress. While I wolfed a bagel with Philly cream cheese, Michael strode into the kitchen, seemingly full of vim under the circumstances.

"No luck at the gun range."

"Why am I not surprised?"

"I'll keep trying, but I have some good news." He set his empty coffee mug in the sink. "They've filed charges on the murder of the pharmacist."

"Why, do they think I did that?"

Michael smiled at my black humor. "It's the garage attendant at Adventist."

I swallowed. "How does that help?"

"Because, my dear, he's innocent. If my theory is right, he'll need lawyers. Real lawyers. Not legal aid wannabes and bloody idealists. *That* will give us another avenue, another case to investigate. Visiting hours run till eleven."

I wasn't entirely sure what the ol' wise one had in mind, but scrambled up and brushed my hair and teeth. Decided to change out of jeans and suit up like a lawyer—powder-blue skirt, pinstripe blouse, heels, and hose. Felt good to look good. Especially since my next outfit would likely be orange.

Thirty minutes later we were at the jail in the waiting area for visiting relatives. Dallas County's jail will make you need Prozac just gazing at the outside of the concrete rectangular monstrosity. It looks like an aboveground fortress.

The inside was even more depressing. Probably a hundred people, most Hispanic or black, milled around. Women with kids, lots of T-shirts stretched over big bodies. A few men, too, looking pissed off at their incarcerated women. The desperation palpable, everybody waited to be called to the viewing room.

Michael wore a gorgeous Corneliani charcoal suit, white shirt showing off his tan, yellow tie, and platinum cuff links. The power look seemed pointless among these poor dregs of humanity, but I kept quiet and watched.

Michael raised his voice over the babble. "Is anyone here to see Lee Beal?"

A tall African-American woman, better dressed than most in a flowered sundress over brawny legs, shyly raised her hand while flashing scarlet fingernails. "Me."

Heart-shaped lips, big eyes, pecan-colored skin—despite her size she was striking.

Michael hurried over to where she'd managed to scrounge a folding chair and introduced himself. She scrunched her face in obvious confusion over why this over-dressed white lawyer approached her.

"I know your husband is innocent. He needs a good lawyer or they'll frame him."

Michael had used his refinery town accent, contrasting with his appearance. He'd probably known more black folks than all the rest of the members of the Dallas Country Club combined, even counting the caddies.

She bit, telling Michael again and again how her husband was being set up because he had a record as a kid. Through tears, she assured Michael he'd been absolutely clean for the ten years they'd been married and that he was a great dad. I believed her and could tell Michael did too.

Michael patted her hand and gave her his pocket square. She hesitated to take a silk hanky, but Michael said, "Go ahead."

She blew her nose and said she'd get it cleaned and return it. He waved the offer off. They'd bonded.

Others in the area scowled with jealousy. Some tried to get Michael's attention, but he remained fixated on Lee's wife, as if they were the only two people in the room.

Michael squeezed her hand. "All you got to do is hire us." He pointed to me. "We can see him now, then I'll go straight to the DA and see what those lyin' bastards got."

"How much?" Her face suddenly plastered with skepticism.

"Nothing. It's my Christian duty to help an innocent man."

I hid my smile. Give him credit, Michael could lay schmooze on as thick as wet cement.

Soon we were in the attorneys' interview room with Lee Beal. Slender with a neat mustache, he wore the familiar orange jumpsuit. He had the stark look of fear of the newly jailed. Both biceps were tattooed with something I didn't understand, but we got off to a great start when he recognized me from my trips to Adventist as their lawyer.

Beal interrupted Michael's first question. "I was workin' that night, and I seen her. Once. I didn't do nothin'!"

His pleading looked legit to me, not that I'm a great expert at sniffing out liars.

"Do you have any idea what they have on you?" Michael asked.

Lee covered his face with his hands and spoke through his fingers. "I helped that lady start her car two nights before. Was on gate duty and she walked down and asked me for help. You gotta believe me."

"I do, man."

Michael nodded at me. They had Beal's prints on the victim's car. With a record—even a sealed juvee charge—that was enough to get the DA rolling.

Lee sighed with relief, then added: "Her car was kinda old. The hood attachment cut my finger. I told the detectives about it. Then they swabbed my mouth."

He held up his forefinger, showing us a nearly healed scratch.

He had probably left a speck of blood on the car. The DA would get a DNA match. Without some break Lee would likely be convicted. Guys sat on death row with less evidence against them.

Michael waited a second. "Did you see anyone with the pharmacist the night she was killed?"

"I was walkin' the floors that night. Jonesy had the gates. I saw her waitin' at the elevator, like she was expectin' somebody, 'stead of goin' to her car."

"Yeah?" Michael asked with encouragement.

"I took the stairs to the next floor. Them stairs is by the elevators. I heard the elevator doors open when I was 'bout halfway down."

We both bobbed our heads, eager for more.

"Sounded like she was talkin' to a babe. I wasn't tryin' to listen in, but it sounded kinda like an argument."

"Any idea who this gal could've been?"

"Nope. Didn't see her."

Michael drew his lips in, his disappointment showing. He started to tell Lee what we were going to do, when the prisoner interrupted.

"You know, a dude can sometimes tell a girl is good-lookin' just by hearin' her?"

Michael smiled, a man-to-man shit-eating grin. "Sure."

I tried to look unfazed by their boy talk.

"I'd swear she was a cutie pie, just from the sound from her darlin' lips. If I'd had time, I woulda gone back up for a look-see, but I had to go down and relieve Jonesy."

Michael and I exchanged glances.

"We'll go to the DA right now."

* * *

Two tedious hours later, we were with a snot-nosed ADA in a conference room in the Frank Crowley Courts building. The tall kid had dark whiskers on his jut jaw. He needed to shave closer, but probably thought stubble passed for sexy. His dirt-blond hair was plastered back and parted down the middle. My little sister would've thought he was a cute.

Now that we were Beal's lawyers, we were entitled to know what the state had and Michael was determined to get it that afternoon without motions and other legal folderol.

Michael and the ADA went three rounds over disclosure of their evidence. The ADA claimed they hadn't compiled their file or some nonsense. They had to pony up sooner or later. Constitutional law said so, but that doesn't mean ADAs always jump to a defense lawyer's commands.

My fiance, ever unflappable, shrugged and said, "If you want to prosecute an innocent man—a *black* innocent man—go ahead. But if you'll let me help, you can nail a serial killer and tie up six deaths. You'll be the assistant of the month."

The kid betrayed his astonishment, keeping his mouth open a bit too long. He got up and dialed an extension from the phone on the table and spoke some DA code into the receiver. In response to whoever was on the other end, he spoke a lot of "yes sirs." The kid hung up, excused himself, and left.

After another excruciating thirty minutes sitting by ourselves, we were escorted to another room. The ADA motioned us over to a desktop computer. He hit the play button and we saw grainy video surveillance of the garage. I figured that at some point they would enhance the quality. The kid had to backtrack to two nights before the pharmacist was murdered.

Lee Beal showed up talking to a woman who looked a lot like the victim, though the image wasn't clear, because they weren't directly in line with the camera. She stood near her car. Everything looked casual.

Beal left the focus of the camera, then returned to the fourth floor in a security pickup. He used jumper cables to start the pharmacist's car, then unhooked them and closed her hood. He even sucked his finger. Blood? She tapped his elbow, looked at his hand, appeared to thank him, got in, and drove out of the picture.

After another tedious search we found video from the first floor showing the pharmacist's car leaving the garage two minutes later. I watched the ADA for his reaction. Sour turned-down lips gave him away.

Lee now had a credible explanation for his prints being on the car. Not to mention his DNA. Without any motive, and no sexual assault, the state's case just fell apart. Of course that didn't mean Beal would be home that night. They don't quit that easily.

Next we scanned the system and found choppy shots from the night of the murder at the time it was thought to have occurred. After five minutes, we spotted the pharmacist strolling to her car with another person who had gotten off the elevator with her. In jerky video they approached the same car from the other night.

The taller and heavier pharmacist shielded the other person. We only saw legs in scrubs and sneakers. They slipped out of the picture. I suspected the other person intentionally kept herself between her victim and the camera, so we only saw her back.

I asked the ADA to run it again slowly. The cops had examined the video, but thought the pharmacist was simply speaking to a friend before going to her car, and had settled on Lee Beal as their man. But whoever it was had to be smaller than the dead woman, who according to the preliminary autopsy report stood five-nine and weighed one-sixty.

So the mystery person could be either a small man or a female. My mind tumbled around the possibilities. Before I locked on to anyone, the pharmacist in the video turned and raised her hand, her index finger pointing at her companion. With a freeze, we got the most fleeting glimpse of the other person's pert nose and layered haircut.

A woman. An attractive woman. Lee wasn't lying.

The raised forefinger conjured an image of arguing with my sister. I caught Michael's gaze. He got it too.

As if she knew the camera angle, the other person's image disappeared as the victim slid into her car. The dead woman's car and body were found on the next floor down.

The kid seemed to sense our growing confidence. "We've found hairs that appear to match your client on the vic's jacket in the backseat. Plus prints all over her car."

Michael gave him a look of utter disdain. "You probably also got prints of the salesman who sold her the car."

The kid smirked. "Your client had an indecent exposure charge when he was seventeen. He was lucky he wasn't older."

Michael snorted. "What? Pissing in a bar parking lot?" Michael glanced at the guy's wedding ring. "Didn't you ever go to a bachelor party?"

I stifled a chuckle. Men can be hilarious.

The ADA mumbled, sounding forlorn, "There's a spot of blood on the hood latch. We'll have DNA next week and try to get his DNA off hair on the girl's jacket."

I guessed this was the coat the woman had on the night before when Lee jumped her car. He probably brushed against her while hooking jumper cables. From my last little escapade with the law, I learned that hair falls everywhere. And gets retrieved by the crime scene guys.

The charge against Beal smacked of a hurry-up indictment designed to comfort all the patients and personnel—i.e. voters—at a big hospital. It would have to be dropped, but maybe Michael didn't care if it lingered a while, letting the real murderer feel over confident.

Michael thanked the pup attorney, like you'd thank a process server delivering a summons. The kid snarled his obvious irritation that an Italian-suited lawyer represented a security guard.

The Beal interlude had taken well into the afternoon. We hurried out.

*　*　*

We could cover more ground splitting up. Michael wanted to track down "Jonesy," the other garage employee. I told Michael I'd pop in on the bartender again. We parted with a kiss. I let my lips and hands linger, knowing I could be pulled over on my way to Tipsters and never touch the love of my life again. Had to sniff hard and blink away tears as I drove off.

I stopped at Patterson's bar, but my buddy didn't come to work until four, so I went on, carefully obeying all traffic laws. Nurse Peyton lingered in that part of the brain where you can't quite remember. I decided to track down a Baylor alumni directory.

The Louise Herrington School of Nursing at Baylor in Dallas sold me an alumni directory for $19.95. I walked back to my car, flipping through the book. Before I reached my visitor parking spot, I realized I couldn't find her. No Emma Peyton. My copy of her licensing file was at the office.

I called Tina. Fortunately she was in the office. She pulled the folder on Nurse Emma and confirmed Baylor was her school. No way to lie to the Nursing Board. They'd check with any purported school before giving a license. No hospital would hand a name tag even to an agency float without seeing credentials.

Tina said she'd check Facebook. She called back and reported that Emma Peyton's page was down. No surprise. My brain was like one of those inflatable bounce bins kids rent for birthday parties, ideas ricocheting off the sides. None made any sense. I felt exhausted and scared shitless.

I fought the traffic back to Patterson's bar. Calling would've been easier, but I had to be doing *something* and driving counted as *something*. At a standstill on the Central, I checked in with Michael.

He'd found Jonesy, who didn't think his comrade could have a thing to do with molesting and murdering some woman. Jones had volunteered, "Lee's old lady would cut his balls off." From what I saw she could.

Unfortunately, he didn't remember anyone unusual coming out about the time the pharmacist was murdered. I figured that meant the culprit worked at the hospital. And we had a suspect.

I clicked off and rang the bar. My source wasn't in yet. I phoned Michael back and volunteered to pick up Sarah, since I was closer. Michael might even be productive, unlike me. Sarah didn't have practice, so I exited at Forest and drove toward ritzy Hockaday, the private school where Sarah took summer session.

Stopped at a light, I tried Tina again. A question had suddenly popped into my frazzled brain. "Tina, think hard. Could one of the people who beat you up have been a woman?'

Tina was silent for a moment. "All I remember is being grabbed when I walked in. They threw a blanket over my head. I didn't see them."

"Did you hear them talk?"

Again, she hesitated. "I only heard one voice. It was a guy, but I know there were two by the way they grabbed me and the number of blows. They didn't talk to each other. Just heard one laughing and threatening me."

If the other were a female, it would make sense for her not to talk. Better to let the victim think two rough thugs had her.

"I'm sure a guy hit me from the front. But it seems like the other one kept kicking me from behind, but not real hard. Maybe not very big. All the bruises are on the front."

"Did he sound Hispanic?"

I could almost hear the shrug. "I was too scared to notice."

I clicked off.

By the time I reached Hockaday, it was nearly four. I texted Sarah to tell her I was in the pick-up lane. She strolled out, chatting with a friend.

Michael had enrolled Sarah in both mid-high summer sessions to keep her busy. He thought sitting around during the day waiting for her ball games would give her too much time to mope and remember. When she learned that one of the summer courses was vampire literature, Sarah jumped all over it.

She introduced me to her pal, Annie. Thankfully Sarah wasn't embarrassed that her dad was engaged to a future convicted felon. After Sarah told her friend good-bye and we pulled away, her smile faded, concern replacing it.

She knew I was in deep trouble. I recounted my day for her and relayed the Emma Peyton trail dead end. I was tired of talking, wanting a drink, and a rub from my man, when Sarah said: "That's easy. She got married or divorced, and changed her name after she got out of school."

Like I said, I was really beat. And the kid's sharp.

CHAPTER 35

WHEN WE GOT TO MICHAEL'S, Sarah offered to help look through the Baylor directory for all the Emmas who'd graduated in the year Peyton did. There couldn't be many in her class, but the directory, six inches thick, was organized by name and by year at the back. I ripped it in two and gave Sarah half. Emma had to be about the most popular name in the '80s, so progress was slow.

We'd found four Emmas the right age when my cell rang. Brady, the bartender at Tipsters.

"*I think I got the name. We joked that he was a big tipper.*"

"Yes?"

"*My partner called him Cash-Wells, but I believe the real name was Caswell.*"

Holy shit.

A relative of the guy I supposedly shot? Who some people still think I killed.

I went mute. A chill traversed my spine and gripped my neck. He had to be the brother of Tony Caswell, the little bastard who fed the cops invented conversations he claimed to have overheard— conversations about how happy Michael and I would be if we could get rid of his wife. A ruthless adversary, if the brother was anything like Tony.

While I was still trying to gather my wits, Brady added, *"My partner said he was in here last night looking for a tall woman, thick hair, nice skin. The guy tipped big for the information."*

I cringed. "And?"

"My buddy said he asked a lot of questions about you. Frankly it sounded like the guy was stalking you."

Great. Just great.

Thanking Brady I clicked off. I realized I'd been followed and hadn't noticed.

Sarah pushed her half of the open directory toward me. "Here's another Emma the right age," she said.

I picked the book up and spotted the name she'd circled.

Emma Caswell.

* * *

Tony Caswell had been an associate lawyer at Michael's old firm. He'd grown up attending prestigious schools all over the world while his father, a big oil exec, tried out trophy wives in various locales. I think his mother played cougar about the same time. For revenge, if no other reason.

Having attended Harrow, the elite boys' school outside London, some ritzy American academy in Paris, and a multicultural institution in Indonesia, Tony was quite the sophisticate. He wound up in Dallas because he'd gone to UT Law, when his father happened to be manipulating energy markets in Houston.

Tony had a problem sticking with anything. He started college at Cornell, dropped out claiming he'd been bullied, and transferred to Virginia. Like UVA's most famous alum—Edgar Allen Poe—Tony drank and gambled too much, left, and wound up finishing his undergrad degree at a commuter school outside Houston. It was the same with law firms. Jackson, Stern & Randolph had been his third stop in six years.

He'd dangled his father's wealth before Michael's partner, Jackson, whose skin had a permanent green hue from greed. Supposedly Tony's dad sat on the board of a big international company and he would bring in the perfect client—rich, mad, and wrong.

As it turned out, Tony's dad did have money, since he bought Tony's stock shares for him a week after Tony finally made partner. Despite his advantages growing up, and his decent looks, Caswell was horribly insecure—especially about his arm, withered since birth.

He was the kind of guy who abraded Michael like a steel file on a brick. Despite Michael's disdain for him, Jackson pushed Caswell's partnership. Michael had vetoed it, until a day he missed a partner's meeting for Sarah's practice. Born a carpenter's son, Jackson never turned down a chance to scoop a nickel off the sidewalk—or rib Michael over his wife's money.

My date with Caswell made me a lifetime enemy. Pete McGee had told me to socialize with Caswell, play the role of *femme fatale*, and learn whether Michael Stern planned to double-cross us in defending the *Layne* case. Stern's firm had the doctor; we represented the hospital.

Having picked up nothing, I foolishly invited him into my townhouse for a drink. He immediately started pawing my chest. I asked him to leave. He started for the door, then caught me by surprise and shoved me to the floor. Then Tony flopped it out and said, "Suck it." Real classy. Even threw a broken glass at me. Caswell didn't know I had a black belt, but found out pretty quick. He left my place barely breathing.

Give me a little credit—Caswell's story was nonsense. Michael, the ol' stud, almost didn't accept my invitation for a weekend, since he had learned of my dark past and was preparing for the custody fight with Diana. He thought I was an eggshell balanced on a unicycle and had decided not to get involved with me.

During the investigation of Diana's murder, the cops suspected he'd hired a hit on his rich wife and were hot on Michael's trail. Caswell, the DA's star witness, suddenly turned up dead in the parking lot of a redneck bar. He'd eaten a couple bullets.

A drunk outside barfing thought he'd seen a tall woman with a gun. That got the cops interested in me. Michael had an alibi—he wasn't a woman and the Highland Park PD had his house staked out with him in it. But the bullets didn't match either my or Michael's gun. And there wasn't even a similar hair at the spot where the killer fired.

The Mesquite police reluctantly called the crime a parking lot dispute outside a rowdy bar. The case was, as far as I knew, open—but considered cold. The Caswell I knew would never have ventured into a dive like that without a lure of some kind. Who or what had been the lure would become a life-or-death question.

* * *

When Michael came home in the evening, I brought him up to date. He grimaced in anger, maybe fear. Obviously none of us were safe from the Caswell clan. A family this into paybacks wouldn't be easy to stop—or, for that matter, easy to find.

Sarah had a softball game that night. We debated whether to go. Not knowing where to look for the Caswells, holing up would be counter-productive since I only had hours before I returned to jail. We checked the court clerk's website—Judge Redhead had finally gotten off the bench for the day and issued a warrant.. Not even the incomparable Michael Stern could stop me from returning to jail.

We drove to Sarah's game in Farmer's Branch. I watched for any tail, but tried not to alarm Sarah. A muggy night, the air weighed heavy on me, reminding me I might never breathe free again. Michael and I eyed the field and stands like Secret Service sharpshooters at a presidential appearance. The other team got run-ruled early and no Caswells showed. Typically for that time of year in Texas, massive black clouds loomed in the sky, while radios and TVs blared about the chance of severe storms, hail, and tornadoes.

Between living in Oklahoma for three years and living in Texas I'd quit worrying and learned that tornadoes seldom hit you. They always seem to smash into poor folks living in trailers—another of life's tragedies.

When the game was over, we hustled Sarah away from her friends, begging off that it was a school night. We decided not to share with Sarah further details about the danger.

That night, I don't think I slept more than an hour, thanks to thunder, wind, and fear. Michael had called the Highland Park police and asked them to keep a special eye on the house. I don't know how close they watched, since he wasn't on their list of favorite citizens.

I gave conceiving a baby boy my best shot. More than once. Michael probably thought that he risked a stress-induced heart attack by marrying me. "Forgot" to tell him about the pills. Maybe I was afraid he'd say, "Let's wait."

The next morning, fallen branches and leaves littered the streets. I reluctantly agreed to let Tina go to class in Denton. We gave her Michael's SL again and my small pistol to stick in the console. I reminded her to stay in very public places and keep her bloody phone charged.

We both took Sarah to school, me riding shotgun. Then we returned to the house and tried to figure out what to do next. This would likely be my last day of freedom, maybe for the rest of my life, and I had to make the most of it.

Before we had agreed on a strategy, Michael's phone rang.

After a minute he hung up, sporting something approximating a smile under our awful circumstances.

"The investigator I hired to help Lee Beal found a set of bloody hospital scrubs in the trash at Adventist."

"Hundreds of blood-stained scrubs go out every day in a hospital."

Michael smiled at me the way he does at Sarah when she asks a naïve question. "I made sure that he searched the general trash—not the hazardous waste. There shouldn't have been any blood where he searched. They have to keep the paper cups and discarded memos separate from the blood, piss, and other fluids."

I nodded, feeling dumb. "Okay."

"Nurse Peyton couldn't have slit the pharmacist's throat without getting blood on her. Regardless of how she slipped out of the garage, she wouldn't have wanted to leave in bloody scrubs. She must've changed in her car and stuffed the evidence in the garage trash."

"That helps Beal, but not me."

Michael squeezed my hand. "I'll call the DA. If we can prove it's the Caswells behind all this, we may be able to get them to drop the charges."

"I'm not so sure."

"I want to see the scrubs before we turn them over. Let's go."

I begged off. Michael didn't need me and was getting something accomplished. Part of me wanted to try to find the Caswell siblings and get the showdown over with, like a condemned criminal sleeplessly awaiting a dawn execution. Also, I guessed if I kept moving I might be less likely to get picked up.

But, in a metroplex of five million people, how the hell was I going to find them?

An idea popped into my head. I told Michael I could follow up some leads on the computer and that I would check in with him after he saw the PI.

* * *

Perhaps David and Emma were using another of Nicky's purloined homes as a safe house for whatever they had ultimately planned. I called the nerdy bank lawyer. He sounded thrilled to hear from me and didn't express much regret over Nicolette's death. I asked if he had a list of other places she'd had access to.

He replied he did and promised to email me what they had, but warned me she might have hooked up with another lender with access to more places. I received his list within a minute. I'd have to spring for *his* lunch, if I ever got out of this.

Thinking I might get lucky and get the jump on them, I started trolling the houses. The drill at each was the same: Gun in pocket, look around, knock; if no answer, quiz neighbors. I eliminated three when it looked like another squatter had taken up residence and two more had been sold. Of course, I tried the address listed in Emma's file. *Shockeroo.* She'd bolted.

I stopped for more coffee, gas, and a Snickers to keep me going. Inside the off-brand convenience store, the clerk had KRLD, the local news radio station, on.

As I paid, a flash bulletin blared that there was a bomb scare at Hockaday. The school was being evacuated.

I was closer than Michael and sent Sarah a text that I was coming. When Michael didn't answer my call I left him a voicemail saying I would get Sarah.

* * *

About a mile away from my exit, traffic ground to a halt.

Shit!

After a minute, police cars and fire trucks, sirens blaring, zoomed along the shoulder past the jam. Then some idiot in front of me jerked to his right to go around on to the shoulder and got creamed by a late-arriving cop.

The collision sent his Yukon spinning three-sixty into a poor guy in the middle lane. In a minute the Central was chaos. I was between exits and could only sit and curse. I sent Sarah a text that I was hung up.

I pounded the wheel and cursed. All I could do. Michael hadn't called back.

Ten miserable minutes later I got a text from an unknown phone: *Going to a movie with Lizzy. They'll take me to practice—Sarah.*

Sarah was under long-standing orders not to go off with anyone she didn't know. But I'm paranoid and didn't like the odd texting from a different phone. I tried Sarah's, but only got her silly recording: *"You've reached Sarah the Stern. Oh not really. Leave a message for Sarah the smiley."*

As I squirmed in frustration rain began peppering my windshield. Practice would be canceled. Bigger drops splattered. Where would she go then? If it weren't raining I could go to the field and wait out the movie. Why the hell didn't she text what movie they were going to see? What theater?

Finally the cops were directing traffic to the median around the confusion. By the time I got to the Forest exit, the bomb had been identified as a fake. An alarm clock and painted paper towel rolls, according to the news, had been an elaborate plot to . . . what?

A spasm of fear hit me. I debated with myself. Surely not. But possibly.

Please, Blessed Mother, not Sarah again.

Her phone was still off. I called Michael, reached him this time, and told him the little I knew. He said he got the same text and vaguely recalled a Lizzy, but did not remember the parents' names.

I told Michael I'd head for Hockaday. Maybe someone would recall seeing her leave. He said he'd go home from Adventist in case Sarah turned up there.

I prayed the Rosary, my anxiety building. By the time I reached Sarah's school, I'd brought the storm with me. Rain slapped my new windshield. I slammed to a stop in the covered pick-up lane and dashed to the door, finding it locked. Of course—keep out kidnappers and fake bombers. I tried the intercom next to the door and got no response. The place seemed totally deserted.

After several minutes, peering through the glass, I finally spotted a security guard carrying a handful of keys, likely locking up. I banged on the door. He must have read the panic in my eyes and hurried over. I introduced myself as Michael Stern's fiancée.

"Do you know Sarah?"

"Of course."

"Did you see her leave?

He looked like a retired cop, droopy creases in his cheeks, lines etched in his forehead, receding hair, but seemed pretty sharp. He stroked his chin a second.

"I watched carpool, but things were wild for summer session. Every kid getting picked up at once."

"Perhaps—"

"Wait." He scrounged in his back pocket and pulled out a cell phone. "Someone found this in the flowerbed. Like it had been thrown from the car line."

I knew bad news was coming.

"Let's see whose it is," the guard said.

Seconds expanded into what seemed like hours as I watched him open the phone.

"Oh my."

He handed it to me.

The screen showed a kid in a softball uniform sliding home with perfect form, kicking up dust, blond hair flying out of her helmet.

Sarah.

CHAPTER 36

I DROVE TO MICHAEL'S THROUGH THE STORM. Miraculously, I killed no one and did not get arrested. I parked in back near the magnolia, carried my shoes, and darted through the downpour—into the kitchen, nearly slipping on the tile. I looked like someone had thrown me into the swimming pool during a frat party.

Michael had beaten me home, his face a frozen expression of terror. I had not seen him while Sarah was missing, but could imagine he looked just as bad.

He continued trying Sarah's friends' parents, trying to figure out who she'd left with. His fingers shook so badly, he had trouble hitting the correct numbers on the phone.

His face paled with each call. In the confusion, nobody had seen anything. The two moms he reached didn't know a friend named Lizzy, making me wonder if there really was a Lizzy or if this was a random name used by the Caswells. None of Sarah's closest friends and teammates were enrolled at Hockaday for the summer, so calls to them netted nothing.

He finished phoning the obvious contacts and collapsed onto a kitchen chair. I poured him a whisky. I suspected action would be required soon, maybe deadly action, and didn't want a drink.

After tossing his down, he told me his PI had found a bank down the street from the infamous dumpster with surveillance video that might show whoever chucked Nicky in the garbage. Like the gun records it would have to be subpoenaed by the DA, who was in no hurry to prove my innocence.

Of course, we tried to tell each other, the day's events could be harmless—a typical teenager losing her phone. But the more we kicked around the possibilities, the more the missing phone screamed like a patient getting a compound fracture set without anesthetic.

Michael sat again, holding his face in his palms. I worried he might have a stroke and flapped nonsense about how innocent it would turn out to be, but for the moment we could only hope someone would call with good news.

When the landline rang, the caller ID said "Unknown." I grabbed it and answered.

"We have Sarah."

The very tone of the man's voice sent my heart rate to the redline. "Who is this?"

"I think you know."

I waved at Michael to get on an extension. He flew out of the kitchen toward the library.

The voice continued, *"Here's the deal. She's in a secure location. But she has, shall we say, limited resources. You come to 1734 Rosewood Lane and she lives. Only you, Kristen."*

I heard Michael lift the receiver in the library.

"Come alone. Unarmed. If we see your boyfriend or the cops, she dies. Get going."

My body went cold. "Okay, but first let Sarah go."

"Another thing. We will be watching Stern's house and calling his landline."

"What?"

"He better not leave. And no busy signal when we call or the kid dies."

324

"Pard', you're fucking dead!" Michael screamed on the extension.

"Alone, Kristen. And no cops."

Click.

In a second, Michael returned carrying the biggest revolver I had ever seen. He was a madman, face aflame, hands shaking.

I ran and blocked the back door. He elbowed past me, but I tugged his wrist for all I was worth.

"Out of my way!"

"Michael, hold it."

He jerked his arm away. Without thinking, I grabbed his wrist again and levered it up, not trying to hurt him, but wanting badly to stop him.

He stopped.

His eyes gaped open in shock and he finally took a deep breath. Hoping I'd bought some time to discuss the conundrum, I eased up and spoke calmly, "They could be bluffing. Sarah could be with any friend, since there's no practice." I tried to make myself believe my own bullshit. Without much success.

Michael pounded his fist against the paneling.

"She knows she has to tell me where she is!"

I couldn't conjure a scenario where Sarah would leave with a total stranger. She was *not* stupid and knew something about danger—a lot about danger. Whoever had taken her either looked familiar or she had been forced.

"This is tied to the fake bomb," I said. "They wanted her out of school, before one of us picked her up."

"Kristen, I'm going after them."

"We can't risk it."

I decided. Time to *act* for the people I love. "I've got to go."

"But you're not leaving without me!"

"It's me they want. Not Sarah. Or you. There's no reason for you to risk it. They think I killed Tony."

"Baby, no!"

This was the same dilemma I'd faced the night I entered a dark house to face a rapist and another thug known to shoot cops. If anything happened to Sarah, Michael and I had no future—jail or no jail. He already carried a conscience full of guilt over Diana.

If I wanted a husband, a father for the baby I might be carrying, I had to go. The whole mess was my fault—for jacking with Larseny. *Why, Kristen? Why didn't you usher Tony Caswell out the door a year ago without beating him half to death?*

He read my mind. "No. I will not let you out of this house."

"Honey, Sarah needs a parent."

"Kristen Kerry, you are the love of my life. You cannot leave without me."

I steered him away from the door. "I love you too, but think logically. For now we have to do what they say until I can get a feel for what's going on—or talk them out of their insanity."

Michael finally put the pistol on the entry table. "I won't have you facing those assholes alone."

I kept thinking. The little gray cells came up with nothing except that this mess was my fault and if anyone had to risk their life it should be me. I added, "We can't call the police. They'll haul me off before I get half the story out."

I stepped into the guest room, my official bedroom. He followed, still arguing, but I tuned him out. Somewhere in the recesses of my brain endorphins sprouted—relief at picking up the gauntlet and getting the battle over with. I felt a strange surge of confidence.

After digging through the pile of gear I hadn't taken the time to stow, I found a pair of sturdy basketball shoes, then put on dark-colored sweatpants and a black tee. I grabbed my pistol from under the bed.

I couldn't slow the momentum or I might chicken out. "I've got to."

He tried to grab me, but I'm good at getting out of the grip of guys.

"Kristen, come back here."

"Don't try to stop me, and don't call the police."

"Please, baby, we'll think of something. We know where they are."

"Michael, I must. Sarah's not at that address. They wouldn't stash her there. They've got other houses."

"Honey, no!"

"Sarah's only bait."

"Kristen—"

"Once they have me, they might let her go . . . *will* let her go and you can come in with reinforcements."

I walked to the kitchen and rummaged in a drawer, finding a short, very sharp paring knife about three inches long. I grabbed a cup towel hanging on the fridge door handle.

Michael stared at me like I was a lunatic. Maybe I was.

"You want to risk Sarah on a SWAT team? That's if you can even get the cops interested until twenty-four hours have passed. We don't have any proof she's been kidnapped."

Michael pointed, a gesture he'd learned to seldom use with me. "If you leave, I'm calling the cops."

"Give me two hours." I tore the towel in half, found some tape, wrapped the blade in cloth, and snuggled the knife to my ankle under my sock.

He stared wide-eyed at my SEAL routine. "No way."

"I'll have my Browning."

I ejected the magazine—twelve rounds, one short of full, army style, to save wear on the mag—slipped it back, and chambered a bullet. What a lovely sound it made. The cold steel felt powerful in my hand. I flipped the safety off. A double-action automatic is okay without it, and I wanted to be able to fire quickly.

Michael's eyes rounded open. He'd never seen me handle weapons. I hoped he was impressed.

"These people are ruthless, crazy . . ."

He stopped, looking nonplussed. Talking about insane people must've made him realize he'd just said Sarah was held by lunatics. His complexion went from neon red to deathly pale. He slumped into a living room chair and pushed the skin on his forehead back and forth.

"There's got to be a better idea. I'll call the police and ask for an Amber alert."

"No, give me a chance. If I don't get anywhere with them, you can call for help."

I knew he was weighing the risk of losing me against even the slim chance that I could find Sarah. He mumbled my own words, "Get anywhere?"

I tried to lighten his burden. "Whatever they have in store for me can't be worse than going back to jail tomorrow."

"I'm working on that. We'll have evidence by morning. Afternoon at the latest."

"We can't wait that long."

He apparently made a decision and hopped up, wagging a finger. "GPS on the car will tell me where you are, but still call me when you get there. Look around, but *don't* go in. You can talk to them on your phone."

Of course I was going in, but didn't want to lie. We walked to the back door. His expression carried obvious skepticism. I'm sure he read my mind and knew I wasn't going to follow orders.

Before he could berate me, an idea popped into my frazzled brain.

I grabbed my phone, found my old pal Jen's number, and punched the shortcut. While it rang I told Michael my plan. He agreed it was better than going in alone.

Jen answered.

"You have a killer working at your hospital."

"*What?*"

"Regardless of the cases, I'm sure you want to do something about it."

She seemed receptive, so I briefed Jen and asked her to tail me, not too close, but in sight. I assumed they would be watching for Michael, cops, or his private eye, not a five-two, spike-haired woman. My friend agreed to a rendezvous point and then to tag along. I felt a little safer.

Michael bought the compromise and quit jamming his finger in my sternum.

One last task. I told Michael I had to pee and ducked into the three-quarter bath in the guest bedroom. My gorgeous engagement ring would not disappear with me in a shallow grave or at the bottom of White Rock Lake.

I took a last glance at it, kissed it like a Rosary, slipped it off, and stuck it in the medicine cabinet. Michael would find it eventually. Maybe it could be reworked for Sarah. Perhaps Michael would fall for Tina and give it to her. That would be okay. Spotting my reflection in the mirror I decided to add my gold earrings to the stash. No point them going to waste.

I slipped my left hand in a pocket before hurrying out, so Michael wouldn't notice my bare finger. Opening the door I absorbed his intense blue eyes for possibly the last time. He wrapped a strong hand around my neck and pulled me closer, his face rough on my cheek. I drew all the strength I could before pulling away. Lord Jesus Christ, no woman was more and better loved than me.

"I promise. No more adventures." I started to add, "Just a boring life raising all the kids you want." But I didn't want to jinx myself.

For the first time in the two years I'd known him, Michael stammered. Tears gathered in his eyes. I'd never seen him cry. And I'd been paranoid about some chick like Donna?

Stupid, Kristen.

Finally he spit out, "Remember—I can't go on without both of you."

I needed to go or my resolve might weaken. Stepping away, I

crossed the threshold. I recalled the classic Spartan oath before battle, "with my shield or on it," and decided not to share it with Michael.

CHAPTER 37

I WAITED HALF AN HOUR at the CVS off Preston for Jen. No nurse buddy. I tried her cell. No answer. I held out another fifteen minutes, pictured Sarah bound frightened, desperate for help, and decided to go on.

Jen had the address. Despite being opponents on the cases, I assumed she wanted to know what really happened and didn't want murderers roaming her hospital. Hopefully Pete didn't either.

Maybe she was only stuck in traffic. I knew she would eventually get there, so I drove to my scheduled ten-rounder. Jen would be worthless in a fight, but maybe if the Caswells realized I had backup they would hesitate to shoot me and I could talk them into letting Sarah go. And convince them I didn't kill their brother. I was working a theory which would give them another suspect. If they agreed it made sense, perhaps I could walk away with Sarah and they'd have somebody else to torture.

The navigation system in my BMW directed me to the street. I slowed before I got to 1734 so I could surveil the area. The block was no more than a year old, judging by the absence of trees. One half-built two-story had a cyclone fence around it to ward off thieves. I counted eight realtor signs. The houses were nice, brick and stone—Dallas style—perhaps built as specs.

Only two cars sat on driveways. At least half the places had to be empty. Nobody outside.

All Quiet on the Western Front.

I parked in front of 1722, three houses down from my destination, and pondered for a minute.

Should I call Michael? No doubt that if I told him Jen wasn't behind me, he'd insist on coming. Would the Caswells really know he'd left the house? Surely they didn't have a lookout.

Surely.

But a few months ago I would have said, "No nurse would murder three kids." I could call the cops, but they'd probably arrest *me*. In an English poetry course in college I had fallen in love with works expressing heroic futility: "The Charge of the Light Brigade," or "The Highwayman." And the maudlin stuff of W.B. Yeats. It all spoke to me of my testimony against Dad and the flight from home. At that moment I felt like I was charging into the cannons.

Back he spurred like a madman.

I wondered if I was madman. Crazy or not—I saw alternatives. Number one: go up and ring the bell. Nothing like getting right to the point. But it might be suicide to walk into a house of homicidal lunatics. Even with the fear of going back to jail, I wasn't quite ready to die.

Two: I could try to slip behind the place and sneak in, but there was still daylight left and I might be spotted anyway.

Three: Figure out a way to talk to them, convince them I was innocent, and leave without eating a bullet.

Four: Chicken out. The sensible choice. But if I was going to puss out, why had I come?

Deciding on number two, I stuffed my 9mm in my waistband, grabbed my phone, and got out of my car. Maybe Jen would still show. Perhaps she was checking out my version of the story, so I took a deep breath and crossed myself. Once I scoped things out, I could decide on the next step.

The rain had morphed to drizzle. Gloomy, clammy weather felt perfect for this adventure. It looked like 1734 backed up to an empty lot. If I could get through the yard of a neighboring house, with luck I could slip closer, unseen.

As I sidled up the drive of 1726, my phone rang.

Michael, leave me alone.

I checked anyway and saw it wasn't my lover, but *Unavailable.*

I answered.

A male voice said: *"Come straight in. No James Bond crap."*

Busted.

The caller clicked off. I tried Jen again. No answer. My heart sped up from its tachycardiac state. Number one it was. I sent Jen a text. *Going in. Park outside. Call cops if not out in fifteen.* I figured if I couldn't convince them in fifteen minutes I never would. Even a federal judge would give you that long for an opening statement.

Nothing about the piled-stone and Tudor-like house suggested a potential murder-kidnapping venue. It looked more like an accountant's house—a guy with two kids and a wife who taught school.

Glancing around, I saw no witnesses who might remember me. Perfect for the Caswells. But hopefully Jen would show any second. I rang the bell. All I had to do was convince the little clan that I hadn't killed their brother. It occurred to me that I might have over-estimated my persuasion skills.

Once more unto the breach.

Although I tried to control my breathing, I felt a weird tingle and an almost sexual, breathless excitement. I guess fear can generate lots of different physiological responses. I was more scared than the two times I had faced Marrs, the parolee. At least I had known I was smarter than that psycho. With these people I wasn't so sure.

Whoever opened the door had to be behind it, as all I could see was an empty house with a bare marble foyer.

"Throw the gun down."

I ran through my options. Roll and fire? Dive onto my belly? Run? The first chance might be my last and if I lost my pistol I'd only have words.

Another voice, female, called from my left opposite the guy on my right. "Now. If you want to see that snotty kid again."

I pulled the big automatic from my sweats, hesitated another second, continuing the debate, and tried to picture a target. The house was dark and I could see no one. I eased my left hand up to double clutch the pistol.

Come on. One of you step into the light.

Silence. Not even a chance to pinpoint the sound. Combat would likely get me killed, and probably Sarah. If by some miracle I shot both of them and survived, I still wouldn't know what they had done with Sarah.

Reluctantly I tossed my gun a few feet toward the far voice.

"Take three steps in."

I launched myself forward, realizing too late that I might have lost my last chance to escape and get help. I glanced behind me. No Jen.

Where the fuck are you?

Emma Peyton appeared from a dining room on my left. She aimed what looked like a big Sig 9mm automatic at me. Fifteen rounds. Very lethal. Appropriately, she wore red scrubs.

Her gaze never left me as she picked up my pistol.

The door closed behind me, revealing the man Tina had described as Dave, about my height, small features, blue eyes, not bad-looking. It took a minute to recall—the guy behind me at the gun range, minus glasses and long hair. Dave pointed a revolver at my chest.

"And the phone."

I pulled my cell out of the sweats pocket and placed it on the floor. He circled behind me.

Nurse Peyton waved her weapon. "Take off your shirt!"

From her shrill voice, she seemed the less stable of the two, but, as I stalled, he pounded me in the back of the neck with the revolver, reminding me who was in charge.

It took a few seconds to shake off the pain. Looking for any opening, but seeing no chance, I pulled off my black tee.

"I did not kill your brother."

"Now the pants!" she barked.

Dave spoke calmly. "We're going to have a trial, counselor."

I pushed my sweats down to my ankles and prayed they wouldn't insist I remove my shoes and crew socks. "I did *not* kill your brother."

She stared at me like an angel of death, her hand white, squeezing her gun. Any nurse who killed three patients to set up this plot had to be totally certifiable. I noticed the cocked hammer and her forefinger on the trigger.

I tried reason. "If we work together, we can figure out who did. I want to solve it as much as you do."

He stepped around in front of me. She slipped to my side, keeping a straight line of fire at my back.

"Now the bra. And raise your arms."

I did. It was so damn humid, sweat beaded in my pits, despite being undressed.

Emma stepped closer and surveyed my bare skin. Keeping her gun pointed at me, she seemed satisfied I wasn't wired. They hadn't spotted the knife.

Keep cool.

Dave looked down. "Check her feet."

Crap. Off went the shoes and socks.

My little trick earned me two more blows on the back. This time I had to bend over to catch my breath. It really hurt.

He unwrapped my blade and tossed it into the dining room, his gaze lingering at my crotch. "Should I check her pussy?"

Another hand rape? Please no. "I didn't hide a rifle in my vagina."

Emma smiled and spared me further humiliation by popping open my panties and peeking inside, averting a pelvic exam by Dave.

What a sweetheart.

"We're going to take a walk," Dave said.

"You don't need these." She threw my sneakers, sports bra, and socks where the knife and the towel had landed. "You just need to be presentable."

Emma tossed me my shirt and sweats. I put them back on, trying to keep my hands steady, but failed—a real profile in courage.

"Where's Sarah? You got me. Let her—"

"Shut up!"

I considered apologizing for my impertinent question and dressed, but couldn't resist another, even at the risk of further angering the good nurse.

"Did you really have to kill three kids to get to me? Why not just grab me off the street?"

She cackled like the Wicked Witch of the West.

Dave spoke evenly without the emotion you would expect from a man seeking cold-blooded revenge, "The first dead kid was an accident. Your former client needs to tell its staff to double check meds before using them."

Snickering, Emma added, "I felt bad for that banker. One of the girls on that floor is a real dumbass. I offed the other two. One was a druggie's kid. Probably brain-damaged. The other was just another wetback and we have plenty of those."

Dave smirked. "And we wanted to make your life as miserable as possible. Enjoy that cell?"

"But why all this? I'm going back to jail."

She snarled, "I decided this would be more fun than watching you rot in prison. Besides, a slick lawyer might get you off. ATF will eventually find the sale of the revolver and tell the DA."

Dave threw open the door. "Change of venue, counselor. We're walking down the street. Very casual suburban stroll. You run or give us trouble, the kid dies."

Emma used her gun to hammer my phone, then apparently not sure that did the trick, she dumped it into the toilet in the powder room next to the entryway. Dave threw the door open.

We strode out. Although the rain had stopped, the street was wet on my bare feet. They shielded their pistols tight against their hips, but I knew they would shoot quickly. Still no Jen in sight. I prayed she had taken a position where she could watch and not be seen. And prayed for a siren approaching.

They directed me to the right. I saw nobody out except some kids on the block well past my car, playing dodgeball. They probably hadn't noticed us in the gathering darkness. We marched toward the far reaches of the development which petered out into a deserted wheat field. After passing eight vacant-looking houses, four on each side, they told me to go up a driveway at a cul-de-sac on my left. The last house on the left. Of course.

I took a count. When Michael or Jen located my car, they'd have more than a dozen houses in the development to search in both directions from my BMW—on just this street. Smart of the Caswells to move me. I gave running serious consideration, but figured the nutcases would not hesitate to shoot me and they would still have Sarah. Also thought about going for Emma's gun, but Dave had one too. I'm good, but not that good.

Dave used a key and pushed me inside. The only furniture was a card table next to the front door with realtor business cards on it and a metal chair in the family room. Wood shutters on the front windows were closed. Pale light coming from bare windows in the back of the house didn't relieve the gloom.

With Emma keeping her gun pointed at me, Dave duct-taped me to the steel folding chair, my ankles tight to the chair's legs. This would be the trial, not *of* my life but *for* my life. No power meant no air conditioning. A sauna would have been cooler. The air was so muggy, I expected the mold to crawl along the floor. Sweat rolled down my sides. My deodorant was failing miserably.

Dave stood over me, his hands on his hips. "You are charged with the murder of my brother. How do you plead?"

"Guys, I didn't kill Tony. I didn't like him, but I didn't shoot him."

"Plead," he snarled.

Emma shrieked, far louder than Dave, "You had every reason to. He told the police about your scam to kill Stern's wife. If Tony hadn't died, you and your boyfriend would be on death row."

I tried to keep calm and direct my response to Dave. If I had any chance of getting out, it depended on him.

CHAPTER 38

"**H**E HATED MICHAEL for denying him partnership, for giving him crap assignments, and ragging him about his arm. That's why he concocted the story about—"

Emma slapped me. So much for my opening statement. Maybe *concocted* wasn't the right word.

"Shut up! Don't tell me my big brother lied."

I absorbed the sting and tried again. "We went out a couple of times. The last date didn't go well. That's part of the reason he—"

She hit me with the pistol this time, the hammer catching the corner of my mouth, tearing skin. I couldn't decide whether to look tough, like it didn't really hurt, or to wail, hoping she would think she didn't need to hit me harder next time.

"Tony told me you were a total skank. You put him in the hospital."

Blood dribbled down my chin. I went with *tough*. Adrenaline pumping, I blurted, "He tried to *rape* me."

She snarled, "Bullshit! You'd have loved it."

Maybe I shouldn't have accused their saintly brother. Should've said I jerked his dick out of his pants, but he wouldn't let me have it. Wanted to save himself for the woman he truly loved.

I went back on the offensive. "Your brother told the cops that we planned to kill Michael's wife. *That's* the bullshit."

She punched my belly. For a small woman she packed a wallop. "He told the truth."

Sucking air, I managed, "Maybe Tony got into an argument over country music or somebody tried to rob him."

She slapped me again. I tried to block out the pain and sputtered, "Why the hell do you think I did it?" If I could figure out what they had beyond insanity I might be able to convince them.

Dave spoke up, much calmer than Emma. "I'll tell you why. After we packed up Tony's stuff, I got into his computer and found the email. *'I KNOW. Meet at 11 Silver Spur.'* He was set up to go to that redneck bar. A perfect place for a murder. Noisy drunks all inside. And his wallet was still in his slacks. The email came from the public library."

I wanted to ask them why they didn't tell the police this little detail, but didn't dare. Had I known about the email I wouldn't have come on this foolhardy mission.

Dave added, "The witness said a tall woman was talking to him while he sat in his car. The 'know' had to mean you knew about his testimony and knew Stern killed his wife. And you are tall."

Emma moved close enough for me to absorb the spray as she shouted, "Enough of this. Confess!"

I had one last card to play. My own theory—my guess. Janet Wharton, Michael's girl Friday. The cops had questioned her. But they had no evidence, just as they didn't against me.

I addressed Dave. "Michael's paralegal was in love with him. Had been for years, but Michael never bit. The cops interviewed her several times, so *she* knew about their theory and who was providing evidence of a motive. Janet's as tall as I am."

Dave scowled, hopefully in thought. He lowered his pistol. I felt a surge of optimism.

But Emma slapped me again with her gun, clipping my ear. "That's horseshit."

"But, Emma—"

She cut Dave off. "Shut up! I'll make her confess."

Holy Mary, where was Jen? My ears strained to hear a siren. A knock on the door. Even a passing car. No luck. Blood trickled from my mouth and my ear. I watched Emma's forefinger, praying that she kept it off the trigger as she waved the automatic pistol around.

"You think Janet could've done it?" Dave asked.

I wasn't sure if the question was directed at me or Emma, but I nodded vigorously.

Seeming at least a bit curious, Emma lowered her weapon to her side.

I went on, "Janet would've done anything for Michael, and disappeared after I shot Marrs. The police checked. My gun didn't kill Tony. If you shot someone, wouldn't you leave town?"

I felt guilty, throwing Janet to these psychos, but hoped I could undo the damage later, assuming I lived to tell the tale. At least Janet wasn't sitting there getting pummeled. I considered telling them I had backup, that Jen would call the cops, but thought they might go ahead and shoot me if they learned they were out of time.

Dave frowned, perhaps considering my tale.

Emma shook her head. She didn't want anything but my blood. Mumbling something I didn't catch, she left the empty room.

"You got any proof?" Dave asked.

"Your brother was putting serious heat on Michael. The cops based their conspiracy theory on Tony's testimony. With him gone, their case fell apart. Janet could then make a grab for Michael. I had dumped him. At that point I didn't care what happened to Stern. He could go to prison, as far as I was concerned."

Dave stroked his chin, giving me as much hope as a forty-foot buzzer-beater. What I'd said was even partly true.

Emma returned with a pair of large tree pruners—the kind with a long handle and short blade. She worked them back and forth, getting an obvious thrill from the clipping sound.

"This talking is a big fucking waste of time."

My fear tripled, but I yammered on, "Janet had to know Tony was the source of inside information. What a heroic act. Kill my lover's tormentor. He'll be so grateful."

Dave still appeared interested. But not his sister.

"I swear. I was finished with Stern!"

Wielding the shears in one hand and her gun in the other, Emma elbowed past her brother. "I'll show you what torment feels like."

"Wait, Sis."

"Don't listen to this crap. She's guilty as sin, and I'm going to get a confession."

Emma put the shears aside and pounded the pistol against my temple. I saw stars, had to blink several times to refocus.

They argued for a minute while I fought to regain coherence.

Emma stuck her nose an inch from mine. "Tony called me the night you beat him up. I met him at the ER. He could have died. He nearly lost a testicle. All over a little fondling. I've wanted a piece of you ever since."

Blinking, I saw Emma had the pruners down by my foot. Then I felt the sharpest, most intense pain of my life. I'd had an ACL tear and a broken nose from a knee in the face during basketball, had taken hundreds of taekwondo blows, and had been shot by Marrs.

But when I looked down and saw that she'd cut off the smallest toe on my left foot, I had to stifle a scream.

The lovely little sadist hopped up and down, holding my bloody toe.

Dave's mouth gaped open. He seemed appalled, but said nothing.

"Spit it out!"

I wailed and cursed, but nothing helped. It wasn't just the pain; it was the visual too. The stump squirted a thin stream of blood and I couldn't avert my gaze.

She clamped the next toe in the blades. I tried to wiggle my foot away, but they had my ankle tied tight against the chair.

"No! Please!"

My eyes pleaded with Dave, but he turned away.

"Emma? Do we really want to . . .?"

She closed the blades, stopping her brother's musing. I stifled my scream. Christ, it hurt, but I didn't want to give her even more satisfaction. For some reason amputation number two hurt even more. Maybe more nerve endings in a bigger toe.

Dave bobbed his Adam's apple like he was going to throw up.

"I'll take another! 'Fess up, whore!"

I retched. As much from the shock as the pain.

Dave backed away, like he feared I would throw up on his slick tan loafers.

Emma stopped her jig and tossed my body parts back into my face. "You'll save twenty percent on pedicures." Another cackle of triumph. "Tell us!"

I choked on my spit, garbled more about my theory. Did my best to look and sound so pitiful that even these loons would feel sorry for me, take their pound of flesh and be done.

While I jabbered through the pain, I heard another snap of breaking bone. Worse this time. If possible. I was scared to look, but did anyway.

Another toe gone. My bladder emptied, soaking my pants.

"Want me to take another? Then we'll do fingers. I might decide to let you go, just to watch you walk like a penguin and eat like a dog out of a bowl." Emma squeezed the shears back and forth. "We'll mail the pieces to Stern."

This was far worse than getting shot. A bullet flies quickly and induces shock, which dulls the pain. Not to mention that, compared to Emma, parolee Leonard Marrs was completely rational. She was a living argument for the return of Victorian insane asylums.

As Emma bent to my foot again, I made the big decision. The same one I made the day Marrs had Sarah and me trapped. Better to die. This *loca* was fully capable of her threat. She'd seen lots of gore in hospitals. So that wasn't a problem for her. Even if, in the next hour, the police stormed the place, and I lived, what good would I be to anybody without fingers? I wouldn't even be able to wipe my butt.

Emma, her face a tomato, cranked the clippers back and forth an inch from toe four. The damn thing made the most horrible screeching sound, echoing in my head. That solidified my choice. Maybe if they disposed of me, Sarah could live.

I sucked as much air as I could get through my staccato breathing. What an incredible fuck-up. Dying at thirty-two. And failing to find Sarah.

Emma grabbed my ankle. She snared the next toe between the blades and yelled, "You did it, didn't you?"

I nodded. I'd gave up.

Dave smirked in triumph, some of the green fading from his complexion.

"I knew it." She shook her fist in the air, tossed the clippers to the side, and jammed the barrel of her gun against my temple.

I shuddered to think that Michael might find my brains splashed on the floor.

I prayed quickly to the Blessed Mother and Saint Teresa, asking them to pray for me, and begged Christ to forgive my many sins and receive me.

"Wait!" Dave shouted. "I want to hear the details."

"What do we care? We got a confession."

"If somebody gave her a gun or drove her, I want them too."

"Who helped you?" Emma asked.

A glimmer of hope, and I took it. I spit out, between waves of pain,

"Janet took me to the bar in her car. . . . She had a different caliber pistol and I used it. . . . We were afraid the cops would spot my car, since I was under suspicion. . . . She dropped her gun in the lake."

"Where the fuck is Janet?"

I garbled out, "I don't know, but Michael might."

Dave grinned, used his phone to call Michael, and pressed the speaker function.

He answered.

"Talk!" Dave barked.

I burned no time on preliminaries, couldn't control the shaking in my voice. "Do you know where Janet Wharton is?"

I sensed in his hesitation his effort to piece the situation together. He didn't have to be psychic to detect my agony.

"Are you with them? Are you okay?" Michael asked.

Dave glowered at me and shook his head.

"Do you know what happened to her?" I asked.

Again he stalled, but then said, "She disappeared right after you met me in the park that day and gave me another chance."

Purplish blood pooled around my bare foot. My breath came choppily when I spoke, "I looked for her just today. Around Frisco."

Hopefully Michael understood I was talking about Sarah, not Janet, and he could eliminate some of the addresses I'd gotten from the bank's lawyer. Michael could start looking for Sarah. If she lived, I could die in peace.

"I have no idea, but Randolph might know where *Janet* went."

He was likely telling me he didn't have a lead on Sarah.

Holy Mary, please.

Michael continued, "I could try to get hold of one of her kids in California. I had a number for emergencies."

"We've got to find her. *Fast.*" I hoped I conveyed urgency—that I couldn't hold out much longer.

I heard him typing on a keyboard. I'd saved the list of Nicky's foreclosures I'd gotten from the bank lawyer. My guess was Sarah was in one of them. Hopefully Michael could get people searching. Unfortunately the area covered two dozen square miles. Then I recalled the lawyer's warning that there might be other lenders getting scammed.

Shit.

"I'm looking on your computer. I'll call you back when I get a lead on . . . Janet," Michael said.

"You better find her, or your cutie will be sent home in pieces," Emma yelled.

A pause before Michael said he would do all he could and hung up.

I risked another beating, but couldn't stand to watch the bleeding. "Would you wrap my foot? Please . . ."

Dave shrugged, grabbed the pruners, and used them to cut a piece of cloth off the front of my shirt, exposing my belly. He wrapped the rag around the wound.

I begged him to tighten it.

He rolled his eyes.

But Emma knelt and did a pretty good job securing it. After all, she was a nurse. Even so, I wondered where the compassion suddenly came from.

For five minutes they whispered behind my back. Thankfully the bleeding slowed.

Finally the cell sounded.

Dave clicked on.

"Randolph said she went to work for a firm in Waco. I left a message with her son in L.A. to get an address. Her phone is unlisted, but I think I can find her. It may take a while."

Dave talked into his phone, "Call this number when you come up with it, but if you alert her or the cops, Kristen and Sarah both die. You've got half an hour."

CHAPTER 39

WHILE WE WAITED, Emma entertained herself by slapping me. I could take anything as long as she didn't have the pruners in her hands. I felt my face swelling and my vision blurred. I fought to stay alert, despite the nasty copper taste of blood filling my mouth.

I lost track of time during the pointless pounding. After a while, my face became so numb that the blows didn't hurt much. Emma must have discerned the diminishing effect and moved on to my chest.

The cell rang.

Dave answered with the phone on speaker.

"I need more time. We found out where she works. Robinson Weinstein, but they're closed for the day. Her home number's unlisted and the son hasn't called me back."

"Tough shit, asshole. She's dead!" Emma shouted.

Dave hushed her. "I'll give you ten more minutes. Your girlfriend's bleeding by the way." He laughed. "And in four pieces."

Michael's response came laced with panic, "I've called a private detective in Waco. He's going to track down a lawyer from the firm. It won't take long."

"Ten minutes." Dave clicked off.

Emma pointed at her brother. "Let's get out of here and head south.

We can be on the way while Stern searches."

"Should we kill her now?"

Emma rubbed the back of her pretty neck. "No. If she's telling the truth, she might help us with this Janet slut. Impress upon her the need to come to Jesus. And it'd be fun to cut her tits off."

"You sure?"

"Yeah. She's harmless."

Hiking his khakis, keeping the cuffs from getting wet with my blood and urine, Dave squatted and ripped the tape off my ankles. He left my wrists bound.

I staggered off the chair. The instant I leaned on my left foot, my leg buckled. Dave caught me. What a gentleman. The stubs started bleeding again through the cloth as I limped in excruciating pain.

They tread cautiously through my mess while escorting me at gunpoint through the empty kitchen. I left a blood trail to the back door leading to the garage. When Dave opened the back door I saw a Lexus sporting a dent the size of Becca in the right quarter panel. Another mystery solved.

Dave tapped the button for the electric garage door. It didn't work. Of course. No power.

Emma shoved me toward the backseat door. I left crimson footprints with each step. Dave walked to the end of the garage and hoisted the door up manually.

All three of us froze.

Because of the cul-de-sac the garage sat at an angle to the street and we could see back to 1734, where the excitement began. Headlights from a car parked in the street revealed a man dressed in khakis and a golf shirt walking up the drive. His belly fought against his belt, his back bent and pace measured, like he needed spine surgery.

He reached the front door, looked around, and appeared to search his chain for the correct key. Another figure sat in the front seat of the waiting car, but I couldn't tell whether it was male or female.

The smart thing to do would've been to scream or run, anything but stand there, leaning against their car on my unmaimed foot. But that's all I did. I just stood useless like one of Madame Tussaud's wax figures. Maybe I was in shock.

"Get back!" Dave said.

Shoving me along with them, they darted back into the house. In their haste, they left the overhead open, revealing their car.

Inside, the siblings argued.

"We left her shit there."

"Fuck! Why didn't you take it?" Emma snapped.

"How was I supposed to know?"

Emma peered through the window blinds. "He's going to the side door. I'm going to slip in and grab them," Emma whispered, as if the place had suddenly been bugged.

While Emma kept her weapon trained on me, Dave taped me back into the chair. He seemed grossed out by my bloody little toes lying on the white tile, and as a result only did a half-ass job. He probably didn't think me much of a threat. Hell, I *wasn't* much of a threat even to a roach crawling on the floor.

Telling her brother not to fuck up, Emma slipped out the back door without offering further encouragement. He rolled his eyes.

At least the looser of the two cannons was gone. I felt for the guy at 1734, with armed and crazy Emma coming.

Dave leaned against the kitchen countertop and eyed me. "I really liked your sister. She's great in the sack. Nice long legs to wrap around a guy's back. Good sense of humor."

"She's a lot of laughs."

He smiled. "Best fuck I ever had. You're almost as pretty, but I guess you're older."

"Yes."

"But I like older women. I bet you're as good as she is."

As I wondered why all of a sudden he was Chatty Cathy, an idea

349

germinated in the recesses of my beaten-up brain. But I knew not to look too eager, so I changed the subject. "You know that ADA, Livermore, would've charged me with Tony's murder if there'd been a shred, and I mean a *shred*, of evidence."

"Tony was helping Livermore get to the truth."

I bit back the pain throbbing with each heartbeat and tried to sound reasonable. "I got claw-raped and nearly killed rescuing Sarah from the worst psycho you can imagine. No matter what you think of Michael Stern, no way he would let that happen to his only child."

"So?"

"So the DA's theory of a grand conspiracy to hire Marrs to kill Diana was bullshit. Bullshit peddled by your bitter brother. For all I know Tony was the one who helped the parolee get inside the Stern house."

Dave laughed. "You think you're going to save Sarah again and be Stern's hero one more time? That he'll give up the booze and babes to marry *you*? What a fucking farce. He's probably already looking for new tail."

"Sarah had nothing to do with any of this. Please let her go."

Guffawing, slapping his thigh, Dave said, "Did we ever hose you! Sarah's at the *movies*."

"What are you talking about?"

"We have a niece at Hockaday. Lizzy. All the girls think Sarah Stern's the cool cat, fighting bad guys and starring in sports."

"What?"

"We got my niece to invite Sarah to the show after school was out early and softball was rained out. She'd been dying to do something with Sarah, but was too shy to ask. We timed our move on a day rain was forecast."

I did a double take. "You've got another sibling? With a girl at Hockaday?"

He shrugged. "A half-sister. Mom had three husbands. She doesn't know much about this business. Emma went to the school and, in the confusion from the bomb scare, Emma slipped Sarah's phone out of her backpack. When Sarah couldn't find her phone, my step-sister told her she'd text her dad."

His dopey grin pissed me off.

"You two planted the fake bomb?"

"Of course."

I cursed my stupidity. I was going to die for nothing.

"Sarah will be dropped off at her dad's. Of course you'll be dead by then. My half-sister has plausible deniability. *If* they find your body."

"So Emma set this whole thing up, got those kids killed, then shot Larsen with the gun I looked at?"

"And it was so fucking easy. Greedy lawyers will bite every time."

"But why kill children? And how did you select Larsen to play the patsy?"

"Well, the first really was a mistake. They had a tired dumbass assigned to that Dunn kid. But Emma was afraid you wouldn't bite on just one case. She even switched a lab report to perk your interest. As you can tell she doesn't like children, Mexicans, or drugged-out strippers."

"Yes, I gathered that."

"She used Sam Larsen two years ago to spy on her ex. She got the divorce in England where the guy was originally from—"

"Which is why I didn't find it."

"Yeah. She got a little carried away. I thought one more kid was enough after the mistake."

"Why did Emma follow Tina from school?"

Dave shrugged. "Her plans are always in flux. She's a little neurotic. Grabbing your sister was always an option."

A little neurotic? Give me a break.

"Was it you who had me attacked in the parking garage? And Tina?" I asked.

His eyes narrowed. "Huh?"

"You tried to scare me off the case?"

"What are you talking about?"

"Threatening me?" I asked.

He shook his head, like the kindergarten teacher admonishing a tyke who can't spell "dog." "Search me. You must have another enemy."

Stunned, my brain became a black hole. After a minute I asked, "Did you run over the girls?"

He nodded. "Too bad about the other kid. It was a spur of the moment opportunity. Just like when you decided to buy a gun. We had originally planned to steal yours."

"You followed me to the range. Bought the revolver I tried?"

"That was real serendipity. Firmed up the plot nicely."

He must've found tugging my chain exciting or was trying to impress me with his vocabulary. He strolled over, getting his face close. I guessed he was going to make a move—I just hoped I had enough time before Emma returned.

"You and Tina have the most luscious lips I ever saw. Something about Italians I guess."

He kissed me, swirled his tongue around. The pressure on my swollen lips was almost unbearable, but I responded. His aftershave and sweat made me want to puke and I could not imagine how he found a bloody face attractive, but I went along.

I eased my head back. "Did Emma kill the pharmacist?"

"Uh-huh. She dispensed the Heparin on the Dunn kid. Emma found out and had her by the short hair to get two more doses. Then she got all squeamish, and was going to confess to the hospital."

"Just to get to me," I muttered through my agony.

He laughed again like I was Amy Schumer. "The others can have more kids or don't need more."

"And Nicky?"

"Another bitch, who was well paid, but asked too many questions.

Servicing the horny slut should've gotten me a discount on the rent."

"I guess you knew I'd wind up at the dumpster."

"We paid a PI to follow you. Told the detective you were cheating on your boyfriend. That always motivates them to keep a close eye."

"The overnight case. Nicky's?"

"Ignorant cow nearly messed up the plans. I thought we could just run her off, but Emma didn't want to take chances with her."

I sensed his growing excitement. Something about talking to me definitely turned him on. "Were you going to grab Tina?"

"That was one possibility to get you here, but she split when she found Nicky's shit, so Emma decided to play it out this way."

"Why all this bother? I'm going back to jail tomorrow."

He smiled. "Emma ran out of patience. And they'll eventually figure out you didn't buy the gun."

Dave strolled toward the front door and set the gun on the card table, the only piece of furniture in the place, besides my execution chair. Dodging the gore, he hurried back, betraying his perverted desire.

He stopped in front of me, pulled my shirt up and fondled my sore breasts. I asked myself how Tina could possibly have slept with such a pile of human debris.

His tongue sticking out, his desperate expression was almost as repulsive as his mitts. But I quickened my breath, pretending to get a thrill, hoping his ego would let him buy my act. He twisted my nipples like they were car radio knobs, but I kept faking building excitement.

His hand slithered down to my crotch. I wanted to tell him his technique was as bad as his big brother's, but turned the volume up on my moaning. A finger probed me, but the discomfort was nothing compared to my injuries.

"Tina would want my dick. One more go-around before dying. You do too, don't you?"

I begged like a smoker, trying to quit, asking for one more Camel.

"Yes, please."

Dave unzipped his pants and flopped it out.

Lord have mercy, I had a chance. Men really are stupid—and I had the dumbest of all in front of me. Like I would put a nipple in his mouth if *he* were tied up?

It was already half-staff. Ironic how if you're not hot and breathless, a penis looks absurd. His looked absurd.

He grinned and waved the thing in my face for a minute.

I opened and he jammed it in my mouth. It tasted like he'd been sweating for hours, but I had to get him to think with the wrong organ.

I did my best for a minute, getting all four or five inches hard.

As he squeezed my breasts I remembered Dana's pal's admonition—you have to make them think you are turned-on. I smacked and moaned. You'd have thought I was humming the All-America quarterback and hoping he'd call me tomorrow.

Thanking God for the invention of oral sex, Dave's eyes drifted up, his breath quickened. I had him all in. My mouth quickly dried out—probably too much body fluid on the floor. Which fit with the plan.

I mumbled, "Let me use my hand too."

So eager and convinced this was the real deal, the moron pulled out. His shaking fingers peeled tape off my left hand. Maybe he thought I was as goofy as Tina—or that beaten up I was no threat. Or that I couldn't do much with my left hand. Or maybe he wasn't thinking at all.

Time to gather whatever energy I had left. I tightened every muscle, sucking oxygen through my nose, readying myself for the final sprint to the finish line.

Climax neared. *La petite mort* as the French say—the little death. And if I had my way Dave would get the big death. I felt the first dribble of semen. He was oblivious to the world and to me.

Time to roll.

I bit down as hard as I could, ground my teeth, tearing at it like a dog after a raw steak. At the same instant my free hand squeezed his balls and pulled as hard as I could, relieving hours of pent-up stress. I thrilled at the sound of crunching testicles and did my best to rip his scrotum off.

He shrieked like a banshee, but I hung on, gnawing and pulling. He wasn't going anywhere without me.

Payback, pal.

He clawed at my head, punched me, trying to pry my mouth apart. In two seconds one of his balls was mulch—totally detached. I dug my nails deeper into his scrotum, shredding a vessel and skin. Blood covered my hand.

Dave shrieked, "No! No! Please stop!"

He slipped in the mess on the floor, pulling the chair and me on top of him. I let go, spit blood, and tore the tape off my other hand and feet, untangling myself from him and the chair.

Dave tried to stand, but failed. Blood spewed from his groin like a fountain. His face screwed into a picture of agony. One hand on his crotch, he slithered for the gun he'd placed on the table.

Even on seven toes I would easily beat him to the weapon and he would soon be toast. But standing erupted more pain than I thought possible. Agony rippled up my leg to my head and my vision blurred. I must have had a concussion. It took a second to see the world as upright again.

Nevertheless I limped to the table, gaining on Dave.

Come on, Kristen. Another step or two.

But my feet flew out from under me as I slipped in the blood and piss on the floor—mine and his. I recovered, tried to stand, and lost my balance again. Damn it to hell. Wet soles would be the death of me.

Having burned so much adrenaline, I couldn't stand. I decided to crawl. My foot screamed relief at no longer supporting my weight. Somehow, Dave had been smarter than me. I should have slid on my ass to the gun like he did.

Despite keeping a hand on what remained of his equipment, Dave reached the table. Rising to his knees, he clawed for the weapon. And snatched it.

I was going to die. I tried one more time to stand. Although I'd reached dry marble my feet were still wet. I couldn't even stand up to face my executioner.

With one bloody hand Dave gripped the revolver, but fumbled it. He wiped his palm on his pants and tried again.

I pulled myself along, hurrying closer. Time seemed to come to a halt. Doomsday would probably feel about like those few seconds.

Dave's slick fingers caused his grip to loosen and his aim to wobble. He transferred the weapon to his left, dragged his wet right hand across his chest, switched hands again, and pointed. His bleeding worsened—a little red fountain driven by his rising heart rate—while using both hands to handle the revolver.

Like a duelist who had already fired, I tried to get small.

Before he could shoot, the doorknob turned.

I froze. Dave turned expectantly toward the door.

When Emma saw her little brother, I'd be returned to Michael in a hundred pieces.

CHAPTER 40

THE DOOR FLEW OPEN, hitting Dave's arm and knocking him off balance. He bobbled the revolver into his bloody lap.

"Hello?" A deep male voice cloaked in curiosity called from the front door, "What's going on?"

A man, maybe fifty, with pasty skin and horn-rimmed glasses resting on a bulbous nose, stood in the entry. Jelly rolls on both sides overlapped his belt. He must have been one of the people in the car at 1734.

"Help!" I screamed. "Get the gun!"

He stared, clueless, eyeballs wide at the sight of Dave—bloody, without pants—and me bloody, barefoot, and without three toes.

I got a bit more specific: "Get the *fucking* gun!"

He finally moved, faster than I would have expected, and snatched the pistol out of Dave's faltering grip.

For a second the guy seemed unable to decide who to assist. He gave my beaten face a quick up and down, stared at my foot a second, then carrying Dave's gun, hurried toward me. The interloper's trouser cuffs skimmed the gore. He slipped, righted himself, and knelt beside me, asking if I was okay.

"There's another one coming!"

He had the wide-eyed, open-mouthed look of "What the hell did I get into?"

I could tell he didn't know who was the villain, and I sure didn't have time to explain.

Somehow I found a surge of energy and, hopping onto my good foot, *ordered* him to give me the gun. I didn't know his experience with killers, but he didn't look like an ex-Green Beret.

He scanned the room, taking in the carnage. I thought for a second he might pass out. His hands shook as he sputtered incoherent questions.

Out of patience I finally ripped the pistol from him, then shuffled with eight-inch steps, like in jail, over to Dave. He was struggling to staunch the stream of blood and his deathly pale complexion reflected sheer terror.

"Please don't kill me. It was all Emma's idea."

What a chicken shit—blaming his sister. I savored a moment of triumph over the miserable sadist. Bad as I wanted to shoot him, I figured the cops would charge me with *his* murder. But pistol whipping him twice across the temple brought me great joy.

The thud Dave made when he hit the floor sounded lovely. He moaned, barely conscious, and the blood kept squirting. I guess he had a strong heart.

"Now call the police!"

I guessed Emma would come in through the kitchen door, where she'd gone out, since the garage was still open. Hopefully she'd missed the other poor soul in 1734.

I tried to gather my wits. No point fleeing for my car. I couldn't outrun a pregnant hippo. Emma could walk back in any second. No cover between the two entrances, only a corner of kitchen granite.

The intruder still hadn't called. He must have thought he'd stumbled into Dante's third level of hell. He asked more questions. If I'd had the energy I would have thrown him out the door. If I had to shoot it out with Emma I needed him out of the way.

"Call the cops and get the hell out of here! These people are killers!" No time for modesty. I turned my back to the guy, pulled off my shirt, and wiped my slick feet, then pulled the sticky thing back on.

Blushing he patted his pockets. "Must have left my phone in the car."

"Then get the fuck out and find it!" He hesitated, apparently unsure he should leave me. "There's going to be shooting in here. Go!"

"I'll get help." He finally shuffled to the front door, taking a last look at Dave exsanguinating on the marble foyer.

I knew I was running out of time and stationed myself in the kitchen behind the built-in granite breakfast bar—the best spot to waste Emma the second she strolled in. All the walking made my foot bleed faster, leaving a trail as I went. As I reached a good sniper spot for the kitchen entrance, I heard a shot from the front door.

I scooted on my butt around the countertop toward the gunfire. Peeking around the corner, I saw the stranger down, bleeding from his torso.

Shit!

Emma slipped around the intruder and grabbed her brother's arm, trying to get him upright and pull his pants up.

I crouched and fired. My line of sight through the dining room was narrow and although I didn't care which Caswell I hit, I didn't want to finish off my angel of rescue. When the gun practically flew out of my hand with the first shot I realized I must have been in worse shape than I thought and that Dave's revolver was a piece of crap, not the smooth-operating Browning automatic I owned. Still bleary, I wasn't sure I could have hit the ocean standing on a dock.

Emma loosed a hail of lead toward me.

In old gangster movie shootouts, the good guy sticks his head up, fires, then ducks when the villain shoots back. Back and forth it goes until the bad guy gets it and dies bloodlessly. Not here. I didn't dare risk a look.

Her gun sent slugs flying in an almost continuous roar chewing into the wood under the granite top. Thank God there was enough material to stop the slugs. I risked sticking my hand around the counter and fired, mainly to keep her from charging behind a shield of lead.

Bullets plowed into the cabinet inches above my head. What an idiot. With all those rounds in a Sig Sauer, she could have advanced behind the cover of her fire and taken me out while I crouched out of sight. But I guess Emma was braver while I was tied up. And when she killed kids.

I shot again, intentionally aiming high. Missed everybody.

More bullets whizzed above my hair. If I'd had my Browning and been able to run, I would have circled out of the garage and taken her by surprise and the world would have been a better place.

More shots. She must have loaded another mag. Or maybe she had my pistol. The destruction pattern moved higher with each shot. Emma obviously didn't know automatics drift up if you empty the magazine too quickly. I guessed she'd fired at least twenty and prayed she didn't have *another* fucking magazine.

The last couple of rounds sounded like they came from farther away, maybe out the doorway. After half a minute of silence, I chanced a peek, then crept into the family room. Emma and her brother had split, leaving a stream of crimson out onto the porch.

The intruder lay in a puddle of blood. By now the first floor of the house looked like a slaughter house. I crept over the litter of spent cartridges and checked his carotid, found a pulse, and decided I'd better help this guy rather than go after the slimeballs, even though I still had two bullets left.

The car in the garage started and pulled out, leaving us behind. Good news at last.

Feeling utter exhaustion I raised his shirt and applied as much pressure to his abdomen as I could muster. Purplish warm blood oozed between my fingers. The wound to his belly must have missed his abdominal aorta, since I stemmed the tide some with my hands, but his guts had been chewed up. If he was lucky it had missed his liver. He groaned and wiggled his feet in pain, actually a good sign.

Surely someone had to have had heard the gunfire. Again time seemed to stop. His breath became irregular, choppy and shallow, like he had asthma. His face had turned ashen.

"Hang on, whoever you are."

The stubs where my toes had once been still trickled blood and screamed in torment, like I could still feel the instant they were sliced. My skull felt pounded by a mallet; my face stung like I'd stuck firecrackers in my mouth and then lit them . . . but it felt incredible to be alive. I felt like I'd been given a new life—one I didn't deserve.

I heard a far-away siren and hoped it meant help was coming.

I kept pressing the poor fellow's belly with blood-stained hands and the noise grew louder.

Thank you, Blessed Mother.

CHAPTER 41

I OPENED MY EYES and realized it was still night. My lids felt like dusty old curtains in an abandoned house, after being taped down by the anesthesiologist during my emergency micro-surgery. I saw Michael sitting on a stool by my bed, holding my hand, and raised my head enough to peer down at the dressing on my foot.

I vaguely recalled the paramedic scooping up my parts, leaving in another ambulance after the realtor had been taken, and briefly waking to find a nurse scrubbing Betadine on my stumps before they slapped the anesthesia mask on my face, with Michael and Tina standing near the OR door until the circulator closed it. And right before I went to sleep a pretty surgeon telling me she would try her best.

Michael, drawn and lined like he'd been up all night, said, "They're all reattached and getting blood flow. You also got a couple stitches around your mouth and on your ear. Your head CT was negative. So they're calling it a concussion."

Slumped in the lounger, Tina joked, "She's so hard-headed I'm surprised the radiation penetrated her skull."

"Don't let this make you miss class," I mumbled.

"I know—you paid for the tuition."

Michael signaled timeout before a sister spat could really get going.

"Sarah?"

"She's at her aunt's."

"Thank God." I felt myself sliding back to sleep.

Sunlight woke me again. It must have been the next day. Before I could ask about her, Sarah bounded into the room, carrying red and yellow roses—obviously fine. Dave hadn't lied, and my ordeal had been totally unnecessary. I'd panicked and played the fool—a common undertaking for me.

Sarah set the flowers next to the bed and kissed my cheek.

Michael squeezed my big toe which stuck out of the dressing. "The surgery went well. The doc said that a sharp sever actually helps, and not much time had elapsed. They'll hurt, though."

A PCA pump sat on my left. My line and the saline bag were on the right. I could juice myself with narcotics as needed, up to what had been prescribed. Right then I needed another jolt and pressed the button. Soothing warmth spread through me and the pain faded. I saw how some people became opioid addicts.

"I'm so sorry," Sarah said.

For a second I thought she might cry. I certainly couldn't blame her and it wasn't my place to lecture Sarah about staying in touch.

Michael continued, "Garden shears aren't exactly clean. You're getting broad-spectrum antibiotics and an anti-fungal." Michael's voice became more serious. "We'll know soon whether there's an infection. Always a danger." He paused, real serious now. "You know we can't risk it getting systemic."

I nodded. A systemic blood infection, bacteremia, would mean they'd take my toes right back off, and close the stumps, and I'd be in danger of sepsis. I decided to do a Scarlet O'Hara.

I'll think about that tomorrow.

"What about the other guy? The one who stumbled into the mess?"

"Max Jennings is his name. His company has the contract to sell houses on that block. He's out of surgery. They're optimistic. He got four units, but the slug missed his liver. He'll poop in a bag for six months, but it can be reversed," Michael said.

"Does he have family?"

"Yes. They want to meet you. You saved his life. His partner called 9-1-1 when he heard the shots. Fortunately Jenkins's pal just missed Emma. Apparently he had decided to go next door when she roared over there to retrieve your stuff."

Through my rising stupor from the morphine hit, I replied, "No, he saved mine."

Michael tucked his chin and eyed me from beneath lowered eyebrows. "By the way, I disobeyed orders. I had already called the cops before he did."

I raised my head an inch and said, "I love you. Both of you."

Sarah piped up. "Let's get a judge or a priest up here. Dad and I'll keep you out of trouble."

"Damn right we will."

I smiled. They probably would. Had I taken him up on his offer months ago, I wouldn't be stitched together. "What about the Caswells?"

"No sign of them. I think Dave's going to need a doctor soon, though, so they're watching hospitals."

I could tell Michael didn't want Sarah to know any details of where poor Dave was injured and especially how he got that way.

"Am I going back to jail?"

"They agreed you can stay out—pending further investigation."

The relief that washed over me felt like a call from the lab saying the biopsy was normal. Maybe they'd even believe me when I told the cops what Emma had admitted to. Maybe.

"Will you get me a toothbrush?"

CHAPTER 42

I WAS A BIG WIMP, taking all the morphine they let me have. Besides dulling the pain, it helped me forget. Forget the blood, the terror, chomping on Dave, and the worry that I might still go back to jail. Call me a cynic, but I didn't trust the system.

Michael left for a nap after the morning commotion of the hospital routine began. Taking over my roll of big-sister-enforcer he had insisted Tina go to class. It wasn't like I was in danger of dying, after all.

My doctor, a micro-surgeon about my age, popped in. Her wide mouth and perfect teeth combined into a wonderful smile for someone who had been up late piecing me together. Her training was in plastic surgery and I admired her for saving limbs, instead of getting rich augmenting boobs.

She told me the circulation in my reattached toes was "acceptable." My CBC showed high white count, but some elevation was to be expected from trauma alone. She'd get another draw in the afternoon. I thanked her as she left.

Though my mouth felt sore I was able to eat oatmeal and some fruit. But the coffee seemed to perk up the pain in my head. After the nurse took my vitals, I went back to sleep. She'd re-dosed my pain pump and I took full advantage. Daughter of the Kerrys—drug addiction must be in my DNA.

Sometime later that morning I heard Sarah and shook off my slumber. She and Becca flanked my bed.

I glanced down and was glad to see Becca putting partial weight on her leg.

"Hey, sister," Becca said.

"Yo, guys. What's up?"

"Dad said we could hang with you and make sure they don't give you an enema or take your gallbladder by mistake."

I chuckled. "Thanks. How you doing, Becca?"

"Good. It only hurts when I do my therapy."

"Dad told me to tell you he would be back after he showered," Sarah said.

"That's okay."

I didn't share with them what I knew about the accident. Better to let Sarah's friend think the world was a safe, happy place. At least for a while.

We chatted for a minute, though I didn't feel much like small talk with teenagers.

"We're going to get Starbucks across the street. Want anything?"

"A pedicure."

They laughed and sauntered out.

I hurt and wanted a hit of narcotic in the PCA pump. I wasn't due another for two hours, but decided to be greedy. I felt myself dozing off.

* * *

Someone whispered my name.

I opened my eyes to see Pete McGee, my old boss, looking at me with that fake sad face I'd seen before.

"I'm so glad that you're all right."

For a second I thought I was dreaming, then said, "Thanks." I figured that was lie number one. I raised the bed, mighty leery of what the hell he was doing here, and waited for the next fib.

Pete set his stocky frame down in the chair. "We had an incident at Adventist late last night while you were getting sewn up."

I wanted to ask why he was telling me, but let him continue.

"It seems someone stole medications from the hospital. Antibiotics, narcotics, lidocaine, even surgery supplies."

Emma. She'd used her ID to get in and grab what she needed to treat her brother.

Pete cleared his throat. "The police today matched prints in the storage area to the ones at the scene of your, shall we say, latest adventure."

"I wonder how he's doing with a stump."

Pete blushed, ever the Southern Baptist. "Quite an injury."

"And where's my ol' pal Jen? She said she'd help me."

"Help you?"

"Follow me to the address. What happened to her?"

"Kristen, I honestly don't know."

I let my skepticism show. If Dave had told me the truth, then Pete or Jen had probably paid for my mugging. Pete was here, Jen wasn't. Even in my condition it was not hard to put two and two together without a calculator. I knew I could never prove it, but they had the incentive to scare me off the cases. But Pete was too big a pussy to order it. So I guessed Jen did it.

Pete wiggled a forefinger at me. That pissed me off. I'd left home sixteen years ago partly to escape finger wagging. My expression warned him.

He took the hint and lowered his hand, but said, "You'd be in one piece had you listened to our advice. But you always were stubborn."

That did it. "You bastard!"

He *had* hired the toughs. I wanted to haul him down to the parking garage and grind his nose in the concrete. And I would have, except it might not have helped my client. That, and I wasn't sure I could walk and lug a man downstairs.

I got some satisfaction seeing his flash of fear and knowing *he knew* I could break his flabby neck.

His Botoxed face blushed. "Please, I didn't *personally*, but I should have stopped it. They went a little overboard. I'm very sorry. Especially about your sister."

"Tina had nothing to do with it. She didn't deserve a beating."

He made another lips-down face of remorse, like he'd hit his golf ball into the water.

"I'm so, so sorry they got rough, but Kristen, listen . . ."

I glared, stopping his blather before it escaped his mouth. "I'm listening." Beating up my little sister was going to cost him plenty.

"We believe we have a legal defense to the last two deaths. We can't be held liable for the criminal conduct of Nurse Peyton. Clearly unforeseeable. Certainly on the Rodriguez child, who was the first she murdered."

"Two cases?"

"Our investigation revealed one syringe was inadvertently mixed up without the LPN checking the dosage. That was the Dunn baby, and the first to die. We will try to settle that case. I understand they're nice folks."

"Yes."

Dave had been honest. Imagine that.

I knew that Pete's wife traced her lineage back to a guy at the Alamo and belonged to some dumb club like Daughters of Texas or something. He sat on the board of every bank and charity in town. They carry their noses so high, I wonder how they can see the sidewalk. I realized his attitude toward Alberto and Sierra wasn't much better than Emma's.

He continued in an unctuous, condescending tone, "The Sayers child was the last to die, and thus perhaps the only intentional death we might owe on a theory of not supervising an obviously insane employee. We will fight the Rodriguez claim, unless their lawyer gets very reasonable."

Ever the bullshitter, Adventist wanted the cases buried with the children. Not good PR to let folks know it hired nurses who murdered patients. By approaching me first, they hoped to defuse the worst problem, the one with notorious little me—the one most likely to land in the paper. Once I settled, the others would probably fall in line.

"So what do you have in mind?"

Pete shifted from one hip to the other, like he needed to fart. He probably wanted me to toss out a number first so he could undercut that. If I offered to take a dollar, he'd counter at fifty cents and hope to get it done for seventy-five. But I was in the power position now, so I let him sweat.

After a minute he said, "I shouldn't be so frank, but Adventist instructed me to settle Sayers for under three million."

"They gave you three in authority and you want to look good by saving the hospital a few grand."

He smirked. "You were always perceptive. That's why I hired you."

He'd want a non-disclosure agreement as part of the deal. He didn't want me sharing what I knew of their Emma Nightingale with the other plaintiffs—or worse, trying to retrieve the files myself now that it looked like I was off the hook on my charges.

I stalled, adjusting the IV line around my arm.

"Kristen, that would mean a million dollar fee."

He offered the kind of smile he'd give his yardman when dispensing his annual fifty-dollar Christmas bonus. I only resisted telling him to fuck off because I wanted to get all I could for Dana.

"Quite a coup for a start-up firm," he added.

That got my Irish up. I'd paid a lot of dues to be called a "start-up" and had a shit load of stitches to prove it. But three was fair. Really more than fair. Adventist had a chance of skating the case entirely under the theory of intervening cause, the act of a madwoman.

If a defendant can't foresee an event, he generally can't be liable. The hotel isn't liable if the bellhop murders guests in their bed, unless the guy wore a picture of the Boston Strangler on his shirt to the job interview.

While I smoldered, Pete tossed in, "That would be a million each, tax-free, for two barely employed young people. Certainly more than Dana can get taking off her clothes."

So he knew Dana stripped. The slimeball was like most rich people. Give the chumps some change and they'll be thrilled, no matter the circumstances. They can always make more babies. He figured they'd just snort or inject it all in a few months anyway.

Gritting my teeth I sat up straighter, more than annoyed that Pete had seen me flat on my back practically naked in a hospital gown, my iodine-stained, bare foot sticking out of the sheet.

He took the hint and rose, his face knotted in perplexity. Maybe he was afraid I was going to lurch out of bed and throttle him.

I made him wait a moment. "I won't take less than four. And though it's not any of your business, my fee is going to be a fourth and I'm giving a quarter million of it to the Jenkins family."

A look of desperation crossed his face. He'd screwed up by being candid—a rare error for him. He seemed to recover and said, "That's more than the authority they gave me. Honestly, Kristen."

Honestly. A real first for Pete.

"I'll give you a release for the hospital and you personally for conspiracy, aggravated assault of both me and my sister, and a confidentiality order. Even promise not to hustle the other cases back. Those items ought to be worth an extra million."

He said nothing. Robert E. Lee must have looked as defeated when he met Grant. It's incredibly enlightening when someone you used to respect hits the bottom of the snake hole.

Michael had been right all along. Pete, my former father figure, was a sanctimonious hypocrite. And a thug. And I'd gotten sucked into his act. It was a bit like falling for a guy because his lantern jaw and overbite were endearing, then after the relationship ends deciding they were repulsive.

"Thanks for coming by," I said with barely disguised sarcasm.

Sucking on his lips, looking like his dog had just been run over, Pete said, "I'll get the four."

An extra million dollars just fell into my lap. And I didn't give a damn.

* * *

It took a while, but I finally calmed down enough to slip back into a narcotic semi-sleep. I saw Emma cranking the shears. My fingers flying across the room as she dismembered me. A Quentin Tarantino movie. Then I saw Marrs, the parolee, pointing my own gun at me and Sarah gagged and bound. I screamed.

Someone said, "Are you all right?" pulling me out of the nightmare spiral.

My anesthesiologist, a guy I'd met on a case while at Wright McGee, had poked his head in the door. "Doing okay?" he asked.

"Yes. I think so."

"Need anything more for the pain?"

I didn't want to look like an addict and shook my head.

"Hang in there. By the way . . . Your sister's darling."

I recalled Tina chatting with him before I went under. Hope he asked for her number.

"Thanks for gassing me."

He smiled. A very nice smile. Maybe something good would come out of this mess.

I tried the pump again and mercifully got a hit. This time I dreamed of the wedding. Picking up Brandon and Beth at DFW. Michael looking resplendent. Sarah beaming with excitement.

* * *

I sensed, more than heard, a nurse putting something in the bag hanging over me. To the extent I had any awareness, I assumed it was more Vancomycin or Amphotericin. Through my stupor I noticed the small, freckled woman, with cropped hair and a button nose, who wore the correct uniform.

She leaned over and whispered in my ear, "You cost three nurses their careers. Did you think I'd let you get away with that?"

I recognized the voice. Jen.

"I loved Casey. She left me, moved to Maryland and hung herself. You didn't even know or care."

"What are you doing?"

My ol' buddy from Wright McGee closed the bag with a chuckle. A friend, supposed to tail me to Dave's, to protect me; who wanted to stop a psycho at her beloved hospital; who mysteriously got lost.

The room spun. My veins burned like she had lit them with a torch. I couldn't hold my head up. Then vision faded. My heart sped. I thought it might explode.

She whispered: "Payback, girlfriend."

Somehow I managed to reach up and grab a handful of her hair. She let out an "Eek."

I had little strength, but pulled as hard as I could.

I heard the kids bound back in just as Jen yanked her head back.

"Hey," Sarah said. "What's going on?"

"Were they *fighting*?" Becca asked.

I could only mumble, "Stop the line." I doubt it came out louder than a whisper.

"What's that?" Sarah asked, likely not hearing me.

I tried again, "Stop." I felt like I had shouted, but nobody seemed to hear.

"Medicine," Jen answered, fixing her hair.

"Like *duh*. What medicine?"

I faintly heard Becca laugh, then add, "Somebody came in just a while ago and put stuff in there."

Holy Mary, the kids really were watching out for me. My guardian angels.

Jen ignored Sarah and edged close to me again. "I always planned to get even. Emma was the inspiration. They'll blame the pharmacy for your death and there's nobody to sue since you and Scumbag Stern aren't married."

It took a second to process this. I was being murdered. After all I'd survived, a "friend" would be the instrument of my early death.

My heart began to slow. I realized that she had put, whatever it was that was killing me, into the bag instead of directly into my IV so she could be out of the hospital when I arrested.

"Pete and I warned you to follow orders and stay away from Stern. But you had to be honest. And horny. Hope that dick was worth it."

Sarah must've overheard some of what Jen whispered. "Stay away from who?"

Becca answered, "I think she said your dad. I think she called him *scum*."

"What? Are you talking about my father?"

The vial plopped into the trash and I felt like blood was congealing around my heart, squeezing cardiac muscle. Which it probably was. Panic seized me, but I couldn't react, couldn't do anything.

I managed with maximum effort to keep my eyes open and saw Sarah grab the bottle from the trash.

"Help . . ." I tried again.

"I, uh, think Kristen said, 'Help,'" Becca stammered.

"Potassium chloride? My dad told me they use it to stop people's hearts in bypass surgery. I got to watch part of one once," Sarah said.

"Kristen doesn't look very good. Something's wrong."

"You're not our regular nurse," Sarah snapped.

Sarah grabbed my wrist with one hand and ripped the IV out, tearing my skin. Blood dripped to the sheet. What a brave, confident, assertive kid. Any other teenager would at most have asked questions, maybe gone down the hall or called her dad. The seconds she saved gave me a chance. A slight chance.

Somewhere in my fogging brain I remembered it only took a little to kill, but couldn't remember how much. Jen would know the correct dosage even how much to mix in the bag of fluid. Squeezing the line and putting it straight into the hep-lock would have only taken a second or two, so I was lucky Jen wanted to escape.

Sweat soaked my gown. The last real-world thing I saw was Jen, wearing blue scrubs, hurrying out.

I felt my heart flutter, then stop. Feeling no pain, absolutely nothing, a total void of sensation, I realized I had died.

* * *

And then I saw it. A tunnel. Bright light at the end. Wow! Amazing! The light more beautiful than a cathedral at Christmas.

Hanging at the edge of the tunnel I hovered over the scene like a spectator, totally uninvolved.

The alarm on the pulse ox, hooked on my forefinger, went off like a tornado warning. Purplish venous blood ran onto the floor from my arm. The line dangled in the air.

Becca hobbled from the room screaming for help. Sarah leapt onto the bed, tore my gown open and began pushing on my bare chest.

I remembered she'd had CPR training for babysitting jobs. She performed correctly, hand over hand, to the beat of "Stayin' Alive."

The kid was strong and pushed hard. It would've hurt had I been able to feel anything. Her father would be proud. Heck, I was proud even as I floated above her, an angelic stepmom. After the correct thirty pushes, she blew in my mouth.

A lovely kiss good-bye.

My vision of the scene below faded. I saw the four Kerry kids throwing snowballs, wolfing down grandmother Spinello's pie, playing basketball against the Murphys and the Donnellys. Italians against Irish, and we almost always won. Even the boys couldn't outshoot or outrun me, including my brother. The crowd standing and clapping at my twenty-eight straight made free throws as a senior. Still a school record. Finally getting to play in a Division One game. Michael taking me into his arms that night in Vail.

I saw only pleasant memories, no slaps from my father. No guns or knives pointed at me. Things like that must not happen at the other end of the tunnel—a good reason to let go.

As I took it all in one last time, three people rushed into the room with a cart. All had a panicky, harried look, but moved with purpose.

Sarah hollered, "It was potassium!"

The team's faces, as one, went wide-eyed in shock. One young guy in a white jacket shoved Sarah out of the way and hopped onto the bed. His pushes looked harder, yet I still felt nothing.

A gray-haired, short woman slapped defib paddles onto my bare chest.

Another nurse crammed a tube down my throat, then pumped oxygen down it with a bag. Still another started a new line in the other arm and pushed medicine in it. Fast. A young tech wrapped my bleeding arm.

The tunnel beckoned me. It sloped toward the light. How could I resist? Just slide down.

No more pain. No more guilt. Come on, Kristen, let go. They'll all be fine without you.

But I looked back down one more time. The young resident yelled something about "calcium." That seemed to make them redouble their effort.

They hadn't given me a mirror since I arrived. I saw why. Welts rose at the top of each cheekbone. My lips puffed out like I'd been in the ring with Hilary Swank in that boxer movie. The swollen left orbit almost covered my eye. No wonder my vision had been fuzzy. What a mess. Surprised I hadn't scared the kids off. Maybe Michael had warned them not to act grossed out.

The woman I saw should've been embarrassed. So many people were seeing her bruised little boobs. Brown nips from her Italian mother. Her belly looked okay. Not as good as when she ran hurdles in college, but great for a thirty-something lawyer. Why had she been so paranoid about losing her man?

With that I decided to release my grip on the world. The amusing reflection on my body had been a pleasant diversion, but time to go— explore another universe. I only wanted to tell Sarah good-bye first. Michael and my siblings, too. I worried about how Beth in Philly would take the news and hoped Tina could find the maturity to take her in.

The paddles connected to a machine that looked like a telephone. Lots of numbers flashed.

Someone hollered, "Clear!"

My body jumped.

I felt nothing.

Sarah wailed around the corner. "Please, God, save Kristen! Please! Please!"

Becca joined her. They sounded like a Gospel group. Tears rolled down Sarah's beautiful face. Becca's hands shook as she clasped them together in fervent prayer. I guess Donna had taken her to church. There's good in everybody.

Someone touched me at the opening of the tunnel. A woman—I couldn't make her out, more like felt her presence, but she hugged me, like I was a child and she a young mother.

I yearned to go with her down the tunnel. So easy it would be to let go and slide away.

Then she shook her head. Did I see that or just sense it? I can't say.

Maybe I was hallucinating, my remaining live neurons firing. Perhaps I'm spouting nonsense. But I swear, the last instant I saw her, she mouthed: *"Someday, but not now."*

Then she disappeared down the corridor.

I felt overcome with emotion. Maybe I wasn't a bad person after all.

My torso rose again. This time the paddles felt cold. The tunnel disappeared.

I felt a touch on my hand. Sarah had slipped around to the other side of the bed and was squeezing my fingers together.

She cried "No!" over and over again.

They shooed her out, but I heard Sarah from the doorway, "Kristen, you *can't* die."

She sobbed so loudly I worried she might choke.

She needed me. Really. After losing her mother, she might never recover from watching me die. It felt great to be wanted. I did my best to focus on the present, to come back. I grit my teeth and clawed my way back to the world.

"We got a pulse!" one of the nurses shouted.

I felt intense pain in my chest. Had they broken a rib? Damn it hurt.

Air rushed down the tube, filling my empty lungs. The best breath I'd ever taken.

The EKG line started bouncing around. They'd done a great job. Just like the textbook. Even with providers on hand, only about a fourth of arrest victims ever walk out of the hospital. The CPR Sarah had initiated, sending a little oxygen to my brain, probably bought enough time for me to survive.

My heart thumped against my chest wall. Warmth flooded my fingertips. I could feel my face pinking up.

Becca and Sarah cheered and hugged each other. I could hardly wait to hug them. And Michael. And go to Mass.

CHAPTER 43

IDIDN'T GET QUITE ENOUGH of the drug to kill me. On the second defib, with epi and lidocaine, they got my heart restarted. An in-house hospitalist pushed insulin and calcium to counteract the potassium. Once they had a blood pressure, they rolled me out to dialysis to cleanse my blood. Everyone was running, hurrying like I was somebody important. Maybe they guessed I was important to the crying kids.

Later they called my survival "pretty damn miraculous." One young doctor asked me what my religion was. When I told him, he said he was converting. I should let the bishop know I'd won a convert.

Not one doctor or nurse seemed to know or care that I was a plaintiff's lawyer and a traitor on the *Layne* case. Or that I testified against my own surgeon-father. They all seemed to care about *me*. Amazing.

A full arrest can cause permanent brain damage. After reflecting like Descartes I decided if I could worry about it, I didn't have any. Or at least not much.

NMNS—Not Mary but sure not shit.

* * *

Michael must've flown like Superman back to the hospital, since it didn't seem long before he was sitting in my ICU room. He was pale. Frankly I hoped I looked better than he did. The warmth of his hand on mine reaffirmed I was alive. He apologized profusely about leaving me with another murderer.

I managed a little smile. The kiss, which lingered only a second, may have been his best ever. He said wonderful things, words like "forever," "love," and "side-by-side." Tears ran down his cheeks. I think I'd have to do something even more stupid than dealing with Larseny to lose him.

But don't push your luck.

They only let one person in at a time in ICU. Sarah replaced her dad after a while. I got a peck on the cheek as good as Michael's kiss. She was telling me about her new team when I dozed off. Even while I slept, I sensed their presence and knew they'd never let anything happen to me.

By morning I could watch my own vitals on the monitor. I assured the cardiologist that my pressure always ran low. He remarked that my fitness helped save my life, along with the action of a teenage girl. Had I gotten any more potassium, there wouldn't have been a heart left to revive. Those races I'd run after college for no good reason, other than not wanting to sit at the office alone, turned out to have a good reason.

I ate, napped again, and woke to the micro-surgeon examining my foot. She didn't look happy. No wide smile. The shock and collapse of my blood pressure compromised the circulation in the extremities and toes are about as far from the heart as a body part gets.

She said two looked dusky and felt cool. She didn't have to say anything else, and didn't.

They took the two smallest toes off that night. A day later I lost the next one. I'd probably never win a race again.

* * *

With no evidence of infection and my blood cleansed, I got kicked out of the hospital two days later. After a celebratory dinner that night, Michael insisted on no extracurricular activity, though I would've been game.

I called Dana, waking her up early in the afternoon. Through her whoops of joy, I warned her that she had a new mom. Me. No stripping. I would tell Pete most of the money should be assigned to an annuity, paying monthly, with bonus payments for college. No cash sitting around for another slob to steal.

I'd deliver the money for tuition directly to the college of her choice. She agreed to my short leash without protest. Made me feel like I'd actually done some good. Not a common experience for a lawyer. I told Troy he'd have to repay me for his ER bill out of his share.

Not entirely trusting Pete's *mea culpa* on behalf of the hospital, I also phoned Laura Dunn from a landline and, without identifying myself, told her what happened to her precious baby. I decided to let the DA's office break the news of the murder to the Rodriguez family. They would arrange grief counselors or a priest.

* * *

Michael hired a security company to watch Sarah at practice, games, and school. At my office we kept the suite door locked, like we were a storefront firm in Newark. I don't know why I bothered to come in, since I knew my career would soon be over. The Bar investigation was underway.

The DA finally got around to subpoenaing the gun records and identifying Dave on the CCTV, despite his lousy disguise. Michael let me give Dallas police a "full-blown" formal statement. My cell records backed me up and they had DNA at the empty house that matched what they found in the computer store, on the pharmacist's clothes, and in the dumpster on Nicky.

The police doubted Dave's half-sister's yarn, but she negotiated a deal with the DA to cooperate in exchange for no charges. She admitted Aunt Emma had encouraged her niece to ask Sarah to go to the movies. Lizzy's mom had expedited the get-together, but claimed to know zilch about Emma's motives.

A few days later, Dave staggered into the ER at Parkland Hospital, accompanied by a young, attractive woman, who slipped out once Dave had been triaged. Nearly dead, Dave talked, was arrested, and was admitted to ICU under guard. Emma must've diagnosed imminent kidney shutdown and decided prison was better than a grave for her brother. Dave's confession finally got the cops off me. They even issued a public statement of my innocence.

Hail Mary.

A surgeon amputated what remained of Dave's pecker, meaning a lifetime of catheterization. He would likely become a "girlfriend" in prison. Too bad the Sultan isn't hiring eunuchs.

Jen disappeared—her office cleaned out and her apartment empty. I figured she headed for the border the instant she learned I had survived. Emma was arrested at DFW trying to fly to London. Had she settled for driving to Mexico she might have gotten away, but designer threads aren't stylish in Matamoros. She was charged with four counts of first-degree murder, kidnapping, mayhem, and assault with intent to murder. The DA announced he'd seek the death penalty.

Vindictive bitch that I am, I fantasized about posing as her attorney, bringing garden shears to the jail conference room, and leaving with all ten of her toes in my pocket. She could shuffle to the death chair like a penguin.

We remained vigilant.

* * *

My summons for a disciplinary hearing arrived. I mulled it over, carefully plotting my response for ten minutes, then called and copped a plea to the Bar Association effective *after* Adventist paid the money. Childhood abuse, alcoholic father, loony mom, insecurity about the rich boyfriend—I decided none of these constituted a defense. I deserved whatever they cared to dish out.

The Bar ordered me to take a two-year vacation. When you get suspended that long, you have to formally reapply to get your ticket back. Some on the discipline panel emphasized that my return to court was far from certain, despite my once golden status, since I'd gotten a private reprimand for violating privacy laws and burglary the year before—the price of rescuing Sarah.

Quite a record for an eight-year lawyer. I even rated a published opinion in the Texas Bar Reporter as a warning to others. One more slip-up and I could go back to giving kids shooting lessons. Permanently.

Once I became a civilian I found Larsen's daughter, who was struggling to stay in school while working at Wally World. I anonymously left a hundred grand in cash at her front door. Figured there wasn't a law against giving my own money away.

CHAPTER 44

"**I** DO."

Judge Wallace smiled at the two of us, our ring bearer, Sarah, and Tina, our witness, then pronounced us married. As a confirmed Catholic I was supposed to marry in the church. Otherwise I would be living in sin and would be forbidden from receiving Holy Communion. But I couldn't wait any longer. Michael promised to do the months of RCIA, so we could have a proper full wedding Mass later.

Sarah seemed thrilled with our decision. I hoped her attitude wouldn't change once I moved in and she had to share her dad's attention. I toyed with the possibility of adopting her, but knew that shouldn't be rushed. Marrying a divorced guy with a daughter was one thing, but I had dived into motherhood, as Sarah's only adult female figure.

Michael and I considered reprising our Vail affair from the previous fall, but Pete's stunning cabin was probably not available. Given a choice by my wonderfully solicitous husband, I chose Paris. He booked a suite at the George V Hotel—which felt like walking into the nineteenth century, a couple of lifetimes away from the troubles that began the night I went out with Tony Caswell.

We took Air France to Nice and spent four days on the Riviera. I caught several people staring. You know things are weird when people eyeball your foot on a French beach. Folks probably wondered where I'd stepped on a land mine.

With lovely tans, we returned to Paris to meet Sarah and Becca at Charles de Gaulle. Becca had advanced to a cane and had brought a one-leg wheel walker to help her get around. The girl had really busted her little buns on her therapy.

I realized I'd missed a period. I told myself not to get excited. I'd missed before, so I didn't say anything to Michael about it. But wouldn't that be something?

Paris dazzled the girls. They piled into the cab with little jet lag and stayed awake all through their first day in France. Even remained alert for the *Mona Lisa*. We planned to stay in Paris four more days, then head for the Loire Valley and the chateau country. Michael also insisted the kids had to see the D-Day beaches and the American cemetery in Normandy.

The second day started well. I genuinely like big-boned, somewhat awkward Becca, and the girls didn't seem to mind me chaperoning them around the city—giving Michael time to study *Les Invalides*.

I've never spent big money on clothes. Dillard's always stocked the same stuff Neiman had the year before. Diana had been indulgent, but Michael set limits, so the kids did more looking than buying on our shopping trip. Sarah had her own credit card. I didn't know what the limit might be, and was afraid to ask.

To keep from being ignored in the shops on the *Rue du Faubourg Saint-Honoré*, we left the tees and sneakers at the hotel and dressed up a little. Sarah converted her excellent Spanish into something resembling French, and I knew enough Italian from my grandmother to blend the two and keep from being the totally ugly American. So in most boutiques the staff practiced patience as the teenagers tried on outfits.

Late that day Sarah came out of the Blumarine dressing room

wearing a skirt slit up the side almost to her butt and a nearly transparent blouse showing off firm little breasts. I would've loved the outfit for a hot date with my new husband—if we were in a town where we didn't know anybody.

Heat rose up my blushing face.

The clerk's face beamed over a big commission. She complimented the kid in accented English, "Verrry verrry stunnnning."

Becca looked at me, hand over her mouth, stifling a laugh, obviously enjoying my dilemma.

Sarah did look stunning. It was scary how she seemed grown-up and luscious.

I wavered. The kid missed her mother and felt guilty over their lousy relationship. Would this get-up help her ego, even if Michael never let her wear it? Did I have the authority to nix it? What if she told me to buzz off and whipped out her own money? Would Michael be pissed if I let her buy it? Was the beginning of stepmother-hood going to be the end?

All eyes riveted on me.

Damn.

Maybe I could I bring that outfit back to the hotel? Pass it off to Michael as mine? That might get me a quick brownie point with Sarah.

I stuttered, "Uh . . . I think it's a little . . . you might not be old enough yet . . ."

A dead pause. She looked at me a second.

"Okay, Mom."

The reply came without a hint of teenage sarcasm or rebellion. No eye roll. Sarah stepped back into the dressing room. Becca returned to digging through piles of jeans. The scene was as natural as homemade ice cream.

Mom. From the kid I had rescued—the kid who had brought Michael and me back together.

I had to turn away, walk to the other side of the store so nobody could see my face. I wiped my eyes, dried my fingers on my pants, but couldn't stop crying.

All I'd been through in the last year flashed in front of me, beginning with the disastrous Caswell date, getting shot, tortured, cheating death, and returning.

The girl, who fled home at sixteen and endured a long ride, while resting her teary cheek on the bus window's cold glass, had come a long way.